Praise for the novels of Justine Davis (Dare)

"A scorcher. . . . Justine Dare hits the target square on the mark with [this] ingenious, brilliantly plotted thriller." —*Romantic Times*

"Dare has a knack for romance and spins an engrossing tale." —*Publishers Weekly*

"*Dangerous Games* is going to win much acclaim for Justine Dare. The lead characters are a wonderful couple and the villain is as deadly a killer to come along in a novel in a very long time . . . a rousing romantic intrigue novel." —*The Midwest Book Review*

"This is a page-turner, with an emotional and sexual intensity that makes it stand out from the crowd." —*Under the Covers Book Review*

**Books by
Justine Davis**

Dangerous Ground
Dangerous Games
Night Fires
High Stakes
Avenging Angel
Hunter's Way
Angel for Hire
Upon the Storm
Found Father
To Hold an Eagle
Private Reasons
Wicked Secret

HIGH STAKES

Justine Davis

SPEAKING VOLUMES, LLC
NAPLES, FLORIDA
2016

High Stakes

ISBN 978-1-62815-511-2

The passing of the torch is painful and inevitable, but it is our best hope to understand the true meaning of eternity and immortality; one too-short life span is never enough.

For Clifford Delos Davis—beloved father, grandfather, great-grandfather. In memory of a good, simple, loving life. I miss you, Dad.

And Zoe Rachel Vardoulis—beloved daughter, granddaughter, great-granddaughter. In hopes for a bright, joyous, wonderful future. Welcome, little niece.

I love you both.

Chapter One

Shelby Wyatt pumped a quarter into the slot without even glancing at the machine. Her gaze was riveted on the polished brass column beside her. Between the huge photos of previous lucky winners, it reflected the front doors of the Golden Phoenix casino.

She knew the glittering room was full of sound, echoing with the clank of slot machines, the occasional drop of coins into a metal tray, and beneath it all the hum of human voices. She knew it, but barely heard any of it. She was watching the doors.

"You have to push the button," a voice said close beside her.

She nearly yelped aloud. She whirled in panic.

It wasn't him.

She let out a breath of relief, and managed a smile for the young man who was standing at her side.

"Sorry, didn't mean to startle you. You have to push the button," he said again, smiling back at her. A nice, friendly smile. If she'd still trusted smiles at all, she would have trusted this one. "It's not like the old ones with the handle."

He looked almost too young to be in the casino, but since he held some chips and a small wad of money, she assumed he must be over twenty-one.

She tried desperately to think of something to say,

something normal, small talk that would hide her panic; she didn't want to stick in anyone's mind.

"I guess you have the hang of it," she said rather inanely, gesturing at his small bankroll.

"It'll almost buy me a new guitar," he said with a grin that made her think suddenly of early days when life was an endless array of possibilities. She made another effort at normal conversation.

"Maybe I can win enough for a round of riding lessons." *If I ever get out of this,* she thought. Then she forced herself to continue the pretense of normalcy. "Are you a musician?" she asked.

The young man nodded. "My band is playing here tonight. My name's Jason. Jason Wilber."

Shelby nodded, her own name stuck in her throat. She didn't dare, no matter how rude it seemed. To cover her discomfort, she turned and pushed the button labeled "Spin Reels."

All hell broke loose. Bells clanged, lights flashed, sirens whooped.

Heads turned.

"Hey, you won! Big!" Jason exclaimed.

She was barely aware of the flashing sign declaring she was a twenty-five-thousand-dollar winner. She could hardly hear all the tumult over the hammering of her heart. She looked toward the door, half expecting the man to be standing there, drawn by all the commotion and zeroing in on her with deadly intent.

He wasn't. But she was the center of attention. People were staring at her. If they kept staring, they'd remember her. One or two well-placed questions, and some well-meaning gambler would be doing the proverbial "She went thatta way," sealing her fate.

Fighting panic, she looked at Jason, at his small wad of cash. "Have you won this much?"

"Never," he said. Then, looking past her, he added,

"Here comes your prize. I'll bet you'll have to go to the cashier's window."

Shelby glanced back, saw a woman in the uniform of the casino approaching with her cart. The cashier's window. A memory stabbed her, something she'd read about any gambling win over twelve hundred dollars having to be reported. Papers to fill out. Names to be given, addresses. A paper trail, leading right to her.

"Maybe they'll hang your picture up there," Jason said.

Shelby saw he was pointing to the photos on the brass column, imagined her face framed there for anyone to find.

For *him* to find.

She lost her battle with panic.

"Forgive me," she said, gesturing at the berserk slot machine. "It's all yours."

She snatched the small wad of money out of Jason's hand.

And then she ran.

Aaron Montana hit the replay button and leaned forward to watch intently. Not that he really needed to see it again; the odd scenario had registered vividly the first time through. And watching it again wouldn't change the obvious question.

Why would anybody walk away from twenty-five thousand dollars?

He didn't have to ask who would. She was captured quite clearly on the security tape. Small, with short blond hair, cut in wisps around her face, and a lithe quickness that made her seem younger than he would bet she was. She was dressed in slim black jeans and a V-neck top, and carried what appeared to be a small leather backpack over her shoulder.

The scene played out again—the jackpot, the lights, the bells, and the shock on the face of the young man beside her as she gestured as if giving him the clanging slot machine and then grabbed the money out of his hand and ran.

Aaron watched, waiting for the moment when she would turn, when the camera would capture her face. The moment when it would show that expression he knew all too well.

Fear.

Maybe it was that clear, unmistakable look that made her seem older. Or maybe, he thought as the image appeared on the videotape again, those eyes were simply too old for her face, fear or not. He hit the freeze button, locking the frame in place.

"Boy, she's afraid of something."

At her words Aaron glanced at Robin Murphy, his chief of security. It had been Robin who had called him in to look at this when he was walking down the hallway outside the surveillance monitor room on the way to his office.

"Yeah," he muttered, "she is."

"I wonder what? Or who?" Robin mused aloud.

Aaron stared at the woman in the paused frame.

She wasn't asking for his help. He knew that. It was only a fluke that she'd happened to turn so that the surveillance camera caught her face. And only a fluke that he'd been passing by the monitor room when the video crew was showing the clip to Robin and discussing whether to turn it over to management. Meaning him.

"Man, I can't think of anything that'd scare me out of collecting twenty-five grand," one of the crew said.

"Oh, yeah?" hooted his partner. "How about your mother-in-law?"

"Nah, I'd just spend it quick, before she could tell me how."

Aaron ignored the banter. He rewound and watched the scene again, peripherally aware that Robin was watching him instead of the screen. He didn't have to look at her; he knew what he'd see if he did. The same expression his ex-wife wore when she warned him.

You're going to kill yourself, trying to take care of all the birds with a wing down.

For all their problems, Cindy knew him rather well. She even knew she was one of those wounded birds, although she refused to do anything about it. He suspected it was because she had wanted to be the *only* wounded bird he took care of; she hadn't liked it much when anyone intruded on that.

But he knew himself rather well, too. He'd been helpless once. Been unable to make things right for Cindy, who had looked at him with the same eyes, eyes full of that awful fear. Been unable to help the little girl who had once looked at him so adoringly, certain there was nothing in the world her daddy couldn't fix.

Ever since, he'd been unable to walk away. Common sense told him he could never make up for what he hadn't been able to do seven years ago, but his gut kept forcing him to try.

"She didn't use a card, did she?" he asked, referring to the Phoenix Club cards for frequent guests. Slot players inserted the cards into the machine to accumulate points for prizes and discounts, but the cards also allowed the computers to identify the gambler and track the activity. The videotape had isolated only the moment of the win, so he hadn't been able to tell if she had used one.

"No, no card."

Aaron checked the digital readout of the time that ticked by in the lower left corner of the screen, then looked at his watch. Not even fifteen minutes had passed.

"Can you track her?"

Robin lifted an eyebrow, but nodded. "Should be

able to, by switching cameras and matching the times. Doug?"

She nodded to the man who had made the mother-in-law comment, and without questioning he sat back down at his console and began calling up tapes to the bank of more than a hundred VCRs in the rack behind them.

"Sorry," Aaron said to the man he knew worked the early-morning shift. "I know you're supposed to be off."

"S'okay," he said without looking up. "This should only take a couple of minutes."

"Doug likes challenges like this," Robin said.

Aaron smiled at the woman who had become a friend in the five years she'd been on his staff. He'd hired her after the first interview, had given her free rein, and had never had cause to regret it. The ex–Los Angeles police lieutenant was an integral part of the team that kept the Golden Phoenix running smoothly, and a big part of its sparkling reputation among smaller casino hotels in the state of Nevada. She hired the best people, inspired loyalty and dedication in them, and it showed.

Like Doug. Who, in a much shorter time than Aaron would have thought possible, had the tapes ready and fed them through successive monitors. Aaron watched as the blond woman ran through the banks of slot machines by the front doors, crowded even at this morning hour. The Golden Phoenix's reputation drew people at all hours.

On the second monitor he watched her slow to a rapid walk as she reached the blackjack tables, and on the third saw her angle toward the back of the hotel. It became more difficult to track her as she made her way past the bar in the center of the casino floor, the roulette and craps tables, then the main cashier, but he never lost sight of the gleaming cap of wispy blond hair.

She was still moving quickly when she passed out of the range of the last camera in the casino area.

Aaron straightened up. There was only one place she could have gone from there. "Doug," he began.

"Working on it," the man said.

Aaron's mouth quirked. He looked at Robin. "Tell your boss to give this guy a raise."

"You just did," she reminded him.

"Did I? Was it enough?"

Doug laughed, never taking his eyes off his console. "It's never enough," he said. "But it was close, sir."

The new hallway cameras, installed in the hotel room tower after several attacks on lone women in neighboring Reno—there had never been a problem here in Outpost, but Aaron wasn't taking any chances—were part of a different camera system, but Doug handled them just as adroitly as he did the casino cameras.

With a sound of satisfaction Doug said, "There you are, Mr. Montana."

Aaron leaned forward to look at the screen.

Shelby leaned against the wall, breathing hard, willing her heart to slow down. She felt like she'd run up the three floors instead of ridden. She stared at the soda machine so that anyone wandering past the alcove beside the bank of elevators would assume she was just trying to decide what to buy. But her focus was turned inward as she tried to tell herself she'd done the only thing she could. The chances that he would find her here were slim, but slim was still a chance, and she couldn't take it.

Her decision not to take her car this morning, for fear it would be seen and possibly remembered, had turned out to be a bad one. She'd dashed into the casino because it was the closest place she could reach on foot at this hour that had a big enough crowd to lose herself in. And then she'd gone and hit that silly jackpot and drawn the attention of everyone within fifty yards.

She reached into her pocket and pulled out the small wad of bills she'd grabbed. It wasn't stealing, not really. She'd left Jason the jackpot, which was—she did a quick count—almost a hundred times this. He should be happy; he'd gotten a heck of a deal. And she'd gotten some cash she was sure to need. Strolling into her bank, one of too few in Outpost, or using a credit card that would leave a paper trail, was as out of the question as identifying herself and collecting that prize.

She heard voices and made herself hum cheerfully as she kept her gaze fastened on the soda machine, one finger artfully pressed to her mouth in an indecisive gesture. The older couple didn't even glance at her; the man was busy talking, and the woman was putting the gold plastic key card for their room in her purse. She could hear them as they waited for the elevator, discussing whether they should stay another day, since they'd won enough to cover it. The Golden Phoenix, it seemed, was a bountiful place.

The moment she heard the elevator doors close, cutting off the man's protest that he had to get back to work, Shelby peeked around the corner to be sure the elevator lobby was truly empty.

It was amazing, she thought as she retreated to the alcove, how quickly she'd reverted. How quickly the last thirteen years had fallen away. Thirteen years of safety, of polishing the admittedly rough edges left by five formative years on the run, and now those years had vanished. She felt exactly as she had when she'd been a scared twelve-year-old runaway.

Except back then she'd had Tiger.

Tiger Blaine. She hadn't consciously thought about him for a long time. Yet he was always there, with her, in the things he'd done for her, the things he'd taught her.

So do what he taught you, she ordered herself. *Survive.*

She heard more voices. She stuffed the folded bills back into her front pocket and dug some change out of her small backpack. She had just enough for the machine, and as the voices got close she shoved the coins into the slot. A younger couple this time, too wrapped up in each other to notice anyone else.

She made a soda selection without even looking, and the can rattled noisily down into the tray. She picked it up but didn't open it; it was much more valuable as a weapon with its full weight. Tiger had taught her to use what was at hand.

She walked casually toward the hallway. A long row of doors on each side, empty except for a maid's cart about halfway down on the right, in front of the single open door.

Look like you belong. That's half the battle.

Tiger's words came back as vividly as if he were standing there, his eyes shadowed, hard with years of living on the street yet fiercely alive. They'd never beaten Tiger down.

Look like you belong.

Shelby reached into the backpack and dug out her wallet. She extracted a gold-colored credit card, her only one. It wasn't exactly the right size, but she hoped it would work. She covered most of it with her fingers, leaving only the gold edge showing. She walked quickly back to the table in the elevator lobby and grabbed one of the tabloid-size magazines advertising local attractions and a smaller, slick issue that covered the entire state.

For a split second she paused, pondering the oddity

of the flyers for Gambler's Anonymous in a discreet rack at the back of the table, then went back to her arranging. She held her backpack in her hand rather than putting it back over her shoulder, and added the magazines. In the other hand she held the soda can and the credit card.

She looked sufficiently loaded down now, she thought, and she started down the hall, not letting herself think of all the things that could go wrong. Hadn't enough gone wrong already? She'd only been trying to help the one person that she loved and trusted, and now things were completely out of control.

She reached the room with the open door. The maid was out of sight, but Shelby could hear her bustling about. She sneaked a peek at the clipboard on top of the cart. Each room number on the floor was listed, and beside it the date and a space for a name, then a second date, which appeared to be the date of checkout. On some of the rooms, those spaces were empty. This one was not. And the checkout date was tomorrow.

Shelby backed up the way she had come and waited. After a couple of minutes, the maid stepped out into the hall, tossing used towels into a bag on her cart. Shelby walked toward her as if she'd just arrived.

"Oh, thanks," she said a little breathlessly. "You saved me having to juggle all this."

She lifted the hand with the mostly concealed credit card, saw the maid look at it. "Are you finished?" she said quickly.

"Yes, just now," the woman said with a nod.

"Good. I've got to pack up some things so I don't have to do it all in the morning before we leave."

Shelby gave her a sunny smile.

The woman smiled back. And stepped aside.

Shelby slipped into the room and pulled the door

quietly closed behind her. She thought of dead-bolting it from the inside, but she didn't want to risk it in case the real occupants returned. It was going to be hard enough to bluff her way out, and she didn't want to have to explain why she'd locked the door against the legitimate tenants.

She walked over to the king-size bed and dropped her things on it. She put the credit card back in her wallet, noticing that her fingers were trembling slightly.

She was out of practice. There had been a time when she could have carried off much worse than this without a qualm. Focused on the goal, with no thought of consequences. She returned the wallet to her backpack, then sank down on the edge of the bed. What to do next?

She let her mind run, as Tiger had taught her, considering all the possibilities. True, she rejected most of them, but as he always said, the process of elimination was part of the planning.

She didn't let herself wonder about him, didn't question whether he was even still alive after all these years since she'd last seen him. He had to be. Tiger was too smart, too tough. She had to believe he was out there somewhere, that he'd survived as she had. No other option was acceptable. Not after he had saved her life so many times, in so many ways.

Don't get sappy, little girl. You lose your edge.

She took a deep breath as the long-ago admonition echoed in her head. She steadied herself and went back to reviewing her options. After a few minutes she picked up the telephone book from the lower shelf of the nightstand and flipped to the Yellow Pages.

She found the page she wanted, and the familiar name. The listing with the phone number she needed was in the upper right, so she simply tore the corner off; it seemed doubtful that anybody who came to the

Golden Phoenix for pleasure would be checking those particular listings.

She stood up, stuffing the piece of yellow paper into her pocket. Her legs were steadier, and her hands no longer shaking, she noted. Making the decision had done a great deal to calm her down. She turned to gather up her things.

The door clicked. She whirled, her mind racing. God, she was rusty. She should have thought of a story, should have—

The door swung open.

In the doorway stood one of the biggest, most powerful-looking—and grimmest—men she'd ever seen. The expensive suit he wore did nothing to detract from his size or his rather menacing appearance. He was watching her with unmasked suspicion, and he was blocking her only escape.

She was trapped.

Chapter Two

Detective Mike Delano took a last look at the sprawled body, stepped over the large bloodstain that had soaked into the carpeting, and left the study with the same exquisite care that he had employed when he entered. He would spend enough time in here later, after the room had been gone over.

He kept his hands in his pockets as insurance against inadvertently touching anything, just as he'd pulled small plastic covers over his shoes to avoid contaminating any evidence. He'd heard too much about high-profile cases being blown by shoddy work at the crime scene. He knew whose house this was, and he was pretty sure who was lying there with his brains blown out, and it all added up to nothing but trouble.

Mike wondered briefly what it would be like to work for a big department, where all he would have to do now was turn the scene over to somebody with all the latest gadgets and wait until he was presented with a lovely string of evidence that led him straight to the killer. Unfortunately, here they had to rely on county, state, or even federal agencies for much of the more refined forensics work. He quashed his irritation; Outpost didn't get enough murders for anybody to be exactly practiced at the procedure, and he couldn't be sorry for that. Besides, thanks to the Montanas, they were better equipped than many departments of similar size.

Speaking of the Montanas, Mike thought, he'd better call Aaron and tell him he was going to have to postpone their handball game. Good thing his best friend was used to the demands of police work; this was the second time this week he'd had to cancel on him.

At least the two patrol officers initially on the scene had followed the first five rules of crime-scene protection: don't touch anything. And they'd kept the shaken housekeeper clear of the house until he'd arrived.

He made his way toward the big garage. If the victim had come home as usual last night, he probably would have pulled in there and gone into the house through the interior door. But the maid had found the garage door open when she arrived. Had he been getting ready to leave this morning when he was confronted by his killer?

As he passed, Mike glanced again into the spotless, perfectly outfitted kitchen. There had been no sign of a pause for a late-night snack or morning coffee, no dirty cups or dishes. He made another mental note to ask exactly what the maid had cleaned before her grisly discovery and went on.

An ornate gilt-and-white table sat just inside the door to the garage, and on this was a set of keys with a leather tag bearing the Mercedes-Benz logo. He didn't touch them. The door to the garage had a lever instead of a knob, and he used his pen to press it open without disturbing any possible prints besides the victim's.

At the far end of the three-car garage was a boxy shape under a car cover, an SUV by the look of it. He would check that out later, since it appeared that the low, sleek vehicle before him was the main driver and matched the keys tossed on the table inside.

It also had a flat tire, the left front. He inspected

it, but there were no obvious signs, no slash marks, no nails that he could see. He would have them check it.

Mike lifted the driver's door handle with his pen. He wasn't surprised when it opened; not many people locked their cars in their own garage. He leaned into the car, careful not to touch or even brush against anything while he did a visual search with the aid of his flashlight. There was nothing so obvious—or convenient—as a bloodstain or a bullet hole, but he hadn't expected anything. Still, he'd have them go over it thoroughly.

He backed out of the car. He figured he had about ten more minutes before Outpost's lone crime-scene technician arrived, and he needed to make the most of the time. He took out his small notebook and began writing.

Two vehicles present. One new Mercedes convertible, black, dark-tinted windows, paper plates from Reno dealership, registration not yet on file. Left front tire flat, no immediately obvious cause. Parked in normal manner in garage. Double garage door open (single door closed), door opener on, lights off. Vehicle cold, cursory inspection of interior shows nothing suspicious.

He left a space for future notes about the SUV, then added what the first officer on the scene had told him.

Front door closed and locked upon housekeeper's arrival at 8 A.M. Double garage door open.

Alarm system on but deactivated. (by victim?)

No sign of forced entry, ransacking; housekeeper reports nothing obviously missing.

Deceased discovered at approximately 8:45 A.M., when housekeeper went to clean study.

He made a mental note to contact dispatch for the exact time the call had come in. They'd called him at 9:15. Given the response time for the patrol unit in weekday morning traffic, time for the officers to determine what they had and to request him, and for dispatch to call, there clearly hadn't been any unusual delay, but he would need the exact time anyway. He was going to have to make sure everybody went by the book every step of the way on this one.

He had just started his rough sketch of the scene when he heard the sound of a vehicle arriving. As he stepped outside, he noticed a couple of curious neighbors across the street, talking to a uniformed officer. Mike saw that it was Sue Sylstra and checked that worry off his mental list. Sue knew her job. She would be asking the right questions and taking note of anything that might be relevant.

An SUV that had been converted into a police utility vehicle came to a halt precisely in line with the driveway. Mike counted down in his head: put in park, set brake, check lights—no matter that it was daylight—remove keys, unfasten seat belt. On the count of six the door swung open. John Herrera was a creature of precise habits. It made him the butt of teasing and jokes about anal-retentiveness. It also made him very good at his job. Herrera would never miss a vital piece of evidence because he was tired, in a hurry, or because he'd done this a hundred times before. His meticulous, orderly mind allowed him to treat each crime scene as methodically and with as much energy as if it was the first he'd ever done. Mike hoped the outside world never found out about him, or Outpost would lose him to some big city.

"Nice place," Herrera said.

Mike didn't know if he was serious or joking; Herrera's sense of humor was rather unique. He himself found the place far too gaudy.

Ignoring the comment, he quickly apprised Herrera of the situation. "Keys to the Mercedes are on a table just inside that door," he said with a gesture toward the garage. "Body's in the study, down the hall to the left. I've only been in once."

"Good," Herrera said absently. Mike knew his mind was already far ahead, cataloging what he would do in what order.

"Check the closet in the study," Mike said. "The door was partially open, while everything else was undisturbed."

Herrera nodded. "Where is the victim in the room?"

"Just inside the doorway. Looks like he was shot the moment he walked in."

"Shot?" Herrera said with a lifted brow.

"Yeah, yeah, I'm no medical examiner," Mike said. Herrera was a stickler for procedure. Cause of death didn't exist for him until it had come from the official source. But he would gladly put up with Herrera's little quirks in return for his thoroughness. "Want me to carry anything?"

He always asked, although Herrera had yet to take him up on the offer; he was as meticulous about his equipment as he was about his work.

As expected, Herrera shook his head. "I'll let you know when you can come back in."

Mike nodded. He'd have his own brand of investigating to do after Herrera was through, when he didn't have to worry anymore about destroying possible trace evidence.

But in the meantime he'd might as well start checking the neighborhood. First he would talk to Officer Sylstra, see what she'd found out. With his luck, it would no doubt be that no one had seen or heard a thing.

This time when he stepped outside, he nearly

groaned aloud. The vultures had landed; two of the most ubiquitous newspaper reporters and even one of the local television reporters were setting up outside. More would follow, he knew. They'd be coming in from Reno and points south for this one, if he was right about who that stiff was.

He put a call to the PIO way up on his priority list. Let Webster handle the public information. He was hot for the spotlight anyway, whereas Mike felt a sense of accomplishment every time he managed to keep his face and name off the airwaves. In a case like this, that was going to be a challenge.

"Mrs. Peterson?"

Margaret Peterson snapped back to the present, flushing as she saw the young girl behind the counter of the dry cleaners looking at her oddly.

"Sorry," she said. "I'm a bit preoccupied."

"That's all right. You said you had a dress as well?"

'Yes, my blue beaded gown," Margaret said as she picked up Robert's suit and shirts. She would need the dress for the upcoming gala. It was her favorite, disguising that stubborn extra fifteen pounds, and Robert loved the way she looked in it. And right now she would take all the reassurance she could get. "I'll just take these out to the car and be right back."

She draped the plastic-bagged clothing over her arm and headed out the door. A bag caught on the newspaper rack outside the shop; she tugged it free. She carefully placed the hangers on the hook above the back door of her car, shifting the shoes she'd just picked up from the repair shop and the portfolio that held the papers for the meeting she had later today with the Restoration Society. It had been that kind of day; she'd left the house early and hadn't stopped since.

She put the driver's seat back in place, her hand

lingering for a moment on the rich leather. The expensive new sedan had been a birthday gift from her husband; Robert pampered her shamelessly.

The panic she'd been battling for three weeks welled up anew, forcing tears to her eyes. Eyes that were red-rimmed almost daily now, as she lived day to day with disaster looming over her shoulder. She could lose everything that was most important to her. The husband she adored, this life she had worked so hard for, everything.

And a tiny voice in the back of her mind was saying, "What did you expect?"

A month ago, she would have quieted the voice by remembering that her dream life, the life she'd never hoped to have, had lasted fifteen years now. It had become her reality, and the time before was the dream. A bad dream, to be forgotten. And she had forgotten it, for the most part.

Until three weeks ago, when it had come back to haunt her.

She fought down her rising panic once more. It did no good.

Shelby had assured her everything would be fine. But Margaret found it hard to share her optimism. She loved the girl like a daughter, despite Shelby's being only fifteen years younger than her own forty-five, but she also knew Shelby was much stronger, much tougher than she was. What spelled doom to her was just another challenge to Shelby.

She'd known that from the day she found the young woman, scared, angry, cold, and hungry, hiding in the back of her car in a snowstorm. She had glimpsed the blond head and huge eyes as the girl risked a peek out the window. Margaret wasn't so long removed from the kind of despair she'd seen in that face, and instead of doing the logical, sensible thing and calling the police, she had gotten into her car. By the time she'd gone a mile, she was certain the girl wasn't waiting with a gun or a knife to carjack her, or worse.

The girl had stayed hunkered down on the floor, clearly not sure if Margaret knew she was there. But if Margaret hadn't already seen her, the low but nearly constant growls of the girl's stomach would have given her away. On an impulse, Margaret made a stop at the nearest fast-food drive-through. She placed a large order, heard the growls increase as the smell of French fries invaded the car.

Then she dropped the bag on the backseat and said, "You'd better eat something before your stomach devours itself."

That had been the beginning. Gradually the scared teenager had come to trust her. Now Margaret was well aware of what a miracle that was, given what the girl had been through, surviving five years as a runaway.

Even now Margaret didn't know the whole story. Shelby had told her there were things she'd done that even Margaret wouldn't be able to forgive. Margaret knew that wasn't true. She would forgive the girl anything she'd done in those desperate straits.

It hadn't been easy, but Shelby had proved Margaret's judgment right; she was a daughter anyone would be proud of. And Robert, bless him, had understood her need to help the girl.

Robert.

With Robert she had everything a woman could want, including the knowledge that material possessions meant less than nothing next to the love of a solid, steady, kind, and admirable man.

She shivered. Shelby had insisted that Margaret was not to worry, things would be fine. But then she had vanished. Margaret hadn't heard from her in more than twenty-four hours, and she was worried.

And Robert was going to suspect something soon. Margaret was very much afraid he already did.

He couldn't find out. He simply couldn't.

She controlled herself, then turned to go back into the cleaners. A piece of thin plastic fluttering in the slight breeze caught her eye; a piece of the bag that had caught on the newsstand, she realized. Instinctively she reached out to pull it free as she passed.

She stopped dead in her tracks and stared at the afternoon newspaper in the rack, at the headline on the lower right of the front page, just above the fold:

LOCAL ENTREPRENEUR FOUND DEAD
NO ONE IN CUSTODY IN PRUETT KILLING

"Dear God," she whispered, swaying on her feet. She reached out blindly for support. There was nothing there.

Fumbling, she dug out change and bought the paper. Once she had it she simply stood there, shaking.

"Mrs. Peterson?"

It was the girl from the cleaners, Margaret registered vaguely. She was holding the blue dress. She had to take it, she thought, her mind still reeling.

"Are you all right?"

No, Margaret thought dizzily. *No, I'm not.*

Somehow she managed to take the dress and get back to her car. She tossed it heedlessly in the back, got in, and sat with her trembling hands on the wheel. She could get home, she thought. Surely she could get home.

It was the most surreal experience of her life. Her vision seemed to narrow to the road in front of her. Some part of her numbed mind knew she shouldn't be driving like this, but she had to get home, where it was safe, where she could lock the door and deal with this.

She had little memory of anything before the moment when, shaking, she sat down at her elegant dining table and spread the paper out before her.

She read haphazardly, unable to stop her eyes from darting through the article in a chaotic fashion. She lifted her hands to her face and covered her eyes for a moment. She drew in a deep breath. She didn't try to stop the trembling; she knew she couldn't. It took the greatest of efforts just to make herself start at the beginning and read slowly.

When she at last finished, she sat there shivering as if a freak snowstorm had just blown through her safe, warm home.

Her blackmailer was dead. Murdered.

And Shelby had said Margaret wasn't to worry, that she would take care of it.

She refolded the newspaper neatly, as if the world depended on getting each page perfectly straight. Her mind was racing, but she forced herself to concentrate on aligning the paper, knowing she couldn't deal with it yet. Couldn't even begin to realize all the ramifications. But one thing kept clamoring to be heard.

She couldn't believe Shelby would kill.

She shivered and pushed the newspaper away from her. It slid across the polished cherry wood of the table, the table she'd selected when Robert had gotten his last promotion, knowing he was now in a position where he would have to entertain. And she would have to learn how to be the perfect corporate wife. Once she would have laughed at the idea, but now it was her reality and she wouldn't trade it for anything.

Shelby couldn't possibly murder anyone. Not the Shelby she knew.

But what about the Shelby she had once been? What about the frightened, angry runaway? The

Shelby who had told her she had done things Margaret would hate her for?

Margaret had always assumed Shelby had meant stealing, perhaps even selling herself, and while the idea pained her, it was only because she hated to think of Shelby in such dire need. She could never love the child any less for what she'd had to do. She never dreamt the child could have meant murder.

But three things were indisputable.

The man blackmailing her was dead.

Shelby had promised to take care of it.

And Shelby had vanished.

The ring of the phone jarred her, and she gave a start. She knew she was dazed, but the sudden hammering of her heart told her just how much.

Praying that it was Shelby, she quickly went to the phone and picked up the receiver.

"Shelby?" she said rather breathlessly.

"No, it's me."

Robert's beloved voice was deep and solid in her ear. Normally it would be reassuring, no matter what problem she was facing, but now it only pushed her closer to the edge she was already teetering on. Still, she tried to make her voice sound normal as she greeted him.

Robert, perceptive man that he was, didn't buy it.

"You sound worried. You still haven't heard from her?"

He already knew she'd been concerned, so there was no point in denying it. Besides, better he should think that was what had her disturbed.

"I am worried," she said honestly. *Panicked, in fact,* she added to herself.

"I know it's unusual, honey," Robert said, "but she'll show up soon."

"I hope so," she said. *She has to.*

"Maybe she met someone," Robert suggested hopefully. "You're always so worried about her having no social life. Perhaps she's finally started one."

"I hope you're right," Margaret said. *You have no idea how much I hope you're right.* She made herself go on, changing the subject. "How did your meeting go?"

She knew Vision Tech, the largest optical manufacturer in the area, was looking to merge with the distributor with the best track record west of the Rockies, and today had been the first big meeting.

"Fairly well. Alton's going to go for the deal, I think."

"That's good news."

"Yes. Are you sure Shelby is all that's bothering you?"

He knew her too well. "I've just had a lot on my mind today." Not a lie, really, she told herself. "And I'm a little nervous about my presentation this afternoon."

Again not a lie. Merely the biggest understatement she'd ever made in her life. How would she ever get through this talk? How could she ever convince people that history was worth saving when her own was about to destroy her?

"You'll do fine. You're a dynamic woman. They'll listen to you. Besides, you're right—Outpost is a unique town and the historical side deserves to be preserved."

He always believed she could do anything she set her mind to. He loved her, admired her, and he never, ever lost his faith in her.

If she ever shattered that faith, she would die. Quite literally, she didn't know if she could live with it. She had been thirty years old and had given up on love when he had come into her life and made her believe all over again. She couldn't bear the thought of losing him because of some silly, stupid thing she'd done when she was too young to know better.

Silly and stupid to her, and perhaps some others, but to her conventional, pillar-of-the-community husband—

"I love you, Margaret."

The abrupt declaration startled her, and she wondered how long she'd been standing there silently. His voice had sounded oddly intense, with an undertone that only made her feel worse. He knew something was wrong.

"I love you, too, Robert. With all my heart," she said fervently. "I always, always will."

She realized too late, after they'd hung up, that she'd only confirmed, with her too urgent declaration, that something was indeed wrong.

But speaking with Robert had, as it always did, calmed her. The panic edged away, leaving her with the ability to think clearly for the first time since the headline had jumped out at her.

Her girl was in this mess because of her, which made her feel even more guilty and responsible. She should have stopped her, should never have let her do . . . whatever she'd done. But the first thing was obvious; she couldn't go to the police. Not even to report Shelby missing. Not when she didn't know what had really happened, or how Shelby was involved.

The fact that Robert was on the police commission only complicated things further. No matter what, she could not let him be touched by even the faintest whiff of scandal.

There was only one thing left to her, and it was the thing she least wanted to do.

Wait.

Wait and pray that, wherever she was, Shelby was all right.

*　　*　　*

She was, Aaron thought, eminently believable.

Or, he amended, she had it down pat, the slightly embarrassed and thoroughly abashed delivery, the gesture toward the open phone book on the bed, the half shrug of charming acceptance of being caught in her petty offense.

"I know, I know," she said with just the right note of sheepishness. "It was wrong of me, but I *had* to make a phone call and I dropped my last quarter in one of your slots."

And then walked away from twenty-five thousand dollars, Aaron said to himself.

But he had to give her credit. If he hadn't seen that bit of videotape, he might believe that she had sneaked in here simply to make a phone call because she was out of change. He might even have let her use a house phone and then sent her on her way.

But he didn't believe it. Not a word of it. Because, deep in those striking green eyes, he'd seen it. It was still there—almost hidden now but there.

The fear.

She controlled it well, but to an expert on the subject, like him, it was obvious. Whatever nonchalant demeanor she might manage to project, she was still afraid, down to the bone.

In the face of that fear, it was impossible for Aaron to be a hardnose with her. He knew what that kind of fear felt like. But neither could he simply let her go. There was only one option he could live with. He didn't like it, but he knew himself well enough to know he couldn't just walk away.

He stayed between her and the door, blocking her in. "What's wrong?" he asked, making his voice as soft as possible.

Based on her reaction, he might as well have boomed out with all the considerable force of his voice. The sheepish air vanished and she frowned, her expression filled with distrust.

"What are you, a cop? You moonlight chasing people who run out of quarters?"

"No," Aaron said, wondering why that was her first question, and why she said it in the tone of someone who had had encounters with law enforcement before. "I'm not a cop. But I'd say trespassing is a bit more serious than running out of change."

"Look, I said I'm sorry. It was stupid." She was trying to brazen it out, but the fear was still there, digging at Aaron. "What are you going to do, arrest me?"

"I told you, I'm not a cop."

Her brows furrowed. "If you're not a cop, and this isn't your room, why do you care?"

"Actually, because I run this place."

Her expression shifted from distrust to obvious disbelief. He wondered why, then supposed it was the same reason he usually ran into; many people thought him too young to be where he was. They assumed he had the job of managing the Golden Phoenix because his last name was Montana, and Montanas had been the nucleus of Outpost for generations.

He shrugged at her. "Believe it or not."

"Not," she selected, her chin coming up in a way that made him smile inwardly. She might be small—most women were, next to his six-two, two-ten bulk—and she might be cornered, but she didn't lack for nerve. Which made him wonder all the more what it was that had her so scared.

"You can't be that much older than me," she said.

His mouth twisted wryly. "Oh, I am. In years and in mileage."

She gave him a sideways look. He'd forgotten about the history in her eyes, and wondered if perhaps he was a bit off on the mileage part. Those eyes were ancient, as if she'd seen far too much for her years, and too much of it ugly.

"I'm thirty-seven," he said, not sure why. "I started as a desk clerk twenty years ago and worked my way up."

"Oh. You are older."

He grinned at her undiplomatic words. "Are you always so tactful?"

"Tact," she said, "is for people who have the time for it. Right now I don't."

"So you're what, sixteen?"

It worked, as he'd hoped; with that face and that pixie haircut, he imagined she got mistaken for a girl a lot. Despite, he noticed suddenly, a shape that was decidedly adult.

"Thirty," she snapped. Then she flushed, the color rising in her fair skin, as if she knew perfectly well he'd baited that response out of her. Her voice took on an edge as she said, "Are you going to let me go or not, Mr. —?"

"Montana," he supplied, watching her face. She didn't react, so she either didn't know the name or was a master at concealing her responses. "And I'll be happy to let you walk right on out of here. After you answer one very simple question for me."

"What?" she asked, suspicion gleaming in her narrowed eyes.

"Why," he said, very softly, "did you run from the kind of jackpot most people would be delirious about?"

She exploded into movement so quickly he was caught off guard. She barreled toward him, headed for the door. Instinctively Aaron reached out, knowing she was no match for his size and weight and could hurt herself trying to get past him. He caught her around the ribs.

She clawed at him, kicked, tried her best to unman

him with a well-placed knee. If he hadn't been so much taller, she might have done it, too. She fought fiercely, almost desperately, until Aaron realized he was going to hurt her if he kept trying to hang on to her.

He let go.

She stumbled back, off balance. For a moment she stared at him, puzzlement clear in her face.

Don't say it, he ordered himself. *She's not your problem, and you have enough already anyway.*

He said it. "Whatever it is you're afraid of, let me help."

Her eyes widened. She gave a half-shake of her head. Then she darted toward the door. He didn't move.

She didn't pause to close the door, just ran down the long hallway. Aaron stepped out to watch her go; she took the fire stairs, not the elevator, apparently not willing to wait long enough for a car to appear.

He wondered who she was. What she was running from. What it would take to scare someone who fought a man who had nearly a foot and a hundred pounds on her so fiercely.

Aaron walked over to the bed, glanced at the phone book with its torn page, closed it and put it away, making a mental note to have it replaced. He picked up the phone and dialed the hotel operator. She hadn't made a call from the room, so he'd either interrupted her, or the whole phone call thing was a ruse.

He secured the room and started back to his office.

Yes, she'd fought him, he said to himself thoughtfully as he walked. And left marks, he noted wryly as he reached the elevator lobby where there was a large mirror on the wall; the left side of his neck looked like he'd had a run-in with a cranky bobcat.

Which perhaps he had. She'd kicked, clawed, slugged, scratched, kneed . . .

The elevator doors opened, but for a moment he didn't move.

She'd done everything but the most logical thing for a woman fighting with a man to do. Scream for help.

Perhaps she'd thought no one was around. But the door had been open, there could easily have been someone in the hall. He sensed it was at least in part because she wasn't used to looking for help. Because she was self-reliant? Stubbornly independent? Because help had never been there when she needed it?

Or was she simply afraid to draw any attention to herself, even if she was in trouble?

He sighed inwardly as he stepped into the thankfully empty elevator car. *You're going to kill yourself* . . .

Whoever she was, he wasn't sure she had a wing down. Not yet. She was alive and vibrant and vital and still fighting.

He felt a sudden pang as he remembered another vibrant and vital spirit who had lost the fight. That was what his problem was, he thought. He just couldn't stand to see a spirit like that snuffed out.

Even when it was none of his business.

Chapter Three

Maybe he really wasn't a cop, Shelby thought.

She had dodged into the ladies' room, hoping she would be relatively safe there, at least for the moment. She didn't think he'd followed her. But she didn't think she'd been followed into the hotel tower, either.

But she'd seen the cameras. Tiger had taught her always to watch for them. So maybe he did work for the hotel. She doubted he was really the manager; that was probably just smoke. But then again, he spoke with the kind of quiet authority that commanded respect. If he did work for the hotel, though, and wasn't going to hold her for trespassing, why would he try to get involved?

Stop it, she ordered herself sternly. *You don't have time to worry about things that don't matter.*

She was in more trouble than she'd ever been in in her life, and she knew it. She felt renewed empathy with the people she'd been trying to help with her fledgling career as a victim representative. Problem was, she wasn't sure right now if she needed a victim rep or a criminal lawyer.

She wished Tiger were here now. No one was better at getting out of tight spots than he was. He would just grin at her through that shaggy mop of dark hair, an unholy gleam lighting his vivid blue eyes as he came up with some clever plan.

It wasn't her fault, really, that things had gotten so totally out of control. She'd just been in the wrong place at the wrong time. With, of course, that little added problem of having committed burglary to get there.

She'd meant to help. And instead, she might well have destroyed both herself and the one person she trusted. Gentle, loving, generous Margaret, the woman who had turned Shelby's life around, who had taken her into her home and given her a chance she'd never thought to have, a chance at a normal life.

She stifled a shiver. No time for such weakness. *Gotta be tough, quick, and smart.* Tiger had been right then, and he was right now, because she was back on the mean streets as surely as if she'd never escaped them.

She glanced around, saw the pay phone near the luxurious sofa just inside the door. Reaching into the pocket of her jeans, she pulled out the crumpled piece of a yellow phone book page. She smoothed it out over her knee and stared at it for a long time. Then she walked to the phone.

All of the messages Margaret had left on the machine at Shelby's apartment had gone unanswered, as had the calls to the small, not-yet-officially-open office of Victim's Voice.

Margaret paced her living room, her hands raised and knotted together in a prayerful pose. She had to *do* something. She couldn't just sit here waiting any longer.

She grabbed up her purse and her keys. She'd been to Shelby's apartment already, but she would go back again. It couldn't hurt, and she would at least feel as if she was doing something. She checked to be sure her cell phone was charged, on, and in her purse, then locked up carefully. She'd been doing that a lot lately, obsessing about security. A natural reaction, she supposed, when your world was about to crumble around you.

She used the key Shelby had given her when she'd first moved into the apartment. As before, she saw nothing out of the ordinary. The place, adorned with things acquired not with an eye to decor but to the meaning they held for her, reflected Shelby's casual charm. Never having had much, she was often content with things that were secondhand, so long as they were comfortable or comforting. The colors were bright and cheerful, the rooms tidy but lived in. Displayed proudly over the desk in one corner were both her GED and her University of Nevada degree; it was like Shelby, Margaret thought, not to overshadow the accomplishment of that simple high school–equivalency diploma with the triumph of her college degree. In a way, the GED had been more difficult for her. Believing she could do it, and settling into the disciplined routine necessary to achieve it, had been a tremendous challenge for a girl who had run wild for five years.

And wild she had been, wary and distrustful as any forest creature. That was why earning her trust had meant so much to Margaret. That was why it ate at her to think that she might be the cause of Shelby's disappearance now. That somebody besides herself might pay a price for her youthful stupidity.

She looked once more for any sign, a note that she might have missed, any clue at all to where the girl might be, any sign she had been back here. As before, she came up empty.

She sank down in the upholstered chair beside the telephone.

"God, I should never have told her about Pruett," she whispered to the empty room.

But after days of living with the horror, she'd had to tell someone. And the only person she had been certain would understand, the only person who could possibly know what it felt like to have the life you loved threatened, was Shelby.

And Shelby had understood. While she herself hadn't thought it any big deal, she had understood how Robert might; she loved Margaret too much to say so, but Margaret knew Shelby thought him hopelessly old-fashioned. And graphic nude photos of his wife in sexual poses with a string of different men—taken after a night of drinking, smoking pot, and experimenting with cocaine, all under the direction of her college boyfriend—weren't something he would take lightly.

Shelby also understood Margaret's terror. If those photographs surfaced, it might cost her everything.

What she hadn't counted on was that the dynamic young woman would take matters into her own hands.

Margaret leapt to her feet, the rising tension making it impossible for her to stay still. She caught a glimpse of herself in the mirror beside the door. Odd, she thought, you'd never guess the woman in the mirror was on the verge of hysteria. She looked poised, calm, polished. She was dressed in a sophisticated gray suit, her auburn hair pulled back into a neat French twist. Rich gold gleamed at her throat and ears, and a diamond whose size stopped just on the safe side of ostentatious sparkled on her left hand. A perfect facade to hide her terror behind.

She whirled, suddenly possessed by a need to get out of the apartment, away from her frightening thoughts. She was back in her car and pulling away before the hammering of her heart and the pace of her breathing began to slow.

It was several minutes later before she realized where she was heading. She nearly turned around and went back home, but some morbid sense of necessity kept her going.

She rounded the corner and slowed. Bits of ominous yellow plastic tape, showing where the entire house had been cordoned off, fluttered in the faint breeze. She could see the adhesive seal that closed the front door, marking it as a crime scene that was in the temporary custody of the coroner's office.

The house was as tacky as she remembered: somebody's version of a Southern plantation house, grossly out of place in the foothills of mountains like the Sierra Nevada. The inside was worse, with garish statuary and gilt everything. She was surprised she remembered, she'd been so distraught, but some things were etched in her mind: the gilded cherubs over the study door, the elaborately painted ceiling in the mock rotunda over the foyer. Well-funded bad taste incarnate, she had thought then.

Now all she could do was stare at the yellow tape, at the two cars that looked like unmarked police cars out front, and the four-wheel-drive vehicle with the police seal and the words "Crime Scene Investigator" on the side parked in the driveway.

It had really happened. Jack Pruett was really dead. But was her nightmare over . . . or just beginning?

"I know you were trying to help me, but God, Shelby, what have you done?"

She whispered it to the air, but one of the men in shirtsleeves and a tie that was askew—a big, powerful, strikingly handsome man—turned to look at her as if he'd heard her from a block away.

She did turn around then, making a U-turn in the street and fleeing the scene. She didn't want to be even that close to the police officers who were investigating this. She had little faith in her own ability to withstand any intense questioning; too much of her reserves had already been expended in trying not to panic about Shelby.

Shelby. She *couldn't* talk to the police. If she did,

she would have to tell them about her sorry situation, and if Shelby was really all right, if she had nothing to do with this, Margaret would have blown her own life apart needlessly—and would quite possibly have helped land Shelby in jail. And if Shelby had, God forbid, had something to do with this, she would still end up in jail, and Margaret's secret would be out, making whatever Shelby had done all for nothing.

But other images haunted her as she drove. Shelby needing help, maybe hurt, or worse. She couldn't stand by and let that happen. She couldn't risk Shelby's life to protect her own. Nothing—not her pride, not even her marriage—was more important than Shelby's life.

She had to do something. It was time to stop being such a coward. Time to quit thinking about herself. She had to have answers, and to get those, she had to find Shelby.

By the time she arrived at her house, she had a plan. And she was going to put it in action now. She couldn't wait any longer.

"He's good," Robin said. "Very good. We know he's cheating, but we haven't been able to figure out how yet. He's not using any method Steve has seen before."

Aaron leaned back in his chair, one elbow on the armrest as he ran a finger over his lips thoughtfully.

"Tell him to keep on it," he said.

"Don't have to," Robin said with a grin. "You know how Steve gets. He hates it when somebody comes up with a system he doesn't know."

Aaron laughed. Steve Kalecky was one of the best, if most risky, investments he'd ever made. A former career casino cheater himself, Aaron had hired him, on Robin's recommendation, shortly after he'd been released from jail after getting caught rigging a roulette game in Las Vegas. Aaron has been leery at first, but Robin had been convinced that the young man could go straight, given the opportunity. He'd been in it, she told Aaron, for the thrill, not the money.

"Switch the thrill to catching others doing the same thing, and he'll be just as happy," she said.

Her prediction turned out to be accurate. For three years now, Steve had proved well worth the not inconsiderable amount Aaron paid him. And so far he'd been loyal. His reputation was growing well beyond the Golden Phoenix, and he'd received more than one offer trying to lure him away to newer casinos in Outpost, or Reno, even as far away as Las Vegas. He'd turned them all down, and whatever reason he had for doing it, Aaron was glad.

"Anything else?"

"I've got a meeting with the Secret Service at two."

Aaron winced. "More?"

Robin nodded gravely. "Another five thousand dollars' worth, roughly. It turned up in the soft count this morning."

"All twenties?"

She nodded again. Aaron stifled a sigh; he'd thought, after a week's gap, that their go-round with counterfeit twenty-dollar bills was over. But this counting of bills had destroyed that hope.

"They're still being careful, whoever they are. Not dropping it in large amounts, or all on the cashier for chips, spreading it around, table to table, so it's not caught until it goes through in the count room."

Aaron nodded in turn. The scanner in the bill-counting machine was nearly infallible when it came to picking out the fakes, detecting any variation in color, texture, or dimension of bills, and spitting those out to be inspected by hand. He knew many casinos wrote off small amounts of passed funny money as a cost of doing business. But he was incapable of just ignoring such basic fraud. His people knew it, and kept on top of it.

"Do you need me there?" he asked.

"Not unless you want to be," Robin replied. "I'm just going to turn over the latest bills. Unfortunately we don't have anything more on a possible source."

"All right."

"Want me to look for whoever clawed you?" Robin asked.

Aaron blinked at the unexpected jab. Robin was good at that, sliding things in sideways when you least expected them. And more often than not it worked, and she got you to say something you never would have otherwise.

"Not biting," he told her firmly.

She gave him her most innocent look. "I'll take that as a no."

His mouth quirked. "Do that. I'll be on my pager if you—"

The ringing of his desk phone interrupted him. Robin nodded toward it, knowing routine calls were intercepted by his assistant.

"That was it anyway," she said, rising and leaving him to handle the call.

He picked up the receiver on the third ring.

"Aaron Montana."

"Aaron, it's Mike."

Aaron knew by the tone of Mike Delano's voice that this wasn't a social call, even though it sounded like he was on his cell phone.

"Uh-oh," he said.

"Yeah," Mike said. "It's Hank again. Booking just called me."

Aaron let out a long, weary sigh. "Damn. It's barely been a month since the last time."

"I know."

"Was he driving?"

"No, not this time. Just causing a ruckus outside the Outpost Bar and Grill."

Aaron glanced at his watch, but he already knew it wasn't even ten in the morning yet. "Let me guess," he said tiredly. "He wanted them to open up early so he could get a drink."

"Something along those lines. The manager said he was perfectly nice about it, but he wouldn't go away."

"How drunk is he?"

"No Breathalyzer, since he wasn't driving. But if I had to guess, I'd say he's a good two-oh."

Aaron knew that Mike's guess, after fifteen years on the force, was damn good. He rubbed his forehead; twenty percent blood alcohol at ten in the morning.

"He's in the tank with a couple others," Mike said. "You know how long it will be."

"Yeah." He knew the procedure all too well. It would be at least five hours before they could release his cousin.

"You going to bail him?"

"I don't know."

If he didn't, Aunt Abby would be on the phone, crying about her baby boy, expecting Aaron to handle it, as he always did. He wondered, as he had so often, when she was going to realize that her baby—who was pushing thirty—was a hard-core alcoholic and she was the biggest enabler in his life.

Next to you, maybe, he told himself.

He couldn't just keep bailing Hank out. It wasn't doing him any good.

It would be easier, he thought, if Hank was a jerk. If he was a loud, obnoxious drunk, then maybe even his mother would get fed up with him. But he wasn't. He was a charming, silly drunk, in fact a lot easier to get along with when he was drunk than when he wasn't. Since he was always a tiny bit drunk, he was always charming—only the degree changed.

"I wouldn't have called," Mike said, "but you said to let you know whenever he got picked up."

"It's fine, Mike. Not your fault he's a drunk."

"Want me to deny I ever called you to your aunt?"

Aaron's mouth twisted. "Thanks, but I wouldn't wish that on my worst enemy, let alone my best friend."

Mike laughed. "Thanks. By the way, how's your dad?"

"Hanging in," Aaron said. "I talked to him today. He's still enjoying Palm Springs, even playing a few holes of golf."

"Good. He'll surprise you yet and outlive us all." Aaron hoped his friend was right; he couldn't imagine not having his father around. "Sorry about this week's handball game. Are we still on for next week?" Mike asked.

"Darn right." Their games were fast, furious, and cutthroat, and did a great deal to keep him in shape. "I've got to salvage my pride after you whipped me last time."

"Yeah, sure, after you beat me four straight," Mike said with a laugh. "Hey, I've got to get rolling. Hot murder case."

Aaron smiled at his friend's enthusiasm. Just as in high school he had enjoyed the complexities of a good algebra problem, Mike liked nothing better than a challenging case. "Good luck," he said. "And thanks."

For a long time after they'd hung up, Aaron sat thinking. When he'd been sixteen, his eight-year-old cousin Hank had attached himself to him, following Aaron wherever he went, whether welcome or not. Aaron had acted annoyed, but secretly he'd been flattered by the boy's adoration. Aaron could do no wrong in Hank's book, and he told anyone who would listen that he wanted to be just like him when he grew up.

But they couldn't be more different. Aaron had worked hard to excel in school—in part, he knew, to overcome the assumption that because he was big, homely, and good at sports he must be stupid—while Hank, who had surpassed him at sports, had looks and charm, and the brains to be a top student, had slid by indifferently. Aaron had gone to work at the Golden Phoenix for his father before he'd even graduated from high school; Hank hadn't had a real job until he was twenty-three, and had lost it before he hit twenty-four. Aaron felt a sense of unwavering responsibility toward his family and friends; Hank blithely expected to be taken care of.

Aaron could take or leave alcohol. Hank was addicted.

Aaron leaned back. The leather of the big desk chair—he'd had to special-order it for it to be truly comfortable for his big frame—creaked familiarly.

There was nothing comfortable about his thoughts. In fact, they were chaotic. His father's uncertain health after his heart attack, cheaters, counterfeiters, his alcoholic cousin, his in-denial aunt . . .

And a tough little blond pixie who wouldn't let loose of his mind.

He'd been telling himself to stay out of it, not to try to find the mystery woman or even think about her. It wasn't his problem. The sting of the scratches was already fading. But so far he wasn't having much luck in making the vivid images of her go away.

He threw himself into clearing out paperwork that had been stacking up, then he headed down to make a circuit of the casino, as he often did. Maybe he would even take a tour on the catwalk, the network of walkways and platforms that ran the length and breadth of the casino, hidden above the two-way ceiling mirrors, giving the security staff the opportunity to be out of sight and out of mind.

All the personnel on the casino floor were used to his occasional appearances, knew by now it was nothing to fear, and went about their business. He nodded to those who acknowledged his presence, smiled at the newer ones who seemed nervous, and never stopped moving.

Not for the first time he wondered what he would be doing if running a hotel, and later this casino, hadn't been the family business, if the Montanas hadn't founded this place several generations ago. It was a moot point, however. It had been Montana's Outpost then, and Montanas had been here ever since.

As he passed the small theater, named the Outpost Music Hall, he heard a light little drum riff and the sound of a guitar being tuned. The band getting ready for sound check, he realized, and stopped.

He parted the curtain and peered in. There were only three people on the small stage, and one of them was the house sound technician. As luck would have it, one of the others was the musician the woman had grabbed the money from.

He stepped inside and made his way toward the front of the theater. The young man—Jason Wilber, he recalled from the band's booking—smiled when he introduced himself.

"Hey, thanks. Robin told me you said to take my cash out of the slot machine payoff."

"Seemed only fair. You could have had the whole thing."

He shook his head. "Not mine," he explained. "Besides, it seemed like she needed it even more than me," he added frankly. "And not for riding lessons."

"Riding lessons?"

He nodded. "I said something about buying a new guitar with mine, and she said something about riding lessons."

An image of the blond mystery woman suddenly

flashed through Aaron's mind again. And a memory. He thanked Jason, then strode out of the theater. He headed to the nearest public phone, lifted out the phone book, and turned to the page he wanted. Then he closed his eyes for a second, picturing the page he'd seen before; it had been the upper right corner that was torn out, he was sure.

He looked down again at the page before him. Stables. And the chunk that had been missing was the ad for Outpost Flats Stables.

Riding lessons.

"Gotcha."

Chapter Four

She was being followed.

Shelby could feel it as certainly as she could feel the warmth of the afternoon sun.

She waited until Pete was busy, then snagged the front section of his afternoon newspaper. She retreated to her hiding place in the hayloft of the big barn and settled down to pore over it. She took as much comfort as she could in the quiet sounds from the stalls—chewing, shifting, occasionally a soft whinny—and from the familiar and welcome scent of horses. Maybe she should give up her idea of becoming a victim representative and take to working with horses all the time. Make her childhood dream come true. It seemed an agreeable and happily unstressful life, something she would welcome just now.

Pruett's murder was front-page news. And according to this story, the police had not made an arrest, nor had they indicted that they were closing in on any suspect.

"Clueless," she muttered. The police never had done anything for her except cause trouble. No matter how hard Margaret tried to change her mind about it, or tell her she was going to have to change her attitude if she wanted any cooperation from them in establishing Victim's Voice.

Margaret.

She would be worried by now; they never missed

talking every morning. Shelby was going to have to call her soon, and she would, as soon as she could be sure her shadow wasn't close enough to see what she was doing, and find out about Margaret.

As a sanctuary this place wasn't bad. It was fairly remote and isolated, but it wasn't going to last. Her pursuer was too determined; eventually he would find her, even here. And she didn't want to endanger Pete; he was a friend of Margaret's, and she liked the crusty old guy herself. Especially after he'd helped without question when she'd called, even though it had been years since she used to come out here with Margaret.

Maybe, if she lived through this, she could get him to tell his story someday, how a man named Pierre Aubergon had wound up being called Pete on a ranch in the Sierra Nevada.

In the meantime, she should get moving and help out. It was the least she could do in return for this place to hide, no questions asked. Besides, she liked working around the big animals, currying them and talking to them. But then, she liked any animal better than most people; at least they never turned on you without reason. And she'd always had a soft spot for horses. As a child, she'd dreamed that someday she would have a horse of her own, to carry her away from the pain and fear.

She was shoveling the last bit of soiled straw out of the little strawberry roan's stall when she heard Pete call her name. He sounded odd, almost tense, and her heart leapt to her throat.

He'd found her.

She grabbed up the pitchfork she'd been using, made sure of her grip on it. She wasn't sure what good it would be against a gun, but that didn't matter. She couldn't leave Pete out there with someone looking for her with deadly intent.

She shifted the pitchfork, raised it to waist level. Then she stepped out of the barn.

She blinked.

He's found her, all right. But it wasn't the man—either of the men—she'd seen following her.

It was the man from the hotel.

Pete didn't seem worried. In fact, he was smiling in welcome. It had been excitement in his voice, not fear. Strange. Pete couldn't know him, could he?

The man wasn't looking her way, so she studied him for a moment, as she'd been too edgy to do before. He was even bigger than she remembered, so solidly built that she wondered anew that he'd let her get past him. She eyed his arms, powerful beneath the rolled-up sleeves of his pale blue shirt.

No way he couldn't have held her if he'd wanted to. Of course, she would have continued to fight him and, judging by the size of him, would have gotten hurt in the process. Could that be why he'd let go so abruptly?

He turned slightly, a movement that emphasized the breadth of his shoulders. Her gaze flicked over his face. He wasn't handsome in any conventional sense, not with that slightly crooked nose and those rough-hewn features. If you were generous you could call him rugged, she thought. But he was very, very male.

She saw the faint red marks on his neck. Scratches. Had she done that? She didn't remember. If so, he was probably even less happy with her than he had been in the hotel room.

"Ah, there she is," Pete said. "Shelby, you didn't tell me you knew Mr. Montana."

I don't, she thought as she walked warily toward them, glancing around, looking for any sign that her pursuer had found her. Or had been led here, by the man standing there as if he had every right.

But all she said was, "You know him, Pete?"

Pete laughed. "Everybody who's been in Outpost for a while knows the Montanas. Why, they settled this place back in the Wild West days. Started with a trading post, if I recall, Mr. Montana?"

He looked up at the man beside him. Pete wasn't a small man, but he seemed that way next to this one.

"Aaron, please," the man said. "Yes, a trading post. My great times about five grandfather, who had the good sense to have a brother in St. Louis who kept him in supplies."

Aaron Montana. A solid name for a solid man, Shelby thought. The expensive clothes shouldn't have suited him, not with his rough-edged features and sheer size, but they did. Or maybe it was just that the man himself was too powerful to be affected by anything as mundane as clothes.

Odd, she thought. She didn't feel threatened by him; she merely wondered how he'd found her. Assuming, of course, that was why he'd come here. But it must be, for Pete to call her out.

"And now look at us," Pete was saying. "A booming town. We'll catch up with Reno soon, and your Golden Phoenix the best casino in the whole state!"

Pete sounded downright admiring, Shelby thought.

"Thank you," Montana said graciously. "I'll pass your kind words along to my father. Whatever the Golden Phoenix is today is his doing."

Shelby couldn't deal with much more of this goodwill. Not when her nerves were at such a high pitch. And she didn't like standing around outside, where everyone could see her.

"What are you doing here?" she asked bluntly.

Montana answered before Pete could chide her for being rude. "I came to see you."

"Why?"

"I still want an answer to that question."

Shelby glanced at Pete, who looked puzzled, but

took the hint. He muttered something about chores, told Montana it had been nice to meet him, and left them together.

Shelby hung onto her pitchfork.

"If I'd wanted to hurt you," he said mildly, "I had a fine chance already."

He seemed to be telling the truth, she thought. And from what Pete had said, his personal history was fairly public. She'd even heard of his family, although not by name; Margaret, she thought, had once mentioned that Outpost had begun as a Wild West trading post and that the center of it, including the famous Golden Phoenix hotel and casino, had been owned by the same family for generations.

"I don't get you," she said finally. "If you're not going to have me arrested for trespassing in your hotel, why do you care who or where I am?"

"If I had the answer to that," he said, his voice dry and self-mocking, "my life would be a lot easier. And my family would be a lot happier."

"You make a habit of this, then? Chasing after total strangers? No wonder your family's unhappy with you."

He chuckled. It warmed his stern face, and suddenly he was better-looking than she'd thought. But the laugh and the smile faded.

"Whatever you're running from, I—" he began.

"What makes you think—" She stopped suddenly, remembering that he knew about the jackpot she'd literally run away from.

"Thank you," he said, as if he'd realized exactly why she'd interrupted herself. "Look, I can see that you're . . . frightened of something. Or someone."

She thought about denying it, just to make him go away, but if he was perceptive enough to see that, then he likely wouldn't believe her. Besides, she admitted, she was curious.

"So?" she said, meeting his gaze. His eyes were dark, as near black as his hair, yet she found them unexpectedly warm. In an odd way they reminded her of Margaret's, although there wasn't a trace of vulnerability in them.

"So," he said, "if you're in trouble, you could use some help."

"And you're volunteering?" she said, unable to stop the edge of sarcastic disbelief that crept into her voice.

"I know it's hard to trust a man if you're being stalked by one," he said.

So that's what he thought. That an ex-husband or boyfriend or somebody was after her. "Why would you care? You don't even know me."

"No," he agreed. "But I know what it's like to be afraid. And helpless."

She stared at him. If ever a man looked like he had never been in either of those states, it was this one. Yet she had heard the ring of truth in his words and his voice.

"Let me help," he said softly.

Shelby opened her mouth to tell him she didn't want his help. But what Pete had said stopped her. If this guy was legit, if he really was part of the founding family around here . . . Besides, he was a big, obviously strong, and satisfyingly intimidating man. He'd already made a fairly safe assumption about what her problem was; she could just let him continue to believe she was being stalked. And in his position, he might know something about Pruett. The man had been, by all accounts, a big gambler.

It all came down to how good was she? How long could she go before giving herself away? Or worse, giving Margaret away?

For the first time in a very long time, Shelby found herself in a very uncomfortable position.

She didn't know what to do.

*   *   *

The bitch was smart, all right. But more than that, she was clever. Either she'd had some training or her instincts were very good.

More than once she'd lost him, and that wasn't easy for the average citizen to do. She'd slipped away, never doing what he expected, and never staying still long enough for him to pin her down.

He didn't understand, really. She looked like an ordinary woman. Where had it come from, this knowledge of how to hide so expertly? True, there was a certain air about her. A sort of hyperalertness, and a smooth way of moving, as if she was used to having to move quickly without making noise, and at the same time stay aware of everything—and everyone—around her.

He wasn't used to seeing those characteristics in a woman. Maybe that was what had thrown him so off balance.

He frowned. He couldn't afford to be thrown off.

He shifted uncomfortably against the rock he had stationed himself behind. He turned the heavy gold ring on the little finger of his left hand, liking the feel of the diamond. He was purely a city boy at heart; you could keep this back-to-nature stuff. Why did she have to pick this godforsaken horse farm to hide out at, anyway?

He glanced at his watch. Time for another check. He leaned round the rock, lifting his powerful binoculars to his eye.

He frowned.

He twisted the focus knob, went past the point of focus, then came back, zeroing in on the tall, broad, dark-haired man the lady was talking to.

His frown deepened.

He didn't like the looks of this at all.

*   *   *

Why, Aaron asked himself, *am I still trying?*

She was as skittish as the deer who had sometimes traipsed through the yard of the old family cabin. The deer Megan had spent patient hours trying to tame, trying to get them to eat from her hand—

He cut off the old, worn line of thought quickly, efficiently, and ruthlessly, and turned his attention back to the woman in front of him. And the question he'd asked himself. Why was he still trying?

Disarmed by a pretty face? he wondered ruefully. Because she was that, in a gamine sort of way that he found very attractive. She was, in fact, far too pretty for him; he was well aware of his shortcomings in the looks department. Add in his size, and the mien of toughness that so many people had told him he had, and he was more vinegar than honey to most of the females he came across.

Still, he didn't think it was he who was making her nervous. Not the way she kept looking around as if she expected someone else to jump out at her at any moment. Her stalker?

Clearly she didn't want his help. And just as clearly she needed it, whether she would admit it or not. He could see the battle going on in her eyes.

And he saw the moment when she decided.

"I . . . could use a safe place to be for a while. Just," she added quickly, "long enough to get myself together, figure out what I'm going to do."

"I can arrange that." He grinned at her. "Contrary to what you might think, considering how easily you got past it, our security is top-notch."

She looked startled, and then she smiled. For a moment, it lit up her face, banishing the fear and the tension. Aaron's breath caught. "Pretty" wasn't the right word. When she wasn't terrified, she must be a very beautiful woman.

"Actually, if you recall, I didn't get past it. At least, not for long."

"But if it hadn't been for the jackpot drawing everyone's attention, we never would have known you were in that room."

"If it hadn't been for that blessed jackpot, I wouldn't have *been* in that room."

"That's what you get for playing a machine close to the door," he said, although he doubted she realized that high-paying slots were put there intentionally, to draw in more players.

"Or playing a slot at the Golden Phoenix."

He shook his head. "We're no different from any other casino. The slot payoff is regulated by the state. You just got lucky."

Her mouth quirked. "Or unlucky, depending on your point of view." She hesitated, then asked, "He wasn't angry, was he? Jason, the man I grabbed the money from?"

Interesting, Aaron thought, that she was concerned about that, in the midst of all her own troubles. "No. He turned down the jackpot, but I made sure he was paid back out of the prize."

"Thank you," she said, and there was no doubt she meant it. "And . . . I'm sorry if I put those scratches on your neck."

He'd nearly forgotten about that. He shrugged. "They're already fading."

"I just . . . had to get away."

"Which brings up a point—how did you get *into* that room?"

She eyed him warily. "Deciding if you want to have me arrested after all?"

Lord, she was suspicious, he thought. And wondered what had made her that way. "Just trying to plug a hole in our security," he said, making sure his tone was casual. "But I understand if you don't want to give away a secret."

Her brows furrowed as she looked at him. "You are the strangest man," she muttered.

He sighed. "So I'm told." *You're such a pushover, Aaron. You're a soft touch for anybody with a problem, Aaron. Anybody with a sob story to sell, just come see Aaron.*

She seemed to make up her mind. "I'd better tell Pete I'm leaving." She gave him a sideways look. "He doesn't know anything, by the way."

"I wasn't going to ask," Aaron assured her, appreciating her effort to keep the man out of it.

Whatever *it* was.

He watched her go at a trot toward the barn to find Pete. Once Pete had found out who Aaron was, he had easily told him Shelby had called this morning to see if he was still working at the stables and to ask if she could come and stay for a while. She had arrived on foot, after taking the bus to the end of the line. That meant, Aaron had noticed, a good mile-and-a-half hike up a dirt and gravel road, but she looked fit enough for it, with that leanly muscled kind of strength that could surprise you.

He'd bet Shelby whatever-her-last-name-was was just full of surprises.

Chapter Five

"So did you know that guy who got murdered? The paper said he was a big gambler."

It had taken her ten minutes of the drive in his surprisingly unflashy sport utility vehicle to work up to saying it. She put everything she had into sounding casual, as if the question meant nothing more to her than any other headline.

Still, he seemed startled by the question, and gave her a sideways look before he answered.

"Jack Pruett? Yeah, I knew him." His mouth quirked. "On occasion, up close and personal."

Shelby's breath caught. Had Pruett tried to blackmail *this* man? "I'm sorry," she said carefully. "Were you friends with him?"

"Hardly." His dry tone told her much about his opinion of the slime. "I kicked him out of the Golden Phoenix."

"Oh?"

He nodded. "Unfortunately, it's against hotel policy to have high rollers arrested unless it's unavoidable."

She barely stopped herself from smiling at that. *You just read it in the paper,* she reminded herself. *Like any other citizen.* For a moment she fiddled with her backpack, tightening a strap that didn't need it.

"So he was a . . . high roller?"

"He tried to be," Aaron said. "Most of the time he

had the bucks, but he never had the class to be a real one."

Shelby opened her mouth, then closed it again. What was wrong with her? Why was she all of a sudden ready to blurt out everything to this man she didn't even know, including exactly how Jack Pruett made a lot of his money?

After a few more miles of silence, they reached the main street that led back to Outpost.

"Did your great-great-et cetera grandfather really start this town?" she asked, curious for her own sake now.

"Yep. Although the name wasn't Montana back then," he said with a crooked smile. "Family rumor has it the old guy got himself into some trouble that necessitated a name change."

So the Montanas hadn't always been the pillars of the community they were now, she thought. Comforting, somehow.

"He was in Montana at the time," he went on, "so he became Zachary Aaron Montana. Quite a mouthful."

"You're named for him? Aaron?"

He nodded. "There's been a Zach or an Aaron in every generation since."

"That's . . . nice." He looked at her, and she realized how odd her voice had sounded. Almost wistful. "The . . . continuity of it, I mean," she said rather lamely. "I can't imagine what it's like, to have all that behind you."

"Can't you?"

She chose to take that as a purely rhetorical question, and didn't answer. He let it go, probably because now they were in town and he had traffic to deal with.

Of course she'd seen the Golden Phoenix before she'd darted in there this morning. It was hard to overlook, since it was the anchor that had started Outpost.

There were more casino/hotels now, but the Golden Phoenix was the most successful, and everybody knew its history. But she had never been inside before; her hard-earned money was not, to her mind, for risking on the unfavorable odds of games of chance. She knew perhaps better than most that if there was such a thing as luck, it was mostly bad.

She'd noticed, even in her chaotic mental state, that for a casino it was tastefully done. It glittered, but it didn't glare. Subtlety, an art lost on most casino builders. Perhaps, she thought as they drove past the main entrance, because it had begun as a small operation, it had held on to the feel of genuine hospitality, rising like the phoenix it was named for from trading post to roadside motel to hotel to hotel and casino.

He pulled around to the back, up to a set of plain double doors painted to match and blend into the building. It looked more like a delivery entrance than anything else. He parked under an overhang in a space marked only RESERVED. Subtlety, she thought again. What an odd place to find it.

There was a numerical keypad beside the big doors, and she noted that his generosity didn't run to letting her see what code he punched in. So he wasn't a complete fool, she told herself. Best remember that.

He held the door for her; she'd heard by the sound of it opening that it was a heavy metal fire door. Yet he held it with one hand, the other hooking the dark blue suit coat slung over his shoulder.

They stepped into a long, cool hallway, with utilitarian blue vinyl flooring and walls painted a softer blue. He ushered her to the right, where she saw what looked like a service elevator.

"I have to stop at my office for just a minute," he said. "Then we'll get you settled in."

She nodded, actually looking forward to being able to lock herself in a hotel room and take a long, hot shower. She was going to have to do something about clothes soon, too.

And maybe she'd splurge and spend some of her hoard on a meal, she thought as the doors slid open on the mezzanine level. Room service, eaten out of range of watching eyes—that would be nice and safe. Another upside to this she hadn't thought of before. Her stomach rumbled softly at the thought.

She followed him through a well-lit lobby area, passing another elevator with a numbered pad beside it like the one on the outside doors. From behind him, looking up at the breadth of his shoulders, she was even more aware of his size; the suit, she realized, had to be custom-made. He wasn't bulky, he was really rather lean and narrow-hipped. He was just—big.

They reached the far side of the room, and he stopped before another pair of solid double doors, again keying a code into the pad to the right. This was real security, she thought, far more than the guest room tower. But she supposed security had to be lighter there, what with the occasional tipsy guests trying to find their rooms.

They stepped into a brightly lit office. A woman she couldn't quite see past Montana's bulk greeted him. She sounded happy enough to see him, and Shelby noticed that when he answered the woman, there was both liking and respect in his voce.

"Messages are on your desk," the woman went on. "Robin uploaded her report on her meeting, and the count room reports all clear so far this afternoon."

"Thanks. Anything else?"

"Well—" The woman hesitated. She heard Montana sigh. Curious, Shelby stepped out from behind him.

"How many times did she call?" he asked, sounding weary.

"A dozen," the woman said, her gaze flicking only momentarily to Shelby before focusing once more on her boss. "Six in the last hour. All about Hank. She was pretty hysterical."

"Sorry, Francie."

The woman, who Shelby could see now was a rounded, grandmotherly woman with silver hair, smiled. "That's what I get paid for, Mr. M. Shall I keep telling her you're not back yet?"

"Yes, for a while. Oh, this is . . . Shelby. Shelby, Francine Chapman. Francie, she'll be staying with us for a while, until she can get some things taken care of."

"Welcome, dear," the woman said warmly, as if nothing else was necessary but the implied endorsement of Aaron Montana. She seemed unsurprised, as if he did this sort of thing all the time.

"Come on in," he said, and gestured toward the heavy oak door that had a simple plaque with his name. Subtlety again, she thought.

She went in after him, and he closed the door. He started toward the big desk on the far side of the spacious office. The moment he stepped away from her, Shelby took the opportunity to inspect the place.

On a credenza were some photographs—one was of a couple: a pretty woman with a sixties hairdo and a man who had to be a relative, judging by the line of his jaw and the fierceness in his dark eyes. On the adjoining wall was a large stretch of bookshelves. No ego items, she thought, no photos of him with the mayor, or diplomas from fancy schools, or sports trophies. Functional and simple.

Then she turned, and her eye was instantly drawn to a lone pedestal placed under a bright downlight. Her breath caught. Her eyes widened. She stared unblinkingly.

This was the reason for the simplicity. Nothing else could compete with this, and whoever had done this room knew it. She stared at what was obviously the source of the hotel's name. And no doubt the explanation for the extra security.

A golden phoenix.

"My God!" she whispered.

Her backpack slid from her shoulder to the floor, unnoticed. It had been a very long time since she had been awed by anything. She was awed by this.

The sheen of the metal couldn't be anything less than real gold, but that didn't matter. It was the sculpture itself that was breathtaking. The flames at the base, swirling, twisting so that they seemed alive, real, hot. And out of them, the stylized bird, suggested more than detailed, as was befitting a creature of legend. Rising, flowing lines, the hint of feathers, the sweep of wings, the arch of straining neck, the curve of beak and talon, surging up out of the fire. This phoenix did not rise easily; it fought and clawed every inch of the way. Yet you knew it would break free, for every line of the sculpture communicated triumph and power.

"Do you like it?"

Aaron's voice came softly from behind her. She didn't even look at him.

" 'Like,' " she said, "is an insipid word for *that*."

For a moment he didn't answer. When he finally spoke again, there was an undertone in his voice she couldn't quite name.

"Thank you. On behalf of my grandfather."

She looked at him. "Your grandfather? What did he do, mine the gold?"

He smiled. "No. My great-great-grandfather did that, over the mountains in California. His grandson—my grandfather—was the artist."

She stared at him. "Your grandfather *made* this?"

He nodded. "His grandfather—the miner—left each of his grandkids a gold bar in his will. This is what Gramps did with his. When he told the rest of the family what he was going to do, they thought he was nuts."

"I hope they changed their minds when they saw it."

He grinned. "Yeah, most of them. Except my uncle Henry, who still says it's a waste of perfectly good gold. But then, he's not a Montana by blood."

She felt an odd tug inside at the familial feeling evident in that last, simple sentence. She tried to ignore it.

"Your uncle Henry," she said firmly, "needs his priorities adjusted."

His grin faded. "Yeah. Yeah, he does."

She had the feeling they were suddenly no longer talking about the phoenix. She wasn't sure why she felt compelled to ask him, "Is this Henry the Hank your messages were about?"

"His father."

She remembered what Francie Chapman had said about the caller. "Don't you need to call her back? Whoever it was who was . . . hysterical?"

"Hank's mother. With her, everything is high drama. She'll keep. Come on, let's get you settled," he said, changing the subject abruptly.

She couldn't blame him; she had no business prying into his family life, anyway. And this sounded perhaps like an unpleasant aspect of that life.

But still, she couldn't help wondering what it must be like to have the kind of complex family history he must have. Her own had ended over seventeen years ago, and, as with all her memories of that time, had been mostly banished from her mind. Tiger had, for a while, been family to her heart, but he had warned her so strongly against caring too much for him that she had backed off. And now Margaret was the closest thing she had.

To her surprise, he headed not back toward the

door they'd come in but toward the paneled wall behind the golden phoenix. She saw then a faint seam and realized there was a door. He slid it back, revealing a set of doors to a small elevator.

"Secret passage?" she asked wryly.

One corner of his mouth curled upward. "My great-grandfather had it put in. He was the tiniest bit paranoid."

She couldn't help smiling. "This is the father of the artist, and the son of the guy with the gold bars?"

"Five points," he confirmed with a return smile.

She followed him into the small elevator, thinking. The idea of family that loved you instead of hurt you intrigued her, and, as with anything that interested her, she wanted to know everything about it. But now, obviously, was not the time to ask.

There were no floor indicators and no row of buttons from which to select. He merely inserted a key in the lock on the wall and turned it, then the doors closed and the car began to rise smoothly. She assumed it went to only one place. A private elevator.

She stifled a smile. Even in the midst of her own chaos, it was fun to have a peek at how the richer half lived.

As the elevator doors slid open, he stood back and gestured her past him. She stepped into a large, open room, clearly the main room of a suite or apartment. The focal point was a comfortable-looking deep-green leather sofa and two chairs, arranged front of an iron stove that served as a fireplace. The slender flue of the stove was flanked by expansive windows that looked out not on the valley below and Outpost, but rather on the mountains above.

If you didn't know, you could imagine there was no hotel, casino, or even town at all outside those windows. She'd bet it was spectacular in the winter, with snow all around.

Gradually she noticed other things in the room. The desk held a couple of small stacks of papers and a computer, and the leather office chair matched the couch. Next to an opening that appeared to lead down a hallway was a shelf housing a sound system and, she guessed, a large but not huge television behind closed cabinet doors. Along a long wall was a medium-sized dining table with six chairs upholstered in a dark-green plaid. Next to it, in the opposite corner from the desk and with a view toward the windows, was an open, airy kitchen, divided from the main room by an efficient-looking island.

A kitchen. An elevator that went to only one place. A desk with a computer.

It hit then, yanking her out of her reverie about the view and the comfortable feel of this space. This was no hotel suite. This was someone's home. And it didn't take a giant leap to realize whose it was. She whirled around.

He was over by the desk, speaking quietly into a phone. She'd been so caught up in the view and her inspection that she hadn't even heard him.

He hung up, then walked toward her with a smile on his face.

"Housekeeping's going to bring up our stranded-traveler kit. It'll have a toothbrush, soap, hairbrush, all the essentials. And a robe you can change into, if you'd like to send your clothes to be cleaned. Looks like you had to take off without packing."

"What," she asked stiffly, although she already knew, "is this place?"

His forehead creased in puzzlement. "My apartment. It's the securest place in the hotel section. Even the doors are cypher locked. Nobody can get in here without the code or a passkey."

If Shelby were a bit less suspicious, she might even have believed his motives were altruistic. He might not be drop-dead gorgeous, but he was wealthy, successful, and apparently of great standing around here. Surely he didn't have to resort to such machinations to lure women to his bed.

But it seemed too classic to ignore, an offer of help that really disguised the oldest of ulterior motives.

"You'll be safe here."

"How about getting out?" she asked, wondering miserably if she was well and truly trapped.

For a moment she didn't think he was going to answer. But finally he said, very quietly, "If you feel you have to, those doors"—he gestured to the set of doors on the wall next to the desk—"are to a hotel corridor. You don't need the code going out. Or there's the elevator."

"If you have the key," she said tightly.

"No. It goes down without the key. It just doesn't come up without it." His voice was softer, as if he knew she was spooked to the point of running.

"Oh."

She walked over to the windows. She looked up at the mountains. Given who his family was, she would have thought he'd have chosen to look out on the town his ancestors had built. She wondered if this choice was a statement of some kind, or if it was simply that he preferred, as she did, the view of the wild, untamed place Outpost had once been.

She shook her head sharply, as if that could clear away the muddle and bring her back to dealing with the reality of the present.

"I'll call the gift shop," he was saying, "and have them send up some other clothes. Just give me your sizes. Or you can go down and pick them out yourself if you'd rather. I'll tell them you're coming."

She turned to face him. "I can't afford it," she said bluntly, meaning much more than simply not being able to spend part of her small bankroll needlessly. He answered as if she meant only the monetary cost.

"We can work something out. You can pay for them when you can."

Pay for them how? she wondered. *In your bed?* Maybe she'd misjudged him. Even years after her escape from the streets she was still not a fool. It seemed she was going to have to get away from Aaron Montana.

And, she added wryly to herself, fend him off until she did. She obviously couldn't fight him, but no matter; Tiger had always told her a good bag of tricks beat brawn any day.

"Is there someone you need to call?"

She snapped back to the present. That had to stop, that wandering off into la-la land. Not paying attention could have dire consequences.

"What?" she said.

"Someone who might be worried about you, that you should let know you're all right?"

Margaret. God, she needed to call Margaret. But she couldn't, not from up here, not when she didn't know what this man was up to. He could have the call traced, or track down Margaret's number. It would have to wait. She could slip down to a pay phone later. If not, then she would call as soon as she got free of him.

But for now, this was a good place to be. Until the cops came up with something, she was safe on that front. Right now, what she had to worry about was her shadow. And she was safer from him here than anyplace else she had access to. So for now, she would stay. She would bide her time.

Another thing Tiger had taught her was patience.

Chapter Six

Mike Delano leaned back in his chair, rubbing a hand over his gritty eyes. He should be sleepy, but he wasn't. Instead he was wired so tight he was humming. It was a familiar sensation, this adrenaline-fueled feeling of not being able to shut down. He almost always reached this point on a murder case.

He just didn't usually reach it this soon.

He'd seen this kind of thing before, in his seventeen years as a cop: the facade of respectable businessman hiding a host of nefarious activities. But he'd rarely come across one with as wide a reach as Jack Pruett.

He leaned forward and dragged out the already thick folder. He knew he could access the information on the computer terminal in the reports room next door, but he would probably have to wait in line for time at the keyboard, and the thing was so outdated it took several minutes to find and call up a file this large. The detective division didn't rate a terminal of its own. The chief preferred to spend the department's budget on sleek new police cars to be seen by the public who paid for them with their taxes, a tactic that most deputies chalked up to the fact that his was an elected position.

Besides, Mike was a bit of a traditionalist. He wanted to page through the physical file, in his own time and in the order he preferred, not the way some computer thought he should.

He opened the manila folder and looked down at the photograph attached to the first page. It was a mug shot taken the last time Pruett had been booked, well over three years ago. Not that the charge had stuck, no more than any of them had.

The man was—or had been—a good-looking enough guy, Mike supposed. Or at least he was the type some women went for. His own ex-wife, for instance, he thought wryly. She'd been a sucker for that blond, bronzed look. Personally, he thought the guy had been a bit too smooth—"oily" was the word that came to mind—and way too pleased with himself.

Mike ran a hand over his own very dark hair. *Well*, he thought with an admittedly vindictive sort of pleasure, *he ain't real pleased now.*

"Detective Delano."

He slapped the folder shut and looked up, startled, into the face of Gordon Cushman, the chief of Outpost's police force. Tall and imposing with an impressive head of gray hair, the chief had great presence, as even his detractors had to admit.

He always addressed his people by their rank; he said it was out of professional respect, but most thought it was to be sure they all knew there was a line between him and them, not to be crossed by the peons. But then, it was in the job description of police officers to think that way, Mike admitted with an inward smile.

"Yes, sir?" he asked.

The man sat down in the chair beside Mike's desk. "You landed the Pruett homicide, correct?"

Mike restrained himself from pointing out that since he was the only man assigned the rarely used title of "homicide detective," yes he had. He merely nodded.

"How's it coming?"

"No witnesses," Mike said. "No one saw or heard anything—or if they did they aren't talking. I've been on the phone all afternoon, going through his history, connections, all that. Pruett had his fingers in ventures all over the country."

And enough of them, Mike thought, had been legitimate so that some of the less innocent ones had so far slid by. They'd never been able to prove that Pruett was the slime they thought he was. The district attorney's office was in the same boat; there had never been enough evidence to make charges stick. Pruett might have been sleazy, but he had also been shrewd. And lucky.

Until now.

"He had some very important business partners," Chief Cushman went on.

Was that what this was? Mike wondered. Some sort of pressure because the victim had friends in high places? He felt his temper begin to rise; he did his damned best on any case. In his book, any murder deserved his best shot, whether it was somebody with highly placed friends or a bum out on the street.

"I know about the racing consortium," he said neutrally. The group of powerful men who were trying to bring a racetrack to the county—some of whom it was suspected had made their money by questionable means—were first on his list of people to prod about Pruett. "I have an appointment with them at five."

"Watch out for them," the chief said, with a note of commiseration in his voice. "Those guys have a great deal of clout, beyond Outpost and this county. But Pruett had his fingers in a lot of other pies, too." Cushman paused before adding, "And he wasn't always an open partner."

Mike went still. He'd learned much over the years about body language and vocal inflection, and this meant something. He waited, silently.

"Look," Cushman said at last, sounding sheepish,

"before you're through, you're probably going to come across *my* name."

Mike blinked, startled. Of all the things he might have expected, this wasn't one of them. "Your name? Sir?"

"Yes, damn it. I didn't know at the time, of course. He hid behind one of his cover investment companies, but he was one of the other partial owners of my condo building."

Mike blinked. "The one that burned down?" A couple of years ago it had been headline news in Outpost, both because it had been a spectacular sight and because the chief of police had lived in and owned part of the building.

Cushman nodded. "That's how I found out, it came out during the insurance investigation. I never knew about his connection until then."

Mike's brows lifted. "That must have been a shock."

"You're telling me," the chief said sourly. "I was not a happy man. Like I've always said, he's a petty sleaze, not worth much of our time, but I didn't like finding that out."

Mike never had quite agreed that Pruett wasn't worth their time, but he wasn't going to argue that again now.

Cushman slapped his hands on his knees, then stood up. "Anyway, it's all public record now, but I wanted you to hear it from me first. Figured it would save you having to ask."

Mike nodded. "Thanks. It would have been disconcerting to come across without warning."

That, he thought as the chief strode away, was an understatement. He was grateful the man had saved him the wasted time of having to track him down for an explanation. It would have been time he couldn't afford; he'd already had to appropriate one of the clerks from records to help log in all the evidence they'd gathered at the scene.

He'd still managed to cross some people off his suspect list today. But if the rumors about Pruett were true, and if what they'd found in that locked metal box from the man's desk was what Mike suspected, it could soon become a very long list again.

He glanced at his watch and stood up. Time to go meet the racing consortium. Maybe he'd get lucky and have his suspects nailed by tonight.

Shelby dodged behind a bank of slot machines, her shopping bag of spare clothes clutched to her chest as if it could protect her. She took several deep breaths, steeled herself, and then leaned forward to peek around the corner.

He was here.

She jerked back, even though he was looking out across the casino floor, not toward the row of shops. But she was certain it was him. The only other person who knew what had happened at Pruett's house. The one person above all she had to be afraid of.

The one person she knew with full certainty wanted her dead.

Leaning against the wall, she tried to think clearly. It was difficult, because she knew she was closer to death than she had been since she'd left Tiger. Surely the guy wouldn't try anything here, among all these people. But he'd hunted her down here, which made her uncertain of what he might do.

She'd made her phone call from the pay phone in the back of the gift shop. She'd had to make her message to Margaret hasty and, for Robert's sake, cryptic. But it was done. Margaret would know she was all right.

Wouldn't it just be too ironic for her be killed just moments later?

Any lingering doubts she had about going back up-stairs were vanquished now by the sight of that man, hunting. She didn't like being prey. Tiger always said the best defense was a good offense. But he also said if you can't muster an offense, retreat until you can.

Obviously her shadow must have seen her come in here at some point. He would just stay, circling like a shark, waiting for her to surface. The question was how to get back to her sanctuary without being seen.

She looked around, but there was no way out in front of her except across the casino floor, right under his nose. And there was no exit from the shops behind her, unless there was one in the back of the beauty shop—

She stared at the window, at the impossibly long-necked mannequin heads that held wigs in a display case and the portraits of beautiful people with trendy hairstyles.

She looked back toward the casino. He was closer, although still looking the other way. But if he was going about this methodically, he would trip over her in a few minutes.

She had to move, and she had to move now.

She crouched down and inched backward, under cover of the slots, grateful that there were no players in the row to see her.

An image flashed through her head once more, the startlingly loud report of the gun, the hideous spraying of blood, and worse, the heavy, final thud of the body.

She edged back farther, realizing she was at least drawing attention. Which, she thought, might not be a bad thing. But she wasn't sure the grim-faced man wouldn't kill her right here and simply fade into the crowd.

She glanced behind her once more. A woman came out of the beauty shop, patting her newly styled, bright red hair. Shelby went still. She looked at the hound from hell who was only seconds away from her. Then at the beauty shop, with its open door beckoning.

One more peek to make sure he was still looking the other way, then she left the cover of the slots and darted inside the shop.

Damn the bitch.

He drew a long, deep breath. He had quit smoking five years ago, but being in a place like this, where secondhand smoke drifted freely, made him crazy. It took all of his considerable willpower not to cross the casino—breathing deeply all the way—to the gift shop and buy a pack. Maybe two.

Might as well, he thought sourly, *for all the good this is doing.*

She'd been right there, practically under his nose. And for once, without the man she'd been talking to out at that godforsaken, remote, primitive stable. He'd glanced around, gauging the number of people close to her. He took his eyes off of her for barely a second, but when he looked back, she had vanished.

He'd known this was going to get complicated when she and the man had come back here together and gone in through what was clearly a private entrance.

His mouth tightened. He did not like this new element, the man she'd picked up. His assessment of the woman might have been a bit off, but he'd sized up this guy at a glance and he didn't like the results. Not just big and obviously fit, but strong. Though the big guy might look civilized on the surface, he had a feeling her protector could turn as tough as he had to if the occasion arose. The solid jaw, the slightly crooked nose—oh, yes, he would fight if he had to. And for all the fancy suit and tie, he'd make it a contest.

He waited a few minutes longer, playing with his ring, watching the area where he'd last seen her. With that blond hair, she was usually easy to spot. When she didn't reappear, he slowly began to backtrack to where he'd first seen her. He'd noted the spot simply because he always did; you never knew what bit of knowledge might come in handy in getting the job done.

When he got there, he stood for a moment, looking around. And then he saw it, just beyond where he'd first spotted her—a gap in the wall, well lit compared to the relative dimness of the casino. It was obviously the entrance to something. He moved ahead slowly, casually. His brow furrowed when he saw the telephone symbol. Surely she wouldn't be using a pay phone? Unless she was making a call she didn't want her companion to know about.

As he moved closer, he saw it wasn't just a phone alcove, but a hallway to several offices.

"Now we're getting somewhere," he muttered under his breath. It only made sense that she had come from there, after they'd used that private entrance.

A man in the casino uniform came out of one of the doors on the right, so he backed out of sight. With an inward smile of satisfaction, he began to plan.

His urge for a cigarette was gone.

Margaret fumbled with her keys, dropped them, bent to pick them up, then took a deep breath to steady herself and stepped out of her car.

She was exhausted. Every hour that passed without news made it worse. If something didn't happen soon, she was going to have to risk everything and go to the police. But first, God help her, she would have to explain to Robert.

Once she got inside the house, she set down her purse and keys, intending to fix a cup of herbal tea in an effort to calm her nerves. But first she would check the answering machine, as she did immediately each time she came back. Even when she was home she checked it, just in case she'd somehow missed the phone's ring. That's how close to the edge she was, how near to—

There was a message waiting, from a half hour ago.

"Robert," she told herself, her pulse racing. But she had just spoken to him on her cell phone, and he'd said nothing about calling the house. Not that he would, she thought as she reached out and pushed the button with a trembling finger.

She nearly cried out aloud when the familiar, loved voice came out of the tiny speaker, distorted slightly by some persistent and very strange-sounding background noise.

"Margaret, it's me. I can't talk long, but don't worry. I'm all right. Everything's all right, or will be soon. Just wait, don't do *anything*, and I'll explain as soon as I can." A pause, then, "I love you."

As soon as she heard the click indicating the connection had been broken, Margaret had to fight back tears.

Shelby was alive, and all right.

Well, perhaps all right was a bit too much to hope for; she had sounded strained. Not to mention that noise, wherever she'd been calling from. And she'd said, "I love you." That alone made Margaret worry. Not that she didn't know the girl loved her, but it wasn't something she said very often. It was a conscious effort for Shelby to express what she felt after years of protecting herself.

But, God, why hadn't she said more? Told her where she was, what had happened? If anything had. But something must have, or Shelby would simply come home. But why hadn't she said?

Margaret answered her own question: Shelby knew it was possible that Robert would hear her message first. She'd had to be careful in what she said. Shelby would think about that kind of thing; she always did.

The tears Margaret had fought back welled up anew. She'd always been as honest as she dared with Robert, but there was still that chapter of her youth he knew nothing about. She'd been an out-of-control kid, away from a very strict home for the first time, blindly in love with the most handsome, charismatic guy on campus, and going along with anything she thought would make him love her back.

She'd been a fool; she'd learned from the mistake and moved on, never guessing that nearly twenty-five years later it would come back to haunt her yet again. She hadn't thought of Dan Holowell and his carefully planned seduction in years.

Damn him, she thought now.

She'd been a naive girl, had adored and trusted him completely. He knew it and he'd used it to get her drunk and then high, and while she was barely aware of what was going on, he had arranged his little tableaux to photograph, keeping her in line by mentioning that he'd dumped his last girlfriend because she hadn't cooperated.

She shuddered, knowing how lucky she was that she hadn't wound up pregnant, with no idea who the father was, or contracted some awful disease. Then she groaned inwardly. "Lucky" was not a word she applied to herself of late.

Dan couldn't have planned this part of it, she told herself, because back then the photos wouldn't have been worth anything. She was just an unimportant small-town girl. Not until she married Robert, and he began to move up in the local world, did she have anything worth trying to take away.

Somehow Dan had found out about her new life and had sold the negatives to that piece of slime Pruett, who had known just what they were worth to the wife of the newest member of the police commission. She'd been willing to pay as much cash as she could to avoid the embarrassment to her husband. She'd even been willing to hide it from him, as much as that made her sick inside.

But she wasn't willing to free herself at the cost of Shelby's life. She knew what being locked up would do to a young woman who had already spent too much of her life in one kind of trap or another. Now that she knew Shelby was alive and apparently unhurt, she could only pray she hadn't done something very, very foolish.

Margaret shivered, forcibly changing the path of her thoughts. She had put her plan into action earlier, and now wondered if she should call it off, now that Shelby had contacted her. But the possibility that Shelby was in serious trouble hadn't changed, otherwise she would have just come home. No, she still had to find her, wherever she was hiding.

It suddenly occurred to Margaret that she knew what the background noise in Shelby's call had been. *Finally, a clue*, she breathed to herself as she ran to her purse and dug out the business card she'd been given earlier. Then she headed for the phone. She would find Shelby, and then together they would deal with whatever she had done.

She only wished she could say with utter certainty that Shelby was incapable of killing.

Even if you weren't a gambler, if you ran a casino you tended to think in terms of odds. And right now Aaron was thinking that the odds that Shelby had mentioned Pruett simply because she'd read his name in the papers were very slim.

No matter how he added it up, he didn't like the results.

She was afraid.

She was fleeing something, or someone.

She acted as if she was being followed.

She asked pointed questions about a murdered man.

She had been very worried that he was a cop.

There was one logical explanation for all that. There might be more than one, but the first one that leapt out at him was one he wished he could discard outright.

She didn't look like a killer. Not with that elfin appearance and those wide green eyes.

But he wasn't naive enough to think an innocent appearance couldn't hide a deadly intent. And he couldn't let the fact that he found her attractive get in the way of his judgment.

He heard the shower start in the guest room. Earlier she had gone down to the gift shop. He'd been leery but had let her go alone, figuring he couldn't watch her all the time. And that if she really wanted to run, he had no right to stop her.

But she had come back, with a small bag in hand, holding only simple leggings and a sweatshirt, no doubt the cheapest things in the store. She had seemed jumpier than ever, but had only asked if she could clean up. He'd directed her to the guest room and bath and called for someone to pick up the clothes she'd been wearing and take them to the laundry.

He changed into jeans himself while she was gone. He was through at his office for the day, and his staff could reach him here if they needed him.

More comfortable—he never had liked suits much—he settled down at his desk, turning on the computer, which was linked to the one in his office. He sent an E-mail message to Francie, telling her he would be here and to call if necessary, then opened the report Robin had filed.

But the meeting with the Secret Service had been routine, as much as it could be, and he found it hard to concentrate. His mind kept wandering back to the woman in the other room.

He leaned back in his desk chair, thinking. And finally, almost reluctantly, he reached for the phone, keeping part of his attention on the sound of the shower. He dialed the cell phone number, knowing Mike was rarely in the office during a big investigation.

Mike answered, sounding harried. "Hey, buddy, what's up?"

Aaron didn't waste time with preliminaries. "That murder you mentioned—is it the Pruett case?"

"None other. Why?"

"I heard somebody asking about it. I knew the guy, sort of."

"I'd guess every casino boss between here and Reno, and probably Vegas, knows him. I should have figured you would. You seen him lately?"

"Not since a couple of months ago when I tossed him out of the Golden Phoenix on his expensively dressed butt."

Mike laughed. "Good for you."

"Figure he deserved it, huh?"

"Deserved worse than that. Guy was a sleaze, one of those slippery ones we were never able to make anything stick to."

"He didn't impress me as that smart. Must have had good lawyers."

"And friends in high places," Mike said sourly. "At least, that's the word going around the D.A.'s office."

"As in bribed friends in high places? He always seemed to have plenty of money to throw around."

"No doubt. Know anybody he ran with, aside from his string of arm-candy blondes?"

Aaron winced at the reference, thinking how well it fit Shelby. He hadn't thought of that aspect. "A couple. Jimmy Davalos, but as far as I know he went back to Atlantic City. Gerry Franco's still around, though."

"Ah, now there's a pair to draw to," Mike said. "I'll track down Franco."

A memory came back to Aaron suddenly. "Now that I think about it, the night we booted him I heard from one of our Golden Club members that there was a problem between Pruett and the racing syndicate," he said, referring to the "high-roller" club that catered to the really big spenders who came in to gamble big money.

"Really? What kind of problem?"

"He didn't go into it, but I got the feeling there was some argument about control of some aspects of the deal."

"Is your source directly involved? An investor?"

"No. So it's bad enough that he heard it on the outside."

"Thanks for the tip," Mike said. "You sure you don't want my job?"

Aaron laughed. It was an old joke between them. But he knew the answer. When Mike had been a street cop, he'd gone on more than one ride-along with him, and while he'd been fascinated by the work and how things were done, he knew himself well enough to know that he couldn't handle seeing people at their worst most of the time.

"So Pruett was a real prize?" he asked.

"A peach," Mike said. "I'm sure he's been running pyramid schemes, and my gut tells me probably more."

"More?"

"For starters, some fluff and fold on dirty money."

Aaron's brows rose. Money laundering was always a problem in any business that dealt with large amounts of cash. "I knew I didn't like the guy."

"And getting himself murdered hasn't moved him up to sterling citizen in my book," Mike said.

"You said that was for starters," Aaron prodded. He knew Mike couldn't tell him anything about the investigation, but at least he could get a sense of the way it was going. And he knew where the line was between casual interest and pushing hard enough to raise the detective's considerable curiosity.

"I suspect he had an organization under him, doing his dirty work. And I've been hearing rumors about blackmail. That the guy had a whole lot of people on a string."

"And if that's true," Aaron said slowly, "you've got a whole lot of suspects."

"More than I can shake a stick at, to quote my sainted mother. It's not like the guy hid out. He was always out there, high profile, flashing the cash and the car and the platinum blondes."

"So those same lot of suspects wouldn't find it hard to get to him."

"Motive, access, and opportunity, buddy, that's the tune."

After he'd said his good-byes and hug up, Aaron sat there for a while, Mike's words echoing in his mind.

Motive, access, and opportunity.

A lot of people had all three.

But it was Shelby who was on the run.

Chapter Seven

*N*ow, Aaron thought.

She'd had a chance to shower, had on clean clothes—it was pleasing, somehow, to see her sitting across his dining table in a bright-green Golden Phoenix sweatshirt—and she'd devoured most of the house's special roast chicken with wine and mushroom sauce that he'd ordered sent up.

Now was the time to try again.

He cleared his throat. She raised her head. Wide green eyes looked up at him from beneath a long fringe of silky, wispy bangs. He forgot what he was going to say.

"You look nice," he finally managed. "The green makes your eyes really . . . green," he ended lamely.

She shrugged. "I clean up okay."

"I'm sorry about earlier. When I startled you."

He'd come up quietly behind her as she stood staring out the mountain windows. She had reacted with amazing swiftness, whirling, crouching, instinctively ready to fight even though he towered over her. That kind of instant reaction, he knew, wasn't learned in a matter of days. He wondered where it had come from, what situation had made her ready to fight at any moment.

Another shrug, but no words this time.

Subtlety, he thought, was getting him nowhere.

"You feel like telling me yet what you're running from?"

Her gaze went back to her plate, although there was nothing left but a few bones. "I can't."

Progress, he thought. At least she wasn't denying she was running. "How about just your last name?"

She looked at him again, shaking her head mutely. But she didn't look happy about it; he supposed that was worth something.

Now, he told himself, *while she's looking at you and you can see her eyes.*

"How did you get involved with Pruett?"

She froze, not breathing, eyes wide, for a split second that seemed to last an eternity.

Bull's-eye, Aaron said to himself. But it wasn't triumphant; all he felt was a sick churning low in his gut. He hadn't wanted to believe it, but her reaction, although quickly hidden, had betrayed her.

She jumped to her feet. "Thank you for the meal, and the clothes," she said stiffly. "I'll send you the money when I can."

She turned and just as stiffly picked up the shopping bag she had brought out of the bathroom with her. She set it on the table in front of him.

"I'd appreciate it if you would send this back down to the beauty shop. I promised them I'd return it intact."

He glanced inside. Saw a mass of red hair. A wig? He frowned, but set it aside when she turned on her heel without another word.

"I'm not going to chase you," he said mildly when she started quickly toward the guest room, as if getting ready to run.

She stopped short. "What?"

He never moved. "Makes running kind of silly, doesn't it, when you're doing it from somebody who isn't chasing?"

For a long, silent moment she just stared at him. Then, in a voice that ripped at his heart, she asked softly, "What do you want from me?"

"What I want is to help."

"Why?" she asked, sounding bewildered.

Was she so completely without anyone to help her that it stunned her to think someone would want to?

"It's a character flaw," he said lightly. "Had it since I was a kid. Ask any of my family."

Slowly, as if her puzzlement made it impossible to stand up any longer, she sank back down onto her chair.

"I used to bring home injured animals. Lost dogs. Friends who had troubles at home. You name it."

She shook her head slowly, but said nothing. He tried an abrupt change of subject.

"That best friend of mine, who's on the police force—he's a really good guy. He'll listen to whatever you have to say. More important, he'll *hear* what you tell him."

She shook her head again. And he saw again the bone-deep fear he'd seen on the videotape. He couldn't push her, not when she was that afraid.

"This is none of your business." Her tone was forced, as if she was having to work hard to maintain the tough demeanor. "You should just butt out."

"I wish I could," he said, meaning it. "My life would be so much easier."

"I don't need you. I've been taking care of myself since I was twelve."

"Have you?"

He said it casually, but inside he was filing away another nugget of knowledge about her. If she'd been on her own since she was twelve, chances were she'd been a runaway.

Visions of his own little girl, who had been so precious, so very wanted, rose up to haunt him, and he knew he couldn't walk away from this. Of course, Shelby was not a little girl anymore. Far from it. He had little doubt that she was as tough and strong as she had to be. No, it wasn't a weakness in her that made him offer his help. Some said it was a weakness in him.

He wished she'd quit looking at him like that, with those unsettling eyes.

And he wished she'd look at him forever like that, with those unsettling eyes.

Knock it off, he ordered himself. *She needs help, not you leering at her like a man who's suddenly realized he's gone without for too long.*

Shelby got up again. She carried the plates to the kitchen, rinsed them and put them in the dishwasher. The glasses were next. Then she began to walk, pace almost, as if she was still on the edge of running.

"Was he here? Is that why you needed the wig? As a disguise?"

The quick flick of her glance gave him his answer. He sensed it was all he was going to get, unless he said exactly the right thing.

"I made some calls this afternoon," he said.

She stopped in midstride, a couple of feet away. She stared at him. "Calls?"

He nodded. "To some folks I know." Who owed him favors he'd never collected on, until now. "In some of the . . . more interesting circles around here, and Reno. They had a lot to say about Mr. Jack Pruett."

He could almost see the battle in her eyes, a need to know warring with the fear of betraying anything more to him. Finally she resorted to the catchall word. "So?"

He went on as if she'd expressed avid interest. "Nearly all of them said they would have knocked off Pruett themselves, if they'd thought they could get away with it. And they were neither surprised nor sorry to hear that somebody had."

She didn't speak this time, but she didn't move as if to leave either. He considered his next words carefully.

"Each one had a theory about who might have done it, too."

"Oh?"

Was it his imagination, or was she suddenly even more tense? He'd meant what he said—each person he'd talked to, whether on the up-and-up or a tad on the shady side, had had someone at the top of the list of probables. None had specifically mentioned a green-eyed pixie, however.

But they had confirmed Mike's words; Pruett went through decorative blondes like a chain-smoker went through cigarettes. And once he decided to discard them, he wasn't particularly nice about it; he'd been known to slap them around. He couldn't picture Shelby with a man like that, but what did he really know?

What he knew was that if Pruett had tried to slap her around she would have fought back. She'd shown him, even in the short time he'd known her, that she was a fighter. She would never give up, she'd go down battling.

She was the polar opposite of his ex-wife. Cindy was soft, frail, and more than a bit timid. Where Cindy was fragile, spun glass, Shelby was tensile steel.

Which meant he would never break her. But he could push and see which way she bent.

"Were you one of Pruett's girls?"

A split second later his head was ringing from her slap. He'd been so focused on getting the truth out of her that he'd neglected to consider that she was liable to try and knock his head off.

There had been a second part to this ingenious plan

of his, he recalled when his head started to clear. But he didn't doubt she would clobber him again if he provoked her.

In for a penny, he thought. "Then it must be blackmail. Did you kill him over it?"

"No!"

He caught her arm before she connected this time. He had to exert himself to halt her swing; strong, he thought, definitely strong. He wondered which she had been denying so furiously, the blackmail or the murder.

She yanked free of his grip. "You can go straight to hell," she hissed. "I don't need your help, and I don't need you butting in where you're not wanted!"

She started toward the room where she'd left her backpack. Then she stopped and looked back at him, her gaze even hotter with anger than before.

"And," she said with fierce emphasis, "even if I wanted your help, I wouldn't sleep with you to get it!"

Aaron gaped at her. "What?".

"You heard me. I don't pay for anything with sex."

Aaron drew back, stung. She thought he expected her to sleep with him in return for his help?

He quashed the unexpected sexual jolt her words had caused. Although it shouldn't have surprised him, he supposed; interest had been stirring since the first time she'd looked up at him from beneath those bangs.

"What," he said, as evenly as he could manage, "led you to the conclusion that I would demand sex for helping you?"

"Oh, please. You brought me here to your place instead of sticking me in a hotel room. You bought me clothes. And a fancy meal. You pretend to be all concerned about my problems, when you don't really give a—"

"Okay," he said, holding up a hand. "I would argue

the accuracy of the last one with you, but I can see where you might . . . misinterpret the rest. But you're wrong. Very, very wrong."

For a long moment she looked at him assessingly. He wondered what thoughts were racing through that agile mind of hers. And then, to his amazement, he saw color rise in her cheeks.

"Oh." She said it in the tone of someone who felt foolish, or had come to a realization she should have reached before. "I'm sorry. I shouldn't have assumed . . . you would even want to . . . I mean, I'm hardly your type, I imagine."

He lifted a brow at her. "And just what," he asked, "do you think my type is?"

Her mouth twisted. She glanced around the apartment. "Expensive," she said.

There was enough self-deprecation in her voice that he didn't feel insulted again, but he decided it wouldn't hurt if she thought so.

"So you're saying I have to buy my women. Is that it?"

"No!" She looked satisfyingly mortified. "I didn't mean that. I just . . . it was arrogant to just assume you would . . ."

"Want you?"

She lowered her gaze and nodded, biting her lip. And in that simple motion of catching her full lower lip between her teeth—one of which, he noticed, was endearingly crooked—she made him face the real answer. The answer his body was already making clear, responding to merely the suggestion.

"Oh, yes," he said, his voice suddenly tight. "I could want you, easily enough."

Her head came up, and he saw the startled look on her face as she recognized what he knew showed in his face—a sudden, surging hunger that surprised him with its strength and swiftness.

"But let me tell *you* something," he went on flatly. "You'd have to strip naked and climb into bed with me before I'd do anything about it. Because there's one thing I require of a lover, and that's honesty. Including honesty about the reasons for having sex. No retroactive mind-changing the morning after in my bed."

She paled, then blushed anew. He wasn't sure if it was something specific that he'd said or just the bluntness with which he'd said it.

"On second thought," he said, abruptly weary of it all, "don't bother. I don't *accept* sex as payment for anything."

She gave him a wide-eyed look he couldn't quite interpret.

And then she turned and walked away.

Shelby dodged into the guest room and shut the door.

She needed time, time to think, to figure out why this man had her so unsettled. Why she was so breathless after that angry little discussion.

It was her own fault, she told herself, for bringing it up in the first place. But she'd been so certain he had to have some ulterior motive, and sex was the only motive she could think of. As far as he knew, it was the only thing she had to offer.

So she'd insulted the man, when in fact something about Aaron Montana appealed to her, made her think of toughness and staying power, qualities that she greatly admired.

So, you're thinking that going to bed with him, even for all the wrong reasons, might not be so bad? In fact, might even be—

Her breath caught as the riotous thought formed, and her pulse began to race. She didn't understand. she *never* thought about a man like this. Any man, let alone a man she'd just met. A man who lived in a world she had never even visited.

A man who was big enough and strong enough to break her in half. But he was also a man who had already shown he could be gentle, a startling quality in a man of his size and power.

She had challenged that power. She'd slapped him. Hard. He could have hurt her badly.

An odd little shiver rippled through her as the ramifications struck. Whatever else he was, on some gut level she had known he wouldn't strike back. She so rarely trusted anyone that it stunned her to realize that she had trusted him, after so short a time.

She tried to rein in her whirling thoughts. Right now she had something else to deal with. Aaron suspected she was the killer. And if he went to his friend the cop . . .

She took a steadying breath.

She was fairly sure the police had nothing on her. She'd left no obvious clues. With modern technology they might be able to prove she was there, but they would have to know about her first, would have to have her to match to the evidence. And until that night she had had no direct connection to the man, no reason to be on a list of suspects that she guessed, given Pruett's propensity for making enemies, was a long one. She should be safe. Unless Aaron turned her in.

And unless her relentless shadow, who had already tracked her here, caught her.

She began to pace, trying to analyze her choices.

Home and Margaret—in her mind and heart too closely bound together to differentiate—were out of the question.

She could run farther. Leave town. The state. Maybe even the country. But she didn't have the money.

She could go to the police, she thought, then quickly discarded the idea. If it was only her call she might do it, but she couldn't risk Margaret's precious secret. She had no right. And she owed her too much.

The last option was starting to look better and better.

Staying put.

She stopped her pacing and sank down on the edge of the Mission-style bed. It was covered in a quietly luxurious cream-colored comforter and piled with welcoming pillows. Margaret would like it, she thought as she absently ran a finger over the heavy damask fabric. She would like the whole room, rich in those fabrics and brightened by touches of green and yellow here and there.

It was elegant, just like Margaret. She'd always admired that. Maybe because she knew that she herself was so far from it. Nobody would ever accuse her of possessing elegance, especially now. She was reverting to the Shelby of the streets. She'd slid completely back into assessing everyone by how much good they could do her, or whether they could or would hurt her. It was as instinctive as it had ever been.

Back on the streets, when she'd been learning from Tiger, it had been life or death. Now it was—

She stopped, nearly moaning aloud at the irony.

Now it was life or death.

Chapter Eight

"Oh, yes, I remember Jack."

It seemed that everybody who had come across Jack Pruett remembered him—and not kindly. Mike had never encountered a guy who had given so many people reason to dislike him. Or worse.

And Mrs. Ruth Washington, a retired Reno high school teacher who was now living in Florida, had as much reason as most. He'd come across her name in Pruett's juvenile file. She had been injured trying to break up the last of a long string of fights between Pruett and a particular classmate. A former school enemy was a long way to go for a suspect, but not impossible. Mike had gotten leads through longer shots, and she'd been listed, so he'd taken advantage of the time difference and called her.

"It's been nearly fifteen years, but I remember. He was a nice young man," Mrs. Washington said, startling Mike into paying closer attention. No one yet had said Pruett was anything even faintly resembling "nice." But then she added an explanatory word. "Once."

He was curious enough at this note that was out of tune with the rest of the symphony he'd heard about Pruett that he asked, "How do you mean?"

"Jack was one of those boys who used money and charm to slide through life. His family was wealthy, and he was quite spoiled. Always had the best cars and clothes. But he was always willing to foot the bill for his friends to join him on this or that adventure."

"Sounds generous," Mike said neutrally.

"I suppose it was, although with his father's money. I got a call about Jack from an old colleague. Is it true?"

"Afraid so."

She sighed. "I'm afraid I saw something like this coming, long ago. After you've been teaching for a while, you can begin to pick out the ones who . . . aren't going to have happy lives. I suppose it must be the same with you in your work, when you deal with children."

"It is," he said. "Sometimes you can just tell it's not even worth trying to help."

"Let me ask you," she said, turning the tables on him, "what about the ones you're not sure about? What do you do?"

"You try," Mike said, without thinking about it.

"Why? There must be so many," she said.

This time he had to think. He wasn't quite sure how he'd lost control of this conversation, but when you were asking for information, it didn't hurt to work on a little rapport.

"Because," he said finally, "you can't risk losing one that could have been saved if just one person had tried. Maybe you're wrong, maybe it's wasted, but you have to, or what's the point?"

There was a pause, and then she said, "I like you, Detective Delano. Ask your questions."

A bit startled by the quick turn, Mike knew instinctively that you'd have to stretch some to keep up with this woman; he felt like he'd been vetted by an expert.

"When did you last see Jack?"

She thought for a moment. "After his mother died, as I recall. Before that, not since he graduated from high school."

"Do you remember breaking up a fight between him and another boy in his senior year?"

"Yes, I do. It was Neal Waldron who gave me the split lip. They never liked each other, and both had sizable chips on their shoulders."

"Do you know if that dislike lasted past high school?"

She guessed his intent and quickly cut to the real answer he needed. "Neal was killed several years ago, in a car accident."

So much for that suspect, Mike thought as she went on.

"Perhaps things might have turned out differently if Jack's father hadn't gotten ill. Some rare form of cancer, I believe it was. They tried everything, all those exotic cures, alternative medicine. Flew him all over the world, but it did nothing for him. Just drained their finances."

"What happened?" Mike wasn't sure what good this was going to do him, but he knew the more he learned about his victim, the better off his investigation would be. Focusing only on looking at suspects, especially the obvious ones, could make you settle on one too early and miss the real one.

"After his mother died, Jack came home from college to take care of things. That was when he found out there was nothing left. Even their home had been mortgaged when his father found one more potential cure in Europe."

"The party was over," Mike said.

"Exactly. And he resented it. Greatly. Excuse me." She paused, and he thought he heard her take a drink of something. "I'm afraid I haven't had my full intake of caffeine yet today, so I'm not quite up to speed."

Mike laughed. She had to be in her seventies, he guessed, since she had retired ten years ago, but he would never have known from her voice or mental acuity. "You're running way ahead of me," he told her.

She laughed in turn, a delightful sound, full of genuine amusement at a world that could still entertain her. Mike hoped he could have her outlook when he hit her age. But he doubted he would. Not if he stayed in this business.

"So it wasn't his father's death that turned him, but the fact that there was no inheritance?"

"That's how it seems. I suppose the true result of his being so spoiled all his life surfaced then. Jack decided—and I do know this firsthand, I heard him say it—that the world was just going to have to pay back what it had taken from him. He wasn't about to give up the life he'd been accustomed to. He deserved it, and he would get it any way he could."

"Entitlement rationale," Mike murmured.

"Is that what you folks call it? Entitlement?"

"Yeah. 'I deserve this,' or 'I'd have this if the world was fair,' or any number of variations on the theme. It's the justification for a heck of a lot of crimes."

He knew now why Pruett had been what he was, but that didn't change the facts. He was still very dead, and there were still a lot of people who weren't unhappy about that.

"Sad," Mrs. Washington said. "Personally, I subscribe to the old philosophy that happiness isn't in getting what you want, it's in wanting what you have."

Mike chuckled. "Mrs. Washington, it's been a real pleasure. Do you date younger men?"

Her laugh came through again, delighted this time. "Thank you, dear. I'm a firm believer in younger men. I'm afraid you might be a bit *too* young, however."

"My loss," he said, and meant it.

Every once in a while, he thought as he hung up, you run into someone who restores a little of your faith in the human race.

* * *

Aaron didn't trust the sudden turnaround.

His quicksilver, skittish visitor had turned into a charming, animated houseguest straight from central casting. She'd straightened up. She was cheerful, helpful, grateful . . .

And it was all full of something else, Aaron thought wryly.

She still wasn't telling him the truth. But he realized it was unfair of him to expect her to. She didn't know him. He'd been forcefully reminded of that when she'd admitted last night that she expected him to want sex for helping her.

And he had wished, just for a moment, that he was the kind of man who would make such a deal.

His jaw tightened. He wasn't very proud of that moment of gut reaction, but there it was. He couldn't deny it. But he could consider it a warning, to be on his guard and not to do something unforgivably stupid.

She had a right to be wary. They'd been out once today, to add to her minimal wardrobe. She was always looking over her shoulder, so edgy that he was seeing shadows following them himself. Except that after a while he began to think they weren't just shadows; he'd seen at least two faces too often. Outpost might be a lot smaller than big brother Reno to the east, but it wasn't small enough to make that a believable coincidence.

The question was, Who was after her? Was he completely wrong in his conviction that it was connected to Pruett's murder? But then why did she react that way to his questions about her relationship with Pruett?

But if the worst were true and she really had killed the man— and done the world a service, it seemed— who would be after her? Was the "organization" Mike had mentioned that strong, that it would hold together after Pruett's death, long enough to go after his killer? Who would care, in that type of operation, if they weren't getting paid?

Hell, maybe the guy left it in his will. A bequest to whoever killed his killer.

He quashed the thought, then yawned widely; he hadn't slept too well. This place had always seemed spacious to him, too large for one person, even one his size. Yet now it seemed that one petite woman, even though she was mouse quiet, filled it so completely that he felt like he could hardly turn around without bumping into her. He knew it wasn't true, but there it was.

He rubbed a hand over his gritty eyes. It didn't help. Sleep was what he needed—

"Can I get you anything? Do you need an aspirin or something?"

There was such concern in her voice he couldn't help wondering what she was up to. He lowered his hand and looked at her.

"You know," he said, his tone thoughtful, "I'm not sure I didn't like your snarly persona better."

He succeeded in making her jerk back, blushing, but it didn't make him feel any better. He felt worse, in fact. He let out a compressed breath.

She spoke a little unevenly. "Maybe I should—"

"Go?" he supplied. "Just run? Again?"

She drew herself up. "*Now* who's snarly?"

In spite of himself he grinned and gave a rueful chuckle. "Don't mind me. I get that way when I'm knee-deep in something and I have no idea what it is because the one person who knows won't tell me."

Perversely, now that he hadn't actually asked her a question, she gave him at least sort of an answer.

"Believe me, you're better off not knowing."

She retreated to the guest room before he could

point out that he'd quit letting other people decide when he was better off a very long time ago.

He sat for a moment, pondering. He'd been down to his office early this morning, even before Francie, and cleaned up most of his morning's work. Then, drawn in a way he didn't quite understand, he'd come back just as Shelby was getting up. He'd waited for her, listening to the sound of the shower, trying not to let his imagination run riot.

He wished she'd never had the silly idea that he wanted her to sleep with him.

Or at least had never spoken it.

Determined to derail his thoughts, he got up and walked over to his desk. He sat down again and reached for the phone. His hand on the receiver, he hesitated, glancing at the clock. Then he picked it up and pushed the speed dial number he wanted.

"Detective Delano."

"You're in early."

"You know I'm always in early, that's why you called me," Mike said reasonably. "What's up? You chickening out on our handball game?"

"Not a chance," Aaron retorted, although he did wonder what he would do if the situation with Shelby weren't resolved by then. And thought perhaps he was being overoptimistic to think it might be.

"Good. My mother spent last night rhapsodizing about her old school friend's daughter and her mate potential, so I need a workout."

"She just worries about you," Aaron said in the excessively soothing tone of voice he always used when Mike's mother meddled. It was part of the old game between them. "Her baby boy all alone in the world. You can't blame her."

"Oh, can't I? Just remember: if she ever gives up on me, she'll turn on you."

"She'll never give up on you. Mother's love and all.

So why don't you just find a nice girl and settle down?"

"Right," Mike said wryly. "The only woman I've run into lately who's the least bit interesting happened to be more than twice my age."

"And you're going to let a little thing like that stop you?"

"Careful, or I'll come after Robin."

Aaron grinned. He knew Mike was a good guy, but he also knew that what a man thought was a good guy didn't necessarily mean the same to a woman. After a painful divorce, Mike was, as he freely admitted, married to his job, and it would take a very confident, strong-minded woman to tolerate that. Many had tried, drawn by his looks. Mike was nearly as big as Aaron, his hair as dark and thick, but there the resemblance stopped. Mike's features were nearly perfect, chiseled, refined. His hair stayed neatly where it was combed; Aaron's became an untidy mop no matter what he did. For a while he'd tried clipping it very short, but all that had done was emphasize the unevenness of his features. When he stood next to Mike, he knew he looked like a caricature of his friend, like a painting moved before the paint was dry, blurred and just a fraction out of focus.

He liked Mike in spite of it. Because he knew Mike suffered from the other edge of the same sword. Women reacted to his looks in the same superficial way they reacted to Aaron's—just in the opposite way.

"So, what has you calling me at this hour?" Mike asked.

Aaron wished for a moment that he'd thought more about what he was going to say. Then he realized it wasn't going to make any difference in the end; Mike was too smart and knew him too well to be snowed.

"I was curious about the Pruett case. How's it going?"

"Curious? At seven a.m. ?"

"Okay, so I woke up with this burning desire to know."

"Bull. What's up, buddy?"

Aaron gave up sooner than he might have if Shelby hadn't been in the other room. "Let's just say I know somebody the guy wasn't very nice to."

Mike snorted inelegantly. "That's a very long list of people." Then, very seriously, he added, "Look, if you know something, out with it. This is the worst kind of high-profile case, and the sooner I close it, the better."

"I don't know anything about your case directly," Aaron said honestly. He *didn't* know anything, not for sure, and certainly not anything to tell Mike. "Not yet."

Mike hesitated, but not for long. He understood the significance of that "yet." "I trust you, buddy. So here's the scoop—what I can tell you, anyway. We've got literally dozens of suspects. Even more motives."

"I gather he wasn't the most well-liked guy in town."

"No. But he had access to cash, in large amounts. That'll always buy you a few friends."

"For a while, anyway," Aaron said.

"You know that, and I know that, but guys like Pruett? Nah, they think they're buying loyalty for life."

And after life? Aaron wondered. *Had Pruett found someone whose allegiance would transcend death? Or had he, knowing his popularity was suspect, paid in advance for just that?*

"And those rumors about blackmail?" Mike was saying. "True. We found a cache of documents, photographs, audio and video recordings, you name it."

Aaron let out a low whistle.

"Yeah, tell me about it. There's a computer disk with what appears to be a master ledger, but the disk is encrypted, and the files probably are too. We're working on it, but it's going to take a while. If it's what I think it is, when we get it all sorted out and the material matched up with names, we'll have an even bigger list of suspects."

After hanging up, Aaron went back to pondering. He wondered what happened to blackmail material once it was in police hands. And to the people who were the blackmailer's victims. He supposed—or perhaps hoped—that unless the material showed them engaged in a criminal act, nothing.

But whatever else, he was sure Shelby knew something about Pruett or his death. And the fact that she was denying it only made it more grimly possible that she was the killer Mike was hunting for.

Mike took note of the audible groan that escaped Gerry Franco as he approached. Sometimes he loved having that effect on people.

"Good morning, Mr. Franco. How are you?" he said with exaggerated politeness. Obviously Aaron's ejection of Pruett had also made his high-roller friend feel less than welcome, for him to be here in the Gold Mine, a poor imitation of the classy Phoenix.

"Just fine, Detective. Isn't gambling on your job a no-no?"

"Sometimes," Mike said as he leaned on the blackjack table, "it is my job. How about you? Isn't poker more your game?"

"Table's full."

Mike lifted a brow. "What's wrong? Can't get a seat without Jack Pruett to toss his weight for you?"

Franco reddened. The dealer asked if he was in or out, and the man gathered his chips and got up. The dealer went on with the hand unconcernedly.

"When did you see him last?" Mike asked, making it clear by his body language as he walked beside

Franco that he was sticking to him until he got answers.

"Last week."

"Want to narrow that down a bit?"

Franco looked like he wanted to growl, but he answered. "Last Tuesday. We ran over to Reno, had dinner. Hit a few clubs, a few casinos."

"Get kicked out of any?"

Franco reddened again. "Your buddy Montana's got a real attitude, you know that?"

Mike grinned. "Yeah, I know. Who drove?"

Franco blinked. "Jack. We took his new Mercedes."

"You and your old friend Jack have a falling-out?"

"No."

The denial came quickly, sharply. Enough so that Mike thought it was worth the risk of asking, "So those people who saw you arguing are mistaken?"

Franco stopped dead. He stared as if they were across a poker table and he was trying to decide if Mike was bluffing. Mike had learned his poker face from playing with Aaron, and it held.

"Look, we just had a little disagreement. Nothing major."

Bingo, Mike thought. "Major enough to get noticed. What was it about?"

"Nothing important."

"He's dead," Mike said flatly. "Everything is important."

"It was something stupid. I don't remember exactly." Franco shook his head. "Look, I can see where you're headed. But you're wrong. Jack may be a prick, and we've had our disputes, but I didn't kill him."

"Where were you night before last and yesterday morning?"

"Out."

"You know," Mike said, "you might want to consider if it's wise to piss me off."

"Look, I was with a friend, okay?"

"Who's the friend, so I can verify that?"

"No." Mike waited, and Franco gave in. "It's a woman, all right? Her husband was out of town. She'll deny everything. So you're just going to have to take my word for it."

"Right. I'll take that straight to the bank," Mike said. "Stay available, Franco."

Mike bet the man would give up his lady friend to save his own skin, if it came down to it. If, of course, she even existed. That was the problem dealing with high rollers. They were used to bluffing, too.

Chapter Nine

He made a circuit of the casino, fixing the layout in his mind. When he was done, he returned to the information desk he'd noted, beside the registration desk. He cleared his throat and put on his best smile for the young woman behind the counter.

"Hi, there. Could you help me? My club is looking for a place to hold a small seminar, and they love to gamble. Is there someone I could talk to about renting a meeting room?"

"Of course," the woman said with a matching smile. "If you'll just walk down past the café there and turn left at the next hallway, you'll see the signs for the offices. The banquet coordinator's office is on the right-hand side."

"Whom should I ask for?" He needed a name to toss out in case someone wondered what he was doing.

"Ask for Mr. Winbridge. He can help you."

He thanked her politely and walked in the direction she'd indicated. When he turned into the hallway, his steps slowed. On the wall was a large portrait of a burly, silver-haired man. The brass plate beneath named him Zachary Montana, chairman of the hotel operation. Beside it was an obviously very old, somewhat worn picture of another Montana, described as the man who had founded Outpost more than a century ago.

But the face that caught his full attention was in the

smaller photograph to one side. Aaron Montana, the current manager of the Golden Phoenix.

It was the man she'd hooked up with.

He frowned as he stared at the face. He had a name to put with it now, and a position. And he didn't like either.

He moved on, slowly, scanning the entire area. It didn't take long for him to zero in on an elevator at the end of the hall, with a numbered keypad beside it. He slowed down, doing his best to look lost. Eventually, a young man in a Golden Phoenix uniform who came out of a room down the hall stopped beside him.

"Can I help you find something?"

"I was looking for Mr. Winbridge," he said.

"His office is right there." The young man wore the smile everybody around here seemed to wear. "Here, I'll show you."

"Thank you, I appreciate it." He chuckled lightly. "This place seems a lot bigger on the inside."

The young man's smile widened. "It's easy to get lost at first."

He gestured toward the elevator he'd spotted earlier. "What's that for?" he asked with another laugh. "Where they count all the money?"

"No, that's to get to the upstairs offices. The chairman and all."

He smiled, one workingman to another. "The bigwigs, huh? Like the manager himself?"

"Exactly. He even lives up there, a few floors above his office," the young man said, accepting the fellowship as if it were sincere. "Has his own private elevator and everything." He stopped beside a door labeled "Banquet Coordinator." "Here you are."

"Thanks. Don't let me keep you from your work."

With a nod the young man hastened away, leaving him alone in the hallway for the moment. He walked over to the security door, noted the name on the system and the layout of the keypad panel. He reached out and quickly pushed one of the numbers. A high-pitched tone was faintly audible.

He walked away smiling his first real smile of the day. It was a good system, one of the best. But he was better. He could get past this sound-based security. He had just the piece of equipment he needed to do it. All he had to do was pick his time.

"Aaron?"

He went still as her voice came from behind him. It had taken him until now to get her to stop calling him Mr. Montana and making him feel seventy years older than she was, rather than seven.

But he hadn't realized how it was going to sound, to hear his name in that low, slightly husky voice. Hadn't realized it was going to feel like a caress.

"I'm sorry I made you angry."

She was being that polite, decorous charmer again. He felt as if the real Shelby, the fiery and fierce woman he'd seen, was unreachable behind this facade of manners. He wanted the other one back, with an urgency that startled him. And bothered him.

"You didn't," he said. "The circumstances do."

She looked relieved, and he wondered if she'd expected he would throw her out on her ear. Given what else she'd expected, that could hardly be a surprise.

He grimaced inwardly as his stubborn body again responded to the idea she'd inadvertently planted.

"How did you end up in Outpost?" he asked rather hastily.

"I came up from Southern California, about a dozen or so years ago. I . . . needed a change."

He lifted an eyebrow at that. "We're coming along, but this town isn't exactly on the Ten Best Places to Relocate list."

She shrugged. "Why do you stay?"

His brows furrowed. "It's home. Always has been."

" 'Montana's Outpost'?"

He nodded. "My family has always been here."

"And you never wanted to get away?"

"I did, a couple of times. To college, and I lived in New York for a while. But I always knew it was temporary. That I would come back here."

"Gambling in your blood?"

His mouth quirked. "I know it sounds odd, but no. I don't gamble. A game of poker with friends is about as far as I go."

She looked thoughtful. "That's probably good."

He hadn't expected her to understand, at least not so quickly. "I always thought a gambler running this place would be like my cousin Hank running a bar, fraught with too much temptation to resist."

She looked at him quizzically. "Is that what his problem is?"

"Yes," Aaron confirmed, and when she looked surprised, he went on wryly, "It's not like it's a big secret. As often as he's gotten hauled in by the police, the whole county probably knows."

"I'm sorry. Does he cause much trouble?"

"Not really." Aaron shrugged. "Hank's a very . . . charming drunk. Nicer, most would say, than when he's sober. So he gets away with it. Nobody really wants to get him into trouble, because he's so sweet about it, as my aunt says."

"This is the aunt who kept calling?"

He nodded. "She wanted me to bail him out, as usual. Like I have a dozen other times." Shelby gave him a surprised look, and he knew she'd realized he'd not been gone long enough to do so. "I didn't do it," he said. "I love the guy, but I told him the last time that it was just that, the last time."

"That must have been a tough decision," she said softly.

It had been, but he didn't want to talk about it. "The hard part," he joked, "was putting up with Aunt Abby's outrage."

"She expects you to be your cousin's keeper?"

"And hers, and every other person with a Montana in the family tree," he said. Surprised by the bitterness that had crept into his tone, he shook his head sharply. "Sorry," he muttered. "I don't know where that came from."

"Exhaustion? Worry? Weariness of being taken for granted?"

If she was guessing, she was doing a damned fine job, Aaron thought as he stared at her.

"It's a lot to expect, on top of running this place," she said with a shrug. "I imagine running a hotel this size is a twenty-four/seven job. I can't imagine what adding a casino on top of that does."

"Makes it about a thirty-six-hours-a-day, ten-days-a-week job sometimes," he admitted. "We've got the best staff and security around, but even they can't be everywhere."

"Is that why the cameras? Like the one you saw me on?"

He nodded. "That way two or three people can monitor what it would take a dozen to do live, out on the floor. And they're in constant contact, so if there's a problem, they can get security there fast. They also have to be in contact with the hotel security staff."

"They're different?"

"Separate staff," he explained. "Different requirements, different job there. Not easier, just different."

"Like?"

She seemed simply curious, so he answered, figuring he wasn't giving away anything that wasn't general knowledge anyway. "Keeping guests safe, quelling disturbances, room security—"

He stopped there, giving her a sideways look. She

lowered her gaze, but didn't comment on her own foray into that area, so he went on.

"We try, but we can't keep things completely clean. I know the call girls come in, but we keep them out of the common areas. The room thieves score occasionally, and the loan sharks circle, but we do the best we can to keep things under control."

"Sounds like you run a tight ship."

"As tight as I can." He leaned back in his chair, looking up at her as she perched on the edge of his desk. "The most important thing to me is to make sure that if there is a problem, none of my own people are involved. That I won't tolerate."

She looked at him for a long, silent moment. Then she said abruptly, "I used a credit card."

He blinked. "What?"

"To get into the room. I saw that people were using card keys that were gold-colored, and I had one that was the same color. So I hid most of it with my fingers, made sure my hands were full, picked a room the maid was working on, and she never questioned it, just let me in."

"Of course," he muttered. "Why wouldn't she? We tell them to be helpful."

"And it's not really her job to be security, so I figured it might work. It could have gone sour, of course, if she'd ever seen the real occupant, but—" She ended with a shrug.

"What if she'd asked to see the key card?"

"I would have laughed that I'd grabbed the credit card by mistake and told her to go on while I dug out my key. Or said my husband must have it down at the blackjack table. Something."

He shook his head in wonder. "You do think on your feet, don't you?"

Her eyes went oddly unfocused, as if she were looking at some other time and place. "I learned from an expert," she said.

He wanted to ask who, wanted to know what put that look on her face, but he sensed he wouldn't get an answer.

"Thanks for the tip," he finally said, when she seemed to come back to the present.

"You're welcome."

He looked at her consideringly. "What made you decide to tell me?"

She seemed surprised by the question, and it was a moment before she answered. "I think because I never thought of a casino as a place where somebody tried so hard to keep order."

"You bought into the slightly seedy, sleazy image, is that it?"

He said it lightly, so she would know he wasn't offended. She gave him a half smile. "Something like that."

"Used to be true," he admitted. "And probably still is, in some places. But I'm proud to say never here."

Her gaze shifted, and after a moment he realized what she was looking at—the framed picture on his desk. His breath stopped in his chest.

"Beautiful little girl," Shelby said.

"Yes."

It was all he could get out past the lump that inevitably formed in his throat whenever he looked at that sunlit, gloriously happy photograph.

"Who is she?"

He couldn't, Aaron thought. Even after seven years, it hurt to talk about it. But neither could he deny the child who had, for too short a time, held his heart.

"Her name was Megan."

She didn't say it. Didn't ask. And when he looked at Shelby's face, he saw she had fully grasped the meaning of that one short, damnable word.

Was.

Most people got flustered, or apologized. Others pushed, for some reason fascinated by tragedy. Shelby simply waited. For him to tell her, or not. And for some reason, the knowledge that she would accept either compelled Aaron to speak. Maybe, he thought, it would work in turn, and she would talk to him.

"My daughter," he said, staring at the framed photograph on the corner of his desk. "She died seven years ago. She was five."

He got up abruptly. He needed to move, he *had* to move. He walked over to the window and stared out at the mountain, seeing only the horrid images that had haunted him for years.

"She went with her mother. To go see her grandmother. In Sacramento."

The story was coming out in chunks, choppy and broken, just like his voice sounded. Shelby walked over to where he stood, but kept a safe distance away, as if she knew he couldn't bear anyone close right now. She simply waited, for him to say as much or as little as he wanted.

He took in a deep breath, tried to concentrate on forming actual sentences. "Cindy was tired. Stopped up the mountain. A little grocery store. Hayne's. About ten miles from here. She fell asleep in the car. Megan—" He stopped, swallowed heavily, tried again. "Megan wandered off."

He stopped, unable to go on. There was so much more, the horror when Cindy had finally called and he'd realized how long his little girl had been gone while her mother had slept, then awakened and panicked, as she was always so wont to do. By the time she called Aaron, three hours had passed. His baby had been out in the woods on the mountain alone for three hours, with no one even looking for her.

He suddenly lost trust in his legs, and barely made

it to the sofa behind him before he went down in an awkward movement that was more like falling than sitting.

"Four days," he said hoarsely. "It took four days. Days of hell. It's so remote up there, rough country, easy to get . . . lost. There's a . . . little lake. Doesn't even have a name."

"Aaron," Shelby said, sinking down on the couch beside him. He knew it meant he could stop, she wouldn't push, but it had been so long since he'd spoken of it that now that he'd started he couldn't stop.

"They almost missed her. It was a search-and-rescue dog who found her. People had already been there, at the lake, but that black dog kept going back, insisting—"

This time when he stopped, Shelby supplied gently, "And the dog was right?"

"She was there. Caught up under a rock overhang. They couldn't see her, but the dog—it was a Belgian something, I think they said—a different kind of dog, really smart—he knew she was there."

He knew he was babbling now, but the next words would bring it all back, the tiny, sodden body brought out of the lake, Megan's cold, pinched, bluish face, her bright-blue eyes closed forever . . .

"I used to go up there . . . . every day, after. There's a spot that overlooks that lake. A ledge you can only get to on foot. I found a . . . really tough trail, going up the back way. I took it so I'd be . . . tired when I got there. I'd . . . sit there for hours. You can see . . . where they found her . . . ."

Shelby let out a tiny sound of pain, a sound he recognized, for all the times he'd made it himself, sitting on that rocky ledge, staring down, looking for an answer that never came.

"I loved that little girl," he whispered, burying his face in his hands. "More than my own life. If I could have traded places with her that day, I would have done it in an instant."

He felt a sudden shift beside him. Shelby slipped her arms around him. She did nothing more, simply held him, but he felt as if he'd been saved from flying out of control.

He didn't look at her. He closed his eyes, feeling the surprising strength of her embrace. And the amount of comforting warmth she generated.

He felt himself sagging against her, knew he was too heavy for her, but couldn't stop. He let his head loll back on his shoulders, and a long, weary exhalation escaped his chest. Eyes still closed, he just sat there, feeling as exhausted as if he'd spent the day once more searching that damned mountain, yet at the same time feeling strangely at peace. As if he'd needed to relive the awful story, as if he'd needed to tell someone.

As if he'd needed to tell this someone.

She did none of the things he always found so hard to deal with. She. didn't murmur platitudes, or say things that were hideously wrong, like "At least you found her, you have closure," or "The water was so cold, she probably didn't feel a thing." She didn't try to distract him, or change the subject.

She simply held him, tightly, as if she could absorb some of the pain.

It almost seemed as if she did.

How did she know just what to do and, more important, what not to? It was as if she'd done it before, comforted someone who was suffering pain beyond bearing.

For the first time in the admittedly short time he'd known her, she wasn't focused on her own situation, but on his. And Aaron knew he was getting a glimpse of the woman she must be when not dogged by fear.

Suddenly he realized she could never have been

mixed up in Pruett's sordid affairs. At least not by choice.

For a long time he simply stayed there, savoring the novelty of letting down, of someone else taking care of *him*. He couldn't remember ever feeling quite like this before, quite so welcomed, so comforted.

Finally, in a voice as tight as when he'd told her, he whispered, "Thank you."

Shelby moved then. When he felt her hands cup his face, his eyes snapped open in shock.

"A father like you," she said, holding his gaze, "should never have to lose a child."

He stared at her, unable to look away from those steady green eyes. He sucked in a breath, and then another when her lips parted.

"Shelby," he said, simply because he had to.

He became abruptly aware that since she had moved she was practically in his lap. Every muscle in his arms tensed with the need to pull her to him. Despite the seeming lack of air in the room, he wanted to kiss her more than he wanted his next breath. The long hours spent lying sleepless in the dark, listening to her move about, the moments spent hearing the sound of the shower and fighting not to picture her, sleek and wet beneath the spray, that fit, compact yet lusciously curved body . . .

Her hands slipped from his face down to his chest as she balanced herself against him. He felt her fingers curl slightly as she looked at him, knew she had to feel the sudden quickness of his breathing. Her gaze shifted to his mouth, the heat of her hands seared him, and he was held motionless, pinned, in a way he'd never known before.

He didn't dare move, didn't dare speak. The moment spun out so wire tight that he thought if he plucked the right bit of air between them it would hum.

Then, so slowly that he nearly screamed with antici-pation, she began to move toward him. The instant her head tilted the slightest bit, he knew she was going to kiss him. His pulse began to hammer, in hot, heavy beats as she came closer, closer—

"Room service!"

The rap on the door and the cheery call shattered the moment. Color rose in Shelby's cheeks, and she scrambled off the couch.

"Breakfast," Aaron muttered. He'd entirely forgot-ten that he'd ordered it sent up.

He headed for the door, willing his unruly body to calm down. Lord, it really had been too long, when even the thought of a kiss was enough to bring him to a boil. The only thing that enabled him to salvage any pride at all was that she had made the move—it had been Shelby about to kiss him.

By the time the steaming omelets and croissants, fresh fruit and coffee were on the table and the waiter tipped and on his way—even the boss tipped at the Golden Phoenix—he had composed himself again.

Shelby tackled the hearty breakfast as if they hadn't had an equally hearty meal last night.

"You could have ordered a midnight snack or some-thing, you know," he said mildly.

For a moment, with a mouthful of eggs and ham and cheese, she looked embarrassed. But then she swallowed and grinned. "Wish I'd thought of it. I've . . . missed a few meals."

"I gathered. We'll have to take care of that."

She shrugged as she took a sip of hot coffee. "I'll survive. It's not the first time."

"I got that impression," he said neutrally.

She glanced at him from beneath those wispy bangs again. "Did you?"

He shrugged in turn, as if it were unimportant. But it was important. He wanted to know, for himself as much as to discover what she was running from. But he didn't push. Just as she hadn't pushed him.

He took a sip of his own coffee, and a bite of the excellent omelet. The chef, a blunt-fingered Welshman who startled them all with his skill, had been a find indeed. Aaron's mother had discovered him ten years ago in London—where, she informed him with her own personal bias, one never expected to find great food—and had exerted all her considerable charm to get him here. Ian Bedwyr had put the Golden Phoenix on the culinary map, something Aaron never would have even thought about aspiring to.

When he looked at Shelby again, she was staring out the windows, up at the mountains.

"It would be hard," she said, almost to herself, "to be a runaway here. Especially in winter."

Aaron winced inwardly at this near admission that he'd been right about her past. He thought of all the times he'd idly wished he could run away from all the pressure of his work and his family. But faced with this woman who'd been forced to do it, he felt ashamed.

With an effort he kept his tone casual. "Better in California, I imagine."

Her gaze snapped back to his face, and for a moment he thought he'd gone too far. But after a moment she slowly nodded. "It's . . . easier there," she agreed. "Warmer, so you don't always need a sheltered place to crash at night. Even the dead of winter isn't too bad, if you've got enough clothes, or a blanket. Especially if you stick to the beach. It's warmer, and there's always leftover food around, if you hunt."

"How long?" he asked, keeping his question short for fear of interrupting her sudden loquaciousness about her past.

"Five years."

He couldn't begin to imagine it. "From when you

were twelve?" She nodded. He shook his head slowly. "No child should ever feel so deserted that running away seems the only answer."

Megan's image rose before him, threatened to send him spiraling down into despair once more. He had put this behind him, as much as it could be, but somehow Shelby's presence, and now his knowledge of her life, brought the memory back in all its raw ugliness.

"No," she agreed. "No child ever should. But I thought it was my fault, something I did, or some flaw in me—"

She broke off suddenly and looked away.

"It's never, ever the child's fault," Aaron said fiercely.

He didn't know why she'd run away, but it wasn't hard to guess that abuse of some kind had been involved. He looked at the top of her head as she stared down at her plate. At the fine, golden silk of her hair, the delicacy of her features, the thick sweep of her golden-brown lashes. The idea of anyone hurting the little sprite of a child she must have been at twelve made him more than a little ill. He wondered if the abuse had been physical or sexual. Or maybe, he thought grimly, both; too often they seemed to go hand in hand.

Even now, when she had poured out a little of her past, she still didn't quite trust him. And he knew simple words couldn't change that. He sensed that she had been betrayed once too often.

Or, he amended grimly, perhaps just once, but by someone she should have been able to trust with her life.

Chapter Ten

"I understand why she went to Pete. I used to take her out there to go riding. But how on earth did she ever get hooked up with Aaron Montana, of all people?" Margaret asked, bewildered.

"You're saying she didn't know him before?"

Margaret shook her head at the man across the restaurant table from her. "I doubt she even knew who he is. I mean, she probably knew the name from my husband, but—"

"Anybody who does business in Outpost knows the Montanas. If this country had aristocrats, they'd be it around here."

"But . . . is he a good man?"

Stan Langford chuckled. "With most folks I'd ask you to define 'good.' But not this one. From what I hear, he's a good man by anybody's definition."

"That's . . . a relief to hear," she said tentatively. "What else do you know about him?"

She'd hired this man because she'd heard he was a competent investigator, knew the territory, and—most important of all—was discreet. Robert had mentioned that Vision Tech had once used him, that he was a retired police sergeant, and the name had stuck in her mind. She'd been doubtful at first, but once she'd called and told him Shelby had called from a casino, he'd located her quickly.

"Montana keeps a low profile, doesn't flaunt his position. Respect rang in Langford's voice, and Margaret guessed there weren't all that many people he respected. "He's got a rep as a straight arrow, who's always helping folks out. But from what I hear, you don't want to mistake him for somebody you can walk over. You'll find out different in a big hurry."

Then Shelby would be safe with him, wouldn't she? From what she'd just been told, the man was acting protectively toward her. That had to be a good sign, that he meant well by her.

But female common sense reared its head. Men and women often had different ideas about what constituted a "straight arrow."

"What about . . . women?"

The man frowned. "He's divorced and hasn't remarried. As for affairs, I'd have to check it out. Do you want me to spend the time?"

Margaret sighed. She didn't care whether Aaron Montana had affairs or not, as long as he didn't try anything with Shelby. And Langford did have a point; there wasn't time to waste on such matters.

"No," she said.

"Do you want me to try and contact her?"

Again Margaret considered the possibility, and again she was uncertain. Especially with this new addition to the equation, this Montana.

Just wait. Don't do anything.

The words from Shelby's cryptic message on her answering machine rang in her head. She had to trust that the girl knew what she was doing.

"No," she said. "Not unless you can make contact when she's completely alone."

"Unlikely," the man said. "Montana's been sticking pretty close."

Margaret frowned. "Is it . . . ? She's not . . . under duress, is she?"

"With Montana? I'd say no. From what I saw, the

lady's a bit jumpy, but not that way. She doesn't seem to mind him being there."

Relieved by that, Margaret lifted her purse to the table, dug into it, and pulled out a plain envelope. It held every bit of cash she'd been able to scrounge up.

"If you can get her alone, give her this. But only if she's alone. I don't want any kind of confrontation with this man."

The man nodded and tucked the envelope into his inside jacket pocket.

"Mrs. Peterson, I have to ask this. Is there someone else . . . looking for her?"

Margaret grew pale. She hadn't thought of that, that the reason Shelby was behaving so oddly was that someone was after her. But Pruett was dead, so who . . . ?

"I don't know. Is there?"

"Maybe not. It was just a feeling," Langford said. "I'd best get back. I have my associate on the hotel, but she's young and inexperienced, and I don't want to leave it in her hands for long."

"Thank you," Margaret said, knowing he was pointing out that he couldn't do his job and meet with her at the same time. She tried not to bother him, but she was getting so horribly anxious.

"I'll contact you if there's any change."

"Yes. And remember, please, that above all I don't want her hurt in any way. Do whatever you have to to prevent that."

After he'd gone, she sat for a long time over her barely touched lunch, thinking.

And wondering again why Shelby hadn't come to her. She had to know that Margaret would move heaven and earth to help her, just as she knew Shelby would do the same for her.

Margaret nearly moaned out loud as her own thoughts echoed in her head.

Move heaven and earth.

Or kill?

Guilt rose up and nearly swamped her. It couldn't be. It just couldn't be. She couldn't believe that Shelby, no matter how much she might think she owed Margaret, would try to pay her back by committing murder.

Margaret sat there until her coffee was stone cold, trying to convince herself.

She couldn't hide out here forever.

Shelby sat curled up on the leather sofa, staring out the big window. She was alone. Aaron was down in his office, catching up on things. Aaron, whose patience with her silence was going to run out eventually.

She'd pored over the newspaper as soon as Aaron had gone down this morning. Pruett still rated several inches of copy, and as yet there had been no arrests.

But from what Aaron had said about his friend Mike—and he rarely missed a chance to suggest that she go to him—the man took his job very seriously. He was, Aaron had said, both tenacious and smart. She wasn't sure if he was trying to reassure her, or warn her.

Maybe she'd be better off with the cops. During their brief foray outside, she'd felt certain she was still being followed, but she caught a glimpse of her persistent pursuer once or twice and it wasn't the man she'd expected. Had he brought in help? Or was she so jumpy that she was seeing shadows where they didn't exist?

For a while she had even thought there were two of them at once, coming at her from different sides. She knew then her nerves were getting the best of her.

With a sigh she got up, rubbing her arms with her hands. She wandered over to the corner where Aaron's desk sat, and looked once more at the photograph framed in silver.

Megan Montana had been adorable, there was no denying that. She must have looked mostly like her mother, Shelby thought, because the only piece of Aaron she could see in the blond, blue-eyed child was that quirky, almost lopsided grin. It softened his face remarkably; on the child, it was endearing.

She shivered. It wasn't that it was cold—she just couldn't seem to get warm. The place seemed huge and empty, and she realized just how much of a presence Aaron Montana was. He filled a room, as much with that sense of power, of strength and quiet integrity, as with his size.

So that's why you wanted to kiss him? His integrity?

She groaned inwardly, still unable to believe she'd done it. If not for the interruption of room service, she would have lip-locked him right there. Even knowing perfectly well that he was off balance, unsettled by the obviously painful recounting of what had to have been the worst days of his life.

True, she had occasionally caught him looking at her rather intensely, with what she thought was pure male interest. But she'd learned long ago never to assume, especially when it came to men—

Oh, yes, I could want you, easily enough.

His words came back to her, as clearly as if he was here, speaking them again.

She shivered again, but this time she knew perfectly well the cause. Aaron Montana was uncompromisingly male, and something deep inside of her, something she'd never even known was there, responded to that maleness viscerally and powerfully.

Someday, Tiger had told her, *he'll turn up. The guy who's man enough for you.*

In an odd way Aaron reminded her of Tiger. He'd had his own code that he lived by, although few who didn't know him would believe it. All they saw was a rough-edged street kid with an attitude. Tiger had been on his own since he was ten, when his alcoholic mother had set their house on fire with herself and her husband inside. Tiger's habit of sneaking out at night after she knocked him around had saved his life that time. He'd arrived back just before dawn to see nothing but smoldering rubble, fire trucks, and police cars.

Even at ten, he'd been under no illusions about his world. If he had any other relatives, he didn't know them, and he didn't want to if they were anything like his brutal mother and ineffectual father. So he'd turned his back and run, with nothing but the clothes on his back and the small wad of cash he'd already pilfered from his mother's booze-money stash.

As she remembered the night he'd told her his story, Tiger's image formed in Shelby's mind with a clarity she hadn't known in years. She could see him as if it were yesterday—his dark hair held back with the white bandanna he wore around his forehead, declaring himself independent of any of the roving street gangs, his blue eyes full of a wisdom far beyond his years, his voice deep and quiet, yet heard when others were shouting.

She had needed him desperately at twelve, and he had let her cling to him, hide behind him, use him as her buffer against a cold and sometimes bloodthirsty world. Even though he was only fifteen himself, he'd helped keep her fed, kept her warm, and kept her from the drugs and prostitution that were the facts of most young girls on the street. Only much later had she realized how amazing that was.

At fifteen, she had fallen completely and utterly in love with him, with all the zeal of a girl who had never known love before. She would have given herself to him without hesitation, had tried more than once to entice him.

He'd gently but firmly stopped her. And finally, he had used her impetuous attempts to impart a lesson that she'd never forgotten.

Don't ever sell yourself, Shel. Not to anyone, for anything. You're worth more than that, no matter what anyone tells you. If you don't believe anything else I say, believe that.

But I love you.

And I love you. But not like that. I'm a hundred years too old for you, little girl.

You're only three years older than me!

Only in time.

What does that mean?

It means I don't deserve your love, Shelby. Save it for someone who does.

She had understood only that he was rejecting her. She had run from him, crying. Later, they had slipped back into a form of their old relationship of teacher and pupil, but for a few days she had been more alone than she'd ever felt before, even in the hell she'd run away from. Tiger had been her anchor, and she was terrified that she had turned him against her with her silly efforts to tempt him.

But when she had finally gone back to him—she had, after all, nowhere else to go, unless she resorted to what Tiger had always protected her from—he had welcomed her as if nothing had ever happened.

"God, Tiger," she whispered into the empty room, "I wish you were here now, to tell me what to do. I never meant for this to happen. I never meant—"

She stopped as Tiger's inevitable answer to such rationalization came back to her.

That's the whining excuse of somebody who didn't think things through.

She sighed. Tiger had been a stern teacher.

But he had protected her. And when it came to the point that he no longer could, he'd bought her a ticket to the farthest destination he could afford—Reno—on the next bus leaving L.A. and told her that if he'd ever meant anything to her, she would never look back.

She'd been terrified. She was leaving the only caring she'd ever known. The one person who had made her feel sheltered, and safe.

Until now.

Aaron made her feel that way. Even in the short time she'd known him, she'd felt the urge to take refuge in his strength.

Take advantage of the fact that he's a sucker for anybody in trouble, you mean, she said to herself.

She looked again at the photograph on his desk, at the picture of the child he'd loved. She was beginning to believe Aaron was a genuine good guy. He didn't deserve to be dragged into her mess.

She should get out.

With a sigh, she walked back over to the window and stood there looking at the mountains. And she wondered what it meant that Aaron lived in this place that forced him to look every day at the mountains where his daughter had died.

Yet another employee came down the hallway, making him dodge once more back into the shadows and hope she missed seeing him. This one went in the same door as the last two, and he wondered if there was some kind of employee break room back there.

He had the equipment he needed to break through the security system now. The problem was doing it. This place never seemed to empty, even late at night and early in the morning. Outside at the private back door they'd used, he stood out even more, and it seemed a guard went by every five minutes. But here in the office area, everybody from employees to slightly tipsy and very lost guests wandered through.

He swore under his breath. Was he never going to be able to get to the bitch? This was cleaning up a mess that never should have happened. He didn't like being outmaneuvered, but it grated on him even more because it was an annoying little urchin of a woman outmaneuvering him.

She'd finally gone outside this fortified castle of Montana's, but he hadn't had a clear chance at her then. That long-faced, broken-nosed hulk had always been right beside her. But now they were back inside, and this was his chance. He needed only ten minutes at most for his electronic emitter to hit the right combination of sounds to open the sonic-based lock, but so far he'd had to pull back and start over three times now.

He pocketed the handheld device and walked hastily back toward the wall of portraits, where he could stand and watch without being too obvious. When the employees came back out, he could pretend interest in the pictures.

He stopped in front of Aaron Montana's photograph. He hated big men. Big, fit, strong men he hated even more. So this one had earned his dislike at first sight, and it had only grown as he found out more about him.

He fiddled with the heavy pinkie ring. This whole thing was turning to shit. It should have been easy, should have been a quick in and out and gone. He should be in the Bahamas by now, lolling on the sand with a cold drink and some island girl beside him, a girl who would be paid not to notice his lack of stature. Women were such shallow, looks-obsessed creatures.

His own mother had simply been a whore who happened to get paid well—until he'd shown her the error of her ways. Silly bitch, she hadn't believed he was going to kill her until it was almost over. Funny, in a way she helped him find his calling in life. She had been the first. The memory warmed him. And proved his point.

No, no woman was ever with an unattractive man unless she was being paid, one way or another.

Which had made him wonder what the little blonde was doing with this guy. At first he had thought it was protection, that she knew he was after her and was using him as a bodyguard. He was sure as hell big enough. But then he had found out who the guy was, and that he or his family owned most of this godforsaken town. So, as usual, it was money. And if you were fucking the owner of this kind of place, money was obviously not a problem.

Too bad he'd already wasted too much time on something that should have been a quick fix; he would have liked to teach her a little lesson first. And if the ape got in the way, so be it. That's what they'd invented the phrase "collateral damage" for.

Chapter Eleven

The afternoon had started out bad, and nothing had happened so far to make Mike change his mind about it. The minute he'd walked into the station after lunch he'd been reminded by the flyers on every bulletin board that he, along with everyone else except patrol officers actually on duty on the street, was expected at the chief's monthly speech.

He'd been to Chief Cushman's motivational talks before and had always come away certain of one thing: he wasn't motivated. The man spoke like a politician, only adding to the general perception among his troops that he was more administrator than cop. He'd spent a very few years actually working on the street in any capacity, and the people who had done their time never forgot that.

This talk had been no different, and Mike had noticed he wasn't the only one fighting to keep from nodding off. But sleeping, even after lunch, during one of the chief's talks was good for a one-twenty-six, a disciplinary slip, in your package, so he'd resorted to going over the Pruett case step by step in his head to stay awake.

It hadn't helped, he thought now as he stared at the file on his desk. At every turn he ran into someone Pruett had pissed off or screwed over. He found more motives to kill than he knew what to do with.

Near the top of the very long list, by virtue of the

recentness and therefore increased heat of their ire, were the people who'd been sucked in at the bottom of his most recent scheme. Pruett was a genius at invoking enthusiasm and the fear of missing out on a great deal that was essential to Ponzi and pyramid schemes. He provided a sham paper trail, brochures, reports and pie charts, and made participants feel secure. He picked the first level of "investors" himself, paying them bonuses to be sure they kept up that level of enthusiasm. Mike was continually amazed at how many people still fell for the "Get rich with just a small investment!" pitch.

He'd pulled records on the last scheme that had gone bust. Pruett had disguised the plan as a multi-level marketing setup, similar to a pyramid but legal, and had done it well enough to get away with it. Barely. But when it had fallen apart, as such things always did when there were no new investors to rope in, the bottom rungs, as usual, paid the price.

One in particular stood out. Mike would be talking to Morris Burt later this morning. The man had made a little money at first in the scheme, and had been so blinded by that success that he poured everything he had into it. It had collapsed a couple of weeks later, leaving Burt broke, and with a wife so furious at his stupidity that she had packed up and left him.

And there was still the racing project. They would be his first afternoon stop. Thanks to Aaron's tip, it hadn't taken him long to find out that Pruett had been a major stumbling block for that group of powerful men. He'd put enough money into the early stages of the quest that he had a loud voice in their dealings. But then he'd angered them all by demanding control of the off-track betting. The consortium refused to give him such a guarantee, and Pruett had dug in his heels and threatened to withdraw. At the time of his death, things were at a standstill, and they had been at that impasse long enough for someone to perhaps decide to remove the problem child from their midst.

But first up now was Pruett's former partner. Mike was looking forward to that interview with the man Pruett had tricked out of his half of a successful electronics business. Lawrence Reichart had started the business on a shoestring twenty years ago, but had recently tried to expand too far too fast. From what Mike had found out so far, he'd been willing to admit the mistake and do what he had to to hold on, but by then his financial report was so grim nobody would touch him.

Except the always eager Pruett. Surprisingly, the man had had a nose for companies desperate for money but still with the potential to turn around. He seldom invested in anything that he wasn't later able to get his investment and more out of when he took over and then destroyed it. As he had Reichart Electronics. Yes, Reichart had very good reason to hate Jack Pruett.

Enough to take revenge? Maybe, Mike thought.

And, he thought wearily, if that ledger turned out to be what they suspected, there would be another large bunch of names to add to the list of people with good reason to want the slick, slippery Pruett dead.

Mike had turned a copy of the encrypted disk over to his favorite computer resource—a young, energetic, and very clever hacker from Outpost High School, a boy he'd once busted for breaking into the mainframe at the state capitol. If the encryption could be broken or bypassed, Eric would find the way. Mike had the official resources working on it too, of course—the techs at the county sheriff's office and some people they used from the state universities. But Mike's money was on Eric and his dancing fingers.

Mike considered making a call to see if the boy had made any progress, but he didn't. Eric would call; he'd be too excited and triumphant not to. And he didn't like being pushed. He worked for Mike because they'd reached an understanding—Mike had taken the time to show the kid how their passions were alike, that solving a case was a lot like hacking, because you just kept at it—but Eric had little patience for authority figures in general.

Mike tried to focus on his schedule for the rest of the day, but in the back of his mind was a nagging little voice reminding him that there was another possibility. The whole thing had been so clean that he had to consider that it might have been a pro. A hit. Pruett had certainly earned it. He—

"Hey, lover!"

Instinctively Mike turned his chair just in time to avoid the little neck nibble that Sunny D'Angelo liked to drop on him whenever she could catch him off guard. The overly stylish brunette was the chief's secretary—reason enough for him to steer clear. But the fact was, he found her a little too calculating for his taste, and too willing to use her position—she could make a cop's life more than a little tough simply because she had the chief's ear—to intimidate.

Besides, he didn't like the way she'd treated Aaron on the single occasion that they'd met. When she'd said they would look exactly alike if Aaron hadn't run into that wall, it hadn't rattled Aaron, but Mike had wanted to dump his pizza on her.

"Good morning, Ms. D'Angelo," he said formally, as he always did, both to avoid any show of anger at her unsubtle flirting and because he knew it irritated her.

She frowned at the appellation, but spoke in a voice that was just a touch too sweet. "Some of us are going out to the Sierra Inn tonight. Want to join us?"

Mike tried not to answer instantly. "Can't," he said, managing a creditable tone of regret. "Sorry."

She'd tried this once a while back, before he'd tumbled to her game. He'd showed up at the local watering hole, expecting a group. He'd found only Sunny, slinkily dressed, erotically perfumed, and loaded for bear. Or more precisely, for him.

He'd thought more than once about making up a girlfriend, so he could tell Sunny he was involved. But considering that she'd made passes at all of the good-looking married guys at one time or another he doubted it would work. Besides, it would get around, and pretty soon people would expect to meet the phantom woman, and if it got out that he'd made her up, he'd be the most pitiful thing this side of the Sierras. Most of the department already thought he was a social cripple. The only person who didn't nag him about his sex life was Aaron, and that, Mike had to admit ruefully, was because he had no room to talk.

And because Aaron knew the truth.

"Surely this case isn't taking up *all* of your time," Sunny said, a pout pursing her lips.

"Pretty much," he said. Sometimes, he thought, you just have to see the signs, and this was a sign that it was time to get out of here. "In fact," he said, "I'm late for an interview right now."

Legwork and paperwork, Mike thought as she finally gave up, the glamorous life of a detective. Plus the occasional predatory female, he added wryly as he grabbed up his jacket. He didn't need it for the weather, but it was a habit most plainclothes cops developed, to cover the weapon on their belt or at the small of their back. He grabbed his cell phone from the charger—his own, since the budget didn't run to that either—slipped it into a pocket, then picked up the keys to the plain unit he was assigned.

Chief Cushman's theory was that the taxpayers couldn't recognize a plain car as a police car, so there was no point in putting a lot of money into them.

Mike didn't think much of his chances if he ever actually had to chase somebody in his car. At five years and a lot of miles old, the thing could barely get out of its own way.

The only address he had for Reichart was fairly close. Mike double-checked the street number as he pulled up in front of an older, rather run-down apartment building. No, this was it. Hardly the kind of place where you'd expect to find a man who had once been president of the local chamber of commerce.

Reichart answered the door himself. Mike sized him up immediately: disheveled and unshaven, still in a not-too-clean bathrobe, he was wearing a sullen expression.

The moment Mike identified himself with his badge and mentioned the investigation, Reichart's expression shifted, a tinge of wariness added to the ill humor.

"What do you want?"

"May I come in?" Mike asked politely. "I just need to ask you a few questions."

The man hesitated. Mike said nothing, just stared him down. Finally, grudgingly, the man moved aside and let him in.

The apartment was small, with yellowed linoleum and a shag carpet that had seen better days. The furniture and various other items were newer and looked expensive, an odd contrast. It didn't take much detective work to guess that the furnishings had been bought for a much nicer residence.

"Great place, isn't it?" Reichart asked sourly as he watched Mike look around. "I've got Pruett to thank for it. We used to live up in Silver Ridge, until he came along."

Mike kept his expression even. Silver Ridge was the ritziest development in Outpost, an upscale residential area with golf course, country club, and riding trails. Expensive European cars were the norm, and Mike knew all too well the financial standing it took to live there. The woman who he'd once imagined was in love with him was one of the premier residents.

"Now we can barely hang on to this place, on what my wife makes."

"You're not working?" Mike asked neutrally.

"I ran a business with a hundred and fifty people working for *me*!"

Definitely bitter, Mike thought. *Question was, Was he bitter enough to kill?*

"A business taken over and then sold by Jack Pruett?" he asked, wanting to see the man's reaction. When it came, it was in the form of a vicious string of oaths. That burst of anger spent, Reichart went on.

"All I needed was that infusion of cash, just to tide me over. It was supposed to be an investment. I'd pay him back plus interest, and he'd turn his share back over to me. We agreed on it!"

"But when the company was back to what it had been worth before, he sold it out from under you?"

"Bastard had his slimy lawyers do some mumbo jumbo with the contracts that gave him a controlling interest."

"And your lawyers let that happen?"

Reichart flushed. "I didn't any lawyer. It was supposed to be a simple loan for collateral."

Mike refrained from pointing out that he obviously had needed a lawyer.

"I built Reichart Electronics up from nothing," Reichart nearly shouted. "It was a success, because of my hard work. I just got caught a little short on the expansion, and—"

Before he could launch into what would clearly be a tirade on ancient history, Mike headed him off. "What happened after Pruett sold you out?"

Reichart looked reluctant to pass up the chance to impress him with the unfairness of it all, but after a moment he said with equivalent anger, "By the time he took his share and deducted the money I'd borrowed from him out of the rest, there was nothing left. I lost my house, my cars, had to file bankruptcy. Now my wife and kid have to exist in this hovel, because the only job she could get is selling perfume and crap at some department store."

And you're too proud to go out and flip burgers or even sell what you used to make, Mike thought. Instead, this guy who called himself a man let his wife carry the load while he sat home and felt sorry for himself.

And let his outrage fester. And grow.

"You must have been pretty angry at Pruett when you realized what he'd done."

"I could have killed him," Reichart snarled. Then, as he realized what he'd said, and remembered why Mike was here, the flush in his face receded slightly.

"Can you account for your time for the last forty-eight hours?"

"I was right here. I'm always right here."

"Anybody who can back that up?"

"My wife." Reichart glared at Mike. "I was mad enough to kill him, but I didn't. I hadn't seen the bastard for over a year. And you can't prove I did. There are probably a dozen people who hated him as much as I did."

More like a hundred or so, Mike thought as he walked back to his car. But Reichart had just moved up to the definite possibility list. He added the man's wife to his list of people to talk to.

Next up was the racing syndicate. The first time he'd been to their office, yesterday, he'd been met with declarations of great distress over their associate's untimely death, avowals of utter ignorance of anything regarding his murder, and a mask of innocence so perfect that Mike immediately doubted it.

He'd never met a slicker bunch outside the Mob. And he wasn't totally convinced all of them *were* outside the Mob.

Since he didn't have any evidence beyond the facts that Pruett had been a problem for them and they were high rollers in the community, he had to tread carefully. But it wouldn't hurt, he thought, to turn up the heat a little. See if he could rattle those smiling men who were too smooth to be believed. And once more he would end up wanting to go home and take a shower.

Sometimes he wished they could just say "good riddance" and move on.

"Robert!" Margaret gasped out his name in shock. Her husband never came home during the day. "What are you doing here?"

"Last time I checked, I lived here," he said.

That was unlike him too—dodging a question, especially with sarcasm. Normally he was the most direct person she'd ever known. "Did you . . . forget something?"

For a long, silent moment he just looked at her. He wasn't a big man, nor was he, she supposed, handsome by most standards. His eyes looked, a neighbor child had once told him, like he'd be the best kind of Santa Claus, which Margaret had thought was the highest of praise. He was kind, gentle, and unfailingly good to her, and she adored him. The thought of losing him tore at some deep, vital part of her, and once more she told herself it wouldn't, couldn't, happen. She would get through this, he would never have to know, and they could go on as they always had.

"I'm looking," he said, "for something I'm afraid I might have lost."

His words were so eerily reminiscent of her thoughts that she nearly panicked, thinking he'd guessed. Or that in trying to save them, she was going to destroy them. She had to get herself under control, she had to be able to act as if nothing was wrong. She'd known that all along, but she'd been a miserable failure at carrying it out. Countless times she had nearly broken down and told him everything, but the deeply held fear prevented her at the last minute.

No, she couldn't risk telling him. Not only for her own selfish reasons, but for Shelby's sake. She couldn't start anything that would point the police in Shelby's direction, not without knowing what had happened.

But now Robert was just looking at her, with an expression on his face that she'd never seen before, and it was shaking her to the core. She knew he was under pressure on a big project at work; as vice president of research and development, he held a great deal of responsibility. And the city council meetings had been tough lately, with a lot of bickering about the budget, although less than before the police chief's home had burned a while back. Robert, as was typical of him, felt bad for the poor man's loss and had been more patient in dealing with him since.

It occurred to her in that moment that she had been forgetting just how patient and generous and tolerant Robert could be, even with people he barely knew. Surely for her, his wife, he would forgive even more? Maybe she *should* tell him, maybe—

"Robert," she whispered, all she could get out before her throat tightened beyond words.

"When I lost Sandra," he said softly, "I didn't think I would ever dare risk loving again. You changed that."

Margaret swallowed tightly. Robert's first wife, his high school sweetheart whom he had married at eighteen, had died from diabetes. It was testament to Robert's love and generosity that, after some initial adjustment, Margaret had never felt like an inferior replacement.

He'd told her before they had married that he knew there were things she hadn't told him. He'd said then that nothing she could say would change his mind about her. But she was certain then, as she was now, that in Robert's quiet, conventional world, the kind of secrets she had to keep would never have occurred to him.

She had tried to picture herself telling him, when Pruett had first contacted her. When the evil, smirking man had promised that if she didn't pay, the photographs would be on their way to the local tabloids, along with copies to the police commission, city council, and Robert's company. It had come to her so vividly, the image of the expression on his face changing from love to puzzlement to disgust, that she had been violently ill. She had instantly decided she could never, ever let him find out about this.

"Margaret?" he said softly.

"Everything is fine," she said, almost desperately. "I'm just . . . distressed over Shelby."

His brow creased. "I thought you'd heard from her."

"She left a message, but I haven't spoken to her, or actually seen her." *And I have to. I have to know what happened.*

Robert looked at her steadily, with those kind, gentle eyes that now were shadowed with hurt. A hurt she had put there.

"I know there's more," he said. "I wish you would tell me."

Don't admit it! Don't admit it! Her every instinct screamed at her, but she literally could not open her mouth to lie to him again. God, what an awful, vicious circle to be in! She could lose him no matter what she did.

Finally, in the face of her agonized silence, he turned to go.

At the door he stopped and looked back at her. "I love you, Margaret. But I don't know how to handle you not trusting me."

And then he was gone.

It was now or never.

As they crossed the casino floor, Shelby searched for a distraction—something, anything, that would draw Aaron's attention long enough for her to slip away from him.

She knew she had to go. She'd fallen asleep on the green leather couch, only to awaken from the dream that haunted her, the vivid images and sounds and memories, of her own terror, of the shot, the unexpected muzzle flash in the darkened corner of the room, the hideous thud of the body falling, the blood, God, all the blood . . .

Shelby had realized then that Aaron didn't deserve to be mired in this mess just because he had a soft spot for people in trouble. And mired he would be, if she gave in to the growing attraction she felt for him. It had nothing to do with feeling that she owed him but everything to do with her own response to every sideways look, every appearance of that crooked grin, every move of his powerful body.

So when he'd come back from his office this afternoon she had talked him into venturing outside, claiming cabin fever. He'd been reluctant, and she hoped he might be distracted enough for her to lose him. She'd even asked if they could go through the casino rather than out the isolated, private back door, hoping that an opportunity would arise amid all the noise and people.

So she waited for her chance as they crossed the casino. When they were close enough to the outside doors, she glanced toward Aaron to see if he was looking her way. She'd noticed he tended to scan regularly when they were in the casino, and supposed it was a habit he was barely aware of, the proprietor checking on his domain.

She'd been hoping something would be going on, anything that would make him focus on it long enough for her to make a move. It didn't happen. He held the door for her, and they stepped outside. He was right in step with her as they started toward the private parking area where he'd left his Yukon.

Okay, Plan B, she told herself. *You'll never outrun him on foot, so get in, and the first time he stops for a light, go for it. You'll have to—*

Her pulse leapt and her heart slammed in her chest. Just beyond Aaron's right shoulder she saw a too familiar face. Not the first man, but the second, the one she had to guess was his cohort, someone he'd hired or coerced into hunting her.

He was coming from the opposite direction, as if he'd parked in the public parking structure, but he was headed quickly toward the doors they'd just exited—and them.

Instinctively she moved, hiding behind Aaron's broad-shouldered height.

"What is it?"

He didn't move, didn't turn to look, did nothing that would betray them to her rapidly approaching shadow. He zeroed in only on her, his dark eyes narrowed.

It took Shelby only an instant to decide on the lesser hazard. Aaron might be a threat to her peace of mind, but this man was a threat to her life.

"That man," she said.

Those were the only words she managed before Aaron reached out and gripped her upper arms, holding her in place. Still shielding her with his body, as if he'd guessed right away that was why she'd moved, he turned his head slightly.

"The one who was following you?" he asked. "In the gray jacket and blue baseball cap?"

"Yes," she said, surprised. As far as she knew, she'd never actually admitted she was being followed. But there had been the wig. He'd guessed then, perhaps.

Aaron just stood there, holding her in the shelter of his body, solid, unmoving and unmovable. "I thought so. I've seen him a few too many times in the last day or so."

"Aaron," she began.

"Shh."

He stood with his head lifted, as if he could see the approaching man even though he was nearly behind him. Shelby didn't dare risk a glance. If the man hadn't spotted her yet, he surely would then. And she had to assume that by now he would recognize Aaron too, and perhaps be looking for him as well, thinking to find her with him.

Aaron waited. The man strode on, still focused on the casino doors.

In the instant before he would have passed them, the man's steady stride faltered. His eyes widened. And Shelby saw his gaze had shifted to Aaron. As if Aaron sensed the man's eyes on him, he turned. Swiftly, he took a step toward the man at the same time.

The man froze, staring up at the man towering over him with wary eyes. Then he whirled and took off running.

Aaron went after him with a speed that belied his size. Shelby started to follow, but suddenly Aaron stopped, letting the man go. He turned back to her, his expression clearly showing his ambivalence. It took Shelby a moment to realize he was torn between chasing the man and staying close to her.

And he had chosen to protect her.

An odd sort of shiver went through her.

When he was beside her again, he pulled out his cell phone and dialed, not a phone number but apparently some kind of two-digit code.

"Robin? Aaron. I need you to have your people watch for someone." He gave a description of the man and what he was wearing, then added, "Get hold of me right away if you find him. I'll be on my cell or the pager." He paused while his security chief apparently spoke, then said, "Yes, hold him if he's anywhere on the property. Let me worry about explaining the reason."

He disconnected and slipped the phone back into his pocket. Shelby looked at him, still a little breathless from what had just happened. And slowly realizing that it was more from Aaron's instant, protective reaction than from the close encounter with her no-doubt-lethal shadow.

"I'm sorry," he said when he saw her looking at him so intently.

"Sorry?"

"That he got away. But I didn't want to leave you, because—"

He broke off, and for a moment Shelby wished he would leave it that way, leave it for her to fill in her own wishful reason that he hadn't wanted to leave her. And that thought alone told her how far gone she was.

"Because?" she prompted, certain that there was another, safer reason, and deciding she needed to hear it before she got in any deeper.

His mouth quirked. "Because this guy wasn't the only one I've seen too many times since you've been here."

Shelby's breath caught. It wasn't the answer she'd

been foolishly wishing for, but it would do. It meant she wasn't crazy. "You've also seen two?"

He nodded. "I wasn't sure at first."

"Neither was I. I thought I was just being paranoid."

"But as they say, being paranoid doesn't mean they're not really after you."

He believed her. With what little she'd told him, he believed her, and even though he might suspect that she had killed Pruett, he was still willing to help her. She didn't understand, but maybe she didn't have to. Maybe all she had to do was trust him.

The hardest thing in the world for her to do.

Not until they were in his car and waiting at a stoplight in front of the Golden Phoenix did she realize she'd changed her mind. She had absolutely no desire to leap out of the car to freedom. She told herself it would be foolish, with her pursuer—or one of them, at least—so close at hand, but she suspected there was much more to her decision than that.

She stayed silent until they left the city limits behind.

"Where are we going?"

He gave her a sideways glance. "You said you were going stir-crazy. So I thought we'd go—where I go when that happens to me."

"You go stir-crazy?" she asked. He seemed so content with his life and work, the idea that he also got restless sometimes surprised her.

"Sometimes," he admitted with a shrug. "The walls seem to close in. Or people. So I go someplace where there aren't any."

"Walls or people?"

"Both."

When he left the main road and started up a narrow gravel road, she gave him a teasing glance. "Wow, an off-road vehicle actually driven off paved roads."

"Novel concept, isn't it?" Aaron agreed with a grin.

As he left the gravel road for a barely discernible trail, she became a bit uneasy. She had the grim thought that this would be a great place to dump a body if one were the murderous sort. She suppressed a shiver, telling herself she was being ridiculous. If he'd wanted to hurt her he'd had a dozen chances by now. She couldn't waste energy dealing with monsters that weren't there.

She needed to save it to deal with the monsters that were.

Chapter Twelve

Aaron caught her sneaking a look at him as he concentrated on maneuvering the Yukon over the rutted road.

"Still don't trust me?" he asked casually.

Shelby flushed. Apparently she'd thought him too preoccupied with driving to notice her wary look and the nervous shiver she'd tried to hide.

"Figure I brought you out to this isolated place to . . . to what? Just how suspicious are you?"

"Sorry," she muttered, not bothering to deny what he'd sensed.

He shrugged. Sadly, he didn't blame her. "You have to be careful. The world's a tough place for a lone woman."

"Men have made it that way," she snapped, sounding more than a little embarrassed that he'd caught her out.

"I can't argue with that as a generalization," he said. "Just don't tar us all with that brush."

Shelby let out a long, audible sigh. "I know. It's just something I'm . . . touchy about."

"Me, too," he said, meaning it. "A woman should be able to walk through any town in this country without worrying about getting assaulted, raped, or worse. Question is, How do we do it?"

"I'm not sure whether the answer is bigger jails, stiffer sentences, better rehabilitation, or simply giving every girl a handgun and shooting lessons along with her first training bra," Shelby said sourly.

"Now there's an idea," Aaron said, barely suppressing a chuckle.

Shelby turned in her seat, shoving the seat belt away from where it was rubbing against her neck. "Maybe we should just ask the guy who designed this belt so that it chokes anybody shorter than the average male."

Aaron did laugh this time, ruefully. "Not very fair, is it, that they build them to accommodate someone as extreme as me, but not the average woman."

She muttered something that sounded like agreement, then looked at him curiously. "What's it like, to be so—"

"Oversize?" he supplied with a wry grimace, slowing as they reached a particularly rough section of the track.

She wrinkled her nose. "That makes it sound like you're overweight, and you're not. You're just . . . big."

"At fifteen, when it happened, it was embarrassing because I was bigger than everybody my age. Now—" He shrugged. "You get used to it. You try to be careful, not to frighten or intimidate people."

"Unless you want to?" she asked.

One corner of his mouth curled up. "Well, there is that," he admitted. "Size does have its uses."

She smiled back at him, apparently having conquered her moment of suspicion. Or at least having gotten it under control, he thought, wondering if she was ever able to take anything at face value.

He pulled off the track onto a flat area where he usually parked. Cindy had hated it here. In the beginning she'd come up for his sake, but he'd always felt like she was only humoring him and couldn't wait to get back down to town. She was constantly looking for snakes or scorpions and never once, he had finally realized, had she been able to relax enough to enjoy it.

Somehow he didn't think a mere scorpion or even a rattler would send Shelby screaming back to the truck.

He led the way, for his own piece of mind, being certain of where he stepped before he put his foot down on one of those rattlers sunning himself. The track was faint, but he knew it well. It began to rise as they neared a small hill, then curved around it. The trail wasn't overly high, but it narrowed as they rounded the knoll, and he slowed a little. He looked back at her. She was close on his heels, watching where she walked, but not looking nervous.

When he got to their destination, he turned, holding his breath, as he always did. Every time he was somehow afraid that it had changed, that it had been taken away or altered in some way that would destroy its effect.

It was as it had always been. Satisfied, he moved over so she could make the final turn. She did, still watching her step.

He watched her, not the view. She made sure of her footing. She turned around. Lifted her head.

And gasped.

He saw her eyes widen, dart around as if trying to take everything in. Her lips parted for breath, as if they were much higher than they were and the air was thin. He knew how she felt. He'd felt the same way the first time he'd come up here. And the second. And third.

The high desert stretched out below and to the right, with rocks of every earth shade tossed in all directions. Occasionally there was an escarpment of angled rocks marching in line, losing their battle with the wind and rain, going from sharp edges to rounded corners. It seemed to go on forever, endlessly, untouched.

A few degrees to the left the mountain began, at first mere hills of the same varied desert colors, but then, almost sharply, a soaring row of forested peaks that looked unreal with their jagged edges and traces of snow at the top.

"My God," she whispered.

"It's better at sunrise or sunset," he said softly.

"How could it be?" she asked, still staring out at the vista before them.

"The sun really throws all her colors into it then, red and orange at sunset, pink and blue at sunrise. Whether you watch it fading away or coming alive, it's . . . breathtaking."

For the first time she looked at him. The wonder he'd always felt in coming up here glowed in her eyes. There was no trace of fear, or wariness, only wonder at the sight. She got it, Aaron thought. In a big way. He felt ridiculously pleased.

"The mountains," she breathed. "They look . . . painted against the sky. Like a postcard you send to people, even though you know it can't ever match the original, that they won't really feel the way you did, looking at the real thing."

"You have to see it," he agreed.

"And the desert . . . it's so vast, so empty, but the colors, all the textures . . . and the air, it's so incredibly clean. . . ."

He saw her take in a deep breath, smiled to himself as he remembered all the times he'd done the same thing.

"After I . . . quit going up to the lake, I used to come up here a lot. It was the only place that helped." He couldn't believe he was telling her this, that he was mentioning it at all. "Maybe it made me feel a little less empty, by comparison."

She looked at him then, her eyes warm, not with painful sympathy but with a deep, heartfelt empathy.

She knew, he thought, what it was like to feel so empty inside that you thought you would never be whole again. And thankfully, she said nothing about the words he'd uttered, but simply let the warmth of her gaze and the softness of her voice say what she didn't put into words.

She turned back to the panorama that fell away from the ledge they stood upon.

"If the mountains weren't there," she said, "I'll bet you could practically see the Pacific."

He blinked. Then laughed. "I remember thinking that once. That the air was really that clear."

She smiled, then turned back to the rugged expanse. They stood there for a long time. Shelby just looked, and looked, showing no sign of being bored or wanting to leave. He leaned back against the outcropping of the bluff and found himself watching her as much as the landscape he loved so much. He realized he was pleased that she was responding this way. What he didn't quite understand was why he felt, oddly, a sense of relief.

He shifted his gaze back to the view. It took a little longer this time, but eventually he felt it. That sense of quiet, of stillness, seeped into him. It didn't make his problems go away, but it brought things into perspective, brought them down to one step at a time, and made him feel like he could handle them.

He didn't know how much time had passed when Shelby finally turned to him. She gave an awed shake of her head. "How did you ever find this place?"

"I didn't. My cousin Hank did."

"Hank? The . . ."

"Drunk?" he supplied. "Yes. He wasn't always a drunk. He used to run out here in the hills, to stay in shape. He brought me out here after my mom died, and I've been coming ever since."

"Looks like a tough place to run."

"It is. But he was manic about it. We thought once he was going to be a star. He was a great baseball player in college. But he blew out his knee his junior year, and that was that. In more ways than one."

"That's when he started drinking?"

Aaron nodded. "I'm not making excuses for him. Sometimes he thought he was God's gift, and he never did deal well with not getting his own way. But after that happened, he got to . . . really hating people. Especially if they had what he'd taken for granted he would have. Success, acclaim, power."

"Bitterness is a crippling thing," she said, her voice soft.

"It sure crippled Hank. It got so the only way he could deal with people at all was with a cloud of alcohol between him and them."

"I've known some people who could make you feel you needed that to deal with them," she said. "But I always figured that was when you needed your wits about you the most."

"And there you have it," Aaron said. "Hank gave up and crawled into a bottle. You're a fighter."

She colored slightly but didn't speak.

"We've all tried to help him, in different ways," Aaron said, wondering why they were standing here jabbering about his thorn-in-the-side cousin. "But he keeps on, and we all know how it's going to end."

"Sometimes there's no helping. Some people . . . just can't change."

He sensed that her words had suddenly gotten very specific, and he wondered who she was thinking of when she said them.

How did we live, Mike wondered, before cell phones?

More peacefully, he answered himself as he answered his on the third ring.

"Didn't see you this afternoon, Detective."

Mike grimaced at the sound of the chief's voice, pointing out that he'd vanished the instant the speech was over. "I've been on interviews all day."

"The Pruett case?"

Considering Cushman had told him to shelve everything else until there was some movement on this, and he'd copied the chief's office with everything so far, Mike thought the question a bit superfluous. But then, Cushman had never been good at rapport with his troops.

"Yes. Reichart's one bitter man. A definite possible. Says his wife will corroborate his alibi, but I'm not sure how much that would be worth."

Cushman made a grunting sound that Mike supposed was acknowledgment before saying, "I just read your report on your first contact with the racing consortium. No surprises?"

"No. They're smooth, and they said all the right things. Presented me with alibis for each one before I even asked. They were expecting me, of course."

"No attorneys present?"

"Not yet." Mike had wondered about that, but had decided it was all part of the plan to present an innocent, cooperative front. "I tried not to spook them, told them it was routine, that we were talking to everyone Pruett had dealings with."

"It may be time to turn up the heat."

"I'm on my way to their office again now."

"Good. They're the most likely in my book."

"I'll push as hard as I can," Mike said carefully, "given that we have nothing on them except that they had motive—along with at least a dozen others. And I know they'll lawyer up the moment we start separating them for individual interviews."

"That kind always does. Push anyway."

"Yes, sir."

Great, Mike muttered to himself as he disconnected. *And guess who takes the heat when one of these high-powered guys goes whining to the mayor about police harassment.*

He wondered if there was another job on earth as complicated as this one.

"Thank you," Shelby said as they headed back toward the main road.

"You're welcome," Aaron returned. "I'm glad you . . . liked it."

" 'Like' is an insipid word for *that,* too," she said, intentionally repeating her words about the golden phoenix in his office.

He smiled at her. "It's a special place. If things are moving too fast, I come out here to slow down. If they're going too slow, I come out here and see what slow really is."

She thought about that for a moment. "I can see where it would work both ways. It must have looked like this for thousands of years."

He nodded. "Nothing changes fast out here. And there's a sort of peace in that."

There had been, and she carried some of it inside her now, even after they'd left that amazing spot. "Thank you," she said again. "For knowing it would . . . help."

He gave her a sideways glance. "I may not even know your last name, but I knew you needed some peace."

Shelby felt a stab of guilt. He'd done so much, helped her without question. She had told herself over and over that he was better off knowing as little as possible, but the more time she spent with him, the more unfair it seemed.

"Wyatt," she said suddenly.

She could risk that, she thought. It really wouldn't

tell him anything except maybe where she lived if he bothered to look it up. And since she hadn't been back there since she'd left that night . . .

"Shelby . . . Wyatt?"

His voice was carefully inflectionless, as if he were afraid she'd somehow take it back.

"Yes."

He didn't say anything more. *If you're waiting for an outpouring of other confidences, don't,* she told him silently. *I can't—won't—risk it.*

And then she realized he was negotiating the turn from the gravel road onto the highway back to Outpost, and felt rather foolish. He hadn't pushed her yet, and there was no reason to think he would now. In fact, she was beginning to wonder if his prodigious patience ever ran out.

They'd been back on the main road for a few minutes when Shelby realized he was frowning. She shifted to look at him, and saw that he was checking the rearview mirrors frequently and intently. She turned to look behind them. At first she saw nothing, then, in the distance, a newer white sedan.

"Aaron?"

He grimaced. "It's the main road, darn near the only road into Outpost, so normally I wouldn't think anything of it."

"Of . . . what?"

"The fact that the same kind of car was behind us on the way out here."

Shelby's breath caught. She'd been so focused on Aaron that she hadn't noticed. But he had.

She stared at the car, which was too far back to make her heart start slamming the way it did. The sedan came to one of the many dips in the roadway, and for a moment vanished from view. But she knew it would reappear. Dogged. Relentless.

"He probably didn't dare follow us off the highway. We'd know right away, and he'd lose his advantage."

Aaron said it calmly, calculatingly, as if it wasn't possibly a killer behind them. Looking to kill her. Did Aaron realize that?

For the first time she realized the ramifications of her decision to stay with Aaron. She'd saved herself for the moment, yes, but she'd also put him in danger. Just being with her, he was in danger.

"What if . . . he tries something now?" she asked, unable to tear her eyes away from the road, waiting for the hunter to reappear. "When we're out here alone?"

"We'll put a little distance between us," he said, and accelerated slightly. When the car crested the rise, Aaron slowed again. Shelby turned to look at him.

"When he's out of our line of sight, we're out of his, for the most part. If we're lucky, we can get a bit more distance between us before he realizes it."

She looked back just as the car dropped out of sight again. In the same moment Aaron sped up again.

"Ah," he said with satisfaction after a moment. Again Shelby turned to look at him.

"Safety in witnesses," he said, nodding toward the road ahead of them.

Shelby looked up and saw a line of three tour buses, full of gamblers eager to offer up their money to the gods of chance.

By some deft maneuvering, Aaron got them solidly placed between the first and second buses. They were creeping along by comparison to their former pace, but Shelby had never been so glad to breathe diesel fumes in her life.

"If they're headed for the Phoenix," Aaron muttered, "I'll give 'em all a free meal."

He would, too, Shelby thought. If she'd learned anything in the past couple of days, it was that Aaron Montana didn't make idle promises.

She settled down in her seat, keeping an eye on the rearview mirror on her side. She'd done this, she thought. She'd brought this dreadful thing here, to this place of beauty and peace. She felt as if she had despoiled Aaron's haven, and the thought made her sick.

She could only imagine how much worse she would feel if he ended up getting hurt.

Or killed.

Chapter Thirteen

He might just go ahead and take that shower as soon as he got out of here, Mike thought.

These guys weren't just polished, they were most definitely slick. Oh, they had it down, all right. This time he'd been treated like visiting royalty. Taken right to the head of the syndicate. Shown every courtesy. Including, he thought wryly, an escort every inch of the way. Red carpet treatment—or just making certain he didn't stick his nose anywhere it didn't belong?

"It's just so very shocking." Leonard Hartwood, in his thousand-dollar suit, silk tie, shirt with a diamond collar pin, and the most unreadable eyes Mike had ever seen, looked suitably distressed. "We still can't quite believe it."

The other two men in the room nodded in unison.

"A life cut short like that," the first said.

"And in such an awful way," the second added.

Ah, yes, Mike thought. The perfect note of shock and regret at their colleague's untimely and unpleasant death. *Platitudes 'R Us.*

"How will his death affect your business here?" Mike asked, careful to keep his voice neutral.

"Our business?" Hartwood seemed surprised that the question was even asked. "Why, hardly at all. The agreement we entered into provided for any . . . unforeseen circumstances."

In case you have to knock off an uncooperative part-

ner? "Farsighted of you," Mike said, a lot less caustically than he was thinking it.

"Our lawyers make sure of such things." Hartwood smiled. "That's why we pay them such outrageous fees."

It was an engaging smile, inviting Mike to join in the universal hobby of sniping at lawyers. Perhaps they assumed that since he was a cop, he would have more reason than most to join in.

"So you were covered if anything happened to him?" Mike said, making the turn he'd planned before he'd begun this interview.

Hartwood frowned. "I suppose you could say that."

"You had his money, so it didn't matter what happened to him after that?"

Hartwood stiffened for a split second, but recovered quickly. "I'm not sure I understand the question," he said coolly.

A crack in the facade? Mike wondered. "You—meaning your syndicate—had some problems with Mr. Pruett." He purposely phrased it as a statement, not a question.

"Dear Jack," Hartwood admitted with just the right note of rueful patience and the perfect air of confidentiality, "was in conflict with most of the syndicate directors, over the terms he'd been demanding."

If he hadn't already known, thanks to Aaron, that this wasn't quite a secret, he might have been impressed with the man's cooperation and forthrightness. As he was sure had been intended.

Call him suspicious, Mike thought, but he couldn't help thinking the whole thing was a facade. Nobody was that grief-stricken by the death of a business partner who, by all accounts, had been a problem for months. Nobody honest, anyway.

"That established, let me rephrase the question. Under the conditions you yourself mentioned, if Mr.

Pruett were to cause you problems, it would have been no financial loss to your organization to . . . remove him, is that correct?"

That did it. Hartwood's note of offended innocence was perfect. "I don't think I like your tone, Detective."

"I get that reaction a lot," Mike said in mock commiseration. "It's a failing of mine."

Hartwood sat up straight, clearly liking this tone no better. "I'm not certain what you're insinuating, Detective Delano. We've given you an account of our whereabouts at the time in question, completely verifiable. We've tried to cooperate since Jack was, for however short a time, a colleague. What else could you possibly want?"

"To know just how far you would go to get this project moving again. And which one of you has the connections to find someone to handle your little problem."

"That's quite enough," Hartwood said sharply. "I think if you come back again, Detective, you'd better have a warrant."

"That can be arranged," Mike said. "Books, bank records, phone records—"

"You should know," Hartwood interrupted, visibly angry now, "that I have friends—"

"Let me guess—in high places. Maybe I'll go talk to them too."

For an instant Mike saw again the crack in that perfect front. He'd accomplished what he'd wanted there today. Neither the polished, perfect Mr. Hartwood nor his equally polished surroundings—and the wealth clearly behind both—had changed Mike's mind. This bunch was way up there on the suspect list.

As he went back to his car, Mike thought of what his great-uncle, a cop in Chicago for decades, used to say: "They reeked of money, and their money reeked."

He'd been talking about gangsters. His tall, strong, brave uncle had worked in the heyday of the later gangsters and had been the one who inspired him to be a cop. But now, for the first time, he knew exactly what Uncle Bud had meant.

"Well, well, well."

Shelby stifled a scream as she whirled and faced the man who had come into the apartment without a sound. When she realized it wasn't either of the men who had been following her, she breathed again. Still, she stayed in the kitchen alcove, where she had access to knives, if nothing else. It had been a long time, but some things you never forgot.

Never raise your hand to stab down. Tiger's instructions had been grimly clear. *It takes too much time, and it leaves you vulnerable. Drive up from below. Jab it under the ribs.*

The man was walking toward her, wearing an expression she couldn't quite define. He moved with a fluid grace, and his eyes were dark and intense, like Aaron's. His hair was dark, too, like Aaron's. But other than that, there was little resemblance; this man was smaller, with regular features, the only distraction a jaw that hinted at the broadness of Aaron's.

But as he got closer, she saw signs of dissipation. The faintest puffiness, bags under the eyes that looked too extreme for his age, which she guessed was even younger than Aaron. In the moment before he spoke and confirmed it, she had figured out who he was.

"Just look at what my sainted cousin has stashed away, without a word to his loving family. No wonder he's been scarce lately. And here we'd all given up on him."

Shelby managed not to blush at the innuendo in his words. "Good afternoon, Hank," she said.

He lifted one dark brow. "I'm flattered. Or should I be insulted? I suppose it depends on what dear Aaron of the perfect reputation has said about me."

Irritation flicked through her then. "If I were you, I'd worry more about what what you said about him says about you."

Both brows shot up this time. "She has teeth," he said, sounding delighted. "Now there's an improvement!"

"She has claws, too," Shelby said dryly. "Want to test them?"

Hank backed up in mock terror. "Oh, no. Not me. I never fight with someone who can beat me. Or a pretty woman. So that's two right there. Ms. . . . ?"

"Shelby," she said. "Shelby Wyatt." It couldn't hurt, since she'd already told Aaron, she thought.

Hank started toward her again, and took a seat on one of the barstools pulled up to the kitchen counter. Only then did Shelby notice the glassy sheen of his eyes and the faint glisten of sweat on his upper lip.

His words weren't slurred, in fact were more clear than most people's; perhaps he was consciously compensating. His gait was as smooth as she'd seen before, and again she wondered if it was just excellent compensation. Because she would swear he had been drinking, at the least. She knew the signs, even if he wasn't belligerent like most of the drinkers in her experience. In fact, he was rather . . . charming.

Hank's a very . . . charming drunk. Nobody really wants to get him into trouble, because he's so sweet about it.

Aaron's words came back to her, and she saw the truth of them before her now as the man with the killer grin looked at her across the counter.

"Well, Miss Shelby Wyatt, if Aaron has finally developed the sense to pick a woman with some spunk, I'm all for it."

She thought about explaining that he was on the wrong track entirely. She thought about telling him that Aaron hadn't "picked" her at all.

But in the end she said only, "Finally?"

"He's got this caretaker thing going on," Hank said. "Always has. That's why he ended up with Cindy."

He stopped, giving her a look that made her think he was just drunk enough to speak first and think later.

"I know about her," Shelby said neutrally. "And Megan."

Hank looked relieved. And interpreted it as she had hoped—perhaps sneakily—he might.

"Then you know why they split?"

"Losing a child damages a lot of marriages."

Hank snorted inelegantly. "Losing Megan may have damaged their marriage, but Cindy destroyed it. Blaming Aaron when it was her fault if it was anyone's."

Shelby didn't speak, hoping he would go on. Why, she wasn't quite sure, but she had suddenly developed a thirst to find out whatever she could about Aaron Montana. And after a moment during which he seemed to contemplate, with what Shelby guessed was a slightly befuddled sense of propriety, whether he should or not, he did go on.

"It wasn't bad enough that she stopped up there on the mountain, barely ten miles from home, and fell asleep with a five-year-old running loose, but then to panic like she always did, and not call anyone, for hours . . ."

Shelby stifled a gasp. "She didn't call anybody? Not even Aaron?"

"Or the police."

And Megan had died. "Poor Aaron," she whispered.

Hank snorted again. "Yeah. Especially when Cindy managed to make it his fault. And divorced him over it."

Shelby blinked. "His fault? But . . . I thought he wasn't even there?"

"Exactly. That's what she blamed him for. It was his fault she had to drive all the way to her mother's herself, even though it's less than a two-hour trip. And never mind that she'd decided to go at the last minute and Aaron couldn't get away."

"I don't understand."

Hank studied her for a moment. "No, I don't think you would. Personally, I think she set it up that way, stopping so close to home, as if she just couldn't drive another ten miles. She'd let him worry for a few hours, then call. So she could say he should have been there, that he'd promised to take care of them. But it backfired on her, in a big way."

"And she divorced him over that? Was he supposed to be around twenty-four hours a day?" Shelby asked incredulously.

Hank smiled at her, as if he was pleased by her instinctive defense of his cousin. It was a captivating, warm smile, and she realized suddenly why people kept covering for him. And for all his comments about his "sainted" cousin and his "perfect reputation," Hank was quick to defend Aaron.

"You'd have to know Cindy," he said. "She's pretty . . . helpless on her own. She depended on Aaron. But then, we all do," he added. "He's the linchpin that holds the Montanas together."

"Sounds like a heavy load."

"I couldn't carry it," Hank admitted with that easy charm. "And Lord knows nobody would want me to." He eyed her thoughtfully. "Cindy couldn't make a move on her own. I can't see you ever being that way."

Perceptive, even after a few drinks, Shelby thought. "No. I couldn't stand it. How did Aaron?"

"I told you, it's that thing he has about taking care of people. And Cindy needed taking care of. Still does."

She opened her mouth to speak, then hesitated. She didn't want to seem too interested, but she did want to know, and if whatever Hank had been drinking had loosened his tongue enough, maybe she should take advantage of his garrulousness.

"And does Aaron still . . . take care of her?"

Hank nodded. "I think he feels responsible for her. She was fragile before, but she broke when she realized that divorcing Aaron didn't change anything. Megan was still gone, and deep down she knew it was her fault."

Shelby shook her head slowly. "I don't get it. She blamed him to bury her own guilt, but he still cares?"

"Don't get me wrong," Hank said quickly. "He doesn't love her anymore, but she's Megan's mother. And for Aaron, that's reason enough not to abandon her completely." His mouth twisted wryly. "Unlike his beloved cousin."

'You?" she asked, quickly guessing he meant Aaron's declining to bail him out of jail this time.

"*Moi*," Hank said, flashing that killer smile again. "Not that I hold it against him. I figured even Aaron would give up on me eventually."

"Maybe he didn't give up. Maybe he just doesn't think you're helpless."

Hank winced dramatically. "Zing!" But then he laughed. "You know, you may be the best thing that ever happened to my cousin."

"I doubt he would agree with that," she said, thinking of all the reasons Aaron would have been better off if he'd stayed out of her life.

"Give him time. He'll figure it out. He's a bright guy, for a soft touch."

"So . . . he really is perfect? He was never in trouble, even as a kid?"

Hank laughed. "Sure, he was. He was a terror as a teenager. I think that's why he's such a straight arrow now. He got it all out of his system early. And when he was in New York, he did some real partying. But now . . ."

"He's a caretaking linchpin who's a soft touch."

"Yeah." Hank grinned crookedly, whether by intention or alcohol Shelby didn't know. "Maybe you can teach him to say no."

She looked at Hank consideringly. "I'd think you'd want him to stay as he is, given that you're one of those he's been a soft touch for up until now."

The wince was for real this time. "You don't pull any punches, do you?"

"Should I?" she asked, looking at him levelly.

When he arrived a moment later, Aaron found them that way, in a silent standoff.

"Should I come back later and toast the winner?" he asked as he tossed his coat and a portfolio on the chair.

"Why wait?" Hank said, his tone equally dry. "You can just toast her now."

Aaron raised a brow at his cousin, but when he glanced at Shelby, there was a glint of humor in his eyes that she couldn't help but respond to. She felt the laugh bubbling up before she could stop it.

Aaron's expression changed, softened, warming his rough features. "I've never heard you laugh."

She knew she didn't have to explain that she'd not had much to laugh about; the knowledge was there in his eyes. Embarrassed, she simply shrugged.

"So," Hank said, breaking in on the oddly intimate moment, "where did you find this treasure, why doesn't anybody know about her, and why do you have her hidden away up here?"

"Come on in, make yourself at home, and ask some more questions that are none of your business," retorted Aaron.

"Whoa, hit a nerve," Hank crowed, clearly taking no offense.

"And it's right next to the reflex for my right hook. Don't push your luck."

Shelby listened to the banter in fascination. Beneath the gruff words was an undertone of longtime affection in both their voices. She'd never seen anything quite like it before. She wondered if this was what it was like in normal families, this kind of teasing give-and-take. Aaron might be exasperated with his cousin, but that didn't mean he didn't love him. And Hank might poke fun at Aaron, but Shelby sensed that deep down he depended on the rock-solidness of him.

As, she thought with a start, she was coming to do. She realized he had neatly diverted Hank's inquiries about her, letting him continue to think that she was a girlfriend Aaron had kept quiet about. Even with his family, he was still protecting her.

Hank sat tracing a nonexistent line in the solid countertop, over and over. Then, finally, he lifted his head and looked at his cousin.

"Sorry about Mom," he said.

Aaron shrugged. Hank clearly didn't blame Aaron for not bailing him out. And it seemed Aaron wasn't about to apologize for it, either. Shelby admired that. He'd made his decision, tough though it had been, and now he was sticking by it.

"I didn't mean to sic her on you," Hank said. "I just—you know how I get. I didn't think."

"Yes," Aaron said, "I know how you get."

"I don't blame you for washing your hands of me," Hank said. "I'm such a screwup."

His voice had changed, Shelby thought, taken on a note that detracted greatly from the charm.

Aaron heard it too and said, "If you're going to start whining, go somewhere else." Then, rather forcefully, "And *don't* drive."

"Who the hell elected you boss?" Hank snapped, the charm vanishing altogether for a moment.

"I wasn't elected. I was the only one who would take the damn job," Aaron snapped back.

Hank looked so startled that Shelby wondered if Aaron had ever lost his temper with his cousin before. Hard to believe that if the late-night bail-out calls had been going on as long as it seemed.

"Okay, okay," Hank said hastily. "I just wanted to say I'm sorry about Mom and I've called her off."

"Next time don't start her up," Aaron suggested, an edge still in his voice. "Better yet, don't let there *be* a next time."

"Yeah, yeah. Gotta go." Hank got to his feet, moving with a bit of unsteadiness now. Perhaps the alcohol was really kicking in. At the outside doors he stopped and looked back at Shelby. The charming, heart-breaking grin flashed at her again. "Nice to meet you, Shelby Wyatt. Straighten this boy out, will you? All work and no play makes Aaron a pain in the ass."

Then he was gone, sauntering out into the corridor.

Aaron didn't say a word. He fiddled with the catch on the leather portfolio.

"He didn't seem horribly drunk," Shelby finally said.

"He wasn't. That was pretty sober, for him. But it won't last."

"You were right. He is charming."

"Yes. It's gotten him through life quite nicely."

"All play and no work?"

He looked startled, then grinned. "Something like that." With a negligent shrug, he added, "It isn't all his fault. His father is . . . a difficult man. The only thing he values in life is making money and then using it to make more. That's a knack Hank didn't inherit."

"So . . he didn't value his son?"

Aaron nodded. "No matter what he did, even when he was almost sure to become a pro ballplayer, he couldn't impress his father. Nothing he did was enough, because it wasn't what his father respected."

"Your uncle," she began, then stopped. It was hardly her place.

"I know. And his mother didn't help. She tried to make up for his father's coldness and ended up spoiling him rotten."

"And now . . . ?"

"And now his father doesn't acknowledge him and his mother covers for him."

"And you?"

He sighed. "I . . . bail him out."

"Until now."

"It had to stop. All I was doing was making it easier for him to keep committing a slow suicide."

"Do you think he'll ever stop?"

"I don't know. The only thing I'm sure of is that I can't do it for him, no matter how hard I try."

There was such weariness in his voice that Shelby couldn't stop herself. She stepped around the kitchen bar and slipped her arms around him.

Aaron stiffened, but in the instant before Shelby pulled back, thinking he didn't want her embrace, he relaxed and his arms came around her. She'd startled him, she realized, that was all. And no wonder—she'd startled herself too. She couldn't remember the last time she had wanted to comfort a man. If she ever had.

His chest was a solid wall against her cheek, and she could hear the steady, strong thud of his heart.

She depended on Aaron. But then, we all do. He's the linchpin that holds the Montanas together.

She knew little about families or what held them together, but she knew it couldn't be easy. It had to be a heavy load. She also knew that if there was anyone able to carry a heavy load, it was this man. He'd taken her on without knowing the real story, even though she wouldn't—couldn't—tell him the truth. And if Hank was right, she wasn't the first person he'd helped.

"Shelby?" he whispered.

She looked up at him, and her breath caught at the raw hunger in his dark eyes. She tried to say his name, couldn't, and wet her lips to try again. She felt a shudder go through him as she did it, and an echoing thrill rippled through her at the thought of literally shaking this massive, strong man.

He lowered his head slowly, so slowly that Shelby wondered if he was giving her a chance to escape, to make some sign that she didn't want this. She was a little amazed at herself, that she didn't really even consider doing that.

Amazed to realize that she *did* want this. That it hadn't been just temporary insanity before.

She expected a kiss that was as powerful, as overwhelming as the man himself.

What she got was a delicate, erotic questing. What she got was a lingering, exquisitely gentle, press of firm, warm lips.

What she got, instead of a bursting explosion of strength, was a slow building of heat and sensation that had nearly swamped her by the time she realized what was happening.

She moaned under the force of it. She felt a jolt as his tongue swept over her parted lips, wished he would come back and do it again.

He did, and she murmured his name against his mouth.

His arms tightened around her. For an instant he broke the kiss; she heard his rasping breath. But it wasn't enough. She wasn't done yet. He couldn't be, could he?

She leaned into him, reaching, straining. With a strangled groan he lowered his head once more.

This time the explosion came, for he took her mouth fiercely, possessively, urgently. His lips coaxed even as they plundered, his tongue stroking even as it demanded. She gave in without hesitation, parting her lips for him, welcoming the hot, sweet probing.

When she gave in to the need to do some exploring of her own, when she tasted his lips, pushed on to trace the even ridge of his teeth, he groaned again, harshly, and she felt it rumbling up in his chest an instant before she heard it.

Her head was reeling when he inexplicably backed away. Only then did she hear the sound he must have heard, the phone on his desk ringing insistently. She hadn't even realized . . .

And she wondered where they might have wound up if not for the well- or ill-timed interruption.

Chapter Fourteen

He'd been here too long. This foothill hellhole had nothing to recommend it but the opportunity to gamble, and he could get that in Vegas, a town he much preferred because it was bigger and flashier and easier to go unnoticed in. But he'd never risked leaving loose ends before, and he wasn't about to start now.

It would be over soon. After hours of trying, too many close calls—not to mention that fruitless foray out into the desert—he had the code. And he knew they were up there. He'd seen Montana go up a while ago, and the woman had never come down since they'd gotten back.

He wondered, as he had been wondering for some time now, why she was still walking around loose, why there were no police swarming around her. Montana was the upstanding-citizen type; it went against that kind of character to know something about a murder and not call the cops. Was it possible that he didn't know? That she hadn't told him?

But then why would he be sticking to her like one of those damned desert cholla plants stuck to your pants leg? No woman was *that* good. There had to be a reason he never let her out of his sight. And in the end the reason didn't really matter. Nothing mattered right now except watching that hallway for the right person.

It had been easy enough to get someone to point out Montana's administrative assistant. The Golden Phoenix people were so helpful, all he'd had to do was say she'd helped him over the phone and he wanted to thank her, and within moments he had her name and the knowledge that she usually ate at the deli next to the arcade about this time. The name led him to the correct portrait on the wall, and now he merely had to wait until she came down.

He wandered to a nearby slot machine that was close enough to give him a view of both the hallway and the entrance to the deli across the casino floor, took out a handful of change, and pumped in a quarter. He pushed the button, the video reels spun, and as he'd expected, nothing happened. He waited a minute or so, then dumped in another quarter, with the same results.

He dropped his last quarter into the slot, but before he could push the button he saw her come out of the private elevator, dressed in a neat pink suit, silver hair in a tiny bun at the back of her head. There was no doubt this was the Francine Chapman in the photo. He watched as she walked briskly around the edge of the casino in the direction of the deli. Several people waved to her, smiling, and she returned the gesture. The unrelenting cheer of this bunch was beginning to wear on him.

She went to the deli. It was time to move. Almost as an afterthought he hit the button on the slot machine. He'd already taken a step away when the clanking in the tray stopped him. He'd won ten dollars. He smiled as he scooped up the coins; he would take that as a good omen.

He walked confidently down the hallway to the elevator, surreptitiously pulling on a clear latex glove as he went. With the gloved hand he keyed in the number his expensive sonic detector had finally given him.

Within moments the elevator arrived. He stepped inside, and pushed the button to close the doors; he didn't want anyone to see him studying the panel as if he didn't know where he was going.

As it turned out, the buttons were clearly labeled, and it didn't take much to figure out he wanted the floor labeled "Administrative Offices." He pushed the button, and felt the tug as the car began to ascend.

When it stopped, the doors slid open smoothly, and he stepped out into what appeared to be a lobby area. Several yards down the wall was another secured elevator that apparently came up from another part of the building. He went quickly over to it. He wondered if this was how Montana got to his residence, but it didn't seem to go beyond this floor. He punched the button to call the elevator to this level; having both of them here would give him another escape route, plus it would slow down anybody heading up here.

On the far side of the room was a set of solid double doors, with another keypad. He pondered this for a moment. Most systems allowed you only one goof before triggering an alarm. It was likely that the door and the elevator were coded alike; it would take someone highly paranoid to make everyone who needed access remember different numbers for each location. So he could either risk that they were coded alike or take the time to hook up the sensor again and gamble that no one arrived while it was working. And that was on top of gambling that Montana was in his apartment, not his office, and that no one would show up here in the next few minutes.

That was too much gambling. He reached inside his jacket pocket, checking that his small .380 automatic wasn't hung up. In the deserted office area he didn't bother with the suppressor, although he had it with him and could have it on the weapon in seconds. As soon as this was over he would discard the pistol, as he always did. He never let himself form an attachment to a particular weapon; using a different one each time left no ballistics trail and no pattern for some sharp cop to figure out.

He pushed the same code he'd used on the elevator, and let out a breath when he heard the click of the lock releasing. He nudged the door open with his toe, leaning back out of a possible line of fire. Montana didn't seem the type, but you just never knew.

It appeared dark beyond the doors, and after a moment, he risked a look. It was apparently the woman's office, and she'd turned out the lights when she left for lunch.

He slipped inside, leaving the door slightly ajar. He quickly decided to leave the lights off, and stood to one side to let his eyes adjust.

After a moment he saw the door behind the desk, marked with a discreet nameplate. He couldn't read it from here in the dimness, but he knew it had to be Montana's office. And, he guessed, in it would be the access to his apartment suite above. He crossed the outer office and tried the door. Locked, as he had expected. He pulled a small leather case out of an inner pocket that he'd had added to his jacket. Inside were his picks and a penlight.

He studied the lock for a moment, then selected two picks. Holding the penlight between his teeth, he went to work. He hadn't had to do this in a while, but some things you never forgot. It took him longer than he would have liked, but eventually he got it.

He wasn't sure what he'd expected of Montana's office, but the plain simplicity he found wasn't it. He took a step inside, then stopped dead. There was a single light on in the room, in the far corner. It flooded down on the biggest chunk of gold he'd ever seen. He knew it was real gold; nothing but the real thing had that gleam, that glow. It was apparently some kind of bird, and he supposed it was the phoenix of the name of the place, although it didn't look like much to him.

For the first time in his career, he was seriously tempted to add burglary to his repertoire. Melted down, this thing would make a hell of a retirement fund. He walked toward it, staring. He stopped a couple of feet away; he had no doubt the thing was seriously alarmed. But still . . .

He was so intent that he jumped when he heard a ding through the partially open door. Someone had called for one of the elevators.

He dashed to the lobby, pulling the outer door shut, trusting that the Chapman woman would assume she'd simply not locked Montana's door. The second elevator's up arrow was lit, so he couldn't be sure who it might be. He dodged into the one he'd come up in, and hit the button to close the doors. Just as they slid closed, he heard the sound of two, perhaps three male voices. Cursing to himself, he pressed the button for the ground level. If he hadn't stopped to gape at that dammed gold bird, he might have had time to get to Montana's lair.

Now he would have to try again.

"Robin Murphy, Shelby Wyatt."

Shelby nodded warily at the woman who had come into Aaron's office. She would have simply smiled had it not been for the discreet gold nameplate on the woman's trim black suit that labeled her as "Chief of Security." But as far as she knew, Aaron hadn't called her in; she had come in on her own to deliver some kind of paperwork.

She was relieved when Aaron didn't go into any more detail about who she was, then wary again when Robin didn't even ask, and she wondered if the reason was because he'd already told her.

"I know you'll want to talk to them yourself, but I

think these are the best three of the final candidates," Robin said to Aaron, holding out some files.

He nodded as he took the folders. "And this will put you back to a full complement, right?"

Robin nodded in turn. Shelby took the opportunity, as Aaron glanced through the files, to study the woman. She was inches taller than her own five-one, a little more rounded, but Shelby instinctively sensed that she was fit and strong. Her hair was a lovely shade of copper, which, judging from her brows and eyelashes, and the freckles across her nose, was genuine. Shelby guessed, if for no other reason than her position, that she was at least in her late thirties, although she looked younger.

Shelby found herself wondering if Robin and Aaron had more than a working relationship, then tensed as she realized how much the idea bothered her.

"Do you want to see them now, while they're still here after my interviews?" Robin asked.

Aaron glanced at Shelby. "Look, I know you wanted a change of scene, but—"

"It can wait," Shelby said, although she was more than a little restless. What she really wanted to do was go outside, just take a walk, with no thought of being followed or hunted. But since that was impossible, she would have settled for a trek downstairs, and maybe a stop in the video arcade she'd noticed. But now it seemed even that wasn't going to happen.

"I'll go with you," Robin offered to Shelby without hesitation.

"No, really—"

"Good idea," Aaron said. "Thanks, Robin. That's a big help."

Shelby was feeling like a child needing a baby-sitter, but she tried not to take it out on the woman as they left Aaron to conduct his interviews. They exited via the outside corridor, Shelby noticed, not the private elevator. And she also noticed, as Robin opened the door, that she wore a simple gold band on her left hand. So she was married, this striking redhead. Shelby relaxed a little.

"Does he always do interviews with prospective employees?"

"Not all of them. But security, yes. He feels very strongly about it." Robin smiled at her. "But you must know that."

Shelby was instantly on guard. "Why do you say that?"

"He brought you here, didn't he?"

Shelby stopped in her tracks. Robin looked at her curiously, cocking her head in inquiry. "Just what," Shelby said slowly, "did he tell you about me?"

Robin's arched brows furrowed. "Just that you were having some trouble and needed a safe place. That's all he ever says."

Now it was Shelby's turn to be curious. "Ever?"

Robin shrugged. "He does this all the time," she explained. "He's always bringing in somebody who needs shelter."

"Oh." Shelby nearly winced at the almost forlorn note in her own voice. She sounded as if she were crushed that she was just another in an apparently long line of people he'd helped.

"However," Robin said, as if she'd read Shelby's mind, "I don't recall him ever bringing one literally home before. He usually just gives them a room."

"Oh," Shelby said again, feeling reassured and hating herself for it. To distract Robin, in case she was as perceptive as she seemed, she asked quickly, "Have you worked here long?"

They reached the elevator and Robin pushed the down button before answering. "Five years now. And I wouldn't leave for twice the money. Not," she added with a grin, "that anybody's going to offer that much to me."

"That's nice, that you're so happy here."

"Aaron gave me a chance when no one else would," she said frankly. "I'd left a police department in a suburb down near L.A. after a . . . a personal situation, and when I couldn't hack the harassment any longer. I'd made lieutenant, and there are enough male cops left who don't like taking orders from a woman to make life more trouble than I wanted it to be."

Shelby nodded in commiseration. "How did you end up here?"

"After I'd decided to quit, a friend of mine told Aaron's friend Mike about me. Mike told Aaron, Aaron flew me up for an interview. Except it was like no interview I'd ever had."

"What was it like?"

"A man from the hotel picked me up at the airport in a Golden Phoenix car. He was very nice, friendly, and willing to talk, so I pumped him for all the info I could get. I was really nervous, because I really wanted the job. He put me completely at ease and answered everything, except he wouldn't talk about the boss."

"The boss being Aaron?"

Robin nodded. The elevator arrived, and they stepped inside. As the doors closed, Robin glanced up at the camera in the corner of the elevator car.

"Good thing everybody already knows this story," she said with a wink at the lens, then went on. "During the ride here, I told him why I'd left my police job. He seemed angry about the way I was treated, which made me like the guy. He asked what I would do first, given a free rein. He asked what I thought was the most important function of the job. And what kind of person I would hire."

Shelby was beginning to realize where this was going. And she couldn't help starting to smile.

"Uh-huh," Robin said, correctly reading Shelby's expression. "It was Aaron himself, and I never had a clue. It never occurred to me. I was expecting somebody much older."

"I can understand that. I didn't believe him at first either."

They arrived at the casino level and the door slid open. Instantly the clamor of the casino rolled over them. Shelby hung back, wanting to hear the end of the story before they went out to where it was more difficult to talk quietly.

"So what happened?" Shelby prompted.

"When we got here, he kept me talking, showing me things and asking my opinion as we went through the casino. By the time we got to his office . . . I had the job. And now I'm here until Aaron fires me."

"Not likely," Shelby said.

"I hope so," Robin said. "Aaron's the best man I know, and it's an honor to work for him."

Shelby pondered Robin's story even as they played in the arcade. And Robin did play. She entered into the spirit of the thing with enthusiasm, and soon she and Shelby were cheering each other on in side-by-side Indy cars careening around in a video race. Surprisingly, it was the most carefree she'd felt in days, and when Robin's pager went off and they had to call a halt, she was disappointed.

"Sorry," Robin said after making a brief call on her cell phone. "Looks like we have a small problem. One of the unwelcomes has arrived."

"Unwelcomes?" Shelby said with a laugh. "Is that like the Unwashed?"

Robin chuckled. "Not quite. Just people we've had to escort out before and have asked not to return. Minor cheats."

"Minor?"

"People who try to increase or decrease their bet after the hand is dealt, or nudge their chips onto another number at roulette, that kind of thing."

"You don't arrest them?"

"Not the first time. But we've got a book full of photos, and somebody just spotted one. Come on, I'll walk you to Aaron's elevator. It's closer."

"No, that's okay. I can go myself. You need to go."

"Uh-uh. Aaron'd have my head. They'll hold him until I get there."

There was a note of unwavering decision in her voice, and Shelby realized that for all her good humor, Robin was as rock-solid as Aaron.

Aaron, who had kept her secret, even from his own people.

Robin saw her safely to the private elevator, and sent it up with her own key. When Shelby stepped back into the apartment, Aaron was on the phone. He looked a bit tense, and when she heard him speak, she realized why.

"I'll take care of it, Cindy. Don't worry."

Shelby hesitated, not certain what to do. She could hardly turn around and go back down in the elevator; that would be a bit too blatant. Yet she didn't really feel comfortable hearing him talk to his ex-wife.

Especially after that blazing kiss and what had roared to life between them.

"I'll call someone to come out. Just leave the water off. No, don't use the other shower until a plumber takes a look."

She's pretty helpless on her own.

Indeed, Shelby thought as Hank's words came back to her, if she couldn't even call a plumber but relied on her ex-husband to do it. She wanted to think Aaron was weak somehow, for letting himself be used like that. It would be easier to stay away from him that way. But she couldn't help thinking it was simple proof of his strength, that he just carried the load.

When he hung up, he didn't explain. She supposed he guessed she'd figured it out. Instead, after he looked up a number and made a call, obviously to a plumber, he suggested that they have dinner in the top-floor restaurant. Not quite an escape, he said, but the best he could manage right now.

When they arrived, Shelby quickly decided that while not exactly an escape, it would do very nicely. Zachary's was pure, understated elegance. She saw instantly that she was grossly underdressed in her leggings and sweatshirt, but obviously being in the company of the big boss made up for any lack.

When the exquisitely dressed maître d' led them to a small private dining room, she wondered if it was at Aaron's request or just to keep her out of sight of the other, better-dressed patrons.

"Do you mind?" Aaron asked as they were seated. "We don't have the best view, but you'll be safely out of sight, just in case."

She nearly blushed, ashamed of herself. He'd requested this room, all right, but for her sake, to keep her safe.

"You," she said, "are really something, Mr. Montana. Just how deep does this caretaking thing go?"

He grimaced. "Hank talked a lot, I see."

"He had an opinion or two, yes."

"I'm sure. I know what he thinks of me."

"You might be surprised," Shelby said, remembering how Hank had defended his cousin, until face-to-face with him. And the way he'd been so clearly on Aaron's side when he'd told the ugly story of Megan's death.

"Hmm," he said noncommittally before answering her question. "I don't know. My mom kept trying to figure out what she'd done to ingrain it in me, but my dad says it was always there. According to him, all the oldest Montana sons have it. He says that, if I was going to have a wearisome habit, it wasn't a bad one to have."

Shelby smiled at that. "I think I'd like your dad."

He gave her a look that was startling in its intensity, even for Aaron.

He handled the formal dining experience with an ease that spoke of long familiarity. She supposed being brought up in a wealthy, prestigious family made this kind of thing old hat. Maybe it was ingrained in such families, the courtly manners, the easy acceptance of luxury. But even Margaret's Robert, who had grown up fairly well-to-do, didn't have quite this air of easy grace.

Just as they finished dessert—a flaming affair that Shelby had watched with fascination and eaten with some trepidation, although it was luscious—Aaron's pager went off. He checked the number, excused himself, and pulled his cell phone out. He'd turned it off for the meal, she thought, feeling a little strange. It wasn't like this was a date. He didn't have to do that.

"Montana," he said into the phone. After less than five seconds of listening, he went tautly alert. "Who?" His face tightened at the answer. "You have the device?" A pause just long enough for an answer. "Good. Have somebody clean out his locker. I'll call Kitty at home and tell her I'm pulling his personnel file. I'll be down to talk to him before we turn him over."

When he disconnected, the tension remained.

"Something wrong?" she asked.

"Very. One of my people was caught skimming credit card numbers."

She noted the way he said "one of my people," but she only asked, "Doing what?"

"Electronically recording customer credit card numbers." His voice was a taut as his posture. "There's a device to do it, small enough to fit in a pocket. You just run the card through. Then they turn around and sell the numbers to crooks, who use them until the victim catches on and reports it."

"Nice racket," she said.

"Yeah. One of those things can hold hundreds of numbers, and at a hundred bucks or better per number . . . you do the math."

"I didn't realize it was *that* nice," she said, awed. Then, carefully, she asked, "You're angry, aren't you?"

"I'm furious," he said. "That's why I'm waiting a moment. If I had to face him now, I'd want to bang his head on the wall."

"What will you do to him?"

"He's fired, and on his way to the gray bar hotel, as Mike calls it."

"No excuses?"

"Not for one of *my* people stealing from our guests. Nothing incenses me more. Everybody who comes to work here knows that's an offense guaranteed to get you tossed out on your butt. You don't last long in this business if guests can't trust your staff."

"Does it happen a lot?"

"Not here. Not at the Golden Phoenix."

He said it with unmistakable pride, which Shelby was beginning to see was well earned.

"Is this . . . a typical evening?"

"Sometimes." He gave her that crooked smile. "Sometimes I can't get a soul to bother me."

She would be willing to bet those days were rare indeed. "If this is what it takes to make your kind of money, it's more trouble than it's worth."

"There are times," he said, "when I would agree."

He sent her up in the elevator from his office while he went to deal with the hapless thief. For a long time

Shelby sat in what had become her accustomed place, on the sofa in front of the big windows. The moon was waxing, casting enough light now to reveal the looming shape of the mountain. It glowed almost eerily in the silver light.

She pondered the complexities of Aaron Montana. Everything he'd done to help her. The swift, implacable justice he was even now dealing out to an employee who had broken a trust he considered sacred. The tough-love approach—and what it cost him—to the alcoholic cousin he clearly cared for, despite everything.

Even in dealing with his ex-wife, the woman who had so unfairly blamed him for not being God, he was apparently unfailingly kind. She could only guess what that cost him as well, with all the memories and pain tied up in that relationship.

She wondered if there was ever a time when he put himself first, when all those who depended on him had to wait. Wondered if the caretaker ever got a vacation.

Wondered if he ever wanted to just run away.

Not likely, she told herself. *You're the one who runs away.*

Mike turned the cold tap on, ran his hands under it, and splashed the water over his face. He grimaced at the shock, but it helped. He let the water run over his fingers until they were as cold as he could stand, then pressed them to his eyelids. He knew it wouldn't change the grittiness, but for the few moments it lasted, it was relief.

He reached for a towel and stopped midmotion as he caught a glimpse of himself in the mirror.

"You oughta see me now, Sunny," he muttered. With a day's worth of stubble—he'd forgotten the razor he usually left here for times when he pulled an all-nighter—hair he'd rammed his fingers through once too often, and bags under his eyes that you could pack for a world cruise in, he doubted she'd be trying to nibble on his neck at the moment.

He'd added two more to the suspect list: the son of an elderly woman Pruett had conned out of most of her life's savings, who had shown up at Pruett's house threatening his life in front of the entire neighborhood, and a longer shot, a local doctor Pruett had sued, claiming he'd bungled his nose job.

Mike walked back to his desk to find his voice-mail light blinking. He picked up the receiver and dialed in his code.

"Delano? Herrera. I've got your CSI results for you. I'll be here another fifteen or so, if you want to call."

Herrera had come through, working late yet again. Grateful for speed dialing, Mike hit the button still labeled with the last investigator's name. Herrera answered on the first ring.

"Was it as clean as it looked?" he asked, wasting no time on amenities.

"Almost. No fingerprints except the victim's. Marble floors, so no footprints we can find, not without a lot more sophisticated equipment than we have. No sign of forced entry, no shell casings. Speaking of which, the gunshot was the cause of death."

"Time of death?"

"Estimated at about zero-six-hundred."

So it had been in the morning, not the night before, Mike thought. "Weapon?"

"Fired at close range, a .38 Special round."

"Great. That'll only fit a million guns in Nevada alone," Mike said.

"We've got the computer working it, but I don't expect a match anytime soon, if at all. This was all too clean. Efficient."

"I know," Mike said grimly. The chance that they were dealing with a pro had never left his mind. As a matter of course, he'd initiated a check on any movement of known contract killers in the region, but so far nothing had come back that fit the timing. Not that that meant much; there were always a few out there who managed to keep a low enough profile that they didn't get noticed.

Besides, even if it had been a pro, it was the person who had hired him that he really wanted. So who the pro was—if there was one—was an attendant issue.

"Nothing else on the body?"

"Well, I could give you the contents of the deceased's stomach—"

"No, thanks." Mike supposed that was Herrera's form of gallows humor, but right now he was in no mood.

"We found a small hole in a sidewall of that tire. Enough to make it go noticeably flat in maybe a quarter mile. About nail-size."

"But not likely to be a normally picked up nail, in a sidewall," Mike mused. "Anything else?"

For the first time Herrera hesitated. This in itself was unusual enough to catch Mike's attention. "What?" he asked.

"Remember you asked me to check that closet, with the open door?"

"Yes."

"Your report said the housekeeper said she had vacuumed it recently. That the deceased used it only for hanging his custom pool cues."

"Right, that's what she said, and that's what was in there. So?"

"I'm getting there. I noticed that the carpet appeared to have been walked on recently, so I vacuumed it myself."

Mike went very still. "And?"

"I found a hair that does not match the victim's."

Mike let out a long breath. This could be the break he'd been waiting for. "You're sure?"

Sounding offended, Herrera said, "Of course I'm sure."

"I didn't mean it that way," Mike said quickly. "I just meant how—"

"I know what you meant. First off, it's blond. Natural, as far as I can tell. Fairly short. Second, there's no coating of hair gel on it."

Mike didn't know whether to laugh or not; he could never tell when Herrera might be joking.

"Blond," he muttered. The housekeeper—who had dark hair—had said Pruett had been home before she left every night for three days before his murder, and still home when she arrived in the morning. And as far as she knew, there had been no guests in that time, no extra dishes, no extra towels in any of the bathrooms, no other signs of a guest.

"I've already sent it over to county," Herrera said. "But you know hair evidence is iffy, especially when it's naturally shed, as this one apparently was. No root on it that I can see. Until you find us somebody to compare it to . . ."

"I know. Thanks, John."

He hung up, wondering if he was any better off than he had been. Before he could decide, his phone rang. Figuring Herrera had forgotten something, he answered quickly.

"Delano."

"It's Eric."

Mike sat up rigidly straight. He recognized the tone in the boy's voice. "What?"

"I've got it. I broke the code."

Chapter Fifteen

Aaron stretched wearily as he stepped out of the elevator and back into his apartment. He hated scenes like the one that had just played out in his office. In any other situation he would give someone a second chance. But not this one. Not stealing from Phoenix guests.

The place was dark; Shelby must have gone to bed. As soon as the thought formed, it occurred to him to wonder if she was still here at all. Perhaps she'd taken advantage of his absence to decamp. But then he saw her jacket lying across the back of one of the stools at the kitchen counter.

He shucked his own jacket, tossed it down next to hers. He was headed for his bedroom when a faint sound made him turn his head.

He saw the shape on the sofa, curled up so tightly that she took up barely more than a single cushion. He wondered if she'd intended to go to sleep or had just dozed off. He wouldn't be surprised if it had taken her unawares. No matter what the truth of her situation was, she'd been under a lot of strain.

He thought about just leaving her there to sleep; he could get a blanket from the closet. But she would be much more comfortable in a real bed. He'd fallen asleep on that couch a time or two, and while it was very comfortable to sit on, for sleeping it left something to be desired.

He walked to the couch and bent over her, bracing himself on the back of it.

"Shelby?" he said softly.

She made that faint, oddly disturbing sound again and stirred slightly.

He gently touched her shoulder to rouse her.

The instant his fingers made contact she erupted. She came up so fast and hard she nearly broke his nose.

"Not again, Brad!" Flailing wildly, she connected with his jaw forcefully enough to snap his head back.

"Shelby—"

"I'll kill you!"

She struck out again, and reluctantly he enveloped her in a gentle bear hug, overwhelming her with his size and bulk.

"Shelby, wake up. It's me, Aaron. You're safe."

She fought for a second longer. Then his words seemed to penetrate, and she went still.

"It's all right," he said as soothingly as he could. "Wake up."

"A-Aaron?"

"It's okay. You're safe," he repeated.

She sagged in his arms, and he felt as well as heard her take a big gulp of air. He stayed silent, figuring she needed a few moments to orient herself; whatever she'd been dreaming, it clearly hadn't been pleasant.

He continued to hold her. He would until she pulled away or asked him to let go. She was shaken, and she needed someone, anyone, to be there. He'd spent some long nights fighting off vicious dreams himself, and he knew how much harder it was to do that alone.

He felt her gradually relax. And the more she relaxed, the more he became aware of holding her. He gave himself a mental slap. The last thing she needed now was to realize that his libido had kick-started.

Finally she shifted in his arms, trying to sit up. He

released her immediately, expecting her to pull away. Instead, she stayed where she was, just leaned back against the sofa cushions. Still close enough to touch. He didn't, but, God, he wanted to. Badly. He bit the inside of his lip, seeking the pain as distraction.

When he thought he had his voice under control, he asked, "Who's Brad?"

She went very still. He thought she'd even stopped breathing.

When he'd given up on an answer, she whispered, "My brother."

Aaron sucked in a breath. "Your brother?"

She sighed, and he wondered if she regretted saying even that much. But after a moment she went on. "Stepbrother, really. My mother married his father when I was nine, a year after my father left us."

"Left?"

She reached up and tugged at her hair, a gesture he'd never seen her make before. "As in walked out. Never to be seen again. Abandoned. Whatever."

There was a shrug of sorts in her voice, as if she didn't care a bit about the subject. Aaron wondered how long it had taken her to get to that point. Or if it was even real, her utter lack of emotion.

"That must have been rough," he said, feeling it was a rather inane thing to say, but unable to think of anything else. He couldn't conceive of walking out on your own child.

"He wasn't a very nice man, from what I remember. But my mother had stayed with him. She was afraid to be alone, I think. After he left, by the time she met . . . Brad's father, she was pretty desperate."

She was still being careful about what she said, he thought. But she was talking, and that was an improvement. Maybe. He was sure he wasn't going to like what he was going to hear.

"Some people are like that," he said neutrally.

Cindy was one. She didn't want him, but she hated being alone, no one to depend on but herself. Shelby seemed to prefer it that way. Which was why Aaron couldn't help but feel honored by her halting revelations.

"Things were okay for a couple of years, maybe three. I even thought it was nice to be part of a family again. Then Brad turned fifteen."

"And?" Aaron said gently.

"And I matured early." The tug on her hair again.

It took him a moment to realize all the ramifications. When he did, he sucked in a quick breath.

"Your stepbrother . . . he molested you?"

"He raped me," she said flatly. "Repeatedly."

Aaron swore, low and harsh. He had to force down the rising bile in his throat before he could speak.

"Is that why you ran away?" She nodded. "Why didn't you just tell your mother what was happening?"

Shelby gave him a pitying look. "I did."

He blinked. "What?"

Again in that uncaring tone she said, with yet another tug on her hair, "She didn't believe me. In fact, her response was to slap me and tell me I was going to go to hell for lying."

He stared at her. He felt the naive fool her look had said he was. "How the *hell* could a parent think a twelve-year-old girl would make that up?"

"She wasn't concerned with that. All she cared about was hanging on to her husband. And Brad was his father's fair-haired boy. He could do no wrong."

"Bastard," Aaron muttered.

"Oh, no. I was the troublemaker. And Brad knew it. He told me nobody would believe me" She reached up and tugged at her hair again, but this time she seemed to realize she was doing it. "He used to grab me by my hair," she said. "That's how he held me down. So I cut it off."

He wanted to sweep her up in his arms, pull her onto his lap and hold her until she forgot all about the nightmare that had been her life. "God, Shelby, I'm sorry. There wasn't anybody else you could go to?"

"Nobody who would believe me over Brad. Or at least," she amended thoughtfully, "that's the way it seemed then."

"So you ran away."

"On my thirteenth birthday, when Brad promised me a present I would never forget in honor of my becoming a teenager." She shuddered visibly. "He was starting to get really rough by then. I didn't want to stick around and see what he had in mind."

Aaron called the absent Brad a name he rarely used.

"Yes," Shelby agreed. "It was the best thing I could do, really. My mother would never have to face the truth, the three of them could go on living happily. I'm sure she was relieved when I left."

Aaron could barely get his mind around the idea of a child being sacrificed like that. "Where did you go? L.A. ?"

She nodded. "It seemed like the best place to get really lost."

"For five years," he said, shaking his head. At twelve he'd been worrying about heading to junior high school, about algebra, about trying to decide if he wanted to play baseball or football. Shelby had spent those years fighting to survive.

"I had help," she said, and he wondered what she was thinking of, or who, that made her eyes go soft and warm.

"I'm glad," he said quietly, meaning it.

"If it hadn't been for Tiger . . ." she whispered, and he had the feeling she was barely aware of what she was saying.

He didn't want to hear what might have happened to her if it hadn't been for the person with the odd name, so he only asked, "Tiger?"

She seemed to snap back to the present. And went on as if she had never mentioned the mysterious Tiger.

"Eventually I came to Reno. Then I met . . . a friend who helped me. Brought me here to Outpost, and helped me get out of that life, get my GED, and get . . . counseling about what had happened to me. Years of it. Even helped me get into college, later. She saved me. I owe her everything."

Something in her voice, and the way she was so clearly being careful about not giving away the name of her friend, caught Aaron's attention. The friend was apparently still here, or at least still alive, and yet Shelby hadn't gone to her. Why?

"Someone you trust," he said.

"Yes. I'd do anything for her."

"I'm glad there's someone," he said.

She looked at him, as if trying to decide if there had been a note of wryness or irritation in his voice. But he knew there hadn't been; he'd meant it sincerely. He was glad there was someone out there she trusted.

And after what she'd told him tonight, he thought it nothing less than a miracle.

Shelby doubted she would ever have chosen Aaron's business for a career, but if she had ever been considering it, the last couple of hours would have changed her mind. She'd never heard anything like it.

She'd gone with him to his office for a change of scene. She needed it. She wasn't sure if confession was truly good for the soul, but apparently it was catching, she thought. Aaron had told her that heart-wrenching story about his little girl, and boom, her own miserable past had breached the dam.

She'd needed every one of those years of counseling and therapy, at Margaret's insistence, to work through her feelings about what had happened to her. Probably thanks to Tiger, she had never become afraid of men in general. Besides, what she'd suffered was too closely tied up with her stepbrother as an individual. But the betrayal of such a basic, familial bond had made her wary of trusting anyone too much.

Yet she trusted Aaron enough to tell him. Trusted him . . . and wanted him. That was the real shocker. But did she want him because she trusted him, or was she convincing herself that she trusted him because she wanted him?

The wrong answer could be disastrous.

"—do what you have to. That backup generator has to be functional."

Aaron's voice was firm but calm as he spoke to the man he'd called the facilities manager, responsible for the entire physical plant, the air-conditioning, elevators, hot water, and most of the hotel's power plant.

Finished with that call, he didn't even hang up, just switched to an in-house line and pushed two buttons. "Linda, Aaron. I called Sierra Linens. Did you get your delivery?"

Shelby remembered that call from earlier, about a late delivery of five thousand pounds of clean sheets that was holding up housekeeping. They had already been called by the director of housekeeping, but the sheets had still not arrived, so Aaron had made a follow-up call himself. He had been adamant, yet not rude or demanding. And apparently it had worked.

"Good," he said into the phone. "Yes, I know. Housekeeping should be an invisible art. That's why I hire the best."

He never failed to do that, she thought, to deliver a pat on the back to his people whenever it was warranted.

Before she'd even fully formed that thought he was on to the next call.

"Now what?" she asked out of curiosity.

"Head of food services," he tossed over his shoulder at her. "Marla? Aaron."

As if they wouldn't know immediately who he was, she thought. She listened as in the space of three minutes he okayed the hiring of four people for the Sunday-morning kitchen staff—apparently that was the busiest room-service meal of the week—authorized the replacement of some sort of belt that she gathered was used for an assembly-line production for banquets, and agreed with the woman that room-service food had to be just as good as the restaurant food.

"I had no idea," she said when he finally hung up, "that you'd be so . . . hands-on."

He gave her a wry grin. "We're considered small for a casino/hotel operation. If we were bigger, I'd have more people to delegate to. But we like it that way. We're able to keep service more personalized."

"We?"

He shrugged. "My father sets the standard, the rest of us adhere to it."

Her forehead creased. "I'm sorry. I thought you said your father was . . . no longer working."

"He's had to cut way back after his heart attack, but he's still the chairman. And Zachary Montana will always be the heart of the Golden Phoenix," Aaron said softly, such love and admiration in his voice that Shelby's eyes brimmed.

Fortunately for her poise, the phone rang. Aaron picked it up, and barely a second after he'd said hello his eyes flicked to her again. She understood when she heard him say, "Hi, Mike."

It was the cop.

Shelby forgot to breathe, and her body went tense

as she fought the instinct to run. Common sense told her if he hadn't turned her in yet, he wasn't likely to do it this instant.

But in the aftermath of the jolt, reality set in. She realized with awful clarity that she'd been playing some kind of fantasy game, allowing herself to revel in Aaron's presence, not thinking at all, when she should have been making a plan.

"So it was a ledger, as you suspected?" Aaron said into the phone. Then a pause before, "Ouch. There grows your suspect list."

Margaret. Dear God, Margaret. If she was guessing right, they'd found Pruett's blackmail ledger. And Margaret's name would be on it. God, she should have grabbed everything out of that box, even if Pruett had noticed immediately.

What would the police do? Would they contact all those people? Suspect list, Aaron had said. Of course they would contact all Pruett's victims; they would all have a motive to kill the slime.

Including Margaret. What if they suspected Margaret?

God, she hadn't thought this through. If they came after Margaret, she would have no choice. She would have to—

"I know, Mike."

The tension that had come into Aaron's voice snapped her attention back to his conversation.

"Look, I don't know for sure how . . . my friend is connected."

Even without the way his voice lowered and he avoided looking at her, there was little doubt in Shelby's mind that Aaron was talking about her.

When he hung up at last and turned to face her, she felt the urge to run, to avoid this confrontation. But Tiger had always told her there were times when you simply had to stand your ground.

Aaron looked at her for a long, silent moment, and she made herself hold his gaze.

"Your friend the cop?" she asked finally.

He nodded. "They decoded Pruett's list of blackmail victims."

She was a little stunned that he would just come out with it like that. She couldn't think what to say; if she showed any interest he would be even more convinced she was involved. So she said only, "Oh?"

"Mike's no fool," Aaron said. "He knows I'm not asking about Pruett just to make conversation."

"Why not?" she said, trying for a breezy tone. "I did."

The moment the words were out, her stomach knotted. Once she'd been able to toss off a lie like that without a care or a second thought. Now it ate at her. She had come too far from that street-smart kid, after all.

Or she simply didn't want to lie to this man.

"Did you?" Aaron asked.

The best defense, she decided, and tried to turn it around on him. "You're the one who decided I was somehow connected to Jack Pruett."

Not to her surprise, it bounced off him without diverting him. "Mike's wondering if your name will be on that list."

Shelby let out a tiny breath. They still thought she might be a victim. That gave her time.

And Aaron was protecting her. Mike was obviously pushing him for anything he might know, but Aaron wasn't telling him anything.

"If you've already told him about me," she said, genuinely curious now, "why didn't you just give him my name?"

He lowered his gaze and let out an audible breath. She had the strangest feeling that he was wondering the same thing himself.

"In fact," she said slowly, "given what you apparently think, why haven't you just turned me over to him?"

He looked at her then, and when he spoke his voice held an odd note that tightened Shelby's throat.

"Because I keep hoping you'll tell me something I can believe, so we can go to Mike with proof."

"Proof?" she repeated. Then she realized what he meant. "Proof that I'm not a killer?"

She saw the answer in his eyes. Aaron Montana, upstanding citizen, scion of the oldest family in town, who had been urging her to go to the police since day one, now didn't want her to go until they had proof that she didn't murder Jack Pruett.

Her throat tightened until it hurt, and her eyes stung as moisture pooled behind her eyelids. He was getting pressure from his best friend, yet he wouldn't give in. He was taking heat to protect her. Other than Margaret—and Tiger—no one had ever put themselves on the line for her before. Yet this man had done it without question, without even knowing the full story.

She wanted to say something to him. Wanted to thank him. Wanted more, wanted to hug him, touch him, kiss him. She'd never wanted that with a man before, and it frightened her. She wrapped her arms around herself to try and stop the shivers.

He wanted proof that she hadn't killed Pruett. Proof she didn't have.

"Tell me something," she asked softly. "What will you do if the only thing you find is . . . evidence that I did do it?"

Something dark and troubled flickered in his eyes. When he finally answered her, his voice was low and harsh.

"I don't know."

Chapter Sixteen

"The lady's not moving," Langford said. "She's cozied up there with Montana, never takes a step outside without him. Who knows how long she'll stay holed up?"

"I don't understand," Margaret said, more to herself than to the private investigator. "Shelby just doesn't trust people that easily."

"Well, she trusts him. And I can see why. He's a good man to have on your side. I thought he was going to take me apart yesterday when I stumbled onto them, but he stopped. He wouldn't leave her unprotected."

That comforted Margaret more than the man could ever know. Shelby had never had many who would defend her in her life, especially those she should have been able to count on the most. But for whatever reason, this man had decided to become her guardian. Margaret knew she couldn't be completely at ease until she knew why—she knew as well as Shelby did that some men found decent behavior impossible, or hid their true selves behind a civilized facade—but for now it was enough.

"Look, Mrs. Peterson, I feel guilty taking your money for just sitting outside the Golden Phoenix. And now that Montana's made me, it's going to be even more difficult. Unless you tell me more about what's going on, I don't think I can do you much more good. How long do you want me to keep this up?"

Margaret had been pondering this, during the long, sleepless hours of her nights, but hadn't yet reached a decision. Her natural instinct was to go to Shelby herself. She wanted desperately to talk to the girl, to find out what was going on, to have Shelby explain—and reassure her that of course she hadn't done it.

But something else had occurred to her during the restless nights. Would Shelby be insulted by her doubts? True, she had warned Margaret early on that she had done some terrible things, but surely she would expect Margaret to have complete trust in her by now.

And she should have, she told herself. She should be utterly, totally certain that Shelby would never commit murder. So why wasn't she?

Because, she thought now, she knew what Shelby had been through. She knew the horror of her childhood, a childhood that had been a nightmare of terror and pain and abandonment. The only thing Margaret could be sure of was that she could never blame Shelby for anything she might do, not after that.

"Mrs. Peterson?"

She snapped back to the present. "Oh. I don't know. Let me think a moment."

Money was going to become an issue shortly. She was already over the limit of what she could spend without going through their joint household account. Robert had never questioned her expenditures, but she had never spent this much without consulting him.

But money was nothing against not knowing where Shelby was and that she was all right.

"Keep at it for another day or two," she said. "Then I'll decide."

Langford shrugged. She hadn't told him that this had anything to do with Pruett and his murder. Not when there was a chance Shelby was involved. Still, she'd felt a pang of guilt. It didn't seem quite fair not to tell him that he was dealing with murder in some way.

God, she needed to talk to Shelby, find out what was going on. And she would, she decided suddenly. If nothing had changed by this time tomorrow, she was going to march right over to the Golden Phoenix and demand to see her.

And then . . .

Margaret stopped and took a shaky breath. Even the thought had the power to terrify her. But she knew she couldn't go on, not like this. At first she had thought she loved Robert too much to have him find out this sordid story. Now she knew she loved him too much to continue to lie to him.

She had to trust him.

She had to tell him.

Mike tossed his pen down on top of the yellow legal pad in disgust. A dozen new names already, and they were barely halfway through Pruett's ledger.

He told himself this was no different than any other tough case. Told himself all he had to do was find the one right thread to pull and the whole thing would unravel.

It was true. But it wasn't calming him down.

He knew why. Knew what was eating at him, the one thing that was making this case nag at him like a chronic toothache.

Aaron.

Aaron knew something, and he was hiding it.

Knowing his friend as he did, Mike knew there was only one reason Aaron would hold back any kind of evidence in a criminal case.

He was protecting someone.

That, Mike thought wryly, would be Aaron Mon-

tana to the core. He'd found some poor soul in trouble
and had taken them on. Hell, he'd taken Mike on,
when he'd been on a path to early destruction, after
Emma. If it hadn't been for Aaron, Mike knew he'd
have been long dead.

So, he wondered, who was Aaron protecting? Most
likely somebody on this list. But if Aaron wasn't ready
to talk, no power on earth would move him. Mike
simply had to trust that if and when it became crucial,
Aaron would come through. After all, these people
were victims. From what he'd seen so far, most of
them had simply been caught doing something embarrassing or lewd or adulterous, not illegal. And even if
there were a few crimes scattered among the blackmail material, unless they were serious, Mike would
see that it ended here, in return for any statement
about Pruett the victims were willing to give.

For a while he stared at the list of names on the
legal pad. And finally he went to his last resort, a
method that he knew seemed ancient in this computer
age. He pulled out a stack of index cards. On each
one he wrote the name of one of the primary suspects,
followed by the motive, alibi if any, other evidence
pointing to the person, such as financial situation and
prior record, and anything else that seemed relevant.

He added his impressions of the person's mental
condition and whether he thought he or she was capable of the crime. Handwriting it all, or more likely
running it through his brain again, sometimes turned
up something new, or at least gave him a new angle
to look at in an old suspect.

When he was done, he arranged and rearranged the
cards, first according to the strength of the motive or
what the suspect had to gain or lose, then by opportunity, then by the strength of their alibi, then by the
evidence, and finally, when he'd looked at them from
every other angle, by his gut feeling. That last was the

hardest to validate, almost impossible to explain, and just as hard to prove in court, but he'd been right more often than wrong.

Finally he shook his head and gathered the cards into a stack. He would look at them whenever he had a moment, shuffling them, turning them, hoping something would jump out at him when they were put in just the right order.

"Poor baby, you look tired and cranky."

Sunny's voice, low, husky, and highly suggestive, wrapped around him like a snake. Lord, he was in no mood. And he was getting mightily tired of having to handle her with kid gloves, when what he wanted to do was tell her to take a hike. A permanent one.

"I am," he snapped.

"Well, goodness, don't take it out on me. I just came by to do you a favor."

He shuddered inwardly at what Sunny's idea of a favor might be. "Such as?"

"This."

Only now did Mike notice that she held the remote control to the television in the front of the office. Mike was puzzled. True, they'd used it yesterday for a training film he'd missed while out on interviews, but he doubted that Sunny would know or care about that. And then the screen came to life, and the chief's voice boomed out.

"—progress on the case."

Mike's brow furrowed. He knew the chief was in Reno today, at some meeting of state officials. This appeared to be an impromptu press conference, but knowing Chief Cushman, he doubted the impromptu part.

"And I can safely say we expect to make an arrest at any moment."

"Chief," a reporter asked, "what about the rumors of Pruett being involved in blackmail?"

Mike didn't even hear the answer. What the hell was the man doing announcing an imminent arrest in the Pruett case? "Is he nuts?" Mike muttered.

"I think," Sunny said cheerfully, "this is his way of putting a little pressure on."

Mike swiveled in his seat to stare at her. She'd picked up his stack of index cards and riffled them like a poker deck. "Pressure?"

"He's just not happy with the speed of this investigation."

He frowned. "Did he send you here to tell me that?"

"Of course not." She sounded offended. "I was just trying to be a friend and give you a heads-up."

"Yeah, right."

"I'd hate to see you get pulled off a case that could really make your career."

Mike went still. "Pulled off?"

"Oh, dear," Sunny said. "I'm sure I wasn't supposed to say anything about that. Just forget I said it. Besides"—she ran her thumb over the stack of cards once more—"I'm sure you'll pick the right name out of all these soon."

With a brilliant smile he didn't trust for an instant, she handed him the remote and strolled away.

Pulled off the case.

He leaned back in his chair and stared up at the man who had the power to do it.

"It's nice," Shelby said, "not to run out of hot water."

It was inane, but all she could think to say. Anything else threatened to lead back down a road she didn't want to travel.

Never again did she want to see that look in his eyes. Yet at the same time it had given her a perverse sort of pleasurable jolt to realize that it mattered, genuinely mattered to him, whether she was guilty of a crime. She'd spent her nearly half hour in the shower dwelling on it, trying to decide if the fact that he hadn't turned her over to his Mike meant that he still had hopes that she hadn't killed Pruett. Or did it mean he was certain that she had?

She hadn't been able to decide.

"Two eight-hundred-horsepower steam boilers, at your service," Aaron answered. He seemed more than willing to ignore their last exchange, and go on as if it hadn't happened. For which she was grateful; she couldn't tell him any more than she had, and shutting him out was surprisingly painful.

She grimaced and gestured toward his desk. "I don't know how you do all this. I couldn't keep up."

"But you like your own job?"

"Yes, I do, even though it's just begun. It's—"

She broke off suddenly, realizing she had once more let down her guard and was about to pour out more personal history. What was it about this man that made her want to open up like this? Even when she knew the danger, knew the risk.

"It's what?" he prompted.

"I—Important. To me, anyway."

"That's what counts," he said.

He waited, as if for her to go on. She bit back the words that wanted to flood out. She knew somehow that Aaron would understand.

After a moment he gave up and got to his feet. "I need to go make a walk-through."

Still feeling guilty for avoiding this simplest of disclosures, she got to her feet as well.

"Can I come with you?"

He looked faintly surprised, then lifted one shoulder in a shrug. "If you want."

She did want. And not just to get out of the apartment that had become so familiar. She supposed she should worry about being spotted, but Aaron's solid presence gave her a feeling of security she couldn't deny.

She walked beside him as they went through the casino. He didn't seem to be in a chatty mood—and all things considered, she could hardly blame him. He spoke only when someone called out to him or stopped him to make an inquiry. She was amazed at how much he knew about the tiny details.

"Do people always come to you about things like lightbulbs?" she asked after an employee had left them.

He shrugged. "One of my hard and fast rules is that anybody can come to me with anything, and not get in trouble for jumping chain of command. And that was a good idea, don't you think?"

"Sure. No woman likes the way she looks under fluorescent light."

"So putting peach-tinted lighting in the ladies' room is a good idea." He began to walk again, his eyes scanning the floor constantly. "We want the ladies happy."

"Not to mention she's less likely to want to run to her room and hide or fix her makeup, instead of continuing to gamble," Shelby said.

"That, too," he admitted easily.

"That doesn't bother you?"

He looked at her. "Gambling has been around ever since two people argued over who could throw a rock the farthest, or who could slay the bigger mammoth. It always will be, in some form. It's human nature. People love the thrill, the chance for the big win. We provide that, in a safe, controlled environment."

"And make lots of money."

"It takes lots of money to run this kind of operation. And after overhead comes our eight percent to the gaming commission. I'm not saying we don't make money, we do. But we try to give value for it."

"So it's just a Disneyland variation?"

He stopped in his tracks. "I don't feel the need to defend what I do, Shelby. To me, gambling is entertainment. But that doesn't mean I don't realize that, like with most things, there is a line that can be crossed. I hate compulsive gambling as much as anyone. Perhaps more, since I see it more often. And I've seen other addictions, and the fallout."

She knew he meant Hank, but she didn't say so. Besides, something else had just occurred to her. As they passed the cashier's cage, she grabbed one of the pamphlets from a rack on the counter. "These Gambler's Anonymous fliers that are on every floor, and at almost every counter—that's by your order, isn't it?"

He shrugged again as he resumed his walking patrol. "I don't deny people can get out of control. Those who do, need help."

He waved in acknowledgement to a man behind a bank of blackjack tables, who had looked up from checking the chip racks at each table to nod at Aaron.

"I can't believe the amount of money some people just throw around," she said as they passed a table with a sign indicating the bet limit was five hundred dollars.

"Biggest blackjack bet on record was in Las Vegas. Seven hundred and seventy-seven thousand dollars."

Shelby stared at him. "Lucky sevens, I gather? Did he win?"

Aaron gave her that crooked grin. "I don't know. That wasn't in the promotional brochure."

Shelby couldn't help smiling; that grin just did it to her. "I hope he could afford to lose it," she said. "That's risking a bit more than the rent money."

"That's why there are no ATM machines on our

casino floor," Aaron said. "They're all down near the hotel wing. If people have to go to a little extra effort to get more cash than they have with them at the moment, they might think twice before doing it."

It seemed an odd—yet admirable—way to run this particular business, Shelby thought. She scanned the pamphlet as they turned and headed along the back of the casino, back toward the elevators. Her steps slowed when she spotted a familiar name; not only did Aaron support GA by placing these fliers in his casino, he was also a local director.

She glanced up. Ahead of her now, Aaron had been approached by another casino employee, a woman with a tray full of empty glasses, apparently one of the cocktail waitresses who kept the gamblers supplied with drinks. She was smiling at Aaron, and he was smiling back. Then he laughed, a rumbling, deep laugh that made the woman's smile widen.

An odd sensation swept Shelby. She was miserable because she had never heard him laugh like that, and angry for the same reason. Or that he was laughing so easily with this very attractive woman who looked as if she hadn't a care.

Of course, what had she ever given him to laugh about? Shelby admitted grimly to herself.

She made herself look away. For a moment she stared at the flyer without really seeing it; it had come to her with a little shock that she was reacting as if she were jealous. Jealous that this woman could make him laugh.

She flicked Aaron and the woman another look, only now noticing the woman wore a wedding band. The fact that this relieved her, as seeing Robin's wedding band had done, only made her feel worse.

This time when she looked at the flyer, she made herself actually finish reading it.

Aaron clearly put his money and his mouth where his convictions were, she thought. He—

She yelped when the arm came around her from behind. A hand slapped down over her mouth. Her attacker pulled her back into the darkness of a deserted telephone alcove.

She'd been caught completely unprepared, lulled by Aaron's solid presence into a sense of security. But her temporary illusion of safety was shattered now. He'd picked her off like a turkey at a shoot. It was over, she'd lost, and the price would be her life.

And the only thing she could think was that she wished she could have been the one to make Aaron laugh.

Chapter Seventeen

"Hey, Delano! About time you got back. And turn your damn radio on in the car, will you? Call dispatch, they've got some info for you."

"Yeah, yeah," Mike said, but grinned at Rich Hickerson, the car-theft detective.

"And you just missed the Cush-man. Boy, is he on your case or what?"

"I know," Mike said, his grin fading. "I've been managing to dodge him."

"I heard about his announcement. Funny, last I heard you still had a few suspects."

"I do."

"Ah. I wondered if that was a CYA announcement."

"Nobody covers his ass better," Mike muttered.

Rich considered for a moment before speaking again. "A word to the wise, buddy. Out of the blue today he's asking me about my homicide experience in Seattle."

"Great." So Sunny hadn't been blowing smoke, for once. Cushman was looking to pull him. "You want the job?"

"Not on your life. Not this case." Rich looked thoughtful. "You don't look surprised."

"I'm not. I was warned."

"Warned? Who?"

"Sunny."

Rich let out a low whistle. "Watch that one. She's always got an agenda."

"I know. I just have no clue what it is this time."

"Good luck, buddy."

"Thanks. I'll need it."

Mike fought the tightening in his gut. He couldn't pull a name out of the hopper and make an arrest just to placate public opinion. He didn't work that way. His cases were solid, and unless somebody else down the line fumbled, he rarely lost in court. He could only go on as he always did. He'd be damned if he would change his approach now, after all this time, just because the chief put the pressure on.

He went to his desk and picked up the pink message form. It was a good thing Rich had told him what it said; no way could he have read the scrawled words. If not for the phone number, the inside line to the communications section, he wouldn't have had a clue who had called.

When he dialed the extension and identified himself, he had the senior dispatcher in moments.

"Hey, Mike," Evie Richards said. "Isn't a Lawrence Reichart one of your suspects in the Pruett case?"

"Yes, why?"

"I thought you'd want to know, we rolled on a disturbance at his place about thirty ago."

Mike sat up straighter. A disturbance of any kind involving a prime suspect definitely grabbed his interest. "Was Reichart there?"

"Negative. Apparently he went ballistic on his wife, slapped her around, then left."

"Any weapons?"

"None used, but we're still there, checking the house. Want me to tell them you're rolling?"

"Yes. I'll be there driving time."

"You got it."

Mike hung up, making a mental note to mention

Evie's alertness to her supervisor. The woman was almost painfully shy on a personal basis, but when she was working, she was the best there was. Most of the time the dispatchers were the forgotten ones when it came to glamour and glory, yet they worked as hard as anyone and were often the only reason things came together as they should.

On the other hand, Mike thought as he headed for his car, sometimes being forgotten had a certain appeal.

"Oomph!"

Air rushed out of the man's lungs and Shelby felt a spark of satisfaction. The shock of the attack had vanished almost instantly; she wasn't about to let this slime take her without a fight.

She stomped down with her foot on his instep, wishing she was wearing boots instead of tennis shoes. He swore, softly and viciously. She lashed out with a backward kick, this time connecting with a shin. At the same time she drove her elbow into his soft stomach. And bit down hard on the hand over her mouth. She tasted the metal of a ring, then blood.

This time the oath was louder. But not, Shelby feared, loud enough to attract any attention.

"Behave, bitch, or I'll shoot you right here," he hissed into her ear.

She didn't believe him. If he was going to just shoot her he would have done it already. So she wasn't going to go tamely along with him, hoping for a better chance of escape later.

She twisted in his arms, using every bit of her weight and flailing as wildly as she could. She caught a glimpse of his face before his grip on her tightened until she could barely breathe.

And then she heard Aaron. Heard that deep voice,

calling her name. He wasn't far away. She could hear him so clearly, even over the din of the casino.

The killer had heard him too. He whipped around and then froze, listening.

He'd pulled her around with him. Hope jolted through her.

This time when she kicked, it wasn't wildly. It was full of purpose and carefully aimed.

Her heel hit the edge of a polished brass ashtray. It tilted, seemed to balance on edge. And then it went, clanging on the hard tile floor like a blessed church bell.

Three things happened almost simultaneously. The killer let go. She landed on her backside on the floor of the phone alcove. He ran.

And then Aaron was there, a uniformed security man on his heels. "Are you all right?"

"Yes," she gasped out. "He was here, he grabbed me—"

She didn't get another word out before a door behind the bank of phones slammed shut.

"Stay with her," Aaron ordered the guard sharply. And then he was gone, running in pursuit of a killer.

The paramedics were pulling away as Mike drove up. When he got to the dingy apartment the door was open, and a thin, bedraggled-looking woman was seated on the expensive sofa, an ice pack held to the left side of her face. A small boy was huddled next to her, looking up at her with wide eyes, dark with shock and fear.

Welcome to the ugly side, kid, Mike thought.

She obviously wasn't hurt too badly, or the medics would have taken her to the hospital. Still, he knew she had to be very shaken, so he prepped himself to be as gentle as he could.

"Mrs. Reichart?" he asked, crouching down before

her. "I'm Detective Mike Delano. I know you've been through a lot, had to answer a lot of questions, but I'm afraid I have to ask a couple more."

She looked at him through her unswollen eye. And he saw then that while she was indeed shaken, she wasn't distressed. She was, judging by the glint in her eye, furious.

"I suppose you want to know what brought this on?" she snapped.

Mike glanced over his shoulder to where the patrol officer—Sue Sylstra again—was finishing up her notes. "Sue?" he called. "Could you take our young friend out to see the police car?"

"Of course."

The dark eyes of the child shifted from his mother to Mike to Officer Sylstra, then back to his mother. With a visible effort, Mrs. Reichart hugged her son.

"It's all right, Larry. Go ahead. You've always wanted to sit in a police car, haven't you?"

The boy nodded, and after a moment's hesitation slipped off the couch. Sue held out her hand. After another sideways look at Mike, the child darted past him to take the uniformed woman's hand.

Mike turned back to Mrs. Reichart. "I presume what brought this on was your husband's immaturity and inability to control his temper."

She blinked the one eye he could see. Some of her fury seemed to ebb. "Exactly. And do you know what sparked it? I had the gall to suggest that he get a job, do something to help support his child."

"And he did that?" Mike asked, indicating her bruised face.

"After he smashed up half the apartment, yes."

"With his hand or fist?"

"I told them all this."

"I know. I hate to have to ask you again, but I do."
He shrugged helplessly.

"Yes, with his hand. The back of his hand." She laughed, a bitter, ironic laugh. "The biggest bruise was from that fancy ring of his, the one he won't sell no matter what."

"No weapon?"

"Isn't that weapon enough?" she asked a bit defensively.

"Of course," he said. "And there's no excuse for it. I know it's painful to talk about—"

"What's painful," she said with a gesture at her cheek, "is this. And seeing that look of terror in my little boy's eyes."

Mike nodded. "That's an awful thing to see, a child terrified of his own father."

The woman sighed. "Ask your questions, Detective."

"Has your husband ever struck you before? Or your son?"

"No, never. I mean, he has a temper, but he only yells. At least, until now."

"I don't mean to make this any worse, Mrs. Reichart, but did your husband threaten to do worse, or even mention a weapon like a knife or a gun?"

She looked thoughtful for a moment. "Threaten, yes. To kill everyone from us to you. But he never mentioned a specific weapon or method. Just wild raving."

Then he asked the million-dollar question. "Mrs. Reichart, do you think your husband is capable of killing?"

He didn't like watching her expression change as she considered the question. And when she answered, in a soft, almost broken voice, he knew the answer before she said it.

"If you had asked me that yesterday, I would have said no. But now . . . now I would have to say yes."

She lowered the ice pack, and Mike saw the extent

of the marks that would become bruises before the day was out. "Have you made arrangements for you and your son? Someplace else to go?" he asked with concern. He didn't want either of them here if Reichart came back. "If not, I can get you a room at the Golden Phoenix."

"We can't afford to—"

Mike waved a hand. "No. It's on the house. My best friend runs the place. He does this all the time."

It was true. Aaron had come through for him more than once, always willing to provide shelter for people in desperate straits.

"I don't know," she said doubtfully.

"Please," Mike said. "I really don't want you here. There's good security at the Phoenix. You and your son will be safe there."

The emphasis on her child seemed to decide it for her. "All right. We'll go."

"Good. I'll make the call. Why don't you go gather what you'll need?"

After she'd gone into the bedroom, Mike pulled out his cell phone and pushed the last speed dial number. He got Francie, who told him Aaron was out on the floor. He thought for a moment, then asked for Robin Murphy, the security chief. She would need to be apprised of the situation anyway.

Besides, he thought with an inward smile as he waited for her to answer, it would give him a chance to talk to her again; he could use a laugh, and Robin always managed to give him one. He'd asked her out more than once, but she'd always laughingly told him she loved him but he was far too pretty for her taste. He'd always let it go before, especially after Aaron told him about her husband, Josh, an L.A. cop who'd been killed in the line of duty. Mike figured the fact that Robin still wore his ring meant she hadn't let go yet, so he wasn't going to push.

Especially when Aaron made it clear that he would throttle Mike if, even inadvertently, he hurt her.

Still, he thought as he pictured the bright-eyed, sassy redhead, he wasn't going to give up. Someday she just might say yes.

"Sure, Mike. We're nearly at capacity at the moment, but you know Aaron always finds room. Send them on over."

"Thanks, darlin'." Mike poured on the drawl, knowing it always made her laugh. She did, and he turned serious again. "She's pretty upset. Her husband messed up her face pretty good, and terrorized the kid."

"How old is he? I'll make sure there are some toys and maybe a nice, huggable stuffed animal in the room."

"He's six. And thanks, Robin. That's a great idea."

"No problem. Aaron would want it."

"He would also want you to know there's a chance the husband will try to come after her. And . . . he's a murder suspect. A primary one, after this."

"And here I thought my day was going to be boring," Robin said, and Mike could almost hear her grinning.

"I've got to get on the search for him, so I'll have a plain car drive them over. No need to advertise, she's upset enough. Can you have someone meet them, escort them in?"

"I'll do it myself, or have Kim or Lori do it. Might be easier on them both if it's a woman."

"Again, good idea. Thanks." He hesitated, then shrugged to himself. "So, as long as you're being so agreeable, when are you going to have dinner with me?"

"As soon as you stop being the poster boy for hunk of the month," she quipped, as she usually did. But for some reason Mike wasn't in the mood to let her slip away with a joke this time.

"That's not fair," he said quietly.

Instantly, her voice changed. "No, it's not. You know I'm joking."

He corrected her gently. "Dodging."

"That too," she admitted.

"Josh?"

A pause. "Maybe. But only a little. It's been six years."

"Then what?"

There was a moment of silence. Then, in a voice he'd never heard from the confident, poised Robin, she said hesitantly, "Because you scare me?"

He hadn't expected that one, and he wasn't sure how it made him feel. Before he could decide, he heard a three-tone beep in the background.

"Wait a second," she said, and then, "That's Aaron's code. His urgent one. I've got to go."

"Saved by the bell," Mike muttered.

"Yes." She had the grace not to deny it.

"For now," Mike said, not sure whether it was a promise or a warning.

It was only after he'd hung up that he wondered what Aaron had gotten himself into now.

"He had a car waiting," Aaron said wearily. "He blocked the door with a trash can, so he was pulling away by the time I got outside."

They were back in his office. He leaned back in his chair, watching Shelby pace. She had insisted she was all right, although her face was reddened from the man's grip.

He would never forget the moment when he'd realized she was gone.

He'd been talking to Sandra, another of his cousins who was working part-time, and laughing about the antics of his uncle Vince, who had just taken up skydiving at the age of sixty. In fact, he'd just been thinking that was something Shelby would probably appreciate, and had looked around to find her.

He'd tried to tell himself she'd just wandered off to look at something, but his gut wasn't buying it. Then he thought she might finally have run, but that made no sense. Why would she have run now? And then he'd heard the crash from the darkened alcove just a few feet away.

He rounded the corner in time to see Shelby struggling violently with the man, kicking, biting, elbowing. On some level he'd registered her courage even as rage surged through him. He thought he might have yelled, but he knew he started to run.

And then the man had dropped her onto the tile floor. And fled. The seconds Aaron spent making sure Shelby was okay cost him his chance to catch the attacker, but he couldn't have left her there without knowing she was all right.

"Shall I call the police now, Mr. Montana?" asked the security guard who had come up with them.

"I'll handle it, Dennis. Go on back to work. And thanks."

"You bet," the man said.

"Do you know everybody who works here by name?" Shelby asked after he'd gone.

If not for the tiniest quaver in her voice, Aaron would have thought she hadn't been rattled at all by the incident. He supposed those years as a runaway had taught her such unflappable calm.

He knew she was stalling, but answered anyway. "Most," he said. "But not all."

She stopped her restless pacing in front of the golden phoenix. She stared at the exquisite sculpture, and he saw her fingers curl, as if she wanted to touch it.

His grandfather had told him once, when he'd tried in boyish words to express what looking at the phoenix made him feel, that if he ever found a woman who made him feel the same way, he should grab her and never let go. He'd laughed at the idea then.

He wasn't laughing now.

He turned in his chair, slid back a panel on the credenza, and punched a series of numbers into the keypad that was revealed. Then he got up and walked over to her.

"Go ahead. I turned off the alarm."

She gave him a startled look. "You trust me to touch it?"

"I like to touch it on occasion myself. To feel the detail, the workmanship, the life of it."

She stared at him.

"Besides," he added, "I keep hoping that if I trust you enough, you might return the favor."

She flushed and looked away. She stared at the sculpture for a long, silent moment, but he had the feeling she wasn't seeing it at all. Then, slowly, she lifted a hand and delicately traced a swirling flame with one finger.

"If this had happened to anyone else, a regular guest, you'd have already called the cops, wouldn't you?"

"Yes."

She followed the flame upward. "Why didn't you?"

"You tell me, because I'm damned if I know."

His voice had an edge, but he couldn't help it. He was rapidly approaching the limit of his forbearance, and frustration was threatening to boil over at any moment.

"I know you're . . . angry," she began.

"I'm not angry. I'm tired of flailing around blindly, not knowing what's going on. I want some answers, Shelby."

"I can't," she said, still staring at the phoenix. "I just can't, Aaron. It's better this way, really."

"That man who grabbed you wasn't after your wallet or your body."

"I know that."

"And he came into *my* place after you."

"I'm sorry," Shelby whispered, in a voice so tight that his annoyance receded.

He saw her bite her lip, saw the shiver she tried to suppress. Without hesitation he put his arms around her. This time there was no moment of resistance, no stiffness against his touch. She simply sagged against him, and he held her tight. She'd been alone for so long.

He felt a shudder ripple through her, felt her tighten against it, then draw herself up, as if she'd decided she was allowed only a certain amount of comforting.

"Give me until morning."

He blinked. "What?"

"Give me until morning. To . . . work up to it. Then you can . . . do whatever you feel you need to do."

The tone of finality, of surrender, in her voice made him uneasy. If nothing else, he'd learned that with this woman nothing was simple. And for one of the few times in his life, he was running out of patience. With others, his supply was endless, but with Shelby, he seemed constantly on the edge of eruption. And he had a sinking feeling that he knew exactly why.

He sighed, and hugged her tighter for a moment. "Okay. In the morning."

He also had a sinking feeling he would regret that decision before this was over.

Shelby sat on the edge of the bed, staring into the darkness. The absence of light didn't help her hide from reality, although she wished it would. It was an odd feeling for her. She'd lost faith in hiding from the truth the first time she had gone to her mother with what Brad had done to her, and her mother hadn't believed her. Or if she had, she'd chosen to ignore it for her own sake, which was somehow worse.

Aaron wanted answers. He deserved them. But they were not hers to give.

She had to protect Margaret. She would never have believed anyone would come along who would make her feel conflicted over her loyalty to the woman who had saved her life. But Aaron did.

And Aaron, she admitted, was the bottom line. He wasn't just putting himself out for her, he was risking his life. She was sure he didn't think of it that way; he'd been more concerned about the danger to his staff and guests. And she felt even more guilty that she had brought evil into his peaceful domain.

But she thought about it that way. Because she knew that man would have killed Aaron if necessary. She'd seen it in his eyes.

She got to her feet and walked slowly across the room to the door. She opened it quietly and stood there for a moment, listening. The apartment was silent.

She made her way down the short hallway. Aaron's door was open, as usual. She could hear him breathing deeply.

She almost turned back. But she knew she would regret it for the rest of her life if she did. It had been a very long time since she'd felt this. It had been since Tiger. She had feared that something had died inside her then. But Aaron had shown her it had merely been dormant, waiting. She didn't want to wait another fifteen years for it to happen again. If it ever did.

Just once in her life, she wanted to know what it was like, what it was *supposed* to be like. Done out of genuine emotion, with a man who cared enough to be gentle until she wasn't afraid anymore. She knew instinctively that Aaron would be like that.

Even if, in the end, all she had was memories, surely that was better than nothing.

She drew a deep breath and stepped into his room. He hadn't pulled the drapes, and a beam of silver moonlight sliced the room in two, a swath of light glowing like a path to the bed. Her mouth quirked at the apparent symbolism her mind was attaching to a simple bit of light.

Moments ago, she had been entangled in a web of chaotic emotions. Now they all fell away as she looked at the man asleep in the moonlight. Aaron Montana was everything she'd long thought didn't exist. And she wouldn't be surprised if he was one of a kind, if she never saw his like again, wherever her miserable life took her.

She took another step into the room.

You'd have to strip naked and climb into bed with me before I'd do anything about it.

His words came back to her, bringing a flush to her face, and a burgeoning heat to the rest of her body. Slowly, she reached for the hem of the T-shirt she'd been sleeping in and pulled it over her head.

Stripped naked, she climbed into bed with him. And hoped that in this, as everything else, he was a man of his word.

Aaron stirred sleepily, on some level of consciousness half wishing to wake up so this dream would end, half wanting to stay asleep forever, so he would never have to face that it was a dream.

This wasn't the first night that erotic images of the woman down the hall had plagued him, and it wouldn't be the last, he was sure. He'd told himself when he brought her here that it was the most secure place in the hotel. That was true, but she would have been safe enough in a room, with his people alerted.

He'd finally had to admit that he'd brought her here because he wanted to. That she'd stirred something beyond his instinct to help someone in trouble. That she was different from any woman he'd known. That she was the most fascinating woman he'd ever known. That she was, in her own way, the most attractive. That she was—

She was here.

He came fully awake, sucking in a breath as he realized the silky caress he'd been feeling hadn't been a dream at all. He held that breath, still not sure he believed it. But he could feel her beside him, could hear her slight movements as her hand slid up his arm, then down over his shoulder.

He turned his head, almost afraid that he would see nothing but moonlit air. But she was there, her tousled cap of blond hair shimmering in the silver light, looking at him steadily. She was there, in his bed, her naked skin soft and hot against him.

"Shelby?" he choked out.

"I remembered what you said," she whispered.

Naked. He'd told her she would have to climb into his bed naked. Heat rocketed through him, and he tried desperately to fight against it. But it had been a very long time for him—in fact, forever; he had never wanted a woman the way he wanted her.

"It's safe, Aaron. In all ways. I've not been with anyone in a very long time."

He didn't doubt her. And he knew why, knew what hideous memories she had to fight, what fears she must have overcome to be here with him now.

"Nor have I. But I said something else, too," he ground out between clenched teeth. "About honesty."

"I'm here because I want to be. No doubts, no obligation, and no regrets later."

He should tell her no. There were too many unanswered questions between them.

"I understand," she said, as if she'd read his mind. "But I can't just let this pass by. It doesn't happen often, and never to me."

"What," he asked, a catch in his voice, "doesn't happen?"

"That I really, truly want someone. So much."

That simple, honest declaration did him in. He never even thought of resisting when she reached for him; instead, he pulled her into his arms and let out a low groan when he felt the full length of her pressed against him. She seemed to pull back for an instant, and he wondered if she was changing her mind despite her words. Then she was clinging to him, and he knew she hadn't. He made himself remember that with her history it was only natural she would be uncertain. From that moment on, he moved with as much care as he could manage.

The spark that had always been between them flared quickly and spread even faster. He kissed her, and it was hotter, much hotter even than he remembered. Hotter than any kiss he'd ever known. She didn't just kiss him back, she kissed him as if she was as hungry as he, as desperate. She touched him as if she couldn't get enough, as if he were the personification of every dream she'd ever had. He'd never in his life been touched like that, with a sense of awe and wonder, and it annihilated the last of his barriers, shattered his doubts—and his ability to go slowly.

It was madness, and Aaron reveled in it. He finally felt free of restraint, forgot about having to be the steady one, the reliable one, the one everybody turned to. Instead he gloried in the aching response of his body where she touched him, savored the way she lifted to his hand wherever he caressed her.

And when she moaned his name as he cupped her

breasts, a blast of heat shot through him, nearly sending him over the edge right then. With enormous effort he regained control and lowered his mouth to her nipples to fulfill the fantasy that had haunted his dreams for days now.

He stroked her, petted her, suckled her until she cried out, until her fingers curved intro claws she wasn't afraid to use on him. He arched his back into her nails, loving the sensation of her eagerness made tangible, any lingering fear vanquished. He'd never felt so truly wanted, and his body was already soaring.

When she reached for him, curling those fingers, gently now, around his aching flesh, he heard her name break from his throat in a harsh burst of sound.

"Aaron, please," she said, and when he felt her tremble he knew he couldn't wait any longer.

He shifted over her, in his need barely aware of the shudders rippling through him. Shelby reached for him again, guiding him, and he probed into her slick, soft heat.

Still he hesitated, never more conscious of his sheer size than now, hovering over her small, delicate body, and terrified of hurting or frightening her.

"Aaron, *please*," she repeated, but this time her pleading swamped his reservations.

All subtlety lost, seared to ash in the blaze they'd kindled, he drove forward, burying himself to the hilt, and gasping out her name as she took him hard and deep and home.

Helpless to stop now, he pulled back and plunged again, and again. He was wondering how he would ever hold back long enough when Shelby rose to meet him on the next thrust, and the next, and when her body convulsed around his, clasping him even tighter, and she cried out his name, he let go in a rush of incredible sensation unlike anything he'd ever known.

Gasping, more than a little stunned, he collapsed,

barely remembering to fall to one side so his bulk wouldn't crush her. He heard his own breathing, quick pants that echoed in the quiet room.

"My God!" he muttered when he could form words at all.

Shelby clung to him in answer, a tiny moan her only sound.

He felt, when he could breath normally again, that he should say something, but she seemed content in the silence, and he didn't know where on earth to begin anyway. But finally he knew he was going to fall asleep if he didn't do something.

"Shel—"

"Shh," she urged. "Later. Please."

He subsided into silence. And sooner than he would have thought possible after that crashing climax, his body began to respond anew to the feel of her snuggled close. And as soon as she realized it, she reached for him again.

Her body deliciously tender, her senses still echoing the explosions of pleasure that had shaken her each time they'd come together, Shelby lay quietly staring into the dark once more. Aaron was deeply asleep, and she wished she could smile at the thought of how he had become so exhausted.

Her resolve was weakening. She wanted nothing more than to stay right where she was for a long time. A very long time. She didn't dare to think the word "forever." It wasn't in her vocabulary, especially when it came to people.

She didn't look at Aaron as she slipped silently out of his bed. She didn't dare.

And she didn't have to. His image, the feel of him, the sound of him, would be with her until the day she died. That was the only forever she believed in.

Back in the guest room she dressed and gathered

up her few possessions. She hesitated, then added the things he'd bought for her. She didn't have enough that she could be noble about it. She reluctantly added some other things. Then she found a piece of paper and a pen, and stood at the bar in the kitchen for a long time, staring at the blank page.

In the end, there was only one thing to say, and she wrote it quickly, barely able to see through the tears spilling down her cheeks. She left the note propped where he couldn't miss it.

Then she slipped out the door and closed it carefully behind her.

If only she could close the door on her thoughts as easily.

Chapter Eighteen

When Aaron spotted the familiar face across the casino, it set off a tumult inside him. Before he even thought, he was crossing the floor in long, swift strides. He came up behind the man, grabbed him by the shoulder.

He'd caught the man off guard, but he reacted quickly nevertheless. He ducked and wheeled, twisting free. Aaron grabbed him again. This time an elbow drove into his ribs, but he held on and backed the man up against the wall. It was him, all right, the man he'd seen following Shelby, the man he'd chased toward the parking structure the day he'd taken her out to the desert overlook.

But not the man who had jumped her yesterday.

"I want to know what the hell is going on, and I want to know now," he snarled.

"Look, buddy, you jumped me."

Aaron's grip tightened. "I," he announced warningly, "am in no mood."

It was an understatement; he'd been way beyond touchy ever since he'd awakened to find that the woman he'd just spent the most incredible night of his life with had vanished, with only a two-word note— "I'm sorry"—left behind.

"I don't know what your problem is—"

"I hate stalkers. How's that for starters?"

"Stalker?"

"And I hate hired killers even more."

The man gaped at him. "I'm no killer!"

He looked genuinely startled, but Aaron was just frustrated enough not to buy it. He knew they were drawing too much attention, but he didn't care. Still, he said, "Never mind, don't say a word. I'll just call the cops now."

"Look, Mr. Montana, I—"

The man stopped abruptly when Aaron's eyes narrowed at the use of his name. Making certain of his grip on the man's shirt, Aaron glanced around, saw two of his security people headed his way at a fast clip.

"Problem, sir?" the first one asked.

"Take him to your office. I'll be right behind you."

He waited until they were out of earshot, then beeped Robin on his phone.

"I need you to meet me at the holding room in security. ASAP."

"On my way. Problem?"

"There could be. I may need you to keep me from squashing somebody."

"Sounds entertaining. I'm at the gift shop on my rounds, so I'm close. See you in a minute."

He'd hoped the walk to the security office would cool him off a bit. It didn't. By the time he got there, he was more steamed than he'd been before; all he could think of was Shelby's eyes shadowed with fear.

And that she'd run again.

Aaron strode across the office to the man, seated at a small table, with one of the uniformed security men opposite him. He leaned over the table, using every bit of his considerable height to intimidate.

"I think you'd better tell me what you're up to, and you'd better tell me *now*."

"Nice hospitality," the man said sourly.

"Are you telling me you're a registered guest at the Golden Phoenix?"

"No, but—"

"No buts," Aaron said sharply. He heard the door behind him open, saw out of the corner of his eye that it was Robin, but kept his attention on the man. "You've been harassing a person who *is* a guest here, and I want to know why."

"I haven't been harassing anyone."

"What would you call it, then?"

"He'd probably call it working," Robin said.

Aaron turned to look at her. "What?"

"He's a P.I., Aaron."

Aaron blinked. "A P.I.?"

His gaze swiveled back to the seated man. A P.I. meant someone had hired him. Not likely Pruett, at least not to kill, not a legitimate private investigator.

He shook his head sharply and glanced at Robin again.

"You know him?"

She nodded. "Stan Langford. Ex-cop, as I recall."

The man let out a sigh. "I don't believe I've had the pleasure," he said to Robin.

"Robin Murphy," she said. "And I suggest you answer his question. If there's a man in this town who could make your life miserable, you're looking at him."

"You think I don't know that?"

"Ex-cop from where?" Aaron asked.

"Here," Robin said, then looked back at the man. "Isn't that right?"

He gave another sigh and nodded, now that his cover was completely blown.

"How long ago?" Aaron asked.

"Seven years."

Aaron straightened up and walked to the wall phone. In moments, Mike answered.

"Mike, I need a question answered."

"Sure. Is it about Mrs. Reichart?"

Aaron blinked. "No. Who's Mrs. Reichart?"

"She hasn't arrived yet? I—"

"Wait," Aaron interrupted as Robin waved at him, "Robin's here and she knows."

"I've got Kim Takei waiting for her," Robin said.

Aaron relayed the information to Mike, who said, "Good. Robin can explain, then. What did you need?"

"Stan Langford."

"Yeah? Local P.I., used to be one of ours. Good man, just didn't get along well with the current management. Kind of old school, if you get my drift."

"Honest?"

"To a fault. That was part of his problem."

Meaning, Aaron guessed, that he was honest in his opinion of the brass. Or perhaps a little lacking in the P.C. approach that was necessary for cops today.

"You have a problem with him or for him?" Mike asked.

"Neither, I hope. I'll let you know."

"There's a lot of that 'I'll let you know' piling up, buddy," Mike said.

"The dam's about to break," Aaron promised. "Thanks," he said, and disconnected.

"Mike who, if I might ask?" Langford asked when Aaron turned back to him.

"Delano."

"Ah," Langford said. "Good cop. Good guy."

"Yes. He says you're honest."

"I'd be flattered, but it's the simple truth."

"I'm not sure I like your idea of honesty."

"You're not my client."

"Who is?"

"I can't tell you that."

"Because it's Jack Pruett?"

The man blinked, his expression utterly blank. Aaron sensed that Robin went very still.

"Pruett?" Langford asked. "The slime who got himself murdered? What does he have to do with this?"

If he was acting, he was damn good, Aaron thought. But then, in his line of work, he supposed you had to be.

"If it's not Pruett, then why are you following Shelby Wyatt?"

Aaron watched the man's expression change from puzzlement to thoughtfulness tinged with alarm.

"Are you saying," Langford said slowly, "that Shelby Wyatt is somehow connected to Pruett? Or his murder?"

Langford sounded, Aaron thought, exactly like he himself had felt lately, like a man in a game where half the rules had been kept secret. He glanced at Robin. She lifted both brows in an indication that she, too, thought Langford was as surprised—and alarmed—as he sounded.

"I'm not sure," Aaron said. "But I have a feeling we're both in the same boat, steering without a compass."

If this guy hadn't been hired by somebody connected with Pruett—although it was possible he just didn't know that was the case—then who could have hired him? Who else would have been willing to pay to find Shelby?

From what Shelby had told him, there was only one person.

"She hired you, didn't she? Shelby's . . . friend— her mentor?"

"Mr. Montana, I'm sorry, but I can't tell you that. Client privilege."

"Damn it!" Aaron exploded before he could stop himself. He saw Robin go still again, knew he'd startled her; he rarely lost his temper. "Shelby's in trouble, and if your client doesn't care about that, then I have to assume he or she is connected to whoever tried to grab her last night."

The man frowned. "Someone tried to grab her?"

"Right here in my hotel, so he's getting desperate. And now she's . . ."

Aaron stopped. He wasn't sure of this man, and no matter how worried he was, he couldn't blurt out that Shelby was gone, vanished, back into the shadowy maelstrom that threatened her.

"My client specified that the girl was to be kept safe, at all costs," Langford said slowly.

"So it is her?"

Langford seemed to struggle with his thoughts for a moment, then reached a decision. "I think that, given the circumstances, she would authorize me to tell you. Her main concern is Shelby's safety, and always has been. Her own privacy was important, but secondary."

"I hope so. She's the only person Shelby trusts," Aaron said, trying to keep any trace of bitterness out of his voice. It wasn't her fault that she found it so hard to trust, nor was it his that she couldn't trust him. He couldn't have tried any harder.

"I got the feeling she trusted you," Langford said.

"Not enough," Aaron muttered.

"What do you mean?"

He hesitated, but realized that unless they pooled what information they had, there was little chance of finding Shelby.

"She's gone," he said flatly. The man looked startled. "Yeah, she outwitted you again, didn't she?"

And me, he added silently. *I don't think I was ever a match for her.*

Then, with an effort, he dragged himself back to the matter at hand. "Why did she hire you?"

Langford glanced at the uniformed security guard,

then at Robin. "No offense, please, but I'd prefer to keep this between us."

Aaron nodded to the guard, who turned to go, and then to Robin, who hesitated for a moment, until Aaron added, "It's all right."

She didn't look happy, but nodded in turn. "I'll go see if I can help with Mrs. Reichart."

"Who *is* Mrs. Reichart?"

"One of Mike's rescues. Battered, I think. With a little boy."

"You've got a room for them already?"

"Yes."

"Good. Get something for the boy to play with, will you?"

"Already done."

When Robin left, Aaron turned back to Langford; the man was looking at him intently. "It appears," he said after a moment, "that everything I've heard about you is true."

"Look," Aaron retorted sourly. "I'm on the edge of tarnishing that supposedly sterling reputation of mine. Why did she hire you?"

"She told me that she just needed to know the girl was all right. That Shelby had gotten into some trouble trying to help her."

"And?"

Langford shrugged. "She didn't come out and say blackmail, but that's what it smelled like. Shelby missed her daily call, which was highly unusual. She wanted me to find her, then follow her, try and contact her if I could get to her alone." He grimaced, "Obviously I need to brush up on my tracking skills. You made me pretty quickly."

"I don't want to burst your bubble, but so did Shelby."

His grimace became a wry smile. "She's quite something."

You don't know the half of it, buddy, Aaron thought. "Who is she?"

"Pardon?"

"Your client. What's her name?"

Langford looked surprised. "I thought you knew."

"I know about her, but not her name."

"Margaret Peterson." Langford hesitated again, but after a moment said, "She hinted that her husband was rather well known in Outpost, thus the need for secrecy."

Aaron frowned, thinking, but the name didn't ring a bell. But something else belatedly did.

She told me that Shelby had gotten into some trouble trying to help her. . . .

Of course. He should have guessed sooner.

He felt both relieved and slightly sickened. While he couldn't believe that Shelby would kill, he'd seen how fiercely loyal she was, and he wasn't nearly as sure she wouldn't kill to protect somebody else, somebody she cared about. Like the woman who had taken her in, who had saved her from life on the street and given her a future.

He took out his cell phone and redialed Mike.

"Hey, darlin', what'd you forget to tell me?"

"I love you, too," Aaron said dryly.

"Oops," Mike said, sounding more than a little flustered. "I thought you were Robin calling back."

"Oh?"

"She called to let me know Mrs. Reichart and her boy were there safe and sound."

"Uh-huh," Aaron said, thinking that later on he was going to have to find out just why Mike was calling Robin "darlin'." But right now this was more important. "Where are you?"

"Just coming back into the station. Why?"

"I need to know if a name's on that list of yours."

"List? You mean Pruett's blackmail list?"

"Yes."

"Aaron, you know I'd do anything for you, but—"

"Mike, this is imperative. You know I wouldn't ask if it wasn't."

"You're putting me in a bad spot, my friend. I know you know something about this case, or someone involved in it."

"And you know I'll give you what I have as soon as I'm sure it's for real. Right now it's . . . smoke. It's there, but I can't get a handle on it."

There was a moment's pause when Aaron could hear doors closing and a change in the background noise. Mike must be back inside now.

"Been there," Mike said finally. "Okay. I trust you like a brother, Montana. Don't let me down."

"Have I ever?"

"Well, there was that time when I came to see you in New York—"

"Hey, that wasn't my fault. You're the one who wanted to see the Big Apple on your own."

"And I did. More of it than I ever wanted to," Mike said dryly. "Okay, I'm back at my desk. What's the name?"

"Margaret Peterson."

"Damn."

"What?"

"Of all the names on that list . . ." Mike didn't sound at all happy.

"She is one of them, then?"

"How the hell did you come up with her?"

"Why did you know without looking that her name is there?"

Mike sighed. "She's married to a member of the police commission. Robert Peterson. That kind of thing in a murder investigation tends to stick in your mind."

"Damn."

"I think I said that."

"What did Pruett have on her?"

"Don't know yet. Haven't matched any of the stuff we recovered to her, but we've got a lot to go through yet. Obviously it's pretty volatile because of her connection to Peterson, so I'm trying to keep the lid on for the moment."

"What a mess." Aaron's words were heartfelt on more levels than Mike knew.

"Aaron, you've gotta give. What do you know?"

Aaron knew he was putting a strain on their friendship, and he hated it. But he hated even more the idea of Shelby being out there, all alone and in trouble, with her attacker no doubt still after her. He wondered for a moment if maybe telling Mike might be the best thing he could do for her; Mike could protect her.

"Twenty-four hours, Mike. Just give me that." And then, if he hadn't found her, he'd do just that. She'd hate him, but she'd be alive.

Mike let out a long, audible breath. "I'll try. But if it starts to come apart on me . . ."

"I understand. If it does, there's no choice."

There was a moment's hesitation, then Mike said, "As long as you're in the middle of this thing anyway, you'd better know. Mrs. Reichart is the wife of one of my prime suspects in Pruett's murder."

Aaron's hand tightened on the phone. Mike had a good suspect? "Oh?"

"I only told Robin her husband was a nasty guy who might come after her, and a murder suspect. Didn't mention Pruett."

"How . . . prime is he?"

"Looks pretty good, so far. Tons of motive, and opportunity, although that doesn't make him stand out particularly on the list of people who hated the guy. No weapon yet, but he could have ditched it long ago.

I'll know better when we find him and I can put some pressure on him."

"I hope it's him." Aaron knew he sounded a bit too fervent, and hastily said good-bye and disconnected.

"Good cop, good guy, good friend," Langford said.

"And then some," Aaron agreed.

"What next?" Langford asked.

The moment the question was out, Aaron realized he'd already decided.

"I'll tell you what's next," he said, a little grimly. "Come with me."

He led the man out of the holding room. Langford wasn't going to like this, but Aaron didn't much care. Not anymore.

Chapter Nineteen

Shelby had been riding around all day, going from bus to bus, spending precious cash. But constantly moving on a public bus loaded with other people was the best place she could be right now. She didn't want to really outrun him, he might turn to Aaron in an effort to find out where she was, making this a pointless exercise. She swiped at her eyes, hoping no one on the bus noticed.

Cryin's useless, girl, unless it's going to get you something from somebody. Get over it.

"God, Tiger, I wish you hadn't been so right," she whispered.

She had to stop this. She'd allowed herself some tears, now it was time to move on. She needed to put some distance between her and Aaron, make it clear that she'd left him, that he was no longer involved. Then he'd be safe.

She'd done everything she could think of. She'd packed her backpack with food, a bottle of water, and anything else she thought might help, including a large knife she had reluctantly taken from Aaron's kitchen. Then she walked blatantly right past the alcove where her assailant had grabbed her and out the door where they'd seen the other man. To protect herself she stayed near the large group of tourists she'd followed outside, even struck up a conversation with one of them. But she'd made sure she was visible, frequently running her hands through her hair, hoping the motion and the pale color of her hair would draw his attention, if he really was around.

She had thought about going home, getting some things and her car, but knew she didn't dare. There was too much there that would lead straight to Margaret. She had to leave, had to lead her pursuer away from both Margaret and Aaron. She'd brought this down on them, it was up to her to save them.

Finally she'd boarded a bus, thinking she'd done all she could to make it clear that she was no longer at the Golden Phoenix. She only hoped her pursuer would reach the conclusion that she was also no longer with Aaron.

No longer with Aaron . . .

Shelby tried to fight the shiver that took her by surprise. She'd expected it to hurt to walk away from the man who had shown her so much passion and tenderness in the night, but she hadn't expected it to feel as if her soul had been ripped out.

She forced herself to think. She had to come up with someplace to hide out. When she'd first come here, used to the concrete canyons of L.A., the landscape of the towering Sierras awed her. The high desert in the other direction amazed her. But she'd been used to city streets, so it was Outpost itself that she had learned inside out in those early days, thinking that if this woman was like all the others who supposedly wanted to help, she would need to have a plan of where to run to.

And by the time she learned Margaret was for real, she was already caught up in the wonder of her new life and she'd never gotten around to scouting out the surrounding territory. A big mistake, Tiger would have said. Always know your retreats, even if you're sure you won't need one.

Well, she needed one now. Some place safe enough, and distant enough, where she could lose herself.

It's so remote up there, rough country, easy to get . . . lost.

Aaron's words, in that torn, devastated voice as he talked about his little girl, echoed in her head.

She wasn't equipped for it. She didn't know the terrain. She wasn't even sure she remembered the name of the grocery he'd mentioned. It was a stupid idea.

It was her only idea.

She stared out the bus window until she saw what she wanted. At the next stop, she got off. She darted into a convenience store and spent a few dollars of her stash, then went into the rest room. And a few minutes later she walked out of the back of the convenience store and into the back of the paint store next door.

Shortly after that a petite redhead, in a local tourist-trap T-shirt and a pair of cheap sunglasses, walked casually out the front door of the paint store and strolled down the street studying a handful of paint chips intently.

"Delta-alpha-nine."

The radio under the dash of his car crackled with his unit designation, "Delta" for *D* as in "detectives," "alpha" as in one-man unit, and "nine" for his desk in the detective division office.

That's what I get for turning it on, Mike muttered to himself.

He reached down, unhooked the microphone from the rack, and keyed it. "Delta-alpha-nine."

"Delta-alpha-nine," Evie Richard's voice came back at him, "be advised patrol has a suspicious person in custody at eleven-fifteen North Nevada."

Pruett's house. "Circs?" he asked.

"He was located trying to gain entry via a back window."

Could be a plain old burglary. Or a more specific one, somebody who maybe knew the resident was dead and figured he'd go in and pick it clean. Happened all the time.

Or it could be somebody doing the proverbial return to the scene of the crime. Reichart, maybe?

"I'm en route. Tell them to stand by, ETA driving time from the south end."

"Copy, delta-alpha-nine."

He made a left turn, drove to Front Street, the main access road that ran between the north and south ends of Outpost, and made another. He hoped it was Reichart; at least it would make his wife's and son's lives easier. Not to mention his own. Returning to the scene of the murder would be another choice piece of evidence against the man.

By the time he arrived at the house, which was still festooned with crime-scene tape in that incongruously cheerful shade of yellow, he'd heard the patrol officers on the radio saying they had the man in the back of one of the units parked up the street. He would head up there in a minute; for now he went to the house and greeted the two officers who were outside.

"Neighbor called," the one who had been first on the scene explained when Mike asked for the details. "Saw him lurking around in the back."

"Any idea how he got here?"

The other officer nodded. "I started running plates." He gestured down the street. "The red Beamer is his."

Mike looked at the BMW convertible. It wasn't new but was waxed to a high shine.

"Nice of him to park practically right in front," Mike muttered. "So, you have an ID on him?"

The first officer nodded and handed Mike a driver's license.

"Well, well, well," Mike said. "Hello, again, Mr. Franco."

"You know him?"

"He was a gambling buddy of Pruett's, before they had a little falling-out." He gestured toward the red car. "You search it yet?"

"Not yet. We just wrapped him up," the first officer said.

"You place him under formal arrest yet?"

"Nope. Haven't told him anything yet, or read him his rights. Figured we'd better wait for you."

"Thanks. That helps. So how'd it go down?"

"By the time I got here, he had one foot inside. If he'd been a little quicker—"

"Or more coordinated," one of the others put in.

"Yeah," the first officer agreed. "He's a bit of a klutz. He'd fallen to the inside, with his other leg still hanging out the window. I made sure he didn't have a weapon in his hands, then I just shut the window on him."

"Nice work" Mike said.

"He yelped like a puppy and jerked back upright. I yanked him out and slapped the cuffs on."

"They should all be so easy," Mike said with a grin that earned him two in return.

But as he walked toward the police unit with the prisoner, he wasn't grinning anymore. It had been too easy. Whoever had killed Pruett had been quick, efficient, neat, and smart. From what the officers had said and from his own assessment, Franco was none of those, especially smart. Coming here in broad daylight, with the police tape still in place, parking his own car barely a hundred feet away, was not the mark of a stellar intellect.

He stared in at the man until his head turned.

"Gerry, Gerry," Mike said, shaking his head.

Franco looked sullen and a little bit afraid. The polished veneer was gone. Mike stood there for a moment longer, expressionless, then nodded as if to himself, turned his back, and walked away. It was all part of the plan. Set the guy to worrying, wondering what he'd been nodding about, let him stew for a while, then confront him back at the station in an interview room, where it was clear who was in charge. The approach generally worked when he saw that touch of fear.

By the time he got to the station, stopped by his office to look at the latest news from Eric, and got down to the jail, Franco had been sitting alone in the small interview room near the drunk tank for half an hour. And he wasn't happy. The jailer reported that about every five minutes he yelled about his rights for a bit, then subsided.

So Mike wasn't surprised when he walked into the room and the man's first words were, "You can't do this. I know my rights!"

Mike closed the door, walked to the other side of the table, reversed a chair, and straddled it. He said nothing, just waited. As he'd expected, the man spoke again.

"I get a phone call!"

Mike lifted a brow. "Only if you're under arrest. Are you saying we should do that now?"

Franco blinked. "I said nothing of the kind."

Mike shrugged. "Sorry. It was all this talk of rights and phone calls, when I just wanted to hear your side of the story. I mean, there might be a legitimate reason you were breaking into your old buddy's house. But if you want, we'll play it your way."

The man sputtered, then clamped his mouth shut. *First smart thing you've done,* Mike thought.

"All right," he said agreeably. "We'll just have to guess why you were there, then."

Franco's jaw tightened further.

"Not that it's a tough guess," Mike said casually. "Although I admit, at first I thought this was all going to boil down to that fight you and Jack had the other night. But that isn't it at all, is it?"

Franco's poker face was crumbling. Then, pulling out the ace from the final list of names he'd found when he stopped by his desk, Mike said, "I mean, you being on Pruett's list makes it pretty clear."

It was a moment before Franco broke and asked, "List?"

"Um-hmm." Mike considered a yawn, decided it would be too over the top, and went on. "You didn't think he tracked all those blackmail payments in his head, did you?"

Franco paled. "I don't know what you're talking about!"

Mike watched him carefully. This guy didn't seem like he'd have the guts to kill anyone up close and personal. But maybe it was just an act. A very good act.

"Look," he said, sounding intentionally fed up. "We know, all right? Don't be dancing around the facts. You'll just look like a bigger fool than you do already. I mean, having this guy who's supposedly your best buddy turn on you like this . . ."

Now *that* hit a nerve, Mike thought: Franco obviously didn't care for being called a fool. Abruptly, to keep the man off balance, he changed tacks.

"It's not your fault Pruett was a sleazy blackmailer, right?"

"He was a dirty rat!"

Now the guy sounded like an old gangster movie, Mike thought. "No argument there. Lot of people felt like you do. But only you had the nerve to kill him."

"I didn't kill him! I was just there because I wanted that video back, that's all. I didn't want it to . . . fall into the wrong hands again."

Well, that should make it easier to match Franco's name with the blackmail material in the huge box down in the evidence lockup in the property room. Of course, he'd just confessed to burglary without having been read his rights, but in a murder investigation, sometimes you pay for what you get.

"And you thought it would still be there?" Mike asked.

There was a delay while Franco processed it. Then he paled again. "You have it?"

"Of course we do. All of it. It's evidence."

The man sagged in his seat, clearly realizing he'd just trapped himself for nothing.

"And you're way up on the suspect list—"

The beep of Mike's pager cut off Franco's protest. He never took his cell phone into an interview, just his pager for emergency info that might affect the discussion. He glanced at the small screen, saw the code for urgent, and stepped over to the phone on the wall.

The information was the results of the car search. It was short, indeed urgent, and very, very sweet. He hung up smiling. And turned back to Franco.

"You know, if you'd just waited long enough, somebody else probably would have killed him for you."

"I told you—"

"Can it, Franco. We found it."

The man frowned. "Found what?"

"The gun."

Aaron looked at the expensive black sedan parked in the driveway of the elegant white house. He'd been startled when Langford had given him the directions; the Peterson house was within a block of his parents' old home. Since the car Langford had described was here, he had to assume its owner was also.

He'd insisted that Langford not call Mrs. Peterson to warn her. He wanted her off guard and vulnerable. Not his usual tactics, but he was dealing with Shelby's life. He offered to let Langford off the hook, to confront the woman and not tell her how he'd found out about her, but Langford had refused to opt out, earning him a bit more respect from Aaron.

The woman who answered the door was not quite what he'd expected. She was elegant and poised. Her jewelry was obviously of the best quality, yet there wasn't too much of it, and the diamond on her left hand was large but not showy.

Somehow he'd expected someone a little less . . . polished.

She was staring at him, as if she recognized him. He opened his mouth to speak, but she beat him to it.

"Aaron Montana," she whispered. He lifted a brow at her. "I looked up your photograph in an old magazine after . . . after I found out Shelby was with you. Is she all right?"

"That's what I came to talk to you about, Mrs. Peterson."

She didn't even blink at his use of her name. "Margaret, please. I was about to come to you, anyway, if I hadn't heard anything by noon. So if she sent you, you'd better come in."

Aaron waited until they were inside—the inside matched the outside for taste and elegance, he noted; his mother would have been right at home here—and sitting down before he disabused her of that notion.

"Shelby didn't send me. Stan Langford told me where you live."

She looked surprised. "He did?"

"He didn't have much choice."

She studied him for a moment, then sighed. "I don't suppose he did."

He'd had enough of the niceties. "Has Shelby been here?"

Margaret's forehead creased instantly. "No. I haven't seen her for three days. I thought she was with you."

"She was. Until this morning."

"I don't understand. Where is she?"

"I don't know."

"But—"

"She vanished. During the night."

"But . . . why?"

Aaron felt a faint heat in his face. *I was so horny I scared her to death last night? One night of wild sex was all she wanted? She woke up and looked at what she'd slept with and took off running?*

"I'm not sure," he said. That was true enough. "If you know, you'd best tell me."

"No, I don't." The poised facade faltered. "I only wish I did. I'm so worried about her . . ."

"I know. She got into this mess because of you, didn't she?"

The woman's poise vanished. Her voice broke. "Oh, God! I never should have told her!"

"About Pruett, and that he was blackmailing you." It wasn't a question, and she obviously knew it.

"I never thought she would . . . do anything rash."

"What did you expect her to do?"

"Nothing!" Margaret exclaimed. "Don't you see? I just needed to . . . talk to someone, someone who would understand."

"Are you saying he was blackmailing her, too?"

"No, no, of course not. But Shelby understands what it's like to . . . lose everything."

Aaron's stomach knotted. Yes, Shelby knew all too well.

"I never thought she would do anything rash," Margaret repeated.

"You underestimated her. Her loyalty and her determination."

"I know," Margaret said, her voice hollow.

"Tell me exactly what you know. Everything that was said."

She hesitated, and irritation flashed through Aaron. He quashed it, knowing he'd been just as confused as this woman was since Shelby Wyatt had tumbled into his life, so how could he blame her?

"Look, Margaret, I'm sorry about whatever trouble you're in, but Shelby's life could be in danger. Somebody attacked her last night in the Golden Phoenix."

Her eyes widened. "Attacked her? In your hotel? Was she hurt?"

"No, she fought him off. She's tough when she has to be."

"Yes, she is." She studied Aaron pensively. "So that's it."

"That's what?"

"Why she left. It would be just like her."

He was lost now. "What are you talking about?"

"She would leave if she felt she was endangering you. Just as I finally realized she wouldn't come to me now, for the same reason."

"Endangering me?" Aaron said, astonished. "You're saying she took off to . . . protect *me*?"

"Is that so extraordinary?"

That someone would try to protect him, instead of the other way around? Yes, Aaron realized with an odd rush of emotion, it was extraordinary.

"I see that it is," Margaret said.

It took him a moment to gather his thoughts. "What exactly did you tell her? And when?"

"I told her that Jack Pruett had been blackmailing me for weeks. That he'd gotten hold of some unfortunate, very graphic photographs that were taken when I was in college and was threatening to make them public to damage my husband."

Aaron looked at her steadily. "I wasn't going to ask what he had on you."

Margaret sighed. "Thank you. But you need to know what's at stake to understand, I'm afraid. You see, my husband is not only a traditional, conventional man who would be greatly humiliated, he also holds a position of public trust that wouldn't bear a scandal involving his wife."

Aaron decided now was not the time to tell her that the police already knew she was on Pruett's list. She would find out soon enough.

"And?" he prompted.

"Shelby knew what was at stake, including the man I love more than my life. And that I couldn't bear to lose him. I found him fairly late, you see. I'd given up on love, after I made such a fool of myself with that boy in college." Her mouth twisted painfully. "Little did I know his betrayal then was nothing compared to what he would do later."

"Let me guess. He sold the photos to Pruett."

She nodded wearily. "Pruett said Dan told him he'd just found the negatives again. And at a time when he needed money badly." She grimaced. "Apparently he'd gone from marijuana and cocaine to something a bit more pricey."

"What did Shelby say when you told her?"

"Oh, she was instantly furious, defensive and wonderfully protective. It was just what I needed. But then . . ." Margaret stopped, took a deep breath, and went on. "She leapt to her feet in that decisive way of hers and told me not to worry about it another minute, that she would take care of it."

"Those were her words, that she would 'take care of it'?"

"Yes. And that things would be all right, she would see to it. I tried to stop her, to tell her not to get involved, but . . . she's difficult to stop when her mind is made up."

Aaron felt a chill spreading upward from his gut. It reached his chest, tightening it until he had trouble breathing.

"Just what," he asked slowly, "do you think she did to take care of it?"

Margaret's mouth tightened and she shook her head, but her eyes were wide and dark and agonized, and what she wasn't saying was blindingly obvious.

Margaret was afraid Shelby had killed Pruett.

Chapter Twenty

She hated hitchhiking. She always had, but now it seemed worse than it had as a kid. Maybe it was because she'd gotten used to having her own transport, maybe it was because it brought back old, painful memories, or maybe it was just because she was an adult now and knew exactly what the hungry-eyed look of some of the men who stopped for her meant.

She'd much rather ride with a woman, but few would stop for a hitchhiker, even a female one. She couldn't blame them; too many used hitching as a ruse to get to somebody they thought had a fat wallet that they could lift or a watch they could steal, and some used it as a stepping-stone to far worse things.

So she'd taken two rides, passing up one she truly didn't like the looks of, and hoped that her instincts weren't rusty enough to get her killed. She'd gotten lucky this last time; the driver was a grandfatherly gentleman who had done little except lecture her on the dangers of hitching and talk about his grandchildren.

The dangers of hitching, she thought tiredly, were nothing compared to the dangers of being around her. And the thought of Aaron's somehow being hurt because of her rash actions caused such pain she couldn't bear to think about it. She tightened her hands into fists, praying that she'd left soon enough and that she had led them away, those malevolent shadows.

"You all right?" The man sounded genuinely concerned.

"Yes," Shelby assured him, sounding calmer than she felt.

They passed the turnoff to Pete's ranch, and she felt another qualm at what she was leaving behind. She would have gladly hidden there again, but refused to risk the crusty old man, who could also lead the way to Margaret.

"This is as far as I'm going on the highway," the driver said a mile later, slowing the car.

"This is fine." She picked her backpack up from the floor of the car. "Thank you very much."

"You sure this is where you want to be, young lady? Not much here but this gas station and that old store up the mountain a mile or so."

"This is fine," she assured him again.

"You be careful now," he said as she got out.

"I will. Thanks again."

As he pulled away and turned left away from the mountain, she let out a relieved breath. When the man had said he would take her to his turnoff of the highway, which was what Outpost Boulevard turned into at the city limits, she hadn't dared hope he'd be coming this far. She'd just been satisfied that they were heading in the right direction.

And that she was leaving Aaron far behind.

After a wary glance at the empty blacktop behind her, she squared her shoulders, shifted her backpack, and started up the mountain road.

"She was trying to help me," Margaret said, her voice barely above a whisper.

Now that he had most of the story, Aaron didn't feel much better, and Margaret's unvoiced yet obvious fear that Shelby was the murderer didn't help any.

"I know she's been through some rough times, and

that she did things she wasn't proud of, but I just can't believe . . ."

Neither can I, Aaron thought wearily. But the fact that neither he nor this woman who was closest to Shelby could be completely convinced that she was incapable of murder given the right motivation only increased his agitation.

I'd do anything for her. . . .

"She didn't give you any hint of what she planned to do?"

"No. Just said that she would take care of it, not to worry anymore." She took a shaky breath. "I haven't seen her since. And only one short phone message that didn't tell me anything."

"What exactly did she say in the message?"

"She said again not to worry. That everything was all right, or would be soon. And she told me to wait, not to do anything—she really emphasized that—and that she'd explain as soon as she could."

Aaron sensed there was more, but rather than prod he simply waited. After a moment, in a voice tight with tears, Margaret went on.

"She said . . . that she loved me. She doesn't say that often. I think she was afraid."

"That she might not get another chance?"

"Something like that." She looked at him, her eyes pleading with him to understand. "Shelby doesn't scare easily, Mr. Montana."

"Don't I know it," he muttered.

"I think that frightened me more than anything."

"Does she have a gun?"

"Shelby? Of course not!"

"You're sure? Or are you assuming that because you've never seen one?"

She looked even more troubled. "No, I've never seen one, but we've never talked about it, either. It never occurred to me."

"Did she ever say—"

He broke off at a sound from the back of the house. His heart leapt. Shelby?

"Margaret?" It was a man's voice, deep and resonant.

"Oh, God," Margaret said, turning stark white. "Robert."

Aaron rose as a man came into the room from what was apparently the kitchen. He was about four inches shorter than Aaron, rather stocky, but there was a look of patience in his warm brown eyes that reminded Aaron of his mother.

He stared at Aaron for a moment, and that patient expression changed to one of sheer pain. He shifted his gaze to his wife. The agony Aaron had seen in his face echoed in his voice.

"Here, Margaret? In our home?"

Margaret rose slowly and none too steadily. "Robert—"

"I didn't want to believe it. I tried so hard not to believe it, but when you wouldn't talk to me, when you wouldn't tell me what was wrong although you were obviously hiding something—"

"Robert, I had no choice."

"Does our marriage mean so little to you? To bring him here, under my roof?"

Margaret frowned in puzzlement in the same instant Aaron realized the interpretation her husband had put on his presence here.

Robert Peterson turned on him then. "I may be older than you, and you may be bigger, but I swear to you, I will not give her up easily."

Aaron was taken aback, as much by the fierce determination in the man's voice as by his misinterpretation. He certainly didn't want to get into a fight with a man who had to be at least fifteen years older than he.

"Robert!" This time Margaret's voice was laced with utter shock. "What on earth are you thinking?"

"He's thinking," Aaron said, never taking his eyes off the approaching husband, "that I'm what you've been hiding from him."

Margaret turned to stare at Aaron. "You mean he thinks you and I—" Her head snapped back toward her husband. "You think I'm having an *affair* with this man?"

She sounded so incredulous that Robert stopped in his tracks. As both men watched her, color rose in her cheeks, and Aaron would have sworn there was a touch of pleasure in her blush. As if she were flattered by her husband's assumption.

"You're on the wrong track, Mr. Peterson," Aaron said. "Very wrong."

"Robert," Margaret said, "how could you think I would ever do that to you?"

Peterson, intent on his wife, barely glanced at Aaron before saying in a rush of emotion, "What was I supposed to think? You've been hiding something for weeks, acting so strangely, and you wouldn't talk to me, you were spending money at a rate entirely unlike you but no purchases ever showed up, you jumped at the slightest sound."

"Oh, Robert, I . . ."

Her voice trailed off, and she looked from her husband to Aaron, as if hoping for help.

"Oh, no," Aaron said. "This is between you two." He turned to go, then looked back at Margaret. "You know, with a little honesty, you could have avoided all of this in the first place. You might want to try it now."

He walked out then, leaving Margaret Peterson to explain to her husband however she would. He wanted to be angry with her, but it wasn't really her fault.

Everybody had things in their past that they wouldn't like advertised.

But most of all, he couldn't be angry with the one person on the planet Shelby trusted, even if he did wish he could have been the second.

Aaron was on the stairs—he'd taken to running up and down them to his office since he hadn't had time lately to keep up with his regular workouts—when his cell phone rang.

He stopped on the next landing and answered it.

"Hey, sorry," Mike's voice said, "but I'm going to have to back out of our handball game again."

"Coward," Aaron said, making a mental note to keep to the stairs for the rest of the week.

"Yeah, yeah," Mike retorted.

"The case?" Aaron asked, then wished he hadn't; he'd promised Mike to come clean, and he wanted to do that even less now than before, now that Shelby had slipped away from him. If she really was the killer, Mike was going to have a hard time forgiving that.

"Yeah." Mike hesitated, then added, "We brought in a suspect this morning."

Aaron's breath stopped in his throat. He couldn't have said a word even if he'd known what to say.

"Caught him back at the crime scene."

Him. They'd caught him, not her. He could breathe again.

"You mean they really do that?" he managed to get out.

"Sometimes. Out of compulsion, stupidity, or fear that they left something incriminating behind."

"Which was this?"

"Not sure yet. He says he was just one of Pruett's victims and was after the blackmail stuff, but we found a gun in his car. Of course, we won't know until ballistics comes back, but it's the right caliber. And he's got no alibi for the night of the murder."

"So he's . . . your prime suspect now?"

"Well, he's leading the pack, anyway. We're waiting on a conference with the D.A. right now to formally charge him. It sounds good."

Shelby hadn't done it. Aaron almost slid down to the floor, he was so relieved. He didn't think he said anything, but Mike spoke anyway.

"Look, Aaron, if your friend is just a victim, have them talk to me. They won't be in trouble, and when this is all over, they'll get whatever Pruett had on them back, as long as it's not criminal in nature."

"I'll . . . pass that along." *Assuming I ever have the chance,* he added silently.

He stayed there, leaning against the wall of the stairwell, for a minute after he'd disconnected from Mike. Finally, when he was sure he could trust his legs, he continued his journey up the stairs. His mind was racing every step of the way.

He had to find Shelby. But how? She'd left him no clue, just that damned note, with the splotch as if she'd been crying when she wrote it.

He should at least call Margaret and tell her the murderer had been arrested, or at least was in custody, about to be charged. It would relieve her, he was sure.

But then again, she might well be knee-deep in trying to explain everything to her husband, he thought as he recalled the scene he'd left behind.

"Damn," he muttered in frustration as he finally reached his office. He needed to sit down and think. He couldn't get rid of the feeling that he was overlooking something obvious here, but he needed a chance to sort it all out.

The minute he walked into Francie's outer office, he knew by the look on her face that he wasn't going to get that chance. She rose and followed him silently into his office, closing the door behind her, and he knew it was going to be even worse than he feared.

He sat down, leaned back in the chair and put his feet up on the desk. Rubbing temples that were beginning to throb, he said, "Okay, hit me with it. Digest version first."

"In order of occurrence or priority?"

Aaron sighed. "Occurrence."

"One failure to pay checkout."

"Only one?"

"So far. But housekeeping later reported they also took most of the room with them, including the television."

"Clever. Next?"

"Cletterer was spotted in the casino this morning."

"I thought he was still in jail."

"Robin checked with Derrick Andrews. Apparently he's been spotted in Reno, too."

Aaron didn't ask if they were certain; Derrick was rarely wrong. A few years ago he'd started a casino linkup system like one that was already in place in Las Vegas where he acted as clearinghouse and record keeper for all known cheats in the state, and the computerized facial-recognition program he used had revolutionized the task of catching cheaters. Within seconds, casinos could send him a live shot of a gambler they were suspicious of, and almost instantly get an answer out of the vast database of faces of known cheaters. Aaron had seen the potential immediately and had been one of Andrews's first subscribers.

"Have Robin check and see if he's been released."

"She's already on it."

"Okay." Still without moving, he asked, "Next?"

"One well-endowed female rail thief. At the crap table."

Aaron sighed. This was one of the more frequent problems. Someone stood at the tail of a table and used some kind of distraction—in this case, no doubt, a display of cleavage—to cover her pilfering of chips from other gamblers. If they were good, didn't get greedy, a twenty-dollar chip here, a fifty there, they could walk away with a considerable amount.

"She's been turned over?"

"The police picked her up about an hour ago," Francie said.

Aaron nodded. "Next?"

"They caught somebody at the slots this morning with an electronic programmer."

"Any idea how long he'd been at it?"

"He only had six hundred dollars on him, but the cashier *thinks* she's seen him before today."

"Great," Aaron said sourly. One guy had netted better than fifteen million dollars with one of those handheld gadgets that programmed the slot from the outside to pay off in multiples of the actual prize won. "Ought to go back to manual slots," he muttered. Then, "Next?"

"Ian Bedwyr called. One of his suppliers recalled today's entire purchase of beef, saying it was possibly tainted. He wants to know if you want him to close down or run with a limited menu."

"Beef only?"

"Yes. He said the chicken and seafood are fine."

"But won't be by tomorrow," Aaron said, knowing the Welshman insisted on the freshest of main ingredients. "Have him put whatever he's got at half price, run an ad on the in-house screens, get George to whip up some flyers and get them distributed. Make it a no-red-meat special or some such. He'll think of something."

"Hey, cousin! Top o' the morning to you."

Aaron nearly groaned aloud. The last thing he wanted to deal with right now was Hank. But there he was, strolling past the unguarded gate as jovially as the town jester.

"Sorry," Francie muttered. She was usually at her desk to stop such things.

"And Miss Francine, you're looking gorgeous, as always," Hank said, as if he hadn't heard her at all, although Aaron suspected he had. He had carefully selective hearing, especially when he was drunk. Which, Aaron observed wearily, he was now. He managed not to glance at his watch; he was fairly sure it was past noon at least.

Francie decamped with uncharacteristic haste, leaving him with his cousin, who plopped down in the chair she'd never taken, and put his feet up much as Aaron had.

"So, where's the pixie?"

He had no answer for that, so he ignored it. "Did you want something, Hank, or did you just drop in to round out my already rotten day?"

Hank lifted a dark brow. "Testy, aren't we?"

He was in no mood for his cousin's patented charm. "What is it, Hank?"

"Why are you so sure I want something?"

Aaron just looked at him. Hank sighed. "All right, all right. There's a small matter of . . . er, a bounced check. Or one that's about to."

Well, this was a new one. "To what liquor store?" he asked dryly.

Hank drew himself up. "I would never ask you to cover that. I know how you feel."

"Doesn't stop you, though, does it?"

Hank chose to ignore that, as usual. "It's to a charity. That's the only reason I'm even bringing it up."

Aaron raised a brow. "You wrote a check to a charity?"

"I'm as philanthropic as the next guy, when I can afford it."

"Or when I can," Aaron muttered. "What charity and how much?"

"Horizon House. Five hundred."

The irony bit deep; Horizon House was a drug and alcohol rehab halfway house. "Who talked you into that one?"

"A charming young lady named Max. She's very persuasive. And I adore her."

"So that's it. I knew there had to be an ulterior motive."

"Suspicious type, aren't you?"

Strangely, his cousin's offhand quip struck home. Was he? He'd never thought of himself that way before. Realistic, yes, maybe even cynical at times, but never suspicious. But was he showing his true colors now, by being able to suspect Shelby of a heinous crime? Was he—

The intercom buzzer on his phone interrupted his thoughts. He reached for it, then when Francie spoke, wished he hadn't.

"It's Cindy on line two, Aaron. She sounds . . . nearly hysterical."

Given that that was Cindy's normal state when anything went wrong, Aaron didn't want to think how bad it must be for his unflappable assistant to even mention it.

"I told her I'd see if I could find you," Francie added.

Bless her, she always gave him an out. And right now, for the first time in a very long time, he was tempted to take it. He felt an odd tension in his muscles, a near hum in his head. He felt as if one more wrong thing would shatter his last bit of control.

But he wouldn't stick Francie with lying for him. Not to his ex-wife. He braced himself and picked up the phone.

Hysterical was an understatement. It took him several minutes and virtually all the patience he had left to calm her down enough to understand what she was saying. When he realized it was a car accident, he drew from some deeper well of endurance, feeling even as he did so that he was scraping the bottom.

"Are you hurt?"

"N-No," Cindy stuttered.

"You're sure?"

"The . . . the paramedics said I wasn't."

Paramedics? He didn't like the sound of that. "Where are you?"

She told him, an intersection he recognized, and before he realized what he was doing, the old habits kicked in and he told her he'd be right there.

When he hung up, he slumped, feeling more exhausted than he could remember feeling since his father's nearly fatal heart attack. He propped his elbows on his desk and buried his face in his hands.

"Someday you're going to tell us all to go to hell."

Hank's voice was so soft it took a split second for Aaron to remember he was here.

"And when you do," Hank went on, "I think I'll be cheering, even though I'll probably be first on the list."

To Aaron's shock, his cousin rose and quietly left, without another word about the loan he'd come for. Aaron hated moments like this. It would be so much easier to just hate Hank for throwing away his life. But every now and then he caught a glimpse of what his cousin could be, and he couldn't give up on him.

Francie didn't say a word when he told her he was leaving, but he could see it in her eyes, the wondering when he was ever going to stop this.

Maybe sooner than you all think.

It was a novel sensation for him to consider shucking some of the responsibilities he took for granted. It kept him occupied until he saw the flash of red lights on the side of the road, marking the scene of Cindy's accident.

He saw her car before she saw him. It didn't take him long to assess the situation.

He walked over to the paramedic van. A young man in uniform sat on the back bumper, holding Cindy's hand and patting it gently. She looked as she always did, pale and fragile. She seemed fairly calm at the moment, but if she ran true to form that would end the moment she saw him.

And suddenly he was tired of it. He'd loved her once, and had sworn that, as Megan's mother, he would always look out for her. But she'd become a basket case since Megan's death, and Aaron was weary of always carrying that basket. Everyone had been telling him for years that she would never learn to stand on her own if he kept propping her up. Now, for the first time, he began to see that he hadn't been doing her any favors.

"Aaron!" she wailed the instant she spotted him.

"Cindy," he said levelly.

She leapt up, clearly uninjured, but started to sag against him weakly. He sidestepped her, walking past her to the medics.

"She's all right?"

"Fine. Not a mark. The car either, and barely a scratch on the road barrier. We're only here because . . ."

The young man's voice faded away, but Aaron could guess the rest. "Because she was hysterical?"

"Aaron—" Cindy began to protest. He held up a hand, and surprisingly, she quieted.

"Afraid so," the other medic said gently.

"Thanks for the effort."

"No problem, Mr. Montana."

He winced. Had she told everyone who he was? The Montana name carried some weight with the fire department and paramedics in Outpost; ever since they had revived his father after his heart attack, he'd made sure a nice chunk of the Montana donation budget went to the paramedic program.

"I'm sure you guys have better things to do," he told the medics. The way they scrambled to depart told him a lot about what they'd been dealing with. He knew all too well.

He turned back to Cindy, who was working up to another breakdown.

"Don't even start." He said it flatly, startling her. "Your car is fine. You are fine. Get in, go home."

She stared at him. "But—"

"Do it."

"But I'm far too shaky to drive."

"Then park the car. Take a cab."

Tears began to well up in her eyes. "Why are you being so cold?"

"This is as close to nothing as you can get in an accident. Just *deal* with it, Cindy."

She reacted as if he'd slapped her.

"But *you're* supposed to deal with it! That's why I married you."

It barely hurt; he'd figured out long ago that she'd married him only to have a bulwark between herself and the big, bad world. He should have realized much sooner than he had that there was no other reason a frail beauty like Cindy would have married a man like him.

"And you divorced me because I didn't do it to your standards," he pointed out wearily. "Maybe it's time you found somebody who will. Or," he added, thinking of all the times she'd threatened it, "go home to your mother. I'll even buy the ticket."

Her eyes widened. He expected her to throw Megan up at him, to blame him once more for her death.

Instead she shouted, "Maybe I will!" and whirled and ran to her car.

Great, he mutterd as she drove off faster than she should have. *Watch her have a real accident now. So much for my foray into shirking responsibility.*

All the way back to his office he waited for another panicked phone call. When it didn't come, he couldn't decide if that was good or bad.

He passed up the stairs this time; he felt too tired to do it again.

Francie, thankfully, didn't stand up this time when he came in. But she was on the phone. Probably taking another disaster call, he thought wearily, pausing beside her desk. It was turning into that kind of day. All he wanted to do was find Shelby, and he was stuck here putting out fires. Not that he had any idea where to begin looking anyway.

"Now what?" he asked when she hung up.

"That? That was Ian. He's come up with a shrimp dish to die for that he's going to use as the special for an 'impromptu Mardi Gras' night, according to him."

"Bless him," Aaron said, meaning it.

He was almost to his office door when she spoke again, "Oh, and Shelby called."

He whipped around. "What?"

If Francie was startled by his reaction it didn't show. "Just before Ian called, so I didn't have a chance to call you."

He tried to keep his voice even. "What did she say?"

"She wouldn't leave a message, just wanted to talk to you."

And he'd been out nursemaiding Cindy through something barely worse than a flat tire. "Where was she?"

"She didn't say," Francie said, frowning. "Just left a number. I suppose I should have asked, but she hung up rather quickly. It seems to be your day for upset women."

Aaron went very still. "Upset?"

"Well, perhaps that's not the right word. She wasn't upset like Cindy gets. She sounded . . ."

When she hesitated, Aaron prompted, "Sounded what, Francie?"

"It sounds silly," Francie protested.

"Please," he said, straining for calm.

After a moment she answered, "Scared."

Chapter Twenty-One

Aaron listened to the ringing, his fingers gripping the receiver so tightly they were starting to cramp.

"Come on, answer," he begged fiercely. But fate seemed to have more torture in mind. Seven rings, eight, nine, ten . . .

He was about to give up and have Francie try and track the number down in the reverse directory when he at last heard a click.

"Hello?"

It was a man. He sounded older, and, Aaron realized, puzzled, not suspicious or wary. Still, not wanting to scare the man into hanging up, Aaron chose his words carefully.

"I'm sorry, I'm not sure I have the right number. Where are you?"

"This is Hayne's Grocery, on High Valley Road. Or at least, it's the pay phone out in front."

Aaron nearly dropped the phone. *What the hell?*

In his shock, it was a moment before he could manage to get any words out. "Are you . . . do you work there?"

"I'm Joe Haynes. I own the place. Why are you calling a pay phone?"

"I got an . . . urgent call from this number, about ten minutes ago."

"The girl? The little blonde?"

Hope soared in him, and he nearly gasped with relief. It really had been Shelby. "Yes. Yes, is she
there?"

"No, not anymore. She bought some stuff, waited
maybe about five more minutes, but then some guy in
a fancy white car pulled up, and she took off out the
back door."

Aaron's flash of hope died, and fear rushed in to
take its place. "Did he see her? The man in the car?"
The man hesitated, and Aaron said urgently, "Look,
he's after her, and he's not a nice guy."

"I got that feel. Didn't like the cut of his jib, if you
get my drift. All slicked up and one of those silly
pinky rings. Came in and started asking if she'd been
here. Said he was her brother."

"He's not."

"Didn't think so," the man said. "Didn't like his
eyes, either. So I didn't tell him anything."

"Thank you," Aaron said fervently.

"I got a granddaughter," he said, and Aaron
guessed that was explanation enough.

"If you see her, tell her to stay put. I'm on my way."

"And you would be . . . ?"

"Aaron Montana."

He hung up before the man could respond, noting
absently that his hand was steadier than he would
have expected.

He tried to think. There was something he should
be seeing here, something obvious. But his mind
couldn't quite get past the fact that Shelby was less
than a quarter of a mile from where Megan had died.
That she had called from the store Cindy had stopped
at, from the exact phone she had used when Megan
had wandered away.

The very last thing he wanted to do was return to
the place where he'd spent the worst days of his life.
The place where he'd searched endlessly, uselessly. The

place where he'd finally taken refuge on the ledge overlooking the picturesque lake that had taken the light out of his life, and pondered whether to ever come down.

But he couldn't leave Shelby's call unanswered. He knew just how hard it must have been for her, determined, independent, and stubborn Shelby, to call him for help. He had to go. And he had to go now. It didn't matter where she was.

He pushed himself up, grabbed his jacket and phone, and quickly stepped out from behind his desk. The glint of gold from the corner caught his eye, and he glanced at the phoenix. He remembered how Shelby had looked at it, how she had reacted exactly as he had, how she saw in it not the price of the gold but the value of the vision.

And he remembered the night spent in her arms, the night that would be one of the most treasured memories of his life, no matter what. She had to have known, even then, what she was going to do. Had to have known there was a chance she wouldn't survive. So she'd picked the best way she knew to say good-bye.

By the time he reached the parking area he was running.

He must be getting hardheaded in his old age, Mike thought. Here was a perfect suspect, handed to him on a silver platter, and he still wasn't happy. Franco had motive. Betrayal and blackmail were among the strongest around. Franco would probably kill without a second thought to regain that videotape Pruett had. No self-described ladies' man would want it to get around that he was in the habit of committing interesting acts with an obvious transvestite. He had opportunity, attitude, the right kind of weapon, no alibi, and had been apprehended at the murder scene. What the heck else did he want?

Maybe it was the silver-platter part, Mike told himself tiredly. He didn't trust anything that came that easily. In his work or in his life.

He unlocked his desk and pulled out the now dog-eared printout of Pruett's list. Then he took out the file folder containing his notes on the suspects who were not on the blackmail list. He started to go through it all again, with the doggedness that had broken more than one case for him. But his mind kept bouncing, from suspect to suspect and, more often than he liked, to Aaron. His friend was deeply involved in this somehow, hiding something, and that made Mike very nervous.

He was going to have to do something about Aaron. But for now, he had a prime suspect sitting downstairs, and just because he was sticking to his story didn't mean Mike could give up talking to him.

He had just put his weapon in the gun locker outside the jail doors when his cell phone rang. He shut the locker door and locked it, then pulled out the phone.

"Delano."

"Mike? Chuck Nguyen."

The county ballistics lab. Mike's pulse kicked up a notch. "You got something?"

"You're not going to like it," Chuck warned.

"The gun's not a match?"

"Nope. Sorry. There's no way it fired the round that killed Pruett."

Back to square one.

Shelby, already furious with herself, sat on a boulder and wondered if she'd made the biggest mistake yet, charging off into the wilderness like this.

But that wasn't what she was really angry about.

She was furious that she had weakened, that when she'd spotted her pursuer so close on her tail that she recognized his face, she had panicked and called Aaron. After all her efforts to put distance between herself and Aaron, she'd gone and done that.

She couldn't worry about it anymore now. Now she had to stay alive. And that meant staying a step ahead of the man behind her.

She'd hoped that he was a city type and would hesitate before plunging into the backcountry after her. Problem was, she was a city type herself. All of her talents for survival on the run had been honed on the streets of L.A., not the rugged heights of the Sierra Nevada.

She did know how to start a fire with almost nothing—a skill you picked up if you didn't want to freeze on the rare nights when L.A.'s temperature dropped. She was good at climbing, too, and she was in good shape. She'd picked up some nutrition bars and water in the little store where she'd called Aaron, enough to keep her going for a bit. If she put on all the clothing she had, with her jacket and the sweatshirt from the Golden Phoenix, she might just survive the possible near-freezing temperatures overnight. She set her jaw; she'd just have to get through it.

The directions that the man at the store had given her had been easy enough to follow. She'd found the blaze mark on the tree, and the trail it indicated. It had been mostly uphill, and by the time she'd reached this small clearing she'd needed a rest. The adrenaline jolt of seeing her shadow so close had ebbed, leaving her a little wobbly.

But she was steady now, and she'd better get moving.

She wondered if this mountain was going to claim another life before this was over, if her pursuer's work would be done for him by the unforgiving wilderness that had claimed Aaron's little girl.

She hoped not. While nothing could be as horrible as Megan's death, she didn't want Aaron to have another bad memory of this place to carry around. No matter what his feelings toward her were by now—

She froze. Had that been a footstep, below her? The scrape of a shoe on stone? Was he already here, after her on the mountainside? She held her breath, listening. She heard nothing, but she didn't dare assume it was nothing.

She started upward once more.

It hit him when he was far enough up the mountain road to be desperate for something to distract him from the painfully familiar surroundings. He swore low and harsh, wondering why on earth he hadn't realized it before.

If the murderer was in custody, and it wasn't Shelby, then why was Shelby still being pursued?

Was it possible her situation had nothing to do with Pruett after all? That it was purely coincidental that Pruett had been killed the morning she'd shown up on the Golden Phoenix's cameras?

He couldn't believe it. It all had to be connected. Which narrowed down his choices of feasible answers.

One, Shelby was the real killer. Or, he amended, fighting for rationality, someone thought she was the killer.

Two—

He slowed his pace slightly as the idea formed.

Two, Shelby knew who the real killer was.

He could picture it so clearly—Shelby, loyal and courageous, determined to make everything all right for the one person she loved, using skills she'd learned as a runaway to try and steal Margaret's negatives from Pruett and free her mentor from his bloodsucking grip.

And instead stumbling onto his murder.

And his murderer.

It all fit. It all fit so perfectly.

And then the ramifications sank in, making him shiver. Mike had the wrong man. Which meant the man after Shelby wasn't a simple stalker, he was a killer. And Shelby could put him away.

He *had* to kill her.

"Not again," Aaron whispered. "God, not again."

He jammed the accelerator to the floor, and for the first time in seven years, he drove this road with no further thought of what had happened here then.

Chapter Twenty-Two

Aaron pulled into the dirt and gravel parking area in front of the small grocery store, feeling the tug of unwelcome familiarity. How many times had he parked here before setting off on the endless treks through the hills, searching, always searching? He'd come to know this place and the country around it better than he knew the Golden Phoenix; he thought he could still find his way to that damned lake blindfolded.

He walked quickly inside, looking for the man who had answered the phone. He found him in the back, restocking the soda cooler.

"Mr. Haynes?"

The man straightened—slowly—and turned around. He looked about seventy, wiry and spry, the eyes in his weathered face bright and alert. Before Aaron could say anything more, he frowned.

"I know you, don't I?"

"I used to . . . come in here a lot," Aaron said reluctantly.

The frown deepened, then vanished. "Hey, I recollect now. You're the guy from years ago, with the little girl, aren't you?"

"Yes."

"Awful thing. Still feel bad about it, y'know."

"So do I," Aaron said softly. Then, before the man

could delve any deeper, he changed the subject, reminding the man of his recent call.

"Wait a minute—you're the same guy who called about that little gal?"

"I'll explain it all later," Aaron said, desperation sharpening his tone. "Have you seen her again?"

The man didn't hesitate this time, as if the reminder of the previous tragedy had somehow given Aaron credibility in his eyes.

"No, she never came back inside. But I saw her heading up the road toward the trailheads, alone." He shook his head. "Not a safe thing for a woman, I don't think. But she seemed like a headstrong sort."

You don't know the half of it, Aaron thought.

"And that man I told you about, that slickster? Saw his car headed the same way a minute or two later."

Aaron's nerves tightened another notch.

"She your wife? Doesn't look like the lady I remember from before."

"She's not," Aaron said. *Not even close . . .*

The man looked puzzled. "Then why would she want to go up to the lake where your little girl drowned?"

Aaron went very still. "What?"

"That's what she asked me, when she came in."

With a tremendous effort, Aaron kept himself from yelling. "She asked what?"

"How to get to that lake. Tried to tell her it wasn't an easy trek."

"She's tougher than she looks," Aaron said, his mind racing. He had told her about the lake, he knew, and how isolated it was, but he couldn't remember how much more he'd said. He couldn't remember much of anything about that outpouring, except the incredible relief he'd experienced when it was done.

He had to assume he'd told her everything. He couldn't risk being wrong.

"Mr. Haynes, this is very important. What exactly did you tell her?"

"I told her where the main trail was. And how to get to the overlook."

"From the turnout?" Aaron asked. It was barely a mile up the road, a worn spot where over the years vehicles had stopped to look at the view back down the mountain. Few people knew of the faint trails that laced the mountainside going the other way.

The old man nodded.

Aaron turned on his heel and headed for the door, but after a few steps he stopped. He looked back at Haynes. "Is the shortcut out back over the ridge still passable?"

It was the way he'd always gone, after Megan had been found. By the time the torturous track dumped him out on the ledge, he was too exhausted to seriously consider throwing himself off it. The trail from the turnout had a branch that led there, too, but it was a much longer, easier route.

"Far's I know."

Aaron was out the door in seconds, barely remembering to toss a thank-you over his shoulder at the man. He yanked out his cell phone as he went toward the back of the small building. He didn't know if he would get much reception up here, but it was worth a try. He dialed Mike.

His friend sounded a bit short-tempered when he answered.

"Where . . . you?" Mike asked. "You . . . really breaking up."

"So are you. Quick, then. I think you may have the wrong guy in jail."

". . . know. . . . gun didn't fire the . . . But . . . the hell . . . you know?"

"Because I think there's an eyewitness. If I can keep her alive."

"Damn it . . . ron, you're breaking . . . Did you say . . . thing about a witness?"

This was hopeless. He cut to the essentials. "The killer's here. I may need help." He heard Mike swear, this time loud and clear. "The lake," he said quickly. "Where they found Megan."

Nothing. The phone was completely silent. He had no idea if Mike had heard enough, if he had sworn because of what Aaron had said, or because he couldn't hear him at all.

It didn't change anything. He still had to get up to the lake as fast as he could. Faster. And he'd better not count on any help. Even if Mike had gotten the message, it would take him at least half an hour to get here.

He was on his own.

He suppressed a shudder as he started up the narrow, steep track. He couldn't believe this was happening, that he was heading back to the scene of his own personal hell on earth. But he never even considered turning back.

Not when Shelby had called him for help. Shelby, who didn't need anyone.

He stopped in his tracks as a revelation hit him. He had married Cindy because she needed him. He had kept her in his life even after their divorce, because she needed him.

Shelby didn't need him.

But she had *wanted* him. Enough to come to him in the night, to take what he knew was a great risk for her. To come to him, even knowing she was going to leave.

Needed. Wanted.

He'd never really appreciated the difference between them. Until now.

Oddly buoyed by the realization, he started up again even faster, making any speed he could by jumping from boulder to boulder, or climbing straight up instead of taking the easier switchback.

And every step of the way he prayed he would have a chance to tell Shelby how being wanted made him feel.

And that the place that had nearly destroyed his life once didn't get another try.

Damn the bitch! What the hell did she think she was up to?

He didn't *like* it up here. That podunk burg of Outpost had been bad enough, but at least it was fairly civilized. This road was barely driveable, constantly throwing rocks up against the car's undercarriage, and with a sheer drop-off on the downhill side that should be marked with barricades six feet tall.

A good place to dump a body, he thought; it was about the only good thing he could say about the place.

After she'd somehow vanished back in town, he'd had a hunch that she might run this way. But he thought she would go back to that horse ranch. He'd staked out the turnoff, and been startled when he'd seen her go right past it in that car with that old man. So instead, she was heading into what appeared like total wilderness, and he wondered if she'd finally cracked under the strain.

If only he'd been a few minutes quicker, he could have caught up with her before she'd gone into that store. And that old geezer of a clerk was no help; he was half senile, could barely remember that she'd been in there at all.

He peered ahead as he drove, grimacing at the dust that was blowing. And settling, he was sure, on his carefully gelled hair. He'd dyed it darker and slicked it back, and added a pair of wire-rim glasses, hoping the disguise would enable him to get closer to her.

But she was clearly on the run now. He'd flushed her out into the open, and now she was his.

He squinted into the sun, hating that the glasses prevented him from using his sunglasses. He reached up to yank them off, then froze.

There she was.

There was no mistaking it, she was walking on the side of the road as openly as could be.

The road curved and he lost sight of her. He could simply mow her down and never have to get out of the car, he thought. But then he'd have to have the car repaired, or dump it with damage and evidence, and that was always chancy. Besides, he wanted to do this up close and very personal.

He glanced at the weapon beside him on the seat. When he realized he was heading out into the country, he'd changed to one of his favorites, a Dan Wesson pistol with interchangeable barrels. He'd considered the eight-inch barrel but settled on the six-inch. That should give him more than enough range, and then he would simply destroy the barrel and replace it.

He rolled down the passenger window and reached for the gun; he wasn't about to give her the chance to get away again. He slowed as the turn tightened, then as it eased he leaned forward, ready to speed up the instant she came into view again.

She was gone.

Instinctively he hit the brakes. The car skewed wildly sideways on the gravel, toward the drop.

"Shit!"

He whipped the wheel around. The car came to a shuddering stop barely a yard from the edge. He let out a string of oaths as his heart hammered in his chest.

"God*damn* that bitch!"

Slowly he eased the car across to the wide spot beside the road. He got out and peered over the edge.

There was no sign of life, nothing moving except a couple of birds circling below. He turned to look the other way, at the rugged mountainside. He saw a couple of small signs and what appeared to be a path.

He detested the idea, but he knew he had no choice. He had to get her.

Swearing under his breath, he leaned into the car. He grabbed the pistol from the seat, then started toward the trees.

She'd found Aaron's ledge. She knew it was his because she was looking down on a pristine little lake. It was a mere pond compared to big brother Tahoe farther up in the mountains, but deadly for all its small size. She could picture Aaron here, torturing himself with images of a small body floating in the icy water. He wouldn't need his ex-wife to blame him, she thought. He'd do a fine job of that himself.

She'd come up here because Aaron had said how easy it was to get lost, and right now lost was exactly what she wanted to be. But her pursuer was relentless. She'd managed to elude him so far—by barely seconds down on the road—but she'd gone as far now as she could go.

She knew it was only a matter of time before the killer found her. He was clumsily but doggedly search-ing the slope below. Sooner or later, he would find the faint trail that branched off the main path.

Now she was backed into a small alcove in the rock face above the ledge. She got out the kitchen knife, then gathered what other pitiful weapons she could find; a small limb that looked solid, a longer, thinner one that she sharpened into a fairly pointed makeshift lance, rocks of varying sizes. It was all she could do; if she moved again, he might see her. So she hunkered down and waited, watching, listening.

She shivered involuntarily. She knew it was because

she was tired; it wasn't really cold up here. At least, not yet. Night would be a very different story. She had a handful of Golden Phoenix matchbooks, but she might as well send up a flare as light a fire.

She shivered again. She sat there, wishing she'd told Aaron everything. The whole sorry story of how she'd gotten into this mess. At least then, if she died, he wouldn't remember her just as the woman he'd suspected of murder.

But what she wished she'd told him most of all was how she felt about him.

She should have trusted him. As everyone in his life trusted him, because they knew he would never let them down.

But she hadn't believed it, not in time.

She glanced down the hill, where she could hear a faint rustling. She would rather face a natural predator, a bear or a wolf, than this. At least an animal would only be doing what he'd been born to do. A man who hunted like this was twisted, perverted, and made for a much uglier way to die.

Not that she was going to give up without a fight. But she doubted she was a match for the cold-eyed man she'd seen shoot Jack Pruett down without a second's hesitation.

Something moved in the brush barely ten feet away.

Stifling a cry, Shelby grabbed the knife in one hand and the biggest rock she thought she could throw in the other. Had he made it up behind her without her hearing it? Then what was it that she'd heard down below?

Maybe this was just an animal. The rock first, she decided. She braced herself, ready to throw the instant whatever it was emerged from the underbrush.

She saw a shape through the leaves.

A man.

She held her breath. Cocked her arm.

He took a step closer.

She hurled the rock with all her strength.

The man seemed to sense what she was going to do in the instant before she did it, but he still barely had time to dive sideways for cover. He hit the ground hard, and she heard a grunt of pain as he collided with a sharp outcropping of rock.

He rolled and came up on his knees, hissing out her name.

It was Aaron.

Shelby smothered her gasp; the killer was still out there, and she knew the longer he thought she was alone up here, the better.

"Aaron?" she whispered harshly. She stared at him in disbelief. "How—?"

He got up gingerly and headed toward her, one finger to his lips.

The moment he was close enough he grabbed her, hugging her fiercely, then holding her back by the shoulders as if to inspect her for signs of injury.

"How did you get past him?" she asked, her voice low but tight with shock.

"I didn't. I came up the back way."

She stared past him. "Over that ridge? *That's* the trail you were talking about?"

He nodded. "I know this piece of ground a lot better than I'd like to. And I planned on starting here on the overlook because of the view of the area."

"Starting?"

"My search for you," he said grimly, his voice husky with the effort to keep it a whisper.

The memory of the last time he'd searched this ground crashed in on her. "Oh, God, Aaron. I'm sorry. I should have told you everything long ago."

"Yes." He didn't bother denying it.

"I was just so scared, and trusting . . . isn't easy for me."

"Damn near impossible, apparently," he said.

"I didn't kill anyone, Aaron." The words she'd wished she could say came out in a rush.

"I know."

She blinked. "You do?"

He nodded. "But you saw him"—he nodded toward the slope—"kill Pruett, didn't you?"

She gaped at him. How on earth . . . ?

"It took me a while to put it together, but it's the only thing that makes sense. The only thing that fits with who you are."

She gulped in some air, almost dizzy with the shock of realizing that he'd put it all together himself, with nothing to go on but faith. In her.

Everything else she'd wanted to say—including the most important thing of all—bubbled up, until she wasn't able to hold it back. "I have to tell you—"

"It's got to wait, Shelby."

"But Aaron, please, if something goes wrong, I don't want to die without telling you—"

"You are not," he said fiercely, as if he knew she'd been sitting here resigning herself to dying at the hands of a proven killer, "going to die."

"I don't care about me, but I could never live with it if you died because of me."

He looked as if he wanted to hug her again. She bit back a harsh breath. It didn't matter whether he loved her back, the fact that she loved him was, to her, miracle enough. She didn't want to die regretting that she hadn't told him.

"Nobody's dying up here today," Aaron said grimly. "This damn place has claimed all the lives it's going to. Now, where is he?"

She made herself think. "Only about a third of the way up, I think. He's . . . not rushing."

"He thinks he's got you cornered, no doubt."

"Doesn't he?"

"Not if we move fast." He glanced up the slope. "It's a tough climb. And it'll be tougher going down. Can you manage?"

"I'll manage. But what about him," Shelby asked, glancing warily down the mountain. "Won't he just follow us?"

"If we're quiet, he won't even know until he gets up here and sees that the trail dead-ends. Or seems to." He looked around, spotted the knife she'd dropped when she'd realized it was him.

"Hand me that."

"Sure. It's yours anyway," she said apologetically.

She handed him the blade, keeping a cautious eye downslope. She frowned when she saw he was digging a hole in the spot where he'd come up over the ridgeline—she could see now, the faintest sign of not really a trail but more of an animal track—her brows creased in puzzlement. But when he yanked a full branch off the back side of a nearby greasewood bush, she realized what he was up to.

"I'm trusting he's a city boy," Aaron said as he shoved the branch into the hole. Shelby dropped quickly to her knees beside the makeshift plant and helped him fill in the hole. When she stood up, Aaron smoothed over the dirt, and added a few of her gathered rocks artfully.

It wouldn't stand up to close scrutiny, but at first glance, it looked like a living bush. And it totally hid the narrow track they were about to take. At the least, it would slow him down.

"Let's go," Aaron said, this time casting a glance down the mountain himself.

The words rushed to her lips again, and again she had to bite them back; there truly was no time. Instead, when he turned back to her, she reached up and kissed him.

For a moment, he just stared at her. Then he said

gruffly, "If that was just for luck, I don't want to know."

Before she could answer that it was much more than just for luck, he had turned and started down the track.

Chapter Twenty-Three

Mike wasn't sure what he was doing, what he was looking for. He wasn't even sure he'd interpreted Aaron's broken phone call correctly. But he'd known even before this call that his friend was knee-deep in this somehow.

If he'd heard right, it was neck-deep now.

The big question, Mike thought as he headed up the mountain road, wasn't how Aaron was involved. It wasn't even how he had known the man they had in custody likely wasn't the killer.

The big question was, had he really said he had a witness to the murder?

It was strange, being up here again. He hadn't been since those long ago days he tried to forget, days spent searching from dawn to dark, uselessly, hopelessly. It was hard enough for him, remembering the bright-eyed little sprite who had called him Uncle Mike. He couldn't imagine what would bring Aaron up here again.

For a while Mike had been greatly worried about Aaron's solitary trips to the scene of his daughter's death. He'd half expected to get a late-night call that Aaron had followed the child he'd loved so much.

But Aaron had finally pulled out of his nosedive. As far as Mike knew, after that first three or four months, Aaron had never come back up here.

Until now.

If, of course, he'd heard that right. But the only words that had come through were "Meg" and "lake," and this was the only thing that made sense.

Still, he was uncertain enough to be relieved when he rounded a curve and saw the little grocery store that had been the base for that tragic search seven years ago. And saw Aaron's Yukon parked beside it.

He quickly pulled in next to it, got out, and headed inside.

"Y'know," the old man behind the counter said when Mike identified himself as an officer, "I knew something was going on. First that girl, then that snaky character, then the big fellow."

Girl? Snaky character? It didn't take much to figure out that Aaron was "the big fellow," but who was the rest of the cast here? After the man explained what he'd seen, Mike asked in frustration, "Did Aaron— the big guy—give you any clue as to what the heck is going on?"

The man seemed to appreciate his mood. "Nope. Got the feel he was pretty worried about that little miss, though. And didn't much like the idea of that man being around her."

Mike's mind was racing. If Aaron was worried about the girl, she had to be the witness. As for the man . . .

The killer's here.

He was sure that was what Aaron had said. And according to what this man was saying, Aaron had gone after the girl, toward the lake where Megan had died.

Mike stared at the photograph on the wall over the old-style, noncomputerized cash register. A photograph of that very lake. "Damn it, Aaron, when did you take to being reckless?" he muttered under his breath.

"Why don't you ask him?" the man said, pointing toward the back of the store.

Mike's head whipped around.

Through the window in the back door he could see them, coming down off the last slope of the mountain in a rush. Aaron hit the bottom, then turned to help the person behind him with the last small leap. He moved with exquisite care, as if handling spun glass.

For a moment Mike just stared. Even though the woman looked a bit bedraggled, she was beautiful. And Aaron was looking at her as if he knew that perfectly well. More, his eyes were fastened on her as if she were the only woman in the world. Mike searched his memory, but couldn't remember Aaron ever looking at a woman like that.

In spite of everything, he felt himself start to grin.

But then he saw Aaron staring back up the mountain intently, and the grin faded. Did that mean the killer was that close?

He started toward the back of the store, but when Aaron and the woman began to hurry toward where the cars were parked, he reversed course and headed for the front.

He stepped out onto the wooden porch of the western-style building at the same moment that Aaron's companion stopped dead. She was staring at the cars. More likely, Mike thought, at his car, the stock, boring kind of sedan that shouted "cop."

He stepped down onto the gravel parking area, the sound echoing in the mountain quiet. The woman's head snapped around, and she took a step back so quickly Mike knew it was instinctive. Aaron's arm went around her shoulders, and he said something to her. She looked up at him. Mike could see her expression.

Finally, he thought. Somebody who looks at him and really *sees*.

He started toward them. She watched him warily, and Mike had little doubt that if Aaron hadn't been there she would have run. He slowed his pace, hoping it would look less threatening. After another quiet word from Aaron, the pair started to close the gap from their end.

"Are you all right?" Mike asked Aaron, although he was studying the woman. She was short, maybe five-one or -two, and had a quick, smooth way of moving that spoke of more strength than her appearance might suggest.

"Fine," Aaron said. "Barely."

Mike glanced up at the mountain. "He's up there?"

Aaron nodded. "Looking for her. Near the lake overlook. With luck, he doesn't know she's gone and he'll be out there a while." He belatedly seemed to realize an introduction was in order. "Mike, this is Shelby Wyatt. Shelby—"

"Mike Delano," she finished for him, with a wary nod at Mike, clearly not about to accept his proffered hand. "The cop."

Her tone told Mike a lot about Aaron's problem, and why he had kept this from him. He'd deal with that later.

"Is that really my killer out there?" he asked.

"It is," Shelby said, in the flat, unarguable voice of someone who was utterly positive. She definitely was, Mike thought, the witness.

"I've got to call in for help, then."

"His car is parked up the road," Shelby said.

"At that turnout," Aaron added. "Where the main trail to the lake starts."

"I remember," Mike said, knowing he didn't have to explain why. "Is there any other way out of here than that way and the way you came?"

"Not unless you want to walk to California," Aaron said.

"Then I'll need a description," Mike said.

Aaron had hung around Mike long enough to know

the drill. "He's about five-eight, not heavy but with a bit of a gut, medium-brown hair, kind of . . . fluffy, no facial hair—"

Aaron stopped as Shelby shook her head. "He's changed today. His hair's darker, nearly as dark as yours. And he's got it all slicked back, with gel or something. But it's him."

"That must be what Mr. Haynes meant when he called him a 'slickster.' " Aaron said. A split second later he added, "He must have decided he'd better change his look, now that both Shelby and I got a good look at him when he grabbed her."

"Grabbed her?"

"Inside the Golden Phoenix."

"This is a long story, I see. But right now I just need to know what to look for."

"He's wearing a brown leather jacket. Some kind of dressy pants, brown too," Shelby said. "And he's got a flashy diamond ring on his pinky."

"Does he know you saw him, his new look?"

"I don't think so." Then, with a tiny quirk of her mouth, she added, "He's wearing dress shoes. He's probably slipping all over up there."

"Maybe we'll get lucky and he'll fall off a cliff," Mike muttered. Shelby gave him a rather startled look. "A guy can hope, can't he?"

Slowly, a smile curved Shelby's mouth. Mike's eyes widened. *Wow*, he thought inanely. It seemed a good time to ask the question he had been afraid would put her off. "I'm not doubting you, but I have to ask specifically. You're sure it's the guy who killed Jack Pruett?"

She didn't even blink. "Yes."

"Then I'd better get moving. I'll call for backup, then go sit on his car. And you'd better get her and your truck out of sight so he doesn't see you.'

Shelby gave him an odd look, as if she hadn't expected him to take her word. He didn't have time to explain that if Aaron believed her, so did he. He started toward his car to use the radio.

"If I recall," Aaron said, falling into step and bringing the reluctant Shelby with him, "there's a spot just beyond the turnout where you could be fairly well hidden and still see his car."

"Good." He looked at his friend. "I may need your help watching until backup arrives. *Watching*," he repeated firmly. "I can't be worrying about where you are."

Aaron held up his hands. "I'll pull the Yukon around behind the building, and we'll stay in the store. You're the hero here, not me."

Mike's gaze flicked to Shelby, then back. "Somehow I doubt that," he murmured, so low that only Aaron could hear him. And had the distinct pleasure of seeing his friend flush before he turned and walked with Shelby back to his car.

Mike's radio crackled to life. He answered it, and they heard him repeating directions and the suspect's description. When he hung up the microphone, he said, "They're making the SWAT callout, but it's going to be a while. I'm trying to get an air unit from the sheriff in case he takes off in his car."

"Let's hope he's still here," Aaron said.

"Yeah," Mike said, then headed for his car. He started up the mountain, slowly, windows down. He was acutely aware of everything around him. His hunting blood was up, his every sense in high gear. He was close to his quarry and he knew it, could feel it.

He rounded the curve and saw the turnout. The white car was still there.

Mike picked up the pace, heading for a wider spot in the road just ahead where he could turn around. It seemed logical that the man would move back toward the main highway; the other way led to nothing but more wilderness.

No sooner had he passed the turnout than a man in a brown leather jacket burst out of the trees and hurried toward the parked vehicle. He looked much the worse for wear, his pants dirty and torn on one leg.

"Damn," Mike swore, trying to focus on the man while he got turned around.

The white car roared to life, and gravel sprayed as the obviously angry driver hit the gas hard. He was around the curve heading down to the highway by the time Mike's sedan began to pick up speed.

He knew that help, and most particularly air support, was still a good ten minutes away. He was on his own.

Shelby and Aaron instinctively dodged back from the store window as the white car raced by. Then Mike's sedan sped by.

Aaron muttered something under his breath. Even before he moved, Shelby was running toward the back of the building. He caught up with her at the Yukon. They started after Mike, hanging back the minimum Aaron thought he could get away with and still keep his word.

They didn't see a sign of either car until they rounded the corner past the store; already the white car was pulling onto the highway below, with Mike still a good hundred yards behind him. They lost sight of the main road as they rounded the last foothill before hitting the floor of the high valley that the road was named for. When they reached the bottom and pulled out onto the main road, neither car was anywhere in sight.

"He's alone, Aaron," Shelby said.

"The killer?" he asked, not sure what she meant.

"Mike."

He gave her a startled glance. "You worried about him? A cop?"

"He's your friend."

His chest tightened at the simple declaration. He wanted more than anything to have some time, to go someplace quiet and let her say what he was hoping desperately she wanted to say. But as she said, Mike was up ahead somewhere, in pursuit of the killer, alone.

"Besides," she said, giving him a slightly crooked, sideways grin, "he doesn't seem like a bad guy. For a cop."

She said it jokingly, but Aaron knew it was quite a statement nevertheless, coming from her experience.

He nudged the speedometer up a bit more as they began to climb a deceptive rise; it didn't seem that high, but as they reached the top it became clear that the drop on the other side was considerable as the road crossed what had once been a streambed.

And in the distance, about a mile away, was Mike's car, half off the road.

The white car was gone.

Aaron rammed the accelerator to the floor.

Chapter Twenty-Four

The blue Yukon roared down the highway. Shelby leaned forward, her eyes fastened on that motionless car. Then she saw movement, near the front end.

"He's all right! Look, Aaron, he's walking around the car!"

Aaron let out a long breath. The distant figure appeared to raise the hood of the sedan, and even from here they could see the column of steam rising into the air. Aaron eased off the accelerator slightly.

Shelby turned her head to look at him. "He really is your best friend, isn't he?"

"I've known him almost all my life. Others have come and gone, but Mike . . . Mike has always been there. I never had a brother, but . . ."

"He's the brother you never had," Shelby finished for him. He nodded.

When they reached him, that brother was swearing a string of oaths into his cell phone; he'd obviously decided that this tirade was not suited for the police radio.

"—damn piece of crap!" Mike was venting into the phone. "Seventy miles an hour and it blows a head gasket! But do we need new cars? No, just ask the brass. Not that they have to drive them. No, they get their own cars, new ones every year."

He finally wound down. Aaron couldn't blame him.

He knew how dedicated Mike was, and his killer had just escaped. Nevertheless, he couldn't help being glad that Mike hadn't had to deal with the man without backup.

"Yeah, right," Mike was saying into the phone. "I'll write it up when I get back. No, I'll get a ride. Send a tow truck—or, hell, a hand grenade—for this piece of junk."

He shut the phone off, jammed it into his pocket, and turned to grimace at Aaron and Shelby.

"Sorry. Damn thing blew up on me coming over that rise. He was in the wind by the time I coasted down here."

"It happens," Aaron said.

"I called the state patrol, for all the good it'll do. If he's as smart as I think he is, he'll dump that car in a big hurry."

"Come on, get in and we'll head back," was all Aaron said.

Mike nodded, but he was still clearly disgruntled as he gathered up several items from the broken-down vehicle and tossed them in the back of the Yukon. Then he turned and looked at both of them.

"Now all I have to do is figure out which of our multitude of suspects this is. I barely saw him. Wish I had a photo lineup for you to look at, but I left in kind of a hurry—"

He stopped abruptly. Aaron and Shelby both watched curiously as he pulled what appeared to be a small stack of index cards out of his hip pocket.

"Let me ask you a couple of things about him," he said. Looking at the top card, he asked, "Is he balding?"

Aaron and Shelby glanced at each other before Aaron said, "No."

Mike nodded, and went to the next card. He studied that one for a moment before he asked, "Eye color?"

Again Aaron and Shelby exchanged glances. "Brown," Shelby said, and Aaron nodded. "A sort of muddy brown, not dark, not light."

Mike nodded again, and went to the third card. "Anything distinctive about his nose?"

"Nose?" Slowly Shelby shook her head. "Not that I noticed. Like what?"

"Like," Mike said dryly, "did he look as if he'd been boozing for the last quarter century or so?"

"Oh. No. Not at all."

"Do you think you two could put together a composite of this guy?"

Aaron hesitated, then nodded. Shelby winced. "Does that mean I have to go to the police station?"

"You sound like you're not sure you'd get to leave," Mike said.

"I'm not," she said honestly.

For a moment Mike just looked at her. "Ms. Wyatt, someday I want to hear your whole story. But now, I just want to catch this guy. So, I'm the only cop who knows your connection to this. As far as anybody else at the station is concerned, you're a friend of Aaron's. And I do need to get a statement from you, about that morning."

Aaron got the feeling her resistance had been instinctive. She probably hadn't expected Mike to help, to keep her secret a while longer.

"All right," she said.

"Thanks," Mike said. "Tell you what. Let me drive, and you two can get a head start. I've got an IdentiKit in my trunk. It's not as quick as a computer, but it works. We can polish it up with a sketch artist at the station."

While Mike drove, Aaron and Shelby worked on the IK, which consisted of layering transparent sheets with facial features drawn on them, head shapes, hairlines and styles, then down to eyes, eyebrows, ears, noses, and mouths. Mike gave them the crash course on how they were categorized, and they went to work as he turned the Yukon back toward Outpost. By the time they reached the police station, they were in agreement that the various features they'd picked formed the man they'd seen.

"Great. He doesn't match anybody I've talked to yet." Mike sighed. "I'll start checking him nationwide, and with the feds. If we're lucky, somebody will recognize him."

"The feds?" Aaron asked as they got out of his car.

Mike nodded. "The shooting was too clean, too slick. The average person out for revenge is messy. I keep coming back to the idea that he may be a pro."

"You mean . . . a hit man?" Shelby asked, shaken to think that she had been pursued by someone whose job it was to kill people, who took money for murder. It distracted her completely as they went into the station.

"It's possible," Mike was saying. "Independent of his blackmail schemes, Pruett pissed off some people who have clout and connections."

Mike led them to a small lounge with a couple of tables and a coffee machine. He left them for a few minutes to get the queries started. Then he came back, closed the door behind him, and sat down opposite Shelby.

"You feel like telling me a story?"

Shelby sighed. "I suppose."

As Aaron had expected, once Shelby realized the police already knew that Margaret was one of Pruett's blackmail victims, she had nothing more to protect and was willing to tell the whole story. A story, he thought, that he would be glad to hear himself. But before she could start, Aaron jumped in.

"She needs some guarantee of immunity or something, Mike."

"Immunity?" Mike's voice sharpened. "You mean she had something to do with the murder?"

"No," Aaron said quickly. And then stopped, realizing he really had no idea what she might need immunity for. It had been a gut instinct to try and protect her before she said anything.

"Look, you know I'll do my best, and if she didn't have anything to do with the actual killing . . ."

"I didn't. Let me just tell him, Aaron."

With a sigh, Aaron nodded. In short, concise sentences, she explained about Margaret's situation.

"So when it was time for her to take the next payment—"

"Take it?" Mike asked. "You mean she'd been taking it personally?"

"That was one of his . . . requirements. I think he probably liked making people crawl to him."

"Arrogant bastard."

Shelby blinked at Mike's words. Aaron wondered if she'd thought cops weren't as disgusted as the public by this kind of slime. After a moment, she went on.

"Anyway, I talked her into letting me take it to him."

"Why?" Mike and Aaron chorused, Mike sounding merely puzzled, Aaron alarmed.

"I wanted to see his place. See if I could find out where he kept the stuff, if he had an alarm, that kind of thing."

"In other words, you cased the place," Mike said. She shrugged and nodded. "Do I want to know where you learned all this?"

"No," Shelby said simply, and went on. "It was easy, really. Pruett started bragging, showed me where he kept it all locked up in some kind of strongbox in his desk."

"He showed you?" Mike asked incredulously.

She gave him a sideways look. "I played it dumb blonde."

"So I can add stupid to his list of sins," Mike said. And to Aaron's surprise, Shelby smiled. She apparently really had decided not all cops—well, not this one at least—were her enemy.

"Anyway, early the next morning, I went back. I waited until he left, and then I got in, and—"

"Wait a minute, what about his alarm system?"

"I came in through a utility room, figuring it might not be as well protected as his study would be." She flashed a look at Mike. "I was right. They only had alarm contacts on the door. So I went over the top, through the transom window they had for ventilation."

"They probably weren't counting on a burglar your size," Mike said wryly, but there was a note of admiration in his voice that Aaron was sure Shelby wouldn't miss.

"I got the box out—"

"His desk wasn't locked then, either?"

"It was. I picked it."

Mike's brows shot upward. "I wondered why he'd left it open." Then his brows came down. "That's not just a one-notch lock."

"I'm good."

Mike looked at Aaron, who couldn't help grinning.

"Go on," Mike said, sounding a bit rattled as he tried to reconcile the woman before him with the practiced burglar she was describing.

"I got Margaret's negatives." Her chin came up and she looked at Mike a little defiantly. "I thought about taking it all, so he couldn't hurt any of those people anymore, but I knew I couldn't carry it. So I put the box back and closed everything up. I figured the longer he didn't realize anything had happened, the better."

"I see."

"I just confessed to a felony," Shelby said to Mike, all her wariness back.

"I noticed," Mike said.

"Am I under arrest?"

"My star witness?" Mike asked jokingly. "Are you kid—" He stopped suddenly. He gave a low whistle. "Boy, am I slow. This was the morning he was murdered, wasn't it?"

Shelby took a deep breath and nodded.

I knew it! Aaron stayed quiet, but he couldn't help breathing an inward sigh of relief as Shelby confirmed his guess.

"Great timing, huh?" Shelby said dryly. "I was about to leave when I heard noises outside. I thought Pruett had come back."

"What did you do?" Aaron asked, trying not to imagine how scared she must have been.

"I hid in a closet in the study." She went on quickly then, as if eager to have it over with. "I could hear him moving around. And after a while I knew it wasn't Pruett. He was being too quiet, too careful. But he didn't set off the alarm. He must have turned it off somehow."

When Mike merely nodded, she continued. "I heard him come into the study. And then . . . nothing."

"Nothing?"

"I realized later he was . . . waiting."

"For Pruett," Mike said. It wasn't a question.

She nodded. "The closet door had those slanted louvers. I could see pretty well."

"And?"

She drew in a deep breath, and the end of it came in a grim, stark rush. "Pruett came back. I don't know why."

"The flat fire," Mike said suddenly. "I'll bet the killer set up that slow leak to give himself enough time to get inside, yet not let Pruett get too far away, so he'd likely come back to the house. Which also explains why the car was cold. He didn't drive it far."

He nodded at Shelby to go on.

"He came right to the study. The man hid in the shadows behind the door. Pruett walked in, he shot him in the head and was walking out the door before he hit the ground. If I hadn't jumped at the sound of the shot, and made a noise . . ."

Aaron forgot to breathe. Mike swore under his breath.

"I wouldn't have said a word," Shelby said, sounding a bit militant. "If he hadn't started chasing me, I would have walked away and no one would have ever known I was there. Nobody hurts Margaret and gets away with it, if I can help it. And he had it coming."

After that outburst, she set her jaw and glared at Mike, as if waiting for him to lecture her on the law and taking it into your own hands. She seemed surprised when it didn't come.

"If anybody ever did have it coming, he did," Mike said mildly. Then, with a glance at Aaron, he asked, "Is that it? Your part, I mean?"

She nodded.

"Except," Aaron said, his voice tight, "for being scared to death and on the run ever since."

"And giving a killer the slip rather nicely," Mike said.

"I had help," Shelby said. The softness of her voice and the look she gave Aaron then sent a shiver of an entirely different kind down his spine.

Mike was true to his word; he set Shelby up alone in a small private room where no one could see her, and as far as she knew, he'd told no one she was here. She missed Aaron's solid presence, but she knew he was around, somewhere. He wouldn't abandon her here. He had come for her without question, even after she'd walked out on him. And that gave her an inner warmth she'd never experienced before.

The moment she emerged an hour later, finished with the four pages it had taken to describe the "every little detail" Mike had wanted, Aaron was there, handing her a cup of coffee. They sat in the small lounge again. She'd never thought of a police station as such a busy place, phones ringing, people coming and going all the time.

She was nearly at the bottom of the Styrofoam cup when Mike strode into the room. When he shut the door behind him as he had before, Shelby guessed he had news. Not that she couldn't have figured it out just by looking at him; energy radiated from him, his dead vehicle clearly forgotten.

"We got lucky," he said, tossing a copy of their composite down on the table with what looked to be a fax with a slightly blurred but quite recognizable photograph. "A buddy of mine from the FBI academy knew the face."

Shelby suppressed a shiver as she looked into the eyes of her tormenter.

"No doubt?" Mike asked softly.

"None," she said.

Aaron nodded. "Who is he?"

"Artie Scanlon. He hasn't been around that long, and he usually only works in the East, but he recently started venturing west of the Mississippi."

Shelby stared at the photo. She couldn't even begin to speak. It was Aaron who asked, "Now what?"

"Well, it narrows down my suspects to those who could both afford to fund a contract killing and would know how to find this guy. Which neatly removes a chunk of the people Pruett had already bled dry. Somebody could have mortgaged their house to buy him, I suppose. Or a bunch of the people at the bottom of his pyramid scheme could have pooled what they had left, but my money's on the racing syndicate."

"You think they wanted him out of the way that badly?"

"They couldn't move forward with him dug in like that. Which means they weren't going to see any progress on their venture or return on their investment. And I have no doubts that they have the kind of contacts that could reel this guy in," he said, picking up the faxed photograph.

Mike stood there for a moment, as if undecided. Then he pulled out a chair and sat down facing them. "Shelby," he said softly, "he's going to try again. He can't leave you alive."

"Mike," Aaron said warningly when she shuddered.

"It's the truth, and you know it. She needs to be in protective custody."

"No!" Shelby found her voice at last. She looked from Mike to Aaron a little wildly.

"It's all right," Aaron said, reaching out to cover her hands with his. "You're not doing anything you don't want to." He looked at Mike. "She'll stay with me."

Mike considered that for a moment. "All right. She should be safe enough there. But keep her out of sight."

Coming out of her shock at last, Shelby began to react to being discussed in the third person. But before she could remind them she was right here, Aaron gave her a sideways look and said, "I'll try."

At this veiled reference to her middle of the night departure, she quickly decided to keep her silence. She hadn't yet had a chance to explain to him. Or to tell him all the things she'd so regretted she hadn't told him when she'd been up on his ledge, waiting for her killer to arrive.

And yet, when they were finally alone and on their way back to the Golden Phoenix, she was suddenly too exhausted even to try to put it all into words. She'd been up and running since three a.m. and it was catching up with her.

"Aaron," she began, wanting, needing to try anyway.

"Hush," he said, not unkindly as they walked to the private elevator. "We'll talk later. We have time, now."

"I really am sorry."

"I know."

His voice was gentle and warm, and so was he as he lifted her into his arms. Or maybe it was the elevator lifting. She didn't know. She only knew she was finally safe. She let sleep envelop her.

Mike knew if he was any more wound up he'd be bouncing off the walls. He was having a hard time coming down from being so close and losing the suspect because of a damned piece of wornout equipment the chief was too cheap to replace.

He leaned back in his chair and took a deep breath. He knew he needed to be busy with something when the adrenaline crash hit, or he'd be wiped for the day. But at the moment the only thing he could think of was Aaron, and the expression on his face when he looked at Shelby Wyatt.

Even more important, to him, anyway, was the way Shelby looked at Aaron. And, Mike admitted, the way she *hadn't* looked at him. There was nothing of the expression he so often saw when someone who was with Aaron got their first look at him. Shelby had barely reacted. Of course, she'd been under tremendous strain, but he had a suspicion that that wouldn't matter. From what little he'd seen, Mike was pretty sure that the gutsy Ms. Wyatt was about as far removed from the needy Cindy as you could get.

About time, my friend, he thought.

Speaking of time, it was time for him to get back to work. He pulled the file on the racing consortium out of his desk. He should have gone with his gut from the beginning and pushed the professional hit angle. But he knew perfectly well that if he'd done that to the exclusion of other suspects and been wrong, there would have been hell to pay.

He took out the list of investors. The top name was the urbane Leonard Hartwood, who at last contact had lost his cool and threatened Mike with a harassment suit. Mike had thought he was bluffing, but one of the well-fed attorneys he suspected they kept in cages just out of sight waved what appeared to be legitimate papers, prepared and ready to be filed, in his face.

It could still be a bluff, but it did make Mike wonder. Maybe he was aiming too high. Maybe he should be looking past the front men. He'd done a cursory background check on all of them, but perhaps he should start digging deeper, into the second tier of investors.

He'd run preliminary financial checks on them and had found several who had recently moved large sums of money around, but since that was not unusual for people in that league, no one single person had stood out. The national criminal checks he'd run on them had come back, but he hadn't had a chance to look at them yet, with the hit man angle breaking and then Aaron's call.

He took a careful look at them now, laying the financial reports and the background checks side by side for each name.

Halfway through both stacks, something caught his eye.

"Well, well," he muttered, leaning forward. He rechecked the dates on both sets of papers. "Hello, Mr. Marlon Swiger."

He was sure the occasional tight—relatively speaking—financial situation wasn't unusual in these circles, but Mr. Swiger appeared to be in deep trouble. He wasn't as big a fish as the front men, but a lot of his capital was tied up in the racing project that had been stalled by Pruett's demands.

True, he wasn't the only one on the list who was in that position. But he was the only one who, the last time he'd been in money trouble, had had a business partner who died in a single-car accident, leaving Swiger the sole owner of the business—and the recipient of a healthy insurance policy that had bailed him out of trouble.

He hoped Mr. Swiger wouldn't mind when he showed up without an appointment.

Who the hell are you?
The image of the little blonde popped into Artie Scanlon's head again as he stood at the rental car counter. It just didn't make sense that an ordinary woman could give him this much trouble. He'd tried to find out, asked discreet questions about whatever bimbo Pruett might have been involved with at the time, but nothing matched.

He didn't know how she had gotten away on that mountain. The going had been treacherous, slippery, and he'd spent every step watching for wild animals or, worse, snakes just waiting to strike. He was furious; he'd been out of his element there, and he didn't like the feeling. He'd finally reached the top of the trail she'd taken, and there'd been nothing except a ledge of rock that made you dizzy, hanging out in space over that little puddle of a lake.

As a further annoyance, he'd had to abandon the

other rental car when he'd gotten to Reno; it was too possible that she'd seen it and would see him coming. And he wasn't certain the car that had unexpectedly pulled out behind him hadn't been after him, even though the driver had given up rather easily.

"If you're sure you don't want the insurance, sir, just initial here and sign at the bottom."

He yanked his attention back to the woman behind the counter. He signed the new false name neatly. The credit card and ID in the name he'd used to rent the other car were now useless, just one more irritation to chalk up to the woman.

"Thank you, Mr. Winkleman." The woman took the agreement and handed him a key. "It's in space C-12."

He took the keys and started outside to track down the maroon SUV he'd rented this time. He wouldn't put another off-road run past this woman.

She had made him angry from that first moment, when he'd pulled open that closet door to see what had made the sound. She'd exploded past him, knocking him on his ass in the process, and squirmed out of that impossibly small window over the door in the utility room. She had been gone by the time he got the dead bolts unlocked.

He'd searched the grounds, then the neighborhood, swearing every step of the way. And then, as he'd been cruising the streets of this burg, trying to decide how to find her, or at least find out who she was, he'd caught a glimpse of that hair in the distance and the chase was on.

He found the vehicle and tossed his two bags onto the passenger-side floor. One held his clothes. The other held the tools of his trade. He wanted them close at hand. It had gone on long enough. More than long enough. The next shot he had at her he would take, no matter the place or time, and simply trust to the luck that had never failed him that he would get away clean. Ordinary, untrained people took too long to react, and made for rotten witnesses.

He drove the speed limit, as he always did, all the way back to Outpost. He drove past the back doors he'd seen them go in through before. The adjacent parking spaces were empty; no sign of the big blue SUV. He picked a different place to park this time. He tucked the .380 in his pocket just in case, then got out and walked over to the pay phone just outside the swimming pool area. He called Montana's office, saying he was returning Aaron's call. Without a pause to check, the woman he presumed was Francine Chapman told him Aaron had been unexpectedly called away, and she had no idea when he would return.

He thanked her, declined to leave a message, and went back to his new rental. He settled in for a wait, wishing he'd thought to grab something to eat when he'd stopped to change his clothes.

Then he was glad he hadn't wasted the time, as the Yukon came around the corner of the hotel and pulled up next to the back door.

He watched them get out and go inside. By the time the heavy door had swung shut, he was already moving.

Chapter Twenty-Five

Shelby stirred slightly, letting out a small sigh. Aaron stood over her, wondering if he should wake her or just let her sleep, even if it meant she would probably be awake all night. She'd been through hell. But she'd made it; it would take more than this to beat her.

And he realized with a little jolt that he'd missed part of that revelation. It wasn't simply being wanted rather than needed that was so exhilarating. It was being wanted by such a strong, tough woman. There was something almost electrifying about that.

He looked down at her. She was so rarely still that this was a treat. She had to be hungry by now, and—

She opened her eyes. She looked up at him. And she smiled, a slow, sleepy smile of pleasure that made his heart do a ridiculous trip in his chest.

When he thought how close he'd come to never seeing that smile, how easily she could have died out there today . . .

Something must have shown in his face, because the smile faded and she sat up. He could almost see the memories come rushing back.

"I'm sorry, Aaron," she said contritely. "I never intended for you to have to go back to that place."

He shook his head. "It's over. Don't worry about it. Let's go get something to eat. Then we can talk."

By the time she had showered and dressed, he had

himself convinced he was going to hear the worst. That she'd left in the middle of the night because she didn't want to tell him to his face that she regretted the night they'd shared, or worse, that she'd meant it as charity. She'd told him she never paid for anything with sex, but still . . .

Not wanting to put any extra pressure on the already burdened Ian—Lord, had that only been this morning?—Aaron selected the main restaurant on the casino level. Shelby stayed so close beside him that it almost alleviated some of his fears, but he told himself she was rightfully scared after the events of the day.

The restaurant was across the casino floor, and Aaron chose a direct route, to avoid any alcoves like the one the killer had been lurking in before. They were passing the blackjack tables, Aaron scanning the pit out of habit, when Shelby stopped short. Her grip on his arm tightened fiercely.

"He's here," she hissed.

Every muscle in his body went tight. "Where?"

"Over by the registration desk."

He started moving again, in the same direction as before. When they'd reached the cover of the cashier's cage, he looked toward the desk.

He was standing near the end of the short line. He'd changed clothes, to jeans and a casual shirt, and yet again his hairstyle. He wore dark, horn-rimmed glasses, and had what appeared to be a camera bag over his shoulder. If it hadn't been for Shelby's sharp eyes, Aaron would have looked right past the man; he looked just like a tourist about to check in who had misplaced his wife and was searching for her as best he could without losing his place in line.

That this piece of human scum had come here, into the Golden Phoenix, with every intention of committing murder, made him very, very angry.

"I've had it with you," he murmured.

"Aaron?" Shelby's voice was taut.

When he looked at her, she was staring up at him, wide-eyed. "What?"

"You look fierce. You're not going to do anything crazy, are you?"

"The pot calling the kettle black?" he asked, and she flushed. "I'm going to do what any upstanding citizen would do. I'm going to call the police. And then I'm going to make sure he's still here when they get here."

He pulled out his cell phone and pushed Robin's emergency code.

"Murphy."

He dispensed with the preliminaries. "Did your people get the copies of that photograph?"

"Yes, I gave them out myself."

"Good. Because he's here."

"Where?" The sudden tension in her voice told him she understood completely.

"Near the registration desk."

"I'll radio the doors first. Then I'll put out a general alarm."

"Go."

She already was; he could hear her on her walkie-talkie, giving orders rapid-fire. When she had everyone alerted, she was back. "I presume he's still interested in your guest? Is she with you?"

"Yes. I don't want him scared off. I want his ass nailed down."

'You have a plan? He's armed, right?"

"Likely." He thought for a moment, his eyes never leaving the man who was scanning the casino every minute or two. "Maybe I can lure him, get him to come after me."

"How?"

"I'm not sure. If he sees me, he's liable to just run. I don't—"

"But not if he sees me."

Shelby said it quietly, but it rang in his head as if she'd shouted it. "No," he said instantly.

"It's me he wants. Not you."

"You're not going to hang yourself out as bait, Shelby."

"Aaron?" Robin said in his ear.

"You've got to get him away from all these people, or somebody might get hurt," Shelby said.

"She's right," Robin said, obviously able to hear Shelby's words.

"Yes," he said to both of them, "but I'm not going to risk her life to do it."

"It's my life. And it's the only way. I'm who he's after."

"Maybe we'll just wait for the police," Aaron said.

"By the time they get here, he could be gone," Shelby insisted. "Look," she said, looking around and then back at the man who was trying to kill her, "he's gotten used to seeing us together, right? So it won't be a surprise that we are now."

"Your point?" Aaron asked.

"Have yourself paged, to someplace on this floor. I'll bet he knows your name, and it will draw his attention. Even if he doesn't, when he sees you respond he'll figure it out. He'll be looking for me, and . . . well, I'll let him see me. At a distance, like over by the elevators. As if I'd just left you while you tended to business."

"No," Aaron began.

"It could work," Robin said in his ear. "I'll have uniformed people lined up along the way, not doing anything proactive to spook him, just there. He'll want to dodge them, and we can use that to sort of herd him in the right direction. We can get him into a controlled environment, and then take him."

"Aaron, please, I'll be fine that far away," Shelby

said, as if sensing somehow that Robin was on her side. "I'm not suicidal, or fragile, but I am *tired* of this."

"So am I," he agreed grimly.

His instinct was to protect her, not to shove her out there and give the guy a chance at her. But she *wasn't* fragile. And it would be denying who she was to act as if she were, as if she were Cindy.

"All right," he said abruptly. "Robin, keep this line open."

He pulled out his own small radio, tuned it to a frequency and spoke into it.

"Ernesto? Aaron. I need you to start shutting down the tower elevators as they empty, except one and three."

"Now?" the facilities director asked, startled.

"Sooner. It'll only be for a minute or two. I'll deal with any complaints."

"Okay, boss, wait a sec, I'm in the main control room, let me get to the elevator panel . . ." Aaron's jaw tightened as the silence spun out. Then, "Okay, two and four are already at ground floor and empty. And . . . off now. Number one is on the fourth floor."

"Any commands?"

"No. Just emptied, I think."

Aaron switched to the phone. "Robin? Have the video team check elevator one."

It was barely a moment before the answer came back. "Empty."

Back to the radio. "Send number one to the ground floor and hold it. When I tell you, send it up to the mezzanine level and stop it." That way if something went wrong, Aaron thought, at least the guy wouldn't be roaming a hotel floor with innocent guests.

A second's pause, then Ernesto said. "Done, boss. You want number three ground level, too?"

"Yes. And when it starts up under command, after

you send up number one, I need you to stop three
between floors."

"Uh . . . intentionally?"

"Yes. Try for just above or below the mezzanine
level."

"Copy," the willing but obviously bewildered man
said.

"Wait for my word," Aaron said. He clipped his
radio onto his belt, then leaned into the cashier's cage.
"Marcus, I'm borrowing your backup radio."

The man, busy counting, nodded without comment.
Aaron turned on the unit and switched to the security
channel—he could hear Robin issuing quick, concise
orders—and handed it to Shelby. Then he pulled out
his key ring, detached his master key, and gave her
that.

"There's a door at the end of the elevator alcove.
It goes into the service area. This will unlock it from
this side. Head for the elevators, but go through that
door instead. Don't stop for anything, just keep going
until you're through. Robin will have somebody waiting for you. Keep the radio on, and don't do anything
until you hear Robin or I talk to you. Got it?"

"Yes," she said, hiding the radio under her
sweatshirt. "But what about you? This is my problem, Aaron."

"Which makes it mine," he said. It was as close as
he could come right now to what they had yet to say.
He saw her take a quick breath, and knew she
understood.

He looked back at the desk. The man was still there,
looking, always looking. He wondered how long before he gave up that vantage point and headed for
another. He didn't want to have to revamp the already
hurried plan, so he moved quickly when he heard
Robin say everyone was in place.

He went back to the cell phone. "You're set?"

"Ready. And I've got the video monitors watching the elevator cams live."

Damn, she was good, Aaron thought. But there was no time for pats on the back now. "Have your people hold any guests back from the elevators, as inconspicuously as possible."

"Copy."

"We're on," he said.

Then he reached for the house phone and dialed the operator. He gave quick instructions. The instant he hung up, they started moving toward the registration desk. A moment later, loud and clear, the page came.

"Mr. Montana, to the desk please. Mr. Aaron Montana, please come to the desk."

He'd told her to purposely keep it vague, and not say which desk. It worked; the killer glanced up toward the overhead speaker, then at the registration desk with a frown. Then he glanced toward the cashier's desk—and them.

"Now," Aaron said, and stepped out from the cover of the cage.

It took everything in him not to watch Shelby as she went, coolly waving good-bye to him. Instead he concentrated on using every inch of his height and size to be sure the killer saw him. And then, as she reached up and tousled her hair in an attention-getting gesture, he saw the man spot her and go still.

Aaron kept walking, a casual expression glued determinedly in place. He saw the man's attention split between his approach and Shelby's departure. Aaron waved, as if to someone behind the man, and then walked right past him as if he had never seen him before.

He turned his head slightly, to keep the man in his peripheral vision. When he was ten feet past him, the man broke, heading at a fast walk in the direction

Shelby had taken. Aaron forced himself not to turn until he caught a glimpse of the man looking back over his shoulder as if to be sure Aaron had stayed put. Only when he'd turned back and sped up did Aaron turn.

As promised, Robin had uniforms in place at every possible turnout along the path Shelby was taking. He saw the man register their presence and keep going. In the distance, Shelby made the turn into the elevator lobby. Aaron counted, picturing her reaching the door, unlocking it, getting through and closing it behind her. He keyed his radio.

"Ernesto, start number three up now."

"Copy."

Barely fifteen seconds passed before the killer made the turn. She'd had time, he told himself.

"Number one's heading up," crackled his radio.

"Stand by," he said, returning to his cell phone. "Robin?"

"I'm with her myself. He took the bait, thinks she went up in number three and got off at the mezzanine. He's on one, and he's alone."

Back to the radio. "Ernesto? Do it."

There were three seconds of silence, then, "Got it, boss. It's sitting about halfway between the mezzanine and the maintenance shop level."

"Give yourself a raise, my friend. Hold it there, and start the other cars again."

"Yes, sir."

He ran toward the elevators, heedless of the patrons who had to dodge out of his way, switching to the security channel as he went.

"Montana to the video room."

"Video here. Don't know who this guy is, boss, but he is not happy."

"That," Aaron said, "is the best news I've heard in a week. Just keep watching."

He went back to the cell phone. "Robin?"

"Here."

"Okay?"

"We're fine."

"Meet me at the video room."

"Copy."

He started that way at a fast clip; he wanted Shelby to be able to look at those monitors, to see her pursuer trapped and helpless. He thought it would do her good.

It would certainly make *his* day.

Shelby paced the small coffee room restlessly, although not with the nervous edge she'd felt earlier. For the second time today, she was in a police station.

But this time it was pleasantly different. This time it was with the shadow that had haunted her safely locked in a cell downstairs.

But she was weary of waiting. After the first hour or so, Aaron had acquired a rather suspect-looking sandwich from a vending machine and nagged her until she ate a couple of bites. She'd eaten more of it than she'd expected to, but couldn't remember how it tasted. That had been two hours ago; it was nearly ten now.

"What's taking so long, and why do we have to wait here?" she asked. The moment she heard her own voice, she grimaced. "Sorry," she muttered. "I'm whining."

"You're allowed," Aaron said mildly, "after what you've been through."

She turned to look at him. "I still can't help thinking they're down there deciding what to book me for."

Aaron shook his head. "Mike meant what he said."

As soon as he had talked to the D.A. Mike had—thoughtfully, Shelby admitted—let them know that in return for her testimony Shelby would walk away with minimal consequences. Maybe it was time she got over that distrust; if she made a go of Victim's Voice, she would be dealing with cops every day.

And this cop was Aaron's best friend. She couldn't conceive of Aaron's having a best friend who couldn't be trusted.

Now that it was over, she was beginning to think more clearly. How could a man like Aaron, with his illustrious family and high rank in the community, ever be serious about someone with her past? Someone who wound up sitting in a police station, caught up in blackmail and burglary and murder?

But what else could she have done? Protecting Margaret had been her only goal and, at the time, her highest priority.

"That's a rather fierce expression," Aaron said.

She stopped in her pacing to look at him. "I was just thinking that it seemed like the only thing to do at the time. And I'd do it again. Guess that makes me a criminal. Or stupid."

"It makes you," Aaron said, "loyal, gutsy, and the kind of friend anybody would be glad to have."

His words took the wind right out of her, and she abruptly sat down in the chair she'd deserted for her pacing. She was trying to decide if she liked that she'd used the word "friend" when Mike strode into the room, pulled an empty chair out from a neighboring table, and sat down. He wasted no time.

"The D.A. is in with him now, talking about a deal for information on who hired him."

"Did he tell you anything?" Aaron asked.

"He didn't want to talk at all, but you"—he nodded at Shelby, a glint of what looked almost like admiration in his eyes—"frustrated him so much that he let a few things slip. He's still not saying much, but what he is saying fits. That Pruett got in somebody's way."

"The racing syndicate?" Aaron asked.

"That's my bet." He glanced at Shelby. "He also says he doesn't know a thing about any blackmail. Looked completely blank when I brought it up."

"You believe him?" Shelby asked, unable to keep from sounding doubtful.

"I didn't want to," Mike answered, reading her voice accurately. "But he's about got me convinced. He's got no reason to lie about that, not at this point."

"I guess," Shelby said. It seemed so strange after these long days of living in fear, to think that it all had nothing to do with her, or what she'd done.

As if he'd read her thoughts, Mike said, "You were a loose end. Something it doesn't pay to leave in his business."

Mike yawned suddenly, and Shelby realized he had had a longer day than she; at least she'd gotten a nap. She lowered her gaze, afraid she was going to blush as she remembered Aaron picking her up and carrying her to bed. That it was only to sleep somehow didn't make it any less intimate. The opposite, in fact.

"Do you need us any longer?" Aaron asked.

"No, not really. The D.A. read Shelby's statement and confirmed the deal. Just stay available for questions, okay?"

Aaron nodded as he stood up, and held out a hand for Shelby.

"Oh and, Aaron, ol' buddy?" Mike said as he walked with them to the door and held it open for them to leave.

"What?"

"Nice work. You ever want a real job . . ."

"Yeah, yeah," Aaron said with a grin, and Shelby got the feeling they'd had this conversation many times before.

When they were back in his vehicle, Aaron turned to her. "I think," he said, "we were about to have dinner."

"About a million years ago."

"No wonder I'm starved," he said with a grin.

She smiled back, although a whole new kind of nervousness was building, and she wasn't sure how she felt. "So we pick up where we were . . . so rudely interrupted?"

Something flickered in his eyes, and she wished she had used different words. If anything had rudely interrupted them, it had been her midnight departure.

But he only said, "I was thinking of someplace else, actually. Now that it's safe, I thought you might want to actually be outside the Golden Phoenix. Cabin fever and all."

"As cabins go, the Golden Phoenix isn't bad," she said, her smile steadier. She glanced at her watch, which read just shy of midnight, then gave him a wry smile. "And I suppose Aaron Montana can get served anywhere, even at this hour?"

"I think I can find a place or two."

"That won't care how I'm dressed, I hope," she muttered. Aaron started to speak, then stopped. "What?" she asked.

"I . . ." He sounded as if he didn't at all want to say whatever it was. Then he sighed and said, "You can go home now."

Her eyes widened. She hadn't even thought of that. She hadn't thought of anything beyond the killer's being caught and being able to breathe freely again herself.

"Margaret!" she exclaimed.

Before she finished saying it Aaron was pulling out his cell phone and handing it to her. "I called her earlier to tell her you were all right and would be in touch."

She stared at him. He seemed to think nothing of it, that anyone would have done the same. "Thank you."

"I figured she'd be worried."

"Yes. Yes, she would."

Robert answered the phone, and sounded so happy to hear her voice it startled her; he was usually so reserved. Then he handed her over to Margaret, who sounded a bit breathless. Shelby gave her the condensed version as quickly as she could. Surprisingly, Margaret asked few questions, and Shelby wondered just how much Aaron had told her earlier.

Then Margaret said, "That Aaron of yours is quite something."

That Aaron of mine? Shelby couldn't deny the skip her heart gave at the sound of it. Had it really been only a few days? She felt as if she'd known him forever, loved him forever.

Loved him. The fact should have shaken her, but it didn't. After years of protecting herself from caring, it was amazingly easy to admit that she loved Aaron.

"Yes," she said. "Yes, he is."

Before Margaret could ask her any questions she couldn't answer, Shelby pressed for Margaret's story of the past few days. When she answered, Margaret's tone was emotional, but not at all upset.

"I so badly underestimated Robert. I don't know how he can forgive me. Not for my past—he's already done that—but for not trusting him. I was such a fool."

Shelby winced. That hit a bit close to home, given her own problems with trust. "He sounds happy."

Margaret giggled, a sound Shelby hadn't heard in a while. It made her smile. She could just guess how the two had made up the breach in their marriage.

"He is. So am I. I told him everything, Shelby. As I should have long ago. He's standing by me, no matter what. He says we'll go public if we have to, and anybody who holds it against me can just go to— Well, you know. The only thing he was angry about was my lack of faith."

"I'm glad," Shelby said, meaning it with all her heart. And she smiled at the thought of the quiet, conventional Robert Peterson telling anyone to go to hell.

"If I'd trusted our love in the beginning, this never would have happened, and you never would have been placed in such danger."

"I made my choices, Margaret. It wasn't your fault."

"Both of us could have made better choices," Margaret said frankly. "But that doesn't mean we can't start over from here."

Shelby sensed there was a pointed message in that for her. Message or not, when she disconnected a short time later, it was with a warm feeling about the possibility of a real, genuine love.

"Thank you," she said again as she handed the phone back to Aaron.

"Everything all right?" He turned into the parking lot of what appeared to be a small Italian restaurant.

She nodded. "They're going to be all right, I think. She—and I—underestimated her husband. She could have trusted him to understand."

He stopped the Yukon and looked at her. She waited for some comment about how she could have done the same. When it didn't come, she asked almost irritatedly, "Well, aren't you going to say it?"

"Sometimes saying it is superfluous."

His gentleness somehow made her feel even more guilty. "I did trust you. Eventually."

For a long moment he continued to just look at her. Then he said quietly, "I think you trusted me as soon as you could."

"Aaron, I—" She cut off the words that almost burst out, the words she wasn't sure she was ready to say.

"Let's eat. Then we'll talk." As they headed into

the restaurant, he added, "But I warn you: I'm not above using wine to get to the truth."

She gave him a startled look. And suddenly, looking into his eyes in the warm light of the candlelit restaurant, she realized that he knew. Somehow he knew what she was afraid to say.

"Make it champagne," she whispered. "It makes me babble."

"Champagne it is," he said, his voice suddenly husky.

Shelby followed the hostess, realizing with an odd little shiver that even though her ordeal was over, she was as tightly wound as ever.

Before, it had been because her life was at stake.

And now, in a different way, her life was still at stake.

Chapter Twenty-Six

Seated in a secluded booth, they had just given their order for what Aaron said was the best lasagna in the state, if not west of the Rockies, when the cell phone rang. Aaron grimaced, but answered, muttering that he would toss it off the top floor of the Golden Phoenix if Mike hadn't said to stay available.

His end of the conversation was restricted mainly to acknowledgments and a thank-you at the end. He disconnected, then stuffed it back in his pocket.

"Mike," he said as the champagne arrived. After he okayed it, the waiter neatly popped the bottle open. Aaron indicated he would pour it himself, and told Shelby the rest as he did so. "He's finally on his way home, but he thought we'd want to know that they got a bit more out of Scanlon. They've got enough on him now that he's decided dealing is his best choice."

"What did he say? Was it those racing people who hired him?"

He nodded as he filled her glass. "Said he'd never been given a name, and had been paid in cash delivered to an arranged post office box."

"Then how does he know it's them?"

"He said the guy who hired him told him they needed Pruett out of the way so the 'Blue Mesa project' could get moving. That's where the track is tentatively planned." He filled his own glass and set the bottle down. "That's all he would say, though."

He lifted his glass then and held it toward her. She picked up her own and clinked it against his.

"To the end of the nightmare," he said.

She nodded, then added softly, "And to trust."

Aaron smiled at her so warmly that she felt herself color. She turned her attention to her plate, and what was indeed the best lasagna she'd ever had. And it vanished with a speed that would have been embarrassing had Aaron's not disappeared even more quickly.

She lost track of how many times he refilled her glass, but when she at last stole a glance at the bottle, it was close to empty. Aaron picked it up, topped off both their glasses.

"One more toast," he said. "To intrepid women."

She picked up her glass, and looked at him. "And heroic men."

Aaron's eyes widened. *Now*, she told herself. *Now or never. Let the champagne do the talking.*

"I know you're right, that I could now, but when we're done here . . . I don't want to go home."

She saw him swallow as if his throat were tight. "You don't?"

"I had a lot of time to think, out there on that mountain. I was sure I was going to die, and the only thing I really regretted besides Margaret was you. That I hadn't told you."

He closed his eyes. Shelby winced inwardly, thinking that now he was the one trying to avoid this. She hastened to finish.

"I want you to know it doesn't matter how you feel, and I don't expect anything from you. But I have to tell you."

"Shelby," he said, his voice strained, as if her name were all he could manage to get out.

"I love you," she blurted out before he could stop her. And then she stopped cold; she hadn't thought of a blessed thing to say beyond those words. She stared down at her empty plate. The silence spun out between them, and she was afraid to look up.

"Shelby." She steeled her nerve and lifted her head. The instant their eyes met, he said quietly, "I know."

She blinked. "You do?"

"Margaret told me the only reason you'd take off like that was to protect me." His mouth quirked. "Nobody's ever tried to protect me before."

"I . . ."

"I could think of only one reason for that, but I was afraid to believe it."

"Afraid?" She knew why she'd been afraid, but why on earth would he be?

"I knew money didn't impress you, or my family standing around here. And for sure my looks couldn't."

Her chin came up. "What's wrong with your looks?" she demanded.

He chuckled. "I hang out with Mike Delano, remember?"

"So? He's pretty. You're . . . beautiful."

He nearly choked on his swallow of champagne. He stared at her. "Are you blind?"

"No," she said, shaking her head slowly as an image came to her, an image of Aaron naked in the moonlight, of him moving over her, into her, of him shuddering in her arms, sharing the most intimate moments two people can have. "No, I'm not blind. 'Beautiful' is definitely the word."

Aaron sucked in a harsh breath. "Whatever you just thought, hang on to it."

"I'd rather relive it," Shelby said, amazed that she had the nerve.

Aaron let out a short, compressed breath, as if she'd punched him in the stomach. "Let's get out of here."

His phone rang. He groaned aloud. He yanked out

the phone, and his thumb hovered over the power button. He was going to just shut it off, she realized.

"It's all right," she said. "I'm not going anywhere this time. I promise."

He clearly didn't want to, but at her words he answered the call. "Montana," he growled. "Mike? What's wrong? For a guy who just popped a murderer, you sound pretty grim."

Aaron frowned then, and it deepened as he listened.

"Tonight?" Aaron said, a touch of that groan in his voice now. "Yeah, yeah, okay. I'm clear across town, but I'll get there as soon as I can."

He broke the connection and glared at the little phone resentfully. He closed his eyes as if in pain, then opened them to look at her.

"He says he needs to talk to me. That there's nobody else he can turn to about whatever it is. He wouldn't say over the phone."

Shelby felt a flicker of resentment herself. She'd wanted nothing more than to go back to Aaron's home, back to his bed, and make up for abandoning him. Darn Mike, anyway.

Everyone in his life trusted him, because they knew he would never let them down.

Her own words came back to her, sweeping away her pique. Whatever Mike wanted, it had to be important. She reached out to cover his hand with hers. "We'd better go right now, then." Aaron drew back slightly, looking at her intently. She smiled at him. "It's all part of that trust, isn't it?"

The smile he gave her was almost worth having to postpone what she so badly wanted. And when he ordered a second bottle of champagne to go, she smiled herself. Didn't some things improve with anticipation? Although if she anticipated this much more, she was going to be spinning in place.

Minutes later they were back in his Yukon, headed

north. Aaron was silent, and she couldn't guess what he was thinking about. She tried not to think too much herself. If she did, she was going to linger on the fact that Aaron had never returned her declaration of love.

Mike was going to owe him big time for this one, Aaron thought as he drove through the darkness toward the small house Mike had bought after the fiasco with Emma, choosing, Aaron suspected, the quiet, middle-class neighborhood at the far edge of Outpost as a sort of declaration of where he really belonged.

"Aaron?" Shelby's voice was pensive in the darkness of the car.

"What?"

"Why do you live in that place? Looking out all the time at . . ."

"At where Megan died?"

"Yes."

He let out a breath. "It was my father's place. And my grandfather's. It's convenient for work. When Cindy and I split, it just seemed natural to move in there."

"Doesn't it hurt?"

"Yes," he admitted. "But it's also a way to be . . . close to her, I guess. To make sure I never forget."

"You would never forget."

"No. But I guess I thought that if, every time I looked out those windows, I could hurt a little less and remember a little more of the good part, the joy she brought into my life, it would be a way to heal. To mark the healing."

"Will you ever leave there?"

"I might," he said pointedly. Then he decided it was time to ask a question of his own.

"Who's Tiger?"

He heard her sigh. But she didn't hesitate. "He

was—*is*—another runaway. Three years older than me. What he went through makes what happened to me look like a fairy tale."

Aaron couldn't imagine anything that bad.

"He sort of adopted me, out there. Like a big brother. I never knew why. Maybe I reminded him of someone. But he took care of me, taught me what I needed to know to survive." He felt more than saw her glance at him then. "It's come in handy lately."

"In that case," Aaron said softly, "I owe him thanks."

"I owe him my life," Shelby whispered. "I hope . . ."

"What?" he asked when her voice trailed away.

"I hope he's alive," she said bluntly. "He put me on a bus to Reno to get me out of L.A. It wasn't until later that I realized he must have been expecting trouble. And that when he kissed me that morning, for the first and only time, he was . . . saying good-bye forever. That he expected to die and didn't want me there to see it. I always think about trying to find him, but . . ."

Aaron ached inside at the sound of the pain in her voice. Maybe, after they'd resolved whatever Mike's problem was, he would ask him about the possibility of finding out what had happened to a long ago street kid.

"Aaron?"

"What?"

"I need to tell you, I did some things back then that—"

"I can guess."

"But—"

"You didn't murder anybody then, either, did you?"

"No, I never intentionally hurt anyone, but—"

"Then never mind. I don't care what you had to do to survive. What you had to steal, who you had to steal from, what you had to sell, or anything else. It's what you're doing now that counts."

He heard her make a small sound, he thought it was one of relief. He hoped so, because he meant every word.

"Shelby?"

"What?"

"What *are* you doing now?"

She gave a small laugh. "With Robert's financial help and Margaret's organizational help, I've been setting up a victim assistance program called Victim's Voice."

"Now that sounds like a good fit," he said. "Victims need somebody like you to fight tooth and nail for them."

There was silence in the darkened car for a moment before she said, "Thank you," in a voice so soft and warm it was all he could do not to pull over right there and kiss her.

But he couldn't because Mike had come up with whatever this was.

Shelby understood that, he thought with a glance at her. She'd never even questioned that he had to go, in fact had urged that they do it now. She understood loyalty. She—

The cell phone rang again. As they stopped at a light he answered it, trying not to snap.

There was no one there.

He checked the phone to be sure he'd pushed the right button. Shelby looked at him curiously.

"Nobody there. I was hoping it was Mike to tell us never mind."

She smiled, almost shyly, and his stomach knotted involuntarily. He couldn't stop looking at her as he put the phone back to his ear to double-check before returning it to his pocket.

He frowned, tuning in to the phone once more. Was

that a voice on the other end after all? He pressed it closer to his ear.

When the light changed and he didn't move, Shelby lifted a brow at him. He gave the rearview mirror a quick glance to be sure he wasn't blocking anyone, while still straining to hear.

The voice became a fraction louder, and he realized it was Mike. And that the phone line was simply open in the room on the other end.

"Oops," he said to Shelby. "Mike must have accidentally hit redial and walked away." He wondered who was there, that Mike was apparently talking to. Unless he'd taken to talking to himself.

"That'll run up your cell bill," Shelby quipped.

Aaron grinned. It was so good to hear her joke.

"—you're doing?"

In his ear, Mike's voice was a notch clearer yet, as if he'd come closer to the open line, but Aaron was still looking at her. He was going to have to get to know a new Shelby, a Shelby without the fear, without the shadow hovering over her. He was looking forward to it.

"He's moving closer to the phone. I'll see if I can get his attention," he said finally, ready to deliver the most piercing whistle he could manage.

"—happy about having to do this. You're a good cop, Delano."

Somebody else was there. Somebody who didn't sound too thrilled with Mike. Was this what he'd wanted Aaron there for?

Mike's voice was suddenly loud and clear. "And I'm not happy about having a gun pulled on me in my own house."

Aaron stiffened, biting back an exclamation.

Shelby leaned forward, as if she had picked up on his sudden change in mood. He silently blessed her for having the presence of mind not to speak until he pressed the mute button, so nothing they said could be heard on the other end.

He stamped down on the accelerator, handing Shelby the phone in the same instant.

"Just listen," he said tightly. "Somebody's there with Mike, and he's pulled a gun on him."

"What?" Shelby drew back, startled, but she put the phone to her ear.

"Hitting the redial button on his cordless must have been all he could manage without being spotted," Aaron said, checking for cross traffic before he blew the signal at Outpost and Front.

"It's muted on our end?" she asked, her tone suddenly cool and businesslike.

"Yes." She'd handle it, he thought, and upped his speed to near reckless.

She listened. "He's saying Mike should have left well enough alone. I presume you didn't recognize the voice."

"No." He dodged a late-night shopper who carelessly pulled out of a grocery store lot without looking.

It was a long moment before she spoke again. Her voice was no longer cool, it was low and filled with tension. "Whoever it is, Mike thinks he's there to kill him."

Aaron swore. And pushed the Yukon to the max.

He should call the police, get them started to Mike's, but he didn't dare sever the connection. Nor did he want to take the time to stop. His mind raced.

There was an all-night convenience store near Mike's place. Shelby could call from there. That would solve two problems, getting help on the way and getting her out of potential danger.

The Yukon's tires squealed but held on the corner of Mountain View, the road that led to Mike's house. The first mile was steep, and he jammed the gearshift down into third to maintain speed. It leveled out at the top of the rise, then came the right turn onto Mike's street. He'd have to—

Shelby's sharp breath cut into his thoughts.

"He found the phone," she whispered. "The connection's gone."

"Son of a bitch," Aaron ground out. "Hit memory, then zero. That's Outpost PD. Give them Mike's name and what's happened."

He heard her make the call, and even as she quickly explained to the dispatcher he knew there wasn't time. They were barely three blocks away, and no matter how fast a unit responded, they would beat it there. And he wasn't about to wait, not when Mike's life was in danger.

Recalling what he'd seen the times he'd ridden along with Mike, he stopped the Yukon several houses away. And he left the door open to avoid the noise of shutting it as he got out.

Only then did he realize Shelby had also gotten out.

He looked at her. "Shelby," he began.

"Don't even think about it, Montana. I'm not sitting here doing nothing."

She reached back into the car and picked something up. For a split second he wavered, but her jaw was set, and he knew that look.

"Bring the phone," he said, "and be ready to call back as soon as we get a look at what we're dealing with."

"Already have it," she said, close behind him as he started toward the house.

The front was dark. Aaron prayed it didn't mean they were too late.

"His den's in the back," he whispered, and they moved carefully that way. There was plenty of cover in the form of shrubbery and some larger trees. They went carefully, to keep down the noise. Out of the corner of his eye he saw that Shelby was carrying something, and he was glad she'd thought to have the phone out and ready.

"There's a light," Shelby indicated as they got closer. Aaron nodded and edged farther along. Then stopped suddenly as a voice came clearly from inside.

"—the matter, you don't have the stomach to do it yourself?"

It was Mike. He was still alive. Aaron felt a flood of relief and nearly sagged against the wall of the house. Then the words he was hearing began to register, and his relief vanished.

"—don't understand!" the other male voice was saying.

"Damn right I don't understand," Mike answered. "You want somebody dead that badly, have the guts to do it yourself. Hiring a hit man to keep your hands clean is pretty chickenshit."

Aaron heard Shelby stifle a gasp. He felt the same way. It had to be the man who had hired Artie Scanlon. But what the hell was he doing here? Had Mike found out about him already? Confronted him? But the man had come here, so he had to have known Mike was onto him, before Mike knew that he knew. Was that what Mike had called about?

Whoever it was, he clearly had nothing to lose now, and that made him even more dangerous. The only reason Mike was still alive was the man's apparent reluctance to actually commit a murder himself.

"I had no choice!" the voice exclaimed. "Just like I have no choice now."

"He's going to crack," Shelby whispered, so low Aaron had to strain to hear. He knew she was right. In that instant he heard the metallic sound of the slide on an automatic pistol.

"Mike needs a diversion. Now."

Shelby moved then, held something out to him, gesturing toward the window. "Oughta break it, don't you think?"

It wasn't the phone. It was the bottle of champagne.

For a split second he grinned. This woman would never run out of ideas. He took the bottle and motioned her back out of any possible line of fire. He heaved the bottle as hard as he could.

He dove to his right, after Shelby, in the same instant. Glass shattered. A split second later, the sound of shots. One and two thwacked into a tree just above their heads. Three, four, and five echoed inside the room. Followed by a shout of pain.

Aaron launched himself through the broken window without hesitation. He felt glass snag his clothes, slice at his arms. He came down hard and rolled to his knees, heedless of more broken glass.

Mike was down. But he was alive.

"He's headed for the front door!"

Aaron knew where Mike's priorities were. He went.

It was a dodging, clumsy pursuit. The man shoved furniture and anything else at hand into his path. But every pause to tip something over gave Aaron another split second of gain on him, because Aaron just leapt over the obstacles.

He cleared an overturned table in the entry, his eyes fastened on the already open front door.

He heard a thud from outside. A string of muffled curses. He hit the front porch at full tilt.

The man he'd been chasing was sprawled at the foot of the porch steps, but trying to get his feet under him. Tripped, Aaron thought as he dived after him. Then, airborne, he saw the real reason the man was down.

Shelby was crouched in the shadows of the porch, at the top of those steps.

He came down hard on the figure who was just struggling to his feet. At the man's grunt of pain,

Aaron smiled with nearly vicious pleasure; his size was a weapon he didn't use often, but he was glad of it now. He applied a knee to the small of the man's back, pinning him in place.

He glanced up just as Shelby got to her feet, a look of satisfaction on her face.

"Such a klutz," she said, wiggling her right foot. "Can't imagine what he tripped on."

Aaron laughed. He couldn't believe it, but he laughed. She must have heard Mike's yell and raced to intercept them at the front of the house. And neatly tripped the intruder at the top of the steps.

Shelby grinned at him. And he knew everything was going to be all right.

At a sound from the doorway they both turned. It was Mike, wobbly but upright, clutching his upper right chest, leaning against the doorjamb. Shelby moved quickly, pulling over the bench beside the door.

"Sit down, you idiot," Shelby said gently, and to Aaron's surprise Mike obeyed.

He heard a siren approaching. Only then did he think to look at the man he was sitting on. He had to lean over to see his face. It was dark, and difficult to see, but after a moment recognition of the familiar, high-profile visage clicked into place.

He lifted his head and stared at Mike. Mike grimaced, and Aaron knew it wasn't from pain. No wonder he'd sounded so grim on the phone.

"Damn," Aaron breathed.

Who did you call when you needed the chief of police arrested?

Chapter Twenty-Seven

"Ten more minutes," the nurse said warningly.

"Yes, sir," Aaron said, while Mike made a face at the man's departing back.

They'd said he would probably be able to go home in a few days. No bullet wound was pretty, but this one had at least missed anything more vital than muscle and his collarbone. It had been a through wound, and they'd been able to treat it in fairly short order.

Aaron, sporting a couple of bandages of his own over cuts from the broken glass, turned back to his friend. He doubted he could ever tell Mike how his heart had stopped when he'd first burst through that window and seen him down. For all his loyalty and friendship, there was a part of Mike that was closed off to everyone, even Aaron. But he would make sure he never took the friendship for granted anymore, Aaron vowed silently.

"So you're saying it was those index cards?" Shelby asked, her tone incredulous.

"Yeah," Mike said. "I kept going through them, looking at each angle. About the third time through on the financial aspect, when I was focused on anybody who was connected to both Pruett and money, I realized I'd left somebody out. Somebody who'd been in financial trouble just before he collected a big insurance settlement on a building Pruett had co-owned."

"Cushman," Aaron said.

Mike nodded against the hospital pillow. "I didn't want there to be any question about the thoroughness of the investigation, so I wrote out a card for him, too." His mouth twisted ruefully. "I didn't realize it until now, but I think Sunny, his secretary, must have seen his name and tipped him off."

"That's when you figured it out?" Shelby asked, with every appearance of fascination at the story.

"No," Mike admitted. "I had to get hit over the head. It wasn't until last night. I had brought home the last of the blackmail stuff, the stuff we hadn't been able to match up to anyone." He stopped, then gave Shelby a lopsided grin. "Funny how some of that stuff never turned up. Just had to write it off as unresolved."

Aaron knew he meant Margaret's negatives. Shelby stared at him for a moment, and Aaron saw the sheen of moisture in her eyes. "For a cop," she said softly, "you're a heck of a guy, Delano."

Mike shrugged, winced at the motion, then went on. "Anyway, one of those things was a tape recording of a phone call. That's when I called you, right after I heard it. I needed somebody to tell me I wasn't nuts. Because it was between Cushman and the arsonist who burned down his condo building. Making the deal."

Aaron let out a low whistle. "I thought that was ruled accidental?"

"It was. Cushman must have used some clout to get further investigation quashed. Or maybe Pruett had somebody at the fire department on the string, too."

"So Pruett set the chief up for a fall?"

Mike nodded again. "He made sure that if it was ever found out, Cushman was the only one connected to the arson. And he made sure Cushman knew he had the tape. Which explains why Cushman was always reining us in on the guy, saying we should focus on bigger fish." Mike sighed in disgust. "No wonder we could never put him away."

"So he knew all along that Pruett was the co-owner of his building?"

"I think so. He just came to me with that phony story to divert me from him." Mike grimaced. "Worked damn well, too."

"He's got the background to know it's what an innocent man would do," Aaron said reasonably.

"What about that blackmail list?" Shelby asked.

"He wasn't on it," Mike explained. "He paid in favors, not cash, so Pruett didn't track it like he did the others."

"And the racing syndicate?" Aaron asked.

"Oh, I'm still convinced they're not as pure as they let on, and I'm going to reopen a case on one of them, but as far as I can find out, Cushman heard the rumblings that they weren't happy with Pruett, and grabbed the chance to use them as a cover when he hired Scanlon." Mike shifted awkwardly in the bed. "He must have thought when Pruett was dead, his troubles were over."

"He didn't count on his own best and brightest," Aaron said, and before Mike could blush, added, "And most stubborn."

Mike grinned. Then, with a glance at her, he said, "Or the likes of one Shelby Wyatt."

There was a world of respect in his tone, and Shelby did blush. They were going to get along, Shelby and Mike, Aaron thought with relief.

When Robin arrived moments later, looking worried, Aaron saw the surprise and pleasure in his friend's eyes. Robin seemed to hesitate, and it wasn't until Shelby cleared her throat and said they probably better go now, that Aaron realized he'd been studying them both with far too much interest.

They left them alone. And Aaron suddenly couldn't wait to get Shelby alone himself.

Shelby had been told by her counselor that it was possible she would always feel a modicum of hesitation when it came to sex, at least until she was able to trust someone completely.

Apparently, she thought now as Aaron reached for her, she'd reached that stage with him, because, except for a split second of anxiety when he was towering over her and she realized he was even bigger than she remembered, the only thing she felt was a deep hunger.

She'd never made love in front of a glowing fireplace, either, or with soaring mountains rising just outside the window. She was about to now because there was no way they could have waited to make it to Aaron's bed.

As if he'd sensed that instant of hesitation, he reversed their positions. He pulled her on top of him, draping her naked body over him as if she were a garment he loved the feel of. And then he let go, leaving her to make the next move.

She rose up, shivering with her own need as she looked down at him, not knowing where to start on the luscious, wanton feast before her. She heard him make a low sound, and wondered just what had shown in her face to wring it from him.

He'd been so careful with her before it had almost driven her crazy. Now was her chance to show him she didn't need just his care, she needed the wildness she sensed was lurking just under his controlled surface.

She leaned over him, her breasts brushing his belly as she pressed her lips to his chest. She felt a shiver go through him and marveled that this big, strong man was putting himself completely in her power. She kissed him again, lower this time, then on his belly, and then still lower, until he held his breath, waiting.

"Aaron?" she asked softly.

"Please," he answered, his voice gravel-rough.

She tasted him then, long and deep. He shuddered violently. He reached for her, then stopped, making a sound of great effort as his hands fell back.

Shelby lifted herself up to look into his eyes.

"I am not fragile," she said, as she had once before. "I've dealt with what happened to me. I can't promise I'll never react before thinking, but I will never, ever be afraid of you, Aaron."

Her name broke from deep in his chest, as if wrenched. He reached for her again, and this time he didn't hold back. He urged her over him, and she lowered herself, taking him in with slow, luxurious pleasure.

He cupped her breasts, lifted, then ran his thumbs over her nipples. Her body clenched violently, and she heard him groan as her inner muscles tightened around him.

It was all fire then, wild and uncontrolled, exactly as she had wanted. Aaron might be the steady, solid linchpin of the Montana family, but here, with her, he let loose all the passion she'd sensed was there.

Much later, as she lolled sated and lazy—and more than a little awed—in his arms, she said what she'd meant to say before this inferno had engulfed them.

"You know, I don't *need* you."

"I know." He didn't sound in the least bothered.

"That's all right?"

"Perfect. I have enough people who *need* me."

She sighed contentedly. "Good. Because it sure is nice to have you around."

"I can move furniture."

"Yes."

"And carry groceries."

"Uh-huh."

"All kinds of heavy lifting."

"Yep."

"And I love you."

Shelby smiled. "I know. But you had me going for a while."

Aaron chuckled, and with her head on his chest, Shelby felt it before she heard it.

"I'll drive you crazy," she warned.

"I'm counting on it. I'll be so busy dealing with you I won't have time to bail out anybody else."

It was Shelby who chuckled this time. It still amazed her to think of it. She was going to take a chance on love, the riskiest gamble of all, and she wasn't even afraid.

"What kind of wedding ring are you going to buy me?" Aaron asked cheerfully.

Shelby blinked. She turned her head to stare at him.

"Hey, I happen to know there's twenty-four thousand, seven hundred and fifty dollars of a jackpot sitting in my safe with your name on it. I want a *nice* ring."

Shelby couldn't help it; she burst out laughing.

"That," Aaron said as he grabbed her up in an exaggeratedly dramatic embrace, "is the sound I want to hear for the rest of my life."

When she could get enough breath, Shelby answered him. "I think I can arrange that."

The biggest gamble of all had paid off.

"This is a page-turner, with an emotional and sexual intensity that makes it stand out from the crowd."
—Under the Covers

Four-time Winner of the RITA Award

Visit: www.speakingvolumes.us

"Your pulse will pound and your blood will sizzle . . .
the very best suspense."—*Romantic Times*

Four-time Winner of the RITA Award

Visit: www.speakingvolumes.us

Sign up for free and bargain books

Join the Speaking Volumes mailing list

Text

ILOVEBOOKS

to 22828 to get started.

Message and data rates may apply.